Sailing Lessons

Center Point
Large Print

Also by Hannah McKinnon and available from
Center Point Large Print:

Mystic Summer
The Summer House

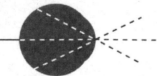

Sailing Lessons

Hannah McKinnon

CENTER POINT LARGE PRINT
THORNDIKE, MAINE

This Center Point Large Print edition
is published in the year 2018 by arrangement with
Atria Books, a division of Simon & Schuster, Inc.

The text of this Large Print edition is unabridged.
In other aspects, this book may vary
from the original edition.
Printed in the United States of America
on permanent paper.
Set in 16-point Times New Roman type.

ISBN: 978-1-68324-922-1

Library of Congress Cataloging-in-Publication Data

Names: McKinnon, Hannah Roberts, author.
Title: Sailing lessons / Hannah McKinnon.
Description: Center Point Large Print edition. | Thorndike, Maine :
    Center Point Large Print, 2018.
Identifiers: LCCN 2018024047 | ISBN 9781683249221
    (hardcover : alk. paper)
Subjects: LCSH: Sisters—Fiction. | Family secrets—Fiction. |
    Families—Fiction. | Domestic fiction. | Large type books.
Classification: LCC PS3613.C5638 S35 2018 | DDC 813/.6—dc23
LC record available at https://lccn.loc.gov/2018024047

To the Jackson girls: Jennifer, Chloe & Ari.
The Bailey girls have nothing on you.

Prologue

Her mother told her not to go outside. She is lying on her grandmother's living room couch, under the "sick blanket." It is plaid and soft and worn in all the right places, and her mother saves it for when any of them are feeling poorly.

Outside the day is gray and thick with fog, the early fingertips of a storm reaching in off the sound and tapping at their shingled house. It has been raining lightly all morning and she is home with strep throat. The doctor advised she rest until her fever broke. And Wren is mad. Missing a day of fifth grade was one thing. But today is Saturday. Her mother and grandmother have just gone out to fetch groceries. Wren had feigned sleep before they left, peeking through one eyelid as they stepped out into the stormy day.

Once again, her father has been sleeping all day. She had wondered aloud if he had strep too, and her mother got a sad strange look on her face. "No, Bird. He's just tired." Her father has been tired a lot lately, ever since they moved into their grandmother's house on School Street. He sleeps whole days when the rest of them go out to school. The clink of the glass on the kitchen table at night is sometimes the only sound of him in the house, the empty beer bottles in the trash bin the next day the only evidence of his having roused. But today he has surprised his three girls by waking up as soon as their mother and grandmother have left. He bursts into the living room in tall rubber boots and a slicker and asks, "Who wants to go fishing on Lighthouse Beach?"

Piper squeals with glee. She has recently been given a child-sized pink fishing rod—a toy, really—and she glares when her older sisters remind her of this fact. It is real! And she wants to use it.

Shannon is worried. She loves to fish with their father, and she is good at it. As the eldest sister, Shannon knows how to drag the skiff down to the water's edge. She can bait a hook without making a face. Her father admires this out loud, robustly, and it is something that makes ten-year-old Wren ache with jealousy.

But Shannon doesn't want to go today. "It's too windy," she worries. "The water will be choppy."

"Nonsense. The fish love this weather," their father insists.

Wren does not think their mother would like this, but she doesn't care; she has been stuck inside for days and despite her achy limbs and woozy head, she wants nothing more than to go. But here their father agrees with their mom. "No,

Wren. You stay home and rest. We'll catch one for you."

This only makes her head burn hotter. Wren watches them suit up and collect rods with disdain. She listens to the din of them getting ready to go followed by the silence that falls on the house like a pillow the second the door closes behind them.

She throws the blanket back and goes to the door. Outside her father and sisters are walking up the street toward Main. They will turn right toward Lighthouse Beach. She tugs her red polka-dot rain boots on over her pajama feet and zips herself into a hooded coat. It won't take her long to catch up. As long as she hangs back until they reach the beach, her father won't send her all the way home.

She trots up School Street. The road is quiet, and at the end of the street lies Lighthouse parking lot. It's empty. When she reaches the steps that lead down to the beach, she pauses. She's more tired than she realized. Her father and sisters have already climbed down the steep stairs leading to the sand and are now small dots near the water, just below their friends', the Jackson's house. The Jacksons own the lovely white house above the beach; they let Caleb store the Beetle Cat there. Wren squints. The beach below is so dense with fog, it's hard to discern sand from sky.

It takes a long time to get down the steps to the beach. Wren is out of breath, and the wind is strong. What she can see of the channel looks rough. Her limbs ache, and she sorely wishes she were back at home under the sick blanket. Wren is about to turn around when she hears the sound of a girl's scream. Wren turns, shielding her face from the blast of sand and wind. The sound comes again. Followed by something else. The sound of a man shouting. Her father!

She kicks off her boots. When her bare feet hit the sand at the bottom of the steps, she pounds at it with her heels, digging her toes in for speed. Ahead she sees the Beetle Cat. It is bobbing on the surf, and her father's yellow slicker is slipping in and out of the water beside it. She realizes then it is flipped over.

By the time she reaches the edge of the water, her lungs are roaring with effort. The boat is not far offshore, and she begins to run toward it. A wave hits her in the knees, knocking her backward. When she regains her footing, the yellow slicker by the boat is gone. Now there is another head bobbing beside the boat. Wren screams. "Shannon!" Where is her father? Where is Piper?

As if he hears her cries through the currents, her father surfaces. He whips his head back and forth, coughing, shaking off water. And then Shannon disappears. Wren screams again. The boat rocks on the water, whitecaps crashing around it.

Shannon is still under the water. "Shannon!" This time it is her father. Wren watches in horror as he reaches into the dark depths, head bent. He dives. Now it is just the boat.

Up the shore, Wren sees two figures walking. No, they are running toward them. With a dog. "Help!" she screams into the gusty wind. She has no idea if they can hear her. Just when she thinks her lungs will explode, Shannon and her father burst through the surface together. Her father swings Shannon up and over, onto the hull of the flipped Beetle. Shannon flops like a rag doll, all soaked hair and clothes and limbs. But she is holding something against her chest. Something slippery and dark. Their father throws his arm over the boat, reaching and scrambling to push Shannon up to safety. To pull himself up. It is then Wren realizes what is stretched across the boat between them. It's the limp form of Piper.

Wren surges through the water. From out of nowhere a man runs past her, leaping over the waves. He dives and makes his way out to the wreckage, his arms cutting through the surf. There are more arms: strong arms that grasp her middle. "It's okay," someone cries in her ear. A woman. "I've got you."

Wren is kicking and paddling toward the boat. She is a good swimmer. This woman doesn't understand. She has to get to her family.

But she can't. The arms are stronger than she

is, the grip relentless. All the air goes out of her. Wren is dragged back to the beach. There is a police siren behind from the parking lot. There are more people now. And hands. So many hands, rubbing her shivering arms and legs. Laying her back on the wet sand. The last thing she sees is the sky. The sun is breaking through.

When she wakes up, the light is bright. Too bright. But it is not the sun. There is the incessant beep she heard in her dreams. The fluorescent hum overhead. Wren blinks and tries to sit up. She's in a bed. Beside her, propped up in another bed, is Shannon, her face as blanched as the sheets enveloping her. Her mother's face appears above her; a sob escapes her throat. She cups Wren's face.

"Piper?" Wren's voice is sandpaper.

Shannon's head turns slowly on the pillow. "I got her, Wrenny. She's okay."

Lindy presses her forehead to Wren's. "Piper's just down the hall, baby. She's having some tests, and we can see her soon," she whispers.

It's then Wren notices her father. He's slumped in a chair. His head is between his knees. A keening sound she has never heard before emanates from his corner of the room.

One

Hank

There would be no sixty-fifth birthday party after all. To be fair it was not the dog's fault. Bowser, oversized in limb as he was overzealous in tongue, could not entirely be blamed.

"He needs hip surgery!" Lindy announced as she fluttered into the kitchen, wringing her hands so that all her silver bracelets jangled nervously up and down her elegant arms. "Oh, and we took your car, honey. I'm afraid there's a rip across the back seat, but that hardly matters now."

Hardly? They (being Lindy and the dog) had just returned from the vet, and Hank could feel the back of his neck prickle. He was so distracted by the news of their chosen mode of transport and the subsequent back seat damage, that he had not fully processed what his wife was saying about the dog. He knew this would happen. To his consternation, he'd discovered his new car was not in the driveway when he'd gone out to retrieve the morning paper from the stoop. Only Lindy's car remained—*the dog car*—aptly named for its age, its wear, and its accompanying odor. It was parked beside the rose bushes, its

13

dented green fender reflecting the morning sun coming up over the house. He groaned.

Lindy had sworn not to let Bowser in the new car. *Hank's* new car: a sensible and pristinely kept Volvo wagon, his only splurge being the buttery leather interior he had no intention of marring with Great Dane toenails, and whose windows he would prefer not be shellacked in dog drool. He pictured Lindy zipping through town, Bowser's head thrust out the back-left window, his tail sticking out the right. "How big is the rip?"

Lindy waved her hand in the air, her new focus on to the hulking espresso maker, which she jiggled and rattled impatiently. "How does this thing . . . ?"

"The lever on the right," Hank began. "You have to pull the lever." Unlike his car the coffee maker was not new, and yet they went through this every morning. But never mind—he was still picturing the back seat of his car.

Lindy tugged the lever twice, and Hank let out his breath as the steaming concoction coursed into her cup. She dumped in a heap of sugar, shaking her head as she spoke. "He was just neutered last month. And now he needs hip surgery. My poor baby."

My poor wallet, is what Hank was thinking but did not dare say. First the Volvo seat and now the dog. Though he should've been used to it by now.

14

His wife was gifted, no—*cursed*—with an attraction for wayward animals. Stray cats who appeared at the back screen door. Baby birds fallen from nests. Just yesterday the slow-moving disc of a snapping turtle that needed to be ferried across a busy road, a move he later learned Lindy did all by herself as the two men, who had also pulled their cars over, stood warily aside verbally noting the dangerous size of its jagged mouth. Animals in distress always found Lindy Bailey. If anyone had bothered to ask Hank, he would've declared himself an animal lover as devout as the next. He'd had plenty of pets as a kid: a handful of hamsters, several cats; he couldn't recall a dogless school year if pressed. But it paled against what Lindy had going on.

The fact of her boundless canine love was the second thing she'd told him on the night they met at the Squire. "I have three headstrong daughters. And we love dogs." Whether it had been a confession or a warning, he had not been sure. Were the headstrong daughters the reason for the dog-loving requirement? Was it a condition they'd set forth for their single mother: the measuring stick against which all prospective suitors of their mother would be judged? Or were the dogs and daughters independent of one another—two equally imperative pieces of information that Hank needed to be made aware of?

It didn't matter. Lindy's unblinking blue eyes had been so earnest it had gone to his heart. The second those words were uttered, she'd swept a lock of blonde hair girlishly behind her ear and tipped back the glass of bourbon that had shown up during her telling. In that moment, had she asked him to join the circus, he would have.

Now, fifteen years later in their Cape Cod kitchen, Hank's adoration for Lindy Bailey had not thinned in its concentration. Her youthful frame still barely filled the kitchen doorway when she entered each morning, blinking, lured from bed by the scent of the espresso he brewed for her. These days there were creases that had etched their paths around her eyes, but they were still eyes that crinkled with easy laughter. What made him happiest was that Lindy now possessed an air of contentedness in her posture that had replaced the too-slow-to-empty recesses of worry she'd carried in her limbs when they'd first met. Back then she was an overwhelmed single mother to three preteen girls who not only needed but also demanded her attention like ravenous eaglets in a nest. Her devotion to them was something that had pulled Hank to her, a surprise since he had no children of his own and could not recall ever wanting any.

In that vein he'd had to learn how to navigate around Lindy, and later, her girls. Like everyone else who crossed their paths, he was helpless in the wake of their glossy hair, their urgent chatter, the beguiling flood of laughter that erupted as easily as their tempers. The Bailey women had that effect on people, and despite his thinking otherwise, his years of worldly travel and education during his quiet bachelor life had been no match for them.

Lindy sipped her espresso and stared absently out the window overlooking the green stretch of backyard and the salt pond beyond it. "I'm afraid we'll have to cancel our trip."

Hank blinked. "Tuscany?"

"I'm sorry, dear. But don't worry, we'll still have a party."

Hank was not an extravagant man. The idea of the birthday party thrown in his honor was not something he relished. That he'd agreed to a party at all had been cause for celebration. Lindy and Shannon had seized upon it, and since then the party had taken on a life of its own, morphing from an intimate backyard gathering into an *event*. His September birthday was still three months away! And yet a caterer had been sought. A tent had been mentioned. Hank cringed at every turn; he hated being the focus of attention. He hated getting older. He hated, most of all, a fuss.

But the real cause for celebration—the sole saving grace of this party—was the trip! He and Lindy would finally be going to Tuscany. The planning for which was as long and winding as the years he'd spent acclimating to family life with the Bailey girls.

The seed for the trip had also been planted that first fabled night they met at the Squire, just after mention of the daughters and the dogs. The third thing she'd told him that night was that she'd never been to Italy. He'd lifted one shoulder in a half-hearted shrug; many people had not been to Italy. But she'd turned to him then, leaning in close and lowering her voice, as in confession. He'd mirrored her, their noses almost touching. He was so engrossed by the lingering smell of bourbon on her lips—fuller lips he'd not seen— that he almost missed what she said next. *That she longed to eat wild boar pappardelle and sip Vin Santo in a trattoria. That she could not imagine her life without biking along a village road and finding a field of sunflowers beside which to set up her art easel.* The images that took root in Hank's mind had caused him to steady himself on his barstool. This woman, who so far had spoken only of wild boar and even wilder children, was unlike any person he had ever met. He'd decided right then they would go together.

No matter that that decision had taken a back seat to fifteen years of ballet lessons and soccer carpools and, later, college tuitions. To leaving Boston and getting married and moving in together in the sleepy seaside hamlet of Chatham.

To walking the ever-quivering wire that was stepparenting three children who on some days clung to him like lovestruck monkeys and on others could wither his insides with their passing glares. On occasions of particular struggle, like the time Piper ran away from Girl Scout camp in upstate Maine to find a boy she'd met at the camp across the lake, or when Shannon and five classmates handcuffed themselves to the band teacher's desk to protest the board of education's defunding of the district arts program, Hank had wondered what on earth he'd gotten himself into by marrying into a full-fledged family. By what stroke of madness had he given up his quiet Brookline apartment with its leather wing-back chair overlooking the cityscape? In those moments of doubt he'd drawn strength from the gauzy memory of that first meeting with his wife at the pub: the burn of bourbon on her lips, the fearless glint in her gaze, and the promise of a Tuscan voyage, just the two of them. And so with that sole reason to steel himself by, Hank had weathered it all, eventually finding himself so bewitched by each of the three Bailey girls that he committed to seeing them through their complicated adolescences into adulthood year after year. Until this year, with all three finally sprung from the family house, when he and Lindy had booked their tickets for his birthday trip to Italy. They had made it. They would, after all, embrace in slumber in some faraway hotel under a Tuscan moon.

Hank stared back at his wife. "We're canceling Tuscany?"

Lindy set her empty mug in the sink and ran the tap. "You poor thing."

But she was not referring to Hank. "I knew hip dysplasia was common in large breeds, but Bowser's so young. The vet quoted the surgery at five thousand dollars. And then there's the physical therapy afterward: at least eight weeks. But I think we can do some of that here at home." She turned to look at Hank, a soapy dish in her hand. "We can't not do it, honey."

As if on cue, Bowser ambled into the kitchen and collapsed on the antique pine floor to nap. Lindy beamed. "Look. Look at that face."

Hank did as he was told, but Bowser did not return the gaze. He was too busy staring back at Lindy with the singular and abiding love a dog holds for its person. Hank was not that person.

Hank sighed and looked instead at his feet that were tucked into worn sheepskin slippers. He needed new slippers. The dog needed a new hip.

Behind him Lindy clattered a pan in the farm-house sink. "Don't worry, darling. Tuscany will still be there."

Two

Wren

D amn it." There were two missing boxes. Maybe three. Wren tore the shipping slip from its plastic sleeve and scrutinized the order. *Bas relief art tiles: clamshell, crab, plover. Seahorse, schooner, shark.* The shark motif had been a custom request, and she was thrilled when Carol, the artist, agreed to make a limited-edition series for her.

Ari, her shop assistant, looked up sympathetically from behind the cash register. "No sharks?"

"No sharks."

Thanks to a rise in great white shark sightings in recent years, Chatham had become famed along the eastern seaboard and was now known as the new shark capital. To the surprise of the chamber of commerce, instead of deterring tourists, so far the influx of sharks along Chatham's shores seemed to be luring them. In that spirit, local shop owners and businesses were trying to embrace the arrival of their finned visitors. The Chatham Merchant's Association launched a shark artwork installation on the front lawn in front of the Eldredge Library. Five-foot-long "sharks" were sponsored and decorated by local businesses and then displayed in front of the library steps. They were quite popular among both locals and tourists, so much so that on a few occasions a shark had been "poached," leading to a reward being offered for information about the stolen piece of art. As her own nod to the great white visitors and as a whimsical touch to her new boutique, the Fisherman's Daughter, Wren had commissioned a special shark tile to be made for her shop. But now it was missing.

Wren scanned the open boxes strewn across the shop's hardwood floor. The crabs, clams, and plovers were accounted for. The rest of the order was not. Wren slapped a box shut.

It was the first week of June, and though tourist season officially started Memorial Day, the real stream of visitors wouldn't clog the Mid-Cape Highway until school let out. It was her deadline to have the store stocked and ready for them.

"Want me to call UPS?" Ari asked. "We placed the order. We know Carol made them."

"Please do. They're custom pieces. It's not like we can refill a missing order by next week." She checked her watch: Lucy would be home from school in twenty minutes. "I've got just enough time to hang these before I go. Though I really want a coffee."

Ari scrutinized the boxes and then the look on

her boss's face. "I'll get it. How about a green tea? It's calming."

"The usual will do: two creams, one sugar, please."

Ari shrugged and took the five-dollar bill Wren handed her on the way out. She was the new hire—the only hire—freshly home from her first year at BC and as new to retail as the boutique was to Main Street. But if she had zero experience in sales, she was also unlike the other candidates who answered questions with an apathetic air, seemingly more interested in scoping out the proximity to the beach or keeping their nights free. Ari, her last interview of the day, had walked in with a book under her arm and then halted in the middle of the store, eyes narrowed.

"What?" Wren had asked. By that point, she'd had no patience and even less hope of finding someone.

Ari shook her head. "Nothing." But her gaze roamed across the painted shelves of maritime artwork that lined the wall, the rack of earth-toned organic cotton clothes, and finally rested on the old pine table in the center of the room where spindly arms of driftwood displayed bracelets, necklaces, and rings crafted by Cape jewelers. Wren watched as she set her book down and moved thoughtfully through the store, peering into the glass jewelry case by the cash register, running her fingers over a teal scarf.

"That scarf is made from seaweed."

"So this is all local?" Ari picked up a necklace, and turned the pearly amulet at its center over in her hand.

"All of it. And eco-friendly. That's an antique button," Wren said, pointing at the necklace in Ari's open palm.

"Huh. It looks like carved oyster shell."

Wren smiled. "Which is why I love it."

Ari looked around once more and nodded, but her expression was hard to place. "Yeah. This place is different."

Wren felt her defense going up. "How so?"

"I don't know. I guess it feels like you brought the ocean indoors." And with that statement, Ari was Wren's right-hand girl for the summer.

But the store had yet to open its doors. Wren had signed the lease that winter and had been fiercely working to ready the space since. There were dark frosted nights when she made dinner for Lucy, tucked her into bed, and left her in Lindy's care only to drive back into town to scrape and sand the baseboards or prime the display shelves with paint into the wee hours. The short gray days had been filled with making phone calls and placing orders to handpicked artisans. Like Carol, from Provincetown, whose ceramic sculpture tiles were glazed and kiln-dried. Or Joseph, from Sandwich, who provided hand-dyed seaweed scarves so soft your fingers lingered in the twists of their fiber. All of the previous fall Wren had driven up and down the Cape to find these wares and their makers, visiting craft fairs and dipping into local boutiques. Main Street Chatham was already teeming with trendy clothing stores, galleries, and gift shops. Wren was purposefully not like them: she did not possess the largest inventory or carry the trendiest souvenirs. A business move that had initially worried her family.

"No Lily Pulitzer?" Shannon had asked, blinking. Wren suppressed her irritation. She'd fully expected her older sister's pragmatism. After all, Shannon did not run a large home over on Stage Harbor and ferry her three children from violin lessons to chess matches to lacrosse prac-tice, while also assisting at her husband, Reid's, office, without running a tight ship. Reid and his family, all Boston natives, owned Whitcomb Group, the largest commercial and residential brokerage on the Cape, and it was he who had tipped Wren off about the upcoming retail space on Main Street before it even listed.

"Not her style," Lindy said, briskly coming to Wren's defense. Lindy had loved the ecofriendly-boutique concept from the start. Of course she had—she was an artist—but she, too, expressed some measure of doubt. "What about a few pairs of sunglasses? This *is* a summer resort town, honey."

"Not my vision," Wren explained. Then, winking, she said, "No pun intended."

Only Lindy laughed.

"What? I want to be unique," Wren said.

Shannon was not giving an inch. "You want to survive past Labor Day, too, don't you?"

Wren told herself she didn't care if her family didn't get it. She knew what downtown Chatham retailers had to offer, and she knew what was missing. There would be no Sperry Top-Siders or *CAPE COD* hoodies in her window. Nor would there be booming music or throngs of teenage girls bent over a basket of sailor-knot bracelets. She wanted her clientele to feel as if they were stepping onto the beach, or back in time. The whitewashed walls were like a stretch of sand bar, the artwork on them like seashells waiting to be picked up and examined. The clothes were fashionable but comfortable: a soft organic cotton sheath, a little girl's brightly printed smock dress. Wren sought out goods that were not only a pleasure to look at or wear but could also make her customers feel good about where they were putting their dollars. Her family would come around, she told herself.

It finally happened last week. Shannon sailed in to the shop on the way home from school with the kids and stopped dead in her tracks. Wren led her around, first to the glass case of silver necklaces, then to the rack of flour-sack dishtowels printed with fish, which Shannon had promptly picked up and blown her nose directly into.

"What on earth?"

"I'll pay for it," Shannon blubbered. "I'm just so proud of you, Wrenny."

Only Piper had yet to weigh in. Wren's little sister had seen the original shop space back in March when she'd come home to the Cape for spring break, when it was still raw and faceless. Curious, she'd tagged along and spent a couple of late nights helping Wren paint the walls a color called "sailcloth." Though "helping" largely meant keeping Wren company, sitting cross-legged on the unfinished pine floors with a flask of Fireball, regaling her sister with anecdotes about her Boston roommates while Wren was perched on a ladder with a roller. Piper had never been a roll-up-your-sleeves kind of girl. But she was reliable entertainment.

Now, Wren glanced around the store. Two weeks until opening day. The walls were painted, the floors finished, the old-fashioned cash register installed. Fliers had been made, social media announcements posted, and an interview with the local paper would run next week. Stocking the last of the inventory was all that remained.

The bell above the shop door dinged. "French

vanilla, cream, two sugars." Ari handed Wren the warm cup. "Oh, and here's the mail."

Wren riffled quickly through the envelopes. Only ten minutes to get across town for Lucy's school bus.

"You'd better hit the road. Lucy will make you pay if you forget her again."

Wren groaned. "I didn't forget her."

"Try telling her that."

It was a half truth. Lately the store had become a bit of a time vortex for her, and the school had called not once, but twice, last week to say that the bus was sitting at the curb in front of Wren's house and *where was she?* Lucy had been returned to the school where Wren had found her, arms crossed and her mouth fixed in a straight line, sitting on an office bench. When Wren tried to explain, Lucy lifted one small hand. "I already know. You were at the store."

Wren glanced at her watch. "You're right. Will you sort the mail for me?" She thrust the pile of envelopes back at Ari, but in her haste they fell out of her hand and spilled across the floor.

"Just go," Ari said. Wren was about to step over the mess when a pale blue envelope caught her eye. She reached down for it.

Wren Livingston Bailey, The Fisherman's Daughter. The scrawled handwriting was as familiar as the veins on the back of her hand. She sucked in her breath.

Ari glanced up at her. "You okay?"

Wren jammed the envelope in her back pocket. "I'm late!" She grabbed her purse and keys from the counter and hurried for the door. "Thanks for the coffee."

When she was safely inside her car, she pulled the envelope out and stared at it. *Livingston* came from her great-grandfather, on Caleb's side. Caleb Bailey was the only person who ever used her full name. Wren swallowed and shoved the envelope in the glove box. It had been twenty-three years since she'd gotten anything in the mail from him, since she'd heard a word, spoken or written, from her estranged father. She threw the Jeep in gear and turned toward home.

Three

Shannon

Avery, you need to get moving. Tennis starts
in ten," Shannon called up the sweeping
staircase. Her oldest daughter had retreated to her
room since school ended to presumably work on
a Mayan civilization social-studies project that
was due the next day.

Shannon had checked the family calendar
twice. George was in red. Winnie in green. Avery
in blue. Reid jokingly called it the command
center. Shannon didn't care; with three busy kids
it was what kept them afloat. "I don't see anything listed here for social studies."

"The teacher assigned it today. It's a graphic
novel."

"You mean like those comic-book stories?"

"I guess. But in French."

"Wait . . . I thought this was for social studies?"

Avery rolled her eyes. "It is."

"In French?"

"Mom. It's interdisciplinary."

"Oh." Interdisciplinary and due tomorrow. She
supposed she should at least be grateful the last-
minute assignment required just colored pencils

and paper, and not a shoe box, an assortment of Styrofoam balls, and acrylic paint. Colored pencils she had.

Shannon returned her attention to the cutting board: two halved carrots, a split stalk of celery, and a cucumber whose green watery depths she'd already scooped the seeds from and sliced.

"I hate celery," George informed her, strolling into the kitchen and peering sideways at her work.

"I know. It's for your sister. And please don't say *hate*. It's such a strong word."

He blinked. "I don't care for cucumber either."

Shannon set down her knife. "George."

"What? I don't." He sat down at the island and rested his six-year-old head on the mahogany surface.

"What's for snack?" Winnie breezed into the kitchen, her soccer bag slung over her shoulder, her cleats making clicking sounds on the new cork floor.

Shannon swiveled around. "Winnie, the floor. Your cleats!"

"Oh, sorry." She reached around her mother and popped a carrot in her mouth.

"Why can't we have Doritos?" George mumbled, his head still resting on the island.

"Because you're growing and I want you to eat something healthy. It's my job."

"What's your job?" Avery appeared in the doorway, tennis racket in hand.

"Vegetables," George replied.

"Didn't I see you get off the bus with a bag of Doritos today?" Avery asked him.

"Did not."

Shannon glanced from her eldest to her youngest. "Is that so?"

George pressed his lips together. "Michael Donnelly gave them to me. His mother lets him have Doritos."

Shannon checked her watch, silently calculating how much time she needed to drive across town and drop Avery at the Chatham Beach and Tennis Club and zip over to Monomoy Middle School for Winnie's scrimmage. She still needed to pick up chicken for dinner. Every Friday was chicken piccata night. "Next time tell Michael Donnelly to keep his Doritos to himself." She thrust a carrot in his direction, and to his credit, he took it. She ruffled his hair.

They piled into the Suburban and eased out of the garage. She still wasn't used to the breadth of the new car. On the way to service at United Methodist that past Sunday, Reid had found himself behind the wheel for the first time and wondered aloud if they really needed the hulking SUV. "It's a beast. A behemoth beast."

Shannon had asked him when the last time was that he'd loaded up dinner to go and ferried half the soccer team to a game in Dennisport. This car was her second home. Though, to be honest, she probably spent more time in it than the house. And as much as she was loath to admit the gas it guzzled or the fumes it spewed, she loved the damn thing. She loved riding high up off the road as others whizzed by balancing coffees and phones on their steering wheels, she loved the safety she felt with her small brood safely ensconced in its steel nest. With all the unpredictability in the world today, Shannon would've driven a tank if she could have.

As soon as she dropped the girls off, she headed south on Route 28 toward Reid's office. It'd been two years since George started school and she'd joined the team at Whitcomb. And she'd loved it. The job was great—but what was best about it was getting dressed, putting on lipstick, and seeing other adults. She didn't care if it was seventy-nine-year-old Sheila, who hadn't sold a single house all year but who brought in cranberry scones for the staff each morning, or if it were a moneyed New York couple fresh off the tarmac at Chatham Airport on the hunt for a beachfront summer residence. It meant she was out of the house and convening with people above the age of twelve. Not that Shannon didn't love her children or her home. Their Stage Harbor residence was a stately, shingled colonial that she and Reid had had their eye on since they were married, right along the water. Since buying it three years ago, they'd renovated it to near perfection. Every drop of her coastal New England taste was etched into that house, from the beveled marble subway tiles over her professional-grade range to the sweeping mahogany island top that her red O&G Colt barstools surrounded. It was a designer Cape Cod dream home, once featured in *Elle Décor*. She'd been raised in her grandmother Beverly's School Street village house, just off Main Street in Chatham proper. She hadn't gone far. Stage Harbor was just across town to the west, but those miles had landed her in another universe entirely.

From the outside, Shannon knew how she appeared to others. She'd married her best friend, moved into the quintessential coastal house, and freelanced for the realty group as a photographer. But what few knew was that none of that squelched the worry that coursed through her flesh and bones at various voltages day in and out. It didn't matter that all three of her children had been born healthy and continued to thrive. Nor did it matter that they were good students, strong athletes, and each had their fair share of equally well-adjusted friends. She knew shortages of those very things were what kept other parents up at night. What kept her awake, on the nights she did not pop one of those sleek Ativan tablets that

Dr. Weber, her psychiatrist, had prescribed for her last spring, was her anxiety over the safety of her children. "The kids are fine, Shannon. They're tucked in their beds, sound asleep. I just checked on them. I don't understand what you're stressed about."

"Anything can happen in a heartbeat," she'd say quietly, pulling the sheets up.

Shannon and Reid had known each other since the summer of their junior year in high school, even though they grew up in different parts of Massachusetts. Reid had lived in Sudbury, in the Boston metro area, and came to Chatham every summer to visit his grandparents, who'd retired on Barcliff Avenue. His grandfather had started the Whitcomb Group, a residential and commercial real-estate agency in the 1960s, where Reid worked each summer. It was now run by his mother, Elizabeth (Bitsy), who'd moved to Chatham when Reid was in college. Even though three generations of his family had Chatham ties, Reid would forever be considered a visitor.

Shannon, however, was a local. Bred and born. Her family ties to Chatham were not as vacationers or summer residents—her great-grandmother Mildred had been the daughter of a farmer turned cod fisherman, and they'd resided above Main Street on Tipcart Lane when it was just a hillside of rolling field and farm animals. Having been raised largely by the

35

women in her family, her upbringing had been less conventional than Reid's. He empathized with her that her father had left the family at a vulnerable time in her adolescence, that he had not been there for her or her sisters when they were growing up. But he also pointed to the fact that Shannon turned out largely unscathed: She was valedictorian of her high school class. She went on to Wellesley, where she majored in both finance and art, which amused him. "See honey? You left no stone unturned, even in your college studies." They'd begun dating seriously during those years and had stayed together since. Now, fourteen years of marriage, three kids, and a dream house later, they were happy, weren't they?

They were. How could they not be? But for her anxieties.

Living on the Cape it was assumed you loved the beaches. You were surrounded by them—Hardings, Ridgevale, Cockle Cove. Oyster Pond, Stage Harbor, Monomoy Island. The ocean was everywhere—in channels and salt ponds. In the protected bay beaches. In the twin harbors, Chatham and Stage Harbor. Beaches were what drew people out to the Cape.

But Shannon was terrified of the water. Of big surf, of deep currents, of boats. It began that morning of the accident on Lighthouse Beach, with her father and sisters, and it had stayed with her, silhouetting the years since like a dark shadow.

Unlike the other mothers on the Cape, Shannon did not take her children to the beach. Rather, she kept them enrolled in summer swim and sailing lessons where professionals could teach them and monitor them on the water while she worked. On weekends, she politely declined offers by friends and neighbors to go out on their boats. She would not go fishing or sailing, claiming instead that she was prone to severe sea sickness. At the yacht club, she kept herself busy with fund-raisers, picnics, and barbecues, all land-based forms of participation. It was manageable that way, living on the water without actually interacting with it.

But Dr. Weber had long warned her that she needed to confront the root of her anxieties head-on before it confronted her. In the meantime, Shannon met with him twice a month and relied on her prescription as needed for the bad days. Shannon was not a pill-popper; she'd heard plenty about dependency and its side effects. Only on those nights that her hands were clammy in the dark and her skin stuck to the sheets with perspiration did she take an Ativan. Though there were other things that helped, things that were more socially acceptable. Like her vodka tonics. She mixed herself one most nights as she cooked dinner. That was fine—all her friends had wine most evenings. And even if she did need a sip or two at lunch on occasion, it wasn't often. Shannon was doing fine—in fact, she'd go so far as to say she was doing great. Now, as she turned the car into town Shannon ticked off the remains of her to-do list for the day. She'd designed a brochure for a contemporary renovation up on Briarcliff, a unique listing against the usual cottage styles and Capes for sale in the area. She wanted to see if the brochures were in from the printer and ready for the open house that weekend.

Unlike most residential realty groups, where nowadays agents worked remotely from their homes and took calls on their cells, Bitsy Whitcomb had put her well-heeled foot down and insisted that their office maintain a level of personal touch. As such, agents were expected to show their faces in the office. The Cape, in full summer, was different, Bitsy said. People wanted last-minute rentals. Tourists rolled through town, finding themselves spontaneously inspired to peruse seller listings after happening upon "the cutest little cottage over by the lighthouse." And the Whitcomb Group would be standing by with glossy listings in hand when they did.

Shirley, the office manager, piped up from behind her desk before Shannon and George were halfway through the front door. "Oh good, you're here! Got a minute?"

"What's up?"

"We have a new seller off of Ridgevale,"

Shirley said. "You know that colossal renovation at the northern end of Nantucket Drive?"

Shannon did. It had been on the market all year, listed at $2.5 million. The owner was notorious both for the four-year renovation timeline and the fact that the house had been listed and pulled from three different brokerages in the last six months. Despite his difficult reputation, Bitsy had been courting the owner. It wasn't about the money. She had plenty of listings in that price range and more; this was about selling the unsalable. Something all the competing firms had so far failed to do. Which meant Bitsy would be the exception. The firm's mission statement stated just that: *Exceptional service for exceptional homes.* Suddenly Shannon had a feeling about who Bitsy had been out of the office having lunch with all afternoon. "The Banks place?"

"That's the one. Everett Banks. Nasty man. Nice house."

"When did we land it?"

Shirley's eyes widened. "Just this afternoon. Bitsy had lunch with him at Chatham Bars. Came back like the cat who swallowed the canary."

Shannon smiled inwardly. She knew just the look on her mother-in-law's face. What she didn't know was why Reid hadn't called to tell her the big news yet.

Shirley twisted her pearl necklace, looking

pained. "It seems the owner wants something different this time around."

"Different?"

"As in marketing and photography. It seems Bitsy is going to arrange a photo shoot for the place. She's planning to bring in an entire film crew with stage lighting and everything—she's even hiring a drone photographer to take aerials."

So that was the reason Reid hadn't told her yet; she had long been the agency's photographer. But now Bitsy was bringing in outside help. *Professionals.* Shannon wondered when they were planning to tell her.

"Your work is so good, honey. I don't know why all the fuss. If it were up to me . . ."

Shannon forced a smile. "It's okay, Shirley. It wasn't your decision."

"I know it's the tip of the weekend, but do you think you could run over there and take some stock photos? Bitsy wants something basic to show potential crews when she interviews them. She won't take anyone out to the property until it's the right team. The seller was very particular about his privacy."

Shannon nodded, ignoring the growing heat that was rising in her cheeks. "So she hasn't hired a crew yet?"

Shirley twisted her necklace again, and Shannon worried it might pop. "Not that I know of."

Shannon felt bad for Shirley. Leave it to Bitsy to hand the nicest person in the office the task of delivering her most unpalatable messages. Reid would never have asked her to do the prep work for an assignment that would ultimately be given away to a third party. He would've insisted that she get the job, or at least a chance at it. But if what Shirley said was true—maybe there was still a chance.

"I'll head right over." There were two things about this deal that stung: the fact she'd been overlooked as the talent. And the fact of the listing's address: Ridgevale Beach.

Shirley's cheeks deflated like a balloon with relief. "Thank you, honey. You know I'd rather it was you—your pictures sell these houses. Reid always says so."

Reid did say that, if his mother didn't. It was one thing about her husband Shannon knew she shouldn't take for granted. He saw her hard work. Her juggling of the kids and the house and the office. In all of that, he saw *her*. But she was still seething about Bitsy's decision. And she wanted to talk with him about it.

"Any idea when Reid will be back?" she asked.

Shirley shrugged. "I think he said six o'clock? Though I'll be gone by then."

"Thanks," Shannon said, grabbing her purse. "C'mon George." They had thirty minutes before she had to pick up the girls.

41

At the tip of Ridgevale Road was a dense grid of sandy lanes and narrow streets that stretched along its same-named beach. It was a very desirable part of town. The sound flanked the road on the left, a shimmering stretch of sea that caused drivers to slow their cars and roll down their windows. For Shannon, however, it had the opposite effect. This was also the road she had grown up on, the last place they had lived as a family of five before Caleb Bailey had left for good.

As she turned right onto Nantucket Drive, she kept her eyes trained straight ahead as she approached number 22. It didn't matter that it had been years since she'd been down this lane; she knew what she'd see by heart. The hydrangea bushes that flanked number 22's front door would be thrust in full-blue bloom. Out of the corner of her eye she noticed a flash of coral pink. Shannon *tsk*ed. Gone was the lobster-red front door. But the rest of the house appeared unchanged, the shingles the same weathered gray cedar. In the rear was the shed in which her father had stored the boats. If you looked carefully, there was even a hedge of wild rose that ran along the picket fence into the back where she and her little sisters used to play on their swing set. But that was long gone now, and there was no life beyond the thrust of vegetation. She accelerated past.

At the end of Nantucket Drive, her childhood

home safely in the rearview mirror, Shannon slowed and pulled in to number 36, the tires of her Suburban crunching on the white shell drive.

"Oh no. We're here to take pictures, aren't we?" It was an accusation. George puffed his cheeks out in the back seat, and she met his exasperated gaze in the mirror.

"Come on. You can help."

"I don't want to help. I want to go home. I'm tired."

Shannon raised an eyebrow. George had taken a "semester off" of soccer, something she did not relish but a move that Reid had encouraged. "These kids have more activities each season than I did in all of my childhood. Give the kid a season off."

"Come on, buddy. I'll let you snap a few photos."

Begrudgingly, George followed her out of the car.

The house had just had a facelift. Like the others on the street, it was a well-kept two story with an inviting front porch. The honey-colored shingle siding was brand-new, untouched by the salt air or the New England seasons. The windows and trim work had a fresh coat of sea-green paint. Her work was halfway done for her.

Shannon set up her camera, opting for a 40-millimeter lens. She didn't have a set routine when it came to photographing the houses for

Reid, rather she walked the property first and got a sense of the place. Sometimes it was the angle of the steps leading up to a sweeping back deck that inspired her; in others it could be the light bathing the smooth arc of a porthole window, the square edges of the front door. She moved about the front of the house, taking shots, and checking them. George trailed her into the backyard, hands stuffed in his pockets.

"Can you guess?" she asked him. It was a game she played when he tagged along on jobs, in part because he seemed interested, unlike his sisters, and this delighted her. And in part because it distracted him so she could get her work done.

George scowled up at the house. He was not going to smile. "The roof," he said, pointing to a shiny line of copper gutter.

"Ah!" she said glancing up. This house was not short on aesthetic appeal. "Good try, but that's not it." She snapped a few shots of the sprawling side deck. Then the outdoor shower, with a half moon carved in the door.

"The windows?" he asked. The windows were wavy glass, and she wondered if they'd had the panes specially made or if they were salvaged originals.

"You're getting closer!" she said, snapping a few more shots. They walked around the rear to a small patio.

George was getting bored. "I give up."

"Whitcombs don't give up."

"Fine. Last one." He glanced around the yard and up to the roofline. "Wait. I know. The whale!"

Shannon grinned. "Attaboy." Atop the roof sat a giant copper weathervane, the same rich patina as the gutters and fascia, in the shape of a whale.

She swapped out her lens and set the camera on its tripod in the far corner of the backyard. The nautical mammal came into view.

Shirley's words came back to her. "Your photos sell these houses." Shannon glanced down the street in the direction of their old family home.

Besides her children and husband, capturing images was one thing that had always brought pleasure. And yet it was the same thing that haunted her. It was the only gift Caleb Bailey had left her with, all those years ago. Shannon turned away from 22 Ridgevale. She looked back in the viewfinder, snapped twice more, and was done.

Four

Piper

She awoke with a start. The morning light was too intense. She leaned over the side of the bed; strewn across the floor were her clothes: her blouse, her wedges. That damn red skirt he liked so much.

Piper lifted the sheets very carefully and rolled out from under them. She tiptoed across the bedroom, scooping up her things as she went. Behind her, Adam stirred. She slipped into the bathroom and dressed quickly. Fuck. She never should've come back here.

She ran the tap until it was good and cold and splashed her face. There was one message on her phone. But it was just Wren: *Please call. Important!*

Piper deleted it.

Staring at her tangled red hair in the mirror, she struggled to recall the night before. Piper had not gone out intending to see Adam; quite the opposite, she'd planned an evening out with her girlfriends, hoping to run into Derek. Some of his Boston University department faculty often met up for a couple beers after Friday classes.

Instead, she'd followed her roommate Claire and their friend Hillary into the dimly lit pub and run smack into Adam. He was seated at the bar with a few guys, dressed similarly in crisp shirts and ties, watching a game on the flat-screen. He broke into a smile when he saw her. "Piper!"

"Adam."

Adam had never been good at containing his feelings. It'd been a few months since she called things off with him, and yet here he was just as bighearted as a Labrador retriever. She ordered three beers and tried to focus on the game on television.

"Want to join us?" Adam introduced her to his colleagues. They'd met at the university last year, but Adam had finished his MBA and now worked downtown.

She'd gestured over her shoulder. "Thanks, but I'm with some friends." Piper watched him look past her with curiosity into the crowd, but Adam was predictably too polite to inquire further. She wished the bartender would hurry up.

Three tall glasses of amber ale arrived and she shoved two twenties across the counter. "Keep the change." Piper really couldn't afford to leave the change. But she couldn't afford to stand there with Adam one second longer either.

"May I?" Before she could object, Adam stood and collected all three pints. She'd always liked his hands. "Where to?"

Piper deflated. His chivalry was ruining her good mood. "There." She pointed to Hillary and Claire, who were waving at them from a corner booth. A booth with plenty of extra room, she noticed with displeasure.

"Want to join us?" they said, when Adam delivered their drinks.

Adam glanced at Piper, but she didn't echo the invitation. "Thanks, but I think I'll leave you ladies to it. Have a good night."

"You, too." Piper slid into the booth.

"So that was Adam?" Hillary leaned across the table to clink glasses. "He's cute."

"And still seems interested," Claire added.

Piper took a long swallow of beer and relished the cold rush in her throat. "Come on, guys. The past is the past."

Hillary leaned in. "How long did you guys date?"

"Long enough to know he's a bore."

Claire narrowed her eyes. "You mean, long enough to know he's one of the good ones. Not to mention *available*."

Hillary feigned deep interest in her drink but Claire stared right at her. Piper knew her friends didn't approve of her new relationship with Derek. It wasn't undeserved.

The first time she'd gone to Professor Derek Cane's office in the English department at BU, it was to recite a poem. Despite the fact that that class was supposed to be an easy elective toward her education degree, she'd gotten a zero on a quiz after sleeping through class after a late night out. Cane had told them at the start of the term that they were allowed one do-over. They had to memorize a piece of work by a poet and recite it. When Piper knocked on his office door, John Donne's "The Ecstasy" dog-eared in the weighty anthology under her arm, redeeming herself academically had been her only intention.

The professor's desk was a mess; stacks of folders flanked a small clearing in the center where he flipped open his laptop, squinting at the screen. He appeared distracted, and she wondered if she'd gotten the time wrong. "Piper Bailey, right?"

She nodded.

"Whenever you're ready," he'd said, leaning back in his office chair. It creaked, the only other sound in the room beyond her breathing. The formality of the assignment was overshadowed by the intimacy of the office—his desk too close, his gaze too absorbing. She'd not noticed his blue eyes before. Nor the way his dark brows knit together, as they did then when she began. He couldn't have been more than ten years older than she was.

She recited the opening stanza too quickly.

"Breathe," he interjected.

Ruffled, she paused and cleared her throat,

beginning again. It seemed like forever to get through the next stanza, although she knew every word and every pause by heart. But by the time she got to the next, she'd relaxed into the flow of the language, the rhythm of the lines. She closed her eyes midway through and the rest poured from her mouth in the same mannered way it had when she'd practiced it in front of the bathroom mirror that morning. On the closing line, she opened her eyes, triumphant and relieved.

Professor Cane nodded indifferently. He opened his ledger and made a note, saying nothing.

Confused, she retrieved her bag from the couch and started for the door. She'd chosen the longest poem, the most complicated stanzas. She hadn't missed a single word.

"Why that one?" he said, finally.

She paused, her hand on the doorknob. "Excuse me?"

He looked amused. "It's a provocative title. An imposing length. What about this poem made you choose it?"

Something in the air shifted. "It's not obvious." She hesitated, wondering if this, too, would be reflected in her grade.

He waited for her to go on.

"The language is erotic, coy. The riverbank is 'like a pillow on the bed.' It's also 'pregnant.' But it's more than that. Donne compares the young lovers to planets, their souls leaving their bodies."

"Meaning?"

Here she did not hesitate. "That love is more than physicality. It's the fusion of the body and the soul. *That* is what makes them ecstatic."

She'd gotten an A. Days later she bumped into the professor at the student center kiosk. He bought her a coffee. Now, five months later, she was sneaking him into her apartment whenever he could get away from home. And hiding the fact that she was desperately in love with him. She'd not thought of Adam Brenner since.

Claire glanced over at Adam at the bar. Piper saw what she saw. The polished suit. The manners. That easy smile. "I don't get it Piper; I just don't get it."

Piper sighed and checked her phone. No messages. She tipped her beer back, emptying half the glass. "No one ever does."

They ordered another round. Then a pitcher and some tapas. Soon the pub filled, rounding out with the hot din of conversation and the clank of dinnerware. Eventually Piper relented and texted Derek: *At the Cambridge Queen's Head.* If he wanted to see her he'd make it happen.

She tried to focus on the conversation. Hillary had just wrapped up her master's in education, like Piper, and was interviewing for teaching positions. She had a second interview lined up at her first-choice school in Watertown. "I'm tired of interviewing. I'm so ready for a paycheck."

"I'd give anything to trade places," Claire said. She was working fifty-hour weeks as a graphic designer in an open-office cubicle downtown. She made great money, often lending some to Piper to cover rent, but she loathed her job. Her real complaint tonight was her soon-to-be mother-in-law's intrusive suggestions concerning her upcoming wedding that fall. "There's so much still to do. In that vein, we need to get together soon to look at bridesmaid dresses."

Hillary pulled up her calendar, but Piper had to try very hard to muster enthusiasm. She adored Claire, but she couldn't imagine getting married at age twenty-six. Hillary, on the other hand, was not far behind. Unlike Piper, both women had boyfriends' apartments to go to that night, and as the night wore on Piper prickled at their constant checking of phones and glances at watches. "You coming home tonight?" she asked Claire.

She shook her head. "I told Dan I'd stay at his place."

Piper understood. Their girls' night was winding down; they wanted to go home to their men.

By midnight Derek had still not responded. Was he tucking in his two kids? Collapsed on the couch with the TV remote and his wife? She ordered another pitcher for the table, and despite

Hillary and Claire's protests she talked them into staying out just a little longer.

Piper's last memory was laying down money at the pool table, cue in hand (had she even played?). The room was starting to spin just a little. She'd looked across the crowd to the doorway, which she now understood Derek would not be walking through. Hillary and Claire were ready to go. She should go, too. She let her eyes roam over the crowd one last time. To her surprise, Adam was still there. He was talking to a young woman on the adjacent barstool.

"We're going to walk to the T. Are you okay to catch a cab back?" The rush of beer and energy of the night had faded, leaving Piper subdued.

"All right," she relented. "Let's call it a night."

They headed to the door together, past Adam. The girl put a hand on his arm, laughed at something he said.

Piper's next memory was pushing through the crowd. She lurched up beside Adam, the blonde turning to notice her first.

"Hey," she said, tapping Adam roughly on the shoulder. His eyes were a little red and tired. But his smile was immediate. That was one thing about Adam Brenner; he had a great smile.

"Come on," Piper said. "Let's get out of here."

Now, Piper tugged on her skirt and tiptoed across the hardwood floors of Adam's bedroom. On the wall hung a Red Sox banner. A small desk in the corner had a picture of the family dog, a black Lab she couldn't remember the name of, and a pile of law books. And there, under the plaid comforter, Adam's sleeping form. Piper went over to the bed. She was furious with herself for landing there last night. She knew what it meant to him; what it did not mean to her. But standing there, looking down at his strong profile on the pillow, she felt some small part inside herself soften.

Outside Adam's door came a clattering sound of pots and pans from the kitchen. Quickly, she slipped into the hall, ducking out the front door before his roommate could see her. By the time she burst through the lobby doors downstairs, she was almost running, startling a young couple walking up the stoop with a toddler. "Sorry," she said. She had to get out of there. She had to call Derek.

Five

Wren

Wren ran the pea pods under water in the kitchen sink. Out in the yard, Lucy laughed aloud and instinctively her gaze went to the window. It'd been a long week. Between finalizing the store for its grand opening and staying on top of Lucy's end-of-the-year school events, Wren had barely been able to catch her breath. There was the kindergarten play, the chorus concert, and the class party she'd completely forgotten she'd volunteered to organize the crafts for back at the beginning of the year on open house night. The classroom mom had called earlier in the week to ask how it was going, and Wren had stammered, "Going great! Can't wait to share." She'd at least had the sense to ask, before the woman hung up, "Um, how many kids are there in the class again?" She'd tried not to take the heavy pause on the other end of the line personally.

There were fourteen students. The craft should account for twenty minutes of activity time. And the theme was "shooting stars." Whatever that meant. Since then, Wren had driven all the way

55

to Michael's craft store in Hyannis to fill her shopping cart with glitter paint, sponge brushes, and small wooden cutouts of moons (there hadn't been a single star between Chatham and Provincetown).

Every parent knew that this time of year was like riding a careening waterslide right down to the last day of school, and as a single parent Wren was especially sensitive about attendance. This was all on her. As was the Fisherman's Daughter's grand opening. This June felt like a tangle of wild *Rosa rugosa* about to burst open along the dune, a culmination of seasons of work and tending leading up to it. Lucy was just as much in bloom as Wren's shop. Wren could not afford a misstep with either, no matter what crossed her path in these final weeks. Including an envelope from her long-estranged father.

Outside, the late afternoon sun was high and bright, and Wren wished her energy level could match it. She kept one eye on Lucy and Badger playing in the yard, the other on the pea pods in the colander. The garden was just beginning to yield, and she longed for the day her window-sill would be lined with its cheerful bounty: tomatoes, zucchini, yellow squash. She opened the window and leaned out. "Lucy! Dinner."

There was the scrabble of dog toenails on the ancient hardwood floors and the slap of a screen door. "Ta-da!" Lucy plopped herself into a chair

56

at the table. Badger stood sentinel beside her, nose daringly close to the edge of the table.

"Hands," Wren said.

"But Mom . . ." Lucy held up her palms as Wren set the plate down in front of her.

"I see chickens. And dog."

Lucy narrowed her eyes, but pushed her chair back obediently. "Cannot."

"Can too. Now, go wash up."

As they ate, Wren watched her six-year-old drag her fork through her mashed potatoes with pleasure. The early summer sun had already colored her limbs peachy from outdoor play. She returned indoors ravenous each afternoon, seemingly growing each day. Lucy popped a pea into her mouth and closed her eyes. "You grew those, you know."

"I know." Lucy looked up from under her row of dark brown bangs. "Do you think Daddy likes peas?"

Wren swallowed. These kinds of questions were coming with more frequency, but they still caught her in the chest each time. "I'm sure he does," she said, carefully. James's dark brown eyes flashed in her mind. The same dark eyes that now watched her from across the table. Wren switched the subject, "Let's finish up, because I have brownies from Grammy."

Wren heaved an internal sigh of relief when Lucy dropped the subject, her six-year-old

57

thoughts turning swiftly to the pan of brownies on the counter.

This was your choice, she reminded herself whenever her thoughts landed on James. Something that was happening more and more lately.

From the moment she found out she was pregnant, Wren knew: she wanted this child and she would do whatever it took to raise her. She didn't need a man beside her to do that. As her mother had told her all her life, "There are things we can do for ourselves." Why not parent? Wren had had a father as a child, and look how that turned out. If Lucy were raised by her, and her alone, Wren could protect her. She could control who and what came into Lucy's life. She could keep her safe. If she missed James at all during those first years, it was in the way one misses a coworker. It would have been nice to have someone to share the burden with, someone to lighten the load.

When Lucy was born Wren was launched into motherhood with such primal force she'd been unable to think of anything else. If she were honest, she'd felt betrayed in those first months. Why hadn't anyone warned her about how hard this was? About the middle-of-the-night feedings, one after the other. About stumbling from darkness into daylight, not knowing what time of day it was but always headed in one direction:

to the crib. Lucy was a fitful baby, hungry and colicky. She needed to be held all the time. For hours Wren would nurse and rock her, rising ever so slowly from the chair and inching her way cautiously to the crib. How her back throbbed from leaning over that crib railing, holding Lucy close as she attempted to lower her softly, so softly, to her bed. To no avail! The moment Lucy detected the touch of the mattress beneath her swaddled backside, she arched angrily and began wailing. Defeated, Wren would scoop her up, and back to the rocker they'd go. If ever she thought she would lose her mind, it was during those early months.

There was no one but her to do it. Sure, Shannon came daily with casseroles and baby clothes and advice. Lindy moved in for a week, and took over household chores, in an attempt to afford Wren a reprieve. Wren wondered if any mother had ever wished to be saved from her own baby, as she did. It was the worst kind of guilt. No, she had not concerned herself with thoughts of James. She had no thoughts of her own during those first years; survival was all she could aim for.

Eventually, things got easier as everyone had promised. Wren learned to read her baby, to differentiate between a hunger cry and a hurt cry. That it was all right to tuck Lucy into bed with her so she could steal some sleep. The pull of love that Lucy projected was the one thing Wren was most unprepared for. When Lucy wrapped her tiny fingers around Wren's own, when she locked eyes on hers, something inside of Wren went still. There was no other person she wanted to be with more, no other place on earth she was needed. *This* was what it was all about.

But even her bottomless love for her child couldn't dampen the struggle of single parenting. When the baby awoke howling with hunger in the middle of the night, there was no one beside Wren in the bed to turn to. As Lucy began to crawl and walk, it was Wren who chased her, picked her up, redirected her from stairs and table edges and open doors. Likewise, the sick days and pediatrician appointments were hers alone to bear, just as the baby music classes and library story times were hers to enjoy. The years of single parenting had left Wren wrung out with exhaustion, her sole focus getting the two of them through each day, each milestone, each year. And then it seemed to ease. Too quickly, Lucy was school-aged and independent. She could tie her shoes and write her name, and was very much her own little self. Wren found that she was soaking up these moments rather than wishing them to pass, as she sometimes had. They were a team, and Lucy was her sidekick, her reason for everything. Surely they were enough for each other.

But lately Wren wasn't so sure about the decision she made all those years ago. Lucy's inquisitions about her father rattled Wren's conviction. They cast a shadow that stretched beyond the limited answers Wren provided. Would Wren and Lucy, just the two of them, still be enough?

For all the complaining Shannon did in private moments about her in-laws, from where Wren stood, Shannon's kids had it all. Happily married parents. Siblings. Two sets of grandparents. Cousins on both sides. Wren knew families came in all shapes and configurations, certainly more so these days than when she had been growing up. Wren wasn't divorced. There had been no upheaval, no grim division of parents and houses and toys. Neither had there been death, like one of the little girls in Lucy's class whose father had suffered a heart attack that year. But still—Lucy's family unit was different than the other kids in her kindergarten, and the more she became aware of it, the more Wren began to question her decision.

Lucy scraped the last forkful of peas across the plate and popped them into her mouth. "Brownie time?"

Wren had meant to tell her mother about the envelope when she popped over that afternoon. But when she arrived Lucy had been sprawled on

61

the couch with a book, and Lindy had seized upon the rare opportunity of her grandchild sitting still and scooped her onto her lap. The sight of the two snuggled and reading aloud together was one that caused Wren to pause in the doorway, envelope in hand; Lucy had enough. They *were* enough. She would not interrupt this moment with overdue words from the past.

Now, as she cleared the dinner plates, listening as Lucy told her about the tiny fairy hole she'd found in the base of a tree outside, she eyed the envelope across the room. It was right where she'd left it, tucked between two of her grand-mother's candlesticks on the fireplace mantel. She still needed to decide how to best share its contents with the rest of the family.

Last night she'd tried, but to no avail. As soon as Lucy was in bed she'd picked up the phone to call her sisters. But even before the first ring Wren already guessed that Shannon would be unreachable, probably at some Tiger Mom–endorsed lesson or other with the kids: chess, cello, or some kind of sailing thing at the club. What would Caleb Bailey have thought of that? As for Piper, her Boston days and nights were not anchored by family routine or suburban life; on any given night she could be engaged in some enviable pursuit that could not be had in their small Cape community, like going clubbing with her girlfriends in the North End or savoring a slow Chianti-sodden dinner in Little Italy on a date.

She'd left Shannon a voice message. "It's me. I know your evenings are busy, but give me a call when the kids are in bed." Next she'd fired a text to Piper, and tried to put the envelope out of her mind until one of them got back to her.

Wren put two large brownies on a plate and followed Lucy out to the front porch. Down the road the hum of a lawnmower rose up over the rooftops. It was her favorite time of year; the lazy promise of summer loomed in the longer hours, and she could spend her evenings on the porch watching Lucy ride her bike. Wren sat in one of the two Adirondack chairs and popped a brownie into her mouth. "Oh, Luce! Come try one of these. Grandma outdid herself."

Lucy climbed the porch steps, the dog on her heels. "Mom. He feels left out."

Wren glanced at Badger. He was staring at Lucy's plate, his big brown eyes wide with hope and a convincing degree of pitiable want. "Dogs can't have chocolate."

"But he wants something." Lucy hopped up and ran back into the house. A moment later she appeared at the door, holding a bag of deli meat Wren had just bought at the market. "Salami!"

"No, Luce. That's for your school lunch."

"But he loves salami! Just one piece? *Please?*"

Badger dragged his gaze from the package of salami to Wren and thumped his tail against the floorboards. "Good grief, you two are a pair. Just one piece."

Her phone rang, startling her. It was Piper. "Okay, okay, I got your messages. Where's the fire?"

"No fire. I was wondering when you were next planning to come home?"

Piper let out a long breath in her ear. "Funny you should ask. I was actually thinking of getting out of here this weekend."

Wren knew what that meant. Except when it came to her nieces and nephew, Piper did not come home when she was invited. Piper came home when she was on the run. Curious as Wren was, it would have to wait.

"How about tonight?" Wren braced herself. Even with her little sister's admission that she was Cape-bound, it usually took days. And several changes of heart. If she ever actually came home at all.

"I can get in the car in five."

Wren sat up. "Five minutes? Really?"

"But I'm not staying with Mom! Too many questions."

"Okay, what about . . . ?"

"And don't even suggest Shannon's house. That place is a crypt. God forbid I drop a crumb on her snow-white furniture or smudge her stainless-steel everything."

Wren was not going to push her good fortune. "Lucy can sleep with me tonight. I'll run upstairs and put fresh sheets on her bed for you."

Piper brightened. "If you insist. See you in two hours."

Shannon picked up on the first ring, like clockwork. "Hey, sorry I missed you last night. I was at the board of ed. meeting. Did you hear what the administration is planning for the new language arts curriculum? I know Lucy is only in kindergarten, but you really need to stay abreast of these school changes . . ."

"You need to come over," Wren interrupted.

"What's wrong?"

"Nothing. There's something I want to share with you. Something important."

Wren could feel her sister's worry coming through the line like the crackling of a bad connection. Shannon had always been like this: a coiled spring.

"What then—is it Lucy? Mom?"

Lucy whizzed by on the sidewalk on her bike. "No, everyone's fine. It's no big thing. Listen, is Reid home tonight to watch the kids?"

"Wrenny. If this is a no-kids visit, it's not *no big thing.*"

She had her there. Shannon was always toting at least two of her three children to Wren's house to play with the dog or snuggle with the chickens, things they did not and would not ever do at their own pet-hair-and-feather-free house.

Wren glanced at her watch. It would take Piper about an hour and a half more to drive down. "How's eight o'clock?"

"I'm not even going to look for my car keys until you tell me what this is about."

They both knew perfectly well Shannon's keys were in the Waterford bowl she kept by the front door. And she was far too nosy not to come, at this point.

But Wren relented. This was not going to be easy. "It's a family thing. I called Piper, too."

There was a beat of silence before Shannon let out her breath. "Jesus. It's him, isn't it?"

"Just come when you can. And bring the gin."

Six

Shannon

Piper hated to be left out of any family theatrics, a grievous act she was forever accusing the rest of them of committing against her. But there were some things Piper did not know that Shannon and Wren needed to discuss first. The older Bailey sisters may have only had a few years on her in age, but with those years came an experience so concentrated that it often felt to Shannon that she'd led a completely different childhood than her youngest sister. Piper's memory of Caleb Bailey was short—colored by the rose-tinged innocence of early childhood—and as such it was often more of a disservice to her. It was not her fault that her memory did not stretch as far down the road of their shared childhood as her sisters' did; arguably, it could be said that it acted as a shield for her, protecting her from what the rest of them had endured. In that vein the other Bailey women did not have the heart to correct Piper when she misspoke about Caleb; her memories were not wrong so much as they were incomplete. Shannon sometimes wondered if it was their job to fill in some of the holes. After all, Piper was not a child any more. She had always possessed an appetite for truths, the more dramatic the better; perhaps it was time to mete some out.

For her part, as the eldest Bailey girl, Shannon often wished she knew less than she did. Their grandmother Beverly liked to say, "Memory has weight. We carry it around with us in our baskets." It had sounded lovely to her ears as a kid, this bountiful collection: a bushel of fruit, a bouquet of flowers. But as she grew, it took on new meaning. There were days Shannon wished to set her basket of memories down; days she wished to abandon it altogether.

Although Shannon was not certain of what awaited her at Wren's house, the anticipation had caused a prickling that ran up and down her limbs like a current. Because of this, she found herself racing out the door in her threadbare yoga pants and hair pulled up in a messy knot, a look appropriated only within the shadowy confines of the family den with a late-night Lifetime movie on demand. But she didn't care; she needed to beat Piper to Wren's house. She'd called Reid to come straight home from the office, waited until she saw his headlights turn into the drive-way and had left the girls with George in the bathtub and a pot of spaghetti simmering on the Viking. Now, she walked through Wren's door without knocking and set the brown bag on the butcher-block island. "Does Mom know?"

Wren was standing in the kitchen as if she'd been waiting for her. Shannon pulled the bottle of gin from the bag and retrieved two limes from the fruit bowl. "That's why we're here tonight."

They clinked their glasses together across the kitchen table. Between them was the envelope. Wren pushed it across the wooden surface to her sister.

"You should probably take another sip before you read it." Shannon ignored this and pulled the letter from its sleeve. "I'll go check on Lucy," Wren added, leaving her for a moment.

When she came back downstairs, Shannon's glass was drained. The letter lay open before her.

"What is he thinking?"

Wren sat back down and studied her sister's expression. "I don't know."

"What the hell could he possibly be thinking?" she repeated. Her voice was hard. She went to the island and began slicing another lime into sharp sections.

Wren reached for the letter as if the answer might be there. She'd read it so many times she knew it by heart. "I think he just wants to see us."

"No. No, he doesn't. He wants something." She pointed the paring knife at Wren. "You don't let twenty-three years go by with no word. Not one Christmas, not one graduation. Jesus, Wren—he wasn't here for the birth of a single grandchild. You don't skip all that and suddenly show up out of the blue, unless you want something." Since she realized that Caleb Bailey was not coming home, Shannon had made a decision: her father was as good as dead to her.

Wren was not about to defend Caleb Bailey. Twenty-three years of silence was indefensible. "The question is, how do we answer him?"

Shannon snorted. "We don't. After all this time, we don't owe him anything." She mixed herself another drink and submerged two wedges of lime into her glass.

There was a sudden squeak from the front door followed by the slap of it closing. Piper appeared in the kitchen doorway, her hair askew, cheeks flushed.

"Pipe!" Wren jumped out of her seat.

But Piper held up both hands. She glanced between her two older sisters. "What's going on?"

They'd used up all the limes. Wren was on her second gin and tonic. Shannon had stopped after three, and was leaning back in her chair, her expression fixed. Piper had already moved on to the Grey Goose in the back of the fridge.

"He wants to come home." Piper said. There was an element of girlish hope in her tone.

Shannon threw Wren a look. "The question is, do we let him?"

"We don't own the Cape, Shannon," Piper said. "It's not like we can shut down the Sagamore Bridge and refuse him entry."

"Careful, Piper. Just because someone wants to come back into your life doesn't mean you have to let them. We've done just fine without him. And what about Mom? What would this do to her?"

"Or to Hank?" Wren added. Since she'd opened the letter, Hank was one of the first people she'd thought of. Hank had been good to them. More importantly, he'd been good for Lindy.

Piper threw up her hands. "Then we don't tell her."

"You can't be serious. After all Mom's gone through and sacrificed for us?"

Wren agreed. "She'd see it as a betrayal."

Piper doubled down. "It's not a betrayal if you're protecting her. Maybe keeping them separate is for the best. I don't want Mom or Hank to be hurt by any of this either. Maybe we could meet up with him first and see how it goes?"

Wren shook her head. "No, it'd be lying to her. Besides, Lindy knows everything we do."

"That's because you two never left the Cape. What do you expect when you stay in your mother's backyard?"

"Hey now," Shannon said.

Piper sipped her vodka. "What? Am I wrong about this?"

"Both of you, please." Wren put her face in her hands. This was the reason she'd hedged before calling her sisters. The two could barely agree on trivial matters.

Shannon pushed the envelope away from her. "I say we throw this away."

Piper swept it up. "This may be the last we ever hear from him! You can't throw it out."

"Isn't that what he did to us?" The ire had gone out of Shannon's voice, and she felt suddenly drained. "I have a family now, a family I can't even imagine leaving. It was awful what he did to all of us then, but, if it's possible, it seems even more awful to me now." Images ran through her mind; a warm hand in the sleeve of yellow rain slicker that reached for her own. Raindrops on waves, as they approached the dinghy with their fishing rods. The gray roll of fog unfolding over the water's edge, encompassing them both. She winced.

Piper did not share these memories. It was something they never talked about, a sort of silent agreement Shannon didn't recall any of them making. Piper knew the story about the ill-fated decision to take the Beetle out on a stormy day. She knew it resulted in the small jagged scar on her forehead, something she'd grown up with, no different than the freckles on her nose. At some point, she'd bumped her head. Soon after her father had left, Shannon was glad she

72

did not remember more. These things Piper did not recall were the very things Shannon had spent the better part of twenty-three years trying to forget.

"I say we tell Mom together at Sunday dinner." Wren turned to Piper. "Does she even know you're here?"

Piper lifted one shoulder. "I was going to call her in the morning."

Shannon scrutinized her little sister. Her expression was so void of the weight that pressed against her own temples daily. Piper had only herself to worry about, only herself to care for. And yet the rest of the women in the family— whose plates were so full—spent much of their time and energy on her.

"What are you doing here, anyway?" Shannon asked her.

"Same as you. Wren called."

"No, no you don't. None of us can ever get you to come home unless someone is being born or buried. What gives?"

Piper feigned incredulity. "Not true."

For the first time that night, Wren smiled. "It is, actually." She glanced at Shannon, and the two burst out laughing. "It's so true."

"Spill," Shannon said.

Piper stared at the table. "I came because Wren said it was important. But if you must know, I was thinking of coming home before I got her message. Things are a little crazy back in Boston. I needed a break."

"You graduated, right?"

"You know I graduated. You didn't come," Piper reminded her.

Shannon scowled. "We've been over this; Avery and Winnie had a tennis match in Orleans. We couldn't. I'm sorry."

Piper shrugged. "Whatever."

"You've sent out job applications, right?" Wren was treading carefully. She'd learned not to ask too much. Piper was like a cat, slinking in and out of Chatham as she pleased. But if you crowded her, she'd slip out the door and race back to Boston before you could think to try to catch her.

"Yes, I've sent out applications. Many of them, if you must know."

Shannon cocked her head. "Then who is he?"

From the look on her little sister's face, she knew she had her. Piper could not lie. Rather, she lied all the time, but not well. Her sisters were too well versed in the averted gaze, the nervous laugh, for it to have any effect on them anymore. Her hands fluttered when she fabricated, just like now as she hurried to the sink to fill her empty glass with water.

"Piper." Wren wasn't letting her off the hook either.

She set the glass down and turned to face them.

74

"You guys remember Adam? I told you about him awhile back."

"From BU? The guy who lived across the hall in your dorm?" Wren asked.

The Bailey women had piled into Lindy's car and visited Piper the fall before, and were pleasantly surprised when Piper brought Adam out to dinner on their last night. They'd all liked him quite a lot. Which meant that shortly after the family crossed the Sagamore Bridge on their way home, Adam's fate was sealed.

"Well, we sort of ran into each other again."

Shannon smacked the table. "Knew it."

"Are you guys back together?" Wren asked hopefully.

Piper shook her head. "There's someone else I've sort of been seeing. His name's Derek. He's different." She felt herself blush.

"Oh, oh."

"He's a little older, though not by much. He's cultured and funny. And we both love going to see the same obscure bands and wandering around the city."

"Then what's the problem?" Shannon asked.

"He's sort of coming out of a relationship. So he's not really available. Yet."

From the change of tone in her voice, Shannon could see this was sensitive territory for her little sister. Which was unusual for Piper. She decided to drop it. "Well, at least you've got options. And excitement. Unlike the rest of us."

It was nearly midnight. Shannon needed to get home; George would be up at six-thirty. There were breakfasts to be made and a family to mobilize for yet another long day ahead. The letter lay between them, no different than their unfinished conversation. Shannon picked it up.

"Have we decided anything?"

Wren nodded. "We tell Mom. Tomorrow."

"What about us? Do we have a consensus about him?"

Piper didn't hesitate. "I want to see him."

"I don't," Shannon said. "But you guys can do what you want."

This upset Piper. "Look, I know it's hard for you guys, but it's hard for me, too. I want to know why."

Shannon sighed. "Why he's back or why he left?"

"Both. I guess. But more than that, I want a chance to know him."

Shannon wouldn't try to argue; Piper's feelings were her own, and she was entitled to them. But what Piper lacked in understanding was the same thing that kept Shannon resisting this so-called reunion. "I don't think you'll get that from him," she cautioned her little sister. "I don't think seeing him again is going to get any of us closer to answers. Are you prepared for that?"

Piper looked back at her with an intensity that

belied her still repose. "I'm open, Shannon. I can't say I'm prepared, but at least I'm open."

Shannon shook her head wearily. "Life isn't all happy endings," she muttered. "I don't want you hanging your hat on a fairy tale that isn't going to happen."

Piper stood. "I don't have to listen to this, again."

Wren put her hand out and gently grabbed the edge of her sleeve. "Hey, wait. This isn't personal."

Piper's eyes were rimmed with tears. "Isn't personal? It's the most personal thing there is."

Shannon felt bad, but she couldn't relent on this. All these years it had felt to her like the three of them against Caleb—against his memory, his leaving the family, and most of all, his absence. Of the three of them, Shannon had been the one to shoulder most of it. As the eldest, she'd had no choice.

She turned to Wren, who had coaxed Piper to sit back down. "What about you?"

Wren pulled her knees up to hcr chest. "I don't know. I'm afraid to let him come back, but I'm also curious. Don't you want to know what he did for all those years?"

Shannon gazed at her sisters levelly. "Has it occurred to either one of you that he may have another family? Because after all this time, that's certainly possible."

"He wouldn't have," Piper said. "No way."

"Why not? We weren't his family."

"That's not true. He was troubled. Like Mom said, he was haunted."

Shannon set the envelope back on the table. "He was an alcoholic."

"It's a disease, Shannon. Not everyone can overcome it."

"Which is why Mom told him to go in the first place."

"No, Mom told him to get *help*."

"And did he?" She stared back at her sisters. "Last we heard he was somewhere down south passed out in a diner. Jesus, Mom couldn't even locate him for six months to get the divorce. Hank had to use his newspaper contacts just to find him!"

"Stop it." Piper swiped at her eyes, her eyes trained on the table. Wren reached over and squeezed her arm.

It hurt Shannon that she couldn't do the same; somewhere inside she wanted to, but on the outside she was the realist. Someone had to be. "Piper, it's the truth."

In the days after the boat accident on Lighthouse Beach, the house had been eerily quiet, like the beach after the storm that day. Beverly swept up the two older girls, taking them to the library, and into town on errands—anything to keep

78

them busy. Their parents wore a look of shocked distraction those first days, coming and going from the hospital like ghosts. Miraculously, aside from a concussion and the gash to her tiny forehead, their little sister had seemed to suffer no other effects. She was released two days later. Shannon remembered the homecoming. It was late afternoon, and Beverly had baked cookies with them to welcome Piper back. Despite the windy day, Shannon paced the porch watching for the car in the driveway. It should have been a celebration.

When her parents pulled in, the first thing Shannon noticed was that Lindy was in the driver's seat. Her father always drove. The next was the look on their faces. Both remained in the car, staring past her as she ran down the steps to greet them. It was Piper who got out first. She was still in her purple pajamas, and she hopped out holding a large stuffed dog. "I got a poodle!" she cried. Only then did Shannon's parents come to life, following her up the steps. Their mother fussed over Piper, ushering her inside. "Quick, you don't want to get cold. Oh, smell that! I think Grandma baked some goodies."

Shannon remained outside on the porch with her father. "Hey, kiddo. Did you hold the fort down?"

His face was drawn, seemingly aged. Shannon

knew they probably hadn't slept in days.

"We baked cookies. Chocolate chip," she told him.

"Did you, now? Let's go in and have some." But once inside, her father headed up the stairs instead of following her to the kitchen.

Later, when they sat down for spaghetti and meatballs—Piper's favorite—their father didn't come down. Lindy waited until they'd eaten, her own plate untouched, before telling them the news. "Daddy is going to be away for a while. On a long trip."

"But you all just got home!" Wren said. "Where is work sending him now?"

Shannon looked to her mother; she sensed this trip was different.

Their mother cleared her throat. "It's not for work. Daddy is not feeling well, and he needs to go away for a little while to get better."

"Where?" Wren wanted to know.

The look in their mother's eyes scared Shannon. This was different than the look she'd had coming and going from the hospital. "He's going to stay at a center outside Boston. It's kind of like a sleepaway camp for grown-ups."

"You mean rehab," Shannon said.

Lindy turned sharply.

"For how long?" Wren asked.

Her mother's eyes remained on Shannon, watery with apology. "Thirty days."

"But that's so long!" Wren protested.

Piper, who had spaghetti sauce stained across her lips, glanced between her two older sisters, gauging their expressions before deciding how she should respond to this news.

"I know, honey, but it's important. It'll go by fast. And we can visit."

Shannon didn't want to talk about visits. She wanted answers. "Is it because of the accident?" She glanced at Piper, but her little sister was now focused on her pasta.

"No, honey. It's because of the drinking that led to the accident. It's a sickness, honey. And Daddy needs help."

Their father left the next morning. Shannon sat in her bedroom window watching him stow his duffel bag onto the back seat of the car. Her mother would drive him to the center and be home by dinner. Shannon could not reconcile the strained calm that had stretched across their otherwise ordinary morning as he prepared to go. They'd eaten breakfast. Her parents had showered and dressed. It was not like the bitter end in a movie: there was no loud confrontation, no splintering of fine china against a kitchen wall. How she wished there had been. As she watched her father standing in the driveway below, something leaden settled within her that morning. A good smashing of plates might have helped dislodge it.

When they had hugged him goodbye, her father's grip left a mark on her arm. But Shannon didn't say a thing. There were tears in his eyes when she looked up at him. "I'm sorry, baby," he said. "I'll write you, okay? And I'll be home before you know it."

That was the plan. But the plan changed. Their father had lasted two weeks in the rehab center outside of Boston. A beautiful brick building with lush gardens that their mother described to them as being like a mansion. But Shannon would never know. Caleb Bailey didn't last long enough for his family to visit.

Piper set her glass down and ran a hand through her long hair. "So what about forgiveness? What about second chances?"

Shannon pointed at Piper but looked at Wren. "See that?"

"See what?" Wren looked between them.

Shannon jabbed her finger at her youngest sister. "That. That look of hope. That's what scares me the most." She glanced around the table at her sisters. "We can't get those years back. This doesn't change what he did."

"But it could change what we have," Piper said. "Don't you want your kids to know their grandpa?"

Shannon scoffed. "Don't bring my kids into this, Pipe. Don't you dare."

But she kept going. "This is about more than us. A lot has happened since Dad left."

Shannon screwed up her nose. "Jesus. How can you even call him that?"

"Because he's still our dad!"

"I can't do this." Shannon pushed her chair back and stood. "I have worried my whole life that this day would never come. It's all we've waited for and all I've wanted since I was a little girl."

"Shan, please. Sit. We can talk through this, all of us," Wren pleaded.

The kitchen began to spin and Shannon gripped the edge of the kitchen table to slow it. "That day is finally here. Twenty-three years have passed, but you know what? It turns out I'm not ready for this. I don't think I ever will be."

Piper stood, too. "Shannon, just hear us out. For once in your life let someone else have a say."

"Enlighten me, Piper. I'm dying to hear what you know that the rest of us don't. Because you were what—three years old—when he took off?"

Shannon hatcd the look that washed over Piper's face because she knew she was responsible for it. It was a look that should have been reserved for their father, not for the sister who had practically raised her in his absence. They were siblings linked by a man they could not feel more differently about. How was it that his absence had spelled hardship for Shannon, yet

Piper seemed to fill in all the missing gaps with a man part hero, part mystery. It was a fictitious history that needed correcting.

Shannon leaned in. "I'll tell you what I know. While you were busy being three years old, I was cooking your dinner and giving you baths because Mom had to go back to school at night so she could support us. Not to mention every weekend I spent my free time doing both your laundry while my friends went out to parties. Remember that?" Shannon raised her voice. "Who do you think taught you to ride your bike? And who patched up your knee when you rode it into Willy McEwan's mailbox? It wasn't *Dad!*"

Piper burst into tears.

"Shannon," Wren begged. "Lucy's sleeping."

At the mention of her niece's name Shannon stopped. The axis of the kitchen seemed to tilt suddenly toward her. The faces around the table jerked into sharp focus. "Oh God." She put her hand to her mouth. "I'm sorry." She fumbled for her purse on the back of her chair. "I'm sorry. I have to go."

"No, let's just calm down. We need to sit a moment with this."

But Shannon was already moving for the door. "I've said too much. I need to go home."

Piper did not follow, but Wren did. "Shannon, please."

She halted in the doorway. Wren came up

84

behind her and leaned her head against Shannon's shoulder. "I didn't want this to happen," Wren whispered.

Shannon turned and pecked her cheek quickly. "It's what always happens when Caleb Bailey is involved." She pushed the screen door open and hurried out into the cloudless night.

Seven

Hank

The antique desk drawer squeaked in protest as he coaxed it open. It was the way of things living by the sea, he thought; salt air was not kind. The shingled sides of houses grayed before giving over to silver. Doorjambs swelled, causing screen doors to stick. Wooden boats weathered, their hulls warping and splintering over time. Hank had become used to this, to the way his neatly combed hair did not lie flat at its part on a humid day. To the way the air in the house had weight on a foggy morning. The sea was everywhere, in their towels hanging over the porch railings and in the cool recesses of the slippers that they slid their feet into in the morning. It was on their skin and even in their blood, as Lindy liked to say. It was a sensation he'd tolerated at first, and if pressed, would admit he had come to love.

The desk drawer gave way with a rough jerk, and he riffled through it. Hank liked order. It was something hard to come by in the house, especially in the earlier years. His den was the one space that was truly his own. Whenever

Hank tired of tripping over the rain boots kicked off carelessly by the front door, or climbing up the staircase whose treads were crowded with stacks of books and errant dolls, or even the refrigerator, whose door could not be opened without disrupting the finger-painted artwork and spelling tests that were precariously affixed to its front by magnets, his den was a refuge from the detritus of children and animals. The girls had dubbed it the Tiger Room when they were younger because if they interrupted his quietude and banged on the door, he would growl playfully from the other side. Piper, especially, loved the game. A turn of the doorknob elicited a roar. A dared peek through the crack might provoke a chase that would send Piper dashing for her mother, a look of delighted horror on her face. Though the girls had grown and moved out, the room still served its purpose as an escape. Against one wall there was the large rolltop desk that held his ledger and computer, and adjacent to it a wall of tall windows overlooking the front lawn and quiet neighborhood street. A leather recliner sat in the far corner. Today he was not escaping. He was looking for something.

Hank examined the contents of the drawer. A box of blue Paper Mate pens, his favorite kind. A lone black stapler. A bundle of rubber bands neatly contained with a twist tie. A tin of thumbtacks, a worn pink eraser. He reached far into the back for what he wanted. The letter he pulled from the desk drawer was postmarked October 9, 1996. The *Boston Globe* address was printed on the return address portion of the envelope.

Hank supposed he could be accused of being sentimental, though he preferred practical. Which is exactly how he thought of his life, to this day. It was neatly divided into two parts: his old life, including childhood, school, and early career days—and the Bailey women years. In that first section, Hank worked as a journalist living in the Boston metro area. He'd started out writing for smaller papers, taking on what he considered the mundane assignments of early reporting. There were city budget meetings, public works projects, crime reports. Most of it he likened to covering the weather, for it was always changing but the selection didn't much vary.

As he worked his way up, Hank did his best to infuse a sense of voice into his pieces. One of his first editors, a sarcastic fellow who doled out assignments like punishments, did not appreciate Hank's personal inflections. "Stick to the news, Henry. The readers want to know what the vote was, not what color pants you wore to the polls." His next job at the *Providence Journal* was different. He worked under a woman who'd been hired as editor in chief the same year he came on the scene. The paper was floundering; she was the lynchpin brought in to keep it afloat. Hank couldn't say that she appreciated his writing any more than his previous editors, but she'd been tasked with the challenge to shake things up, something not well received by a staff long hitched together and loyal to their former boss. In him she recognized both a newcomer and a fresh perspective. She was the first editor who allowed him to pitch ideas for op-eds. And it was like a light went on.

Readers responded to Hank's voice. They liked his level approach, the occasional injections of humor. He tried to stay politically neutral, but he had opinions, and they came through in the text. Within six months he was heading his own column, a weekly that ran in the Sunday paper. Letters poured in. He'd developed an actual readership. CBS News Corp picked up some of his articles and ran them in their local sister papers. He was being quoted. He was a name.

In 1995 he received what he'd long wished for: an offer from the *Globe*. They were looking for someone to spearhead a new op-ed idea they had to invigorate the paper. National news outfits were experiencing the decline with the tech industry balloon, and Hank was well aware that he was in what some insisted was a dying industry. But he loved to hold a book in hand, and he believed in print on paper. And besides, news didn't stop, even if its mode of delivery changed. He accepted the new position with gusto, moved into a downtown apartment with a view of the Boston Harbor, and considered himself on his way. Two months into his new job he met Lindy.

Now, he removed the letter from its worn envelope. The text was brief, but he had no need to read it. He'd long ago memorized it. "We are genuinely sorry to receive your resignation letter, but we wish you all the best in your new life."

He'd been on the job only a year when he asked Lindy to marry him. "But the paper!" she'd said. "You love your job. What will you do without it?"

There was no comparing the *Globe* with the scant local papers out on the sleepy elbow of the Cape. But as much as he did not like to think of leaving the *Globe*, what was impossible to imagine was living without Lindy and the girls. There was no question: it was easier to move one middle-aged bachelor to the coast than it was to uproot a family of four, who'd already endured enough upheaval as it was. In his mind it was the right thing to do. In his heart it was the only thing to do.

He folded the letter and set it on the desk. The same desk that had been in his old Boston apartment overlooking the harbor before being packed up, contents and all, and moved to its current location in this den where little girls once knocked at the door and the doorjambs still swelled with salt air. No, Hank was not a sentimental man. But there were some things that needed hanging on to. This was one of them.

There was a knock at the door. Lindy poked her head in. "Hi, honey. Everyone's expected shortly. Want to start the grill?"

It was Sunday afternoon, which meant the family was soon to amass in his kitchen. All of them, including Mrs. Pruitt from next door. He should probably pour himself a beer before that happened.

Lindy and the girls had long ago dubbed the weekly gathering as the "Something-Rather Dinner Party." Which meant that whoever was available showed up with whatever was on hand. No fuss, more festivity. Hank had never been particularly fond of the term, but he had to admit it sometimes held. While Lindy had meant it in reference to the food, he would argue it could also be applied to some of their discussions over the years. The women in attendance could be long on opinion, and short on temper.

"Right. I'll be out in a minute," he said.

Lindy stepped inside his office and peeked over his shoulder. "Memory lane?"

"Just cleaning out the old desk," he said, tucking the letter back in its envelope.

She placed a kiss on the top of his head and wrapped her arms around his shoulders. "Any regrets?"

Hank shook his head softly. "Just one." He

reached for a red pen and drew a line through the date on the calendar on his ledger.

"What's that?" she asked.

He smiled. "Another Something-Rather Dinner Party."

As usual, Shannon and Reid showed up first, with their kids. They filed in, the girls giving quick hugs to them both, and George inquiring immediately as to the whereabouts of Bowser.

"Oh, he's in the backyard, sweetie. Why don't you go say hello to him?"

George took off through the back of the house, and his sisters followed.

"Hank," Reid said, shook his hand, and held up a six-pack of beer.

"My good man." Hank had always liked Reid. He knew he worked long hours at his family office, but he'd been very successful. He and Shannon had always seemed of the same mindset, and they were the two that Hank and Lindy worried very little over.

Shannon kissed Hank's cheek and deposited something that smelled delicious on the kitchen island.

"This is gorgeous honey, but I don't know where you find the time," Lindy said. "That's the point—bring something simple."

Hank followed to see what the fuss was about. There was a casserole dish of bright summer squash sliced into small half-moons with some kind of crusty cheese topping that looked like it came straight out of *Martha Stewart Living* magazine. "Oh, and I brought dessert, too. Strawberry parfait. The berries are fresh from Cape Cod Organic in Barnstable."

"Shannon!" Lindy scolded.

Wren pulled up in her Jeep next. Hank noticed someone was with her in the front seat, and whoever it was was too big to be Lucy. Perhaps Wren had finally succumbed to her mother's hints to bring someone special to dinner. As women went, Lindy was many things, but not subtle. It had been a long time since James was out of the picture, and Hank didn't like to think of Wren working so hard and being alone. It would be good to have another man in the family.

But when the passenger door opened, he saw it was not a date Wren had brought along. "Lindy!" Hank called.

She was out the door and down the stairs before Piper even made it to the bottom step. "Oh, honey! What a surprise!" Then, looking around at all of them, "Why didn't anyone tell me you were coming?"

Wren hugged her mother. "Blame me; I invited her down last night."

Lindy held Piper at arm's length. "You've been down since last night and didn't come over 'til now?"

"Mom," Piper said.

"Oh, all right, all right." Lindy grabbed Lucy's hand. "Everyone come in. There's a ton of food to be had!"

Within thirty minutes the table was filled. Hank grilled rib eye steaks, Wren tossed a salad she'd picked from her garden, and Shannon's casserole had been heated up. Lindy pulled two trays of garlic bread from the oven. Piper stood at the kitchen island idly picking tomatoes out of Shannon's dish and popping them into her mouth.

Reid handed her a beer. "My wife will kill you if she sees you messing with her dish."

Piper grinned. "Oh, come on. She'll kill one of us before the night's over anyway."

Halfway through the meal, Mrs. Pruitt arrived, late as usual. Widowed and in her seventies, she'd long acted as a sort of aunt to the Bailey girls. As was custom, she let herself in the back door, and they now listened patiently from the dining room as she rummaged through the kitchen drawers and shuffled about the kitchen. The children giggled. Finally she appeared in the doorway holding two lit candles in silver candlesticks. "I found the prettiest beeswax candles in town at Tale of the Cod—they smell so nice! But seeing as you already have these in the sticks, I left them on the kitchen counter for another time."

She set the candlesticks carefully in the center of the table, and it was then she noticed Piper.

"The redhead is back!" she cried, clasping her hands. Mrs. Pruitt had ridden the rises and falls of the family over their many years sharing a backyard fence, and she wasted no time pulling her chair in and filling up her plate to get caught up. "So, what force of nature drove you home, child?"

Piper shrugged casually from her end of the table, but Hank, too, had been waiting for this very answer. "Oh, I don't know. I guess I wanted some family time," she said, her tone a little too honeyed.

"Bullshit," Lindy said brightly.

"Mom!" Shannon pointed a fork in the direction of the kids.

"Sorry, babies. Grandma said a bad thing. Don't you repeat it." She reached for George, who was seated next to her, and clamped both hands over his ears. "I call bullshit!"

Reid smirked and the older grandkids tried to hide their giggles behind their napkins.

Shannon threw up her hands. "Okay, you kids are excused. Nice work, Mom."

Hank shook his head and sipped his wine. It was no use saying anything to Lindy. She was an elegant woman with a foul mouth. He would dare to say he found it maddeningly attractive.

Mrs. Pruitt, who was still mulling over Piper's

answer, chewed her food thoughtfully. "Did someone break your heart, dear?"

"No." Piper set her fork down. "Let me beat you all to the punch. I'm seeing someone new."

Lindy brightened. "Wonderful. When do we meet him?"

"If you actually like this guy, I suggest you might wish to delay that," Reid joked, rising from the table. He began clearing plates as the women settled back into their chairs. This was the usual course of Sunday dinner parties. Everyone pitched in with cooking. The men did the dishes.

"Thank you," Piper said to her brother-in-law. "I had the same thought. Really Mom, everything is fine."

Lindy narrowed her eyes over her wine glass but said no more. She was clearly enjoying having all of her girls around the table, and she would not push the matter.

"Wren, you've barely eaten. Are you feeling all right?"

Wren glanced at her sisters then back at Lindy. "I'm fine, Mama. But there is something I want to share. That we all want to share."

Lindy allowed her eyes to travel around the table, and Hank sensed her apprehension.

Mrs. Pruitt pulled her chair up closer. "Will we be needing more wine?"

Hank stood and refilled glasses, as they all

watched Wren pull an envelope from her purse. She set it down by her mother. "This came in the mail. It was addressed to my shop."

Lindy pulled her reading glasses, which dangled around her neck, up onto her nose. Her eyes widened with recognition. She yanked her reading glasses off and looked around the table at all of them.

"How long?" she asked.

Hank felt something protective rise in his chest. "What is it?"

But Lindy's eyes were trained on the faces of her three daughters. Very softly, holding the envelope up between them, she asked again. "How long have the three of you had this?"

Lindy seemed to know, without even opening it, what was in the envelope. Hank didn't like the sense of being suddenly thrust into the dark.

Wren turned to him, her green eyes flickering with apology. "It's a letter. From our father."

Hank and Lindy locked eyes from each end of the table. He searched her face, the very face he had woken up beside for the last twenty years, whose complex arrangement of features dictated the kind of day he was going to have. For the first time in all those years, as if a compass had been reset, he could not read it. It occurred to him then that it did not matter what the letter said: this was between them, and once again, Hank was an outsider looking in.

Lindy cleared her throat. "He's coming back, isn't he?"

It was a statement, not a question.

Mrs. Pruitt excused herself from the table. "I'm fetching the good candles. This is going to be a long night."

At the other end of the table, Hank could see the change in his wife already. The space between them opened and stretched, like a lifeline uncoiling. "I think I'll leave you ladies to yourselves," he said, rising from his chair.

"No, wait." Wren said. "We want you to stay."

Hank hesitated. Wren had always been the one hardest to reach. Once, when she was eleven years old, after a stormy day, they had taken a walk at the beach. All five of them. Hank had known the girls for several months then. Or at least had been trying to. Piper, desperate to connect, had clambered into his lap—too full of trust, her need visceral as a heartbeat. Shannon had tolerated his company, aloof, but polite. It was Wren who held back longest, her eyes always on him when he turned around. He could feel her watching him when he spoke to her mother in the kitchen, he could feel her eyes on his back as he walked out the door after dinner on a Friday night. He would look up at the house as he backed his car out of the dark driveway and see her silhouette in her bedroom window, her wavy hair spilling around the pale oval of her small face. Always, she kept a safe distance between them. Until that gray afternoon walk on the beach. They'd been walking along the high-tide mark, stopping every now and then to poke around in the detritus washed ashore from the storm, when Wren appeared at his side and suddenly slipped her hand in his. He'd looked down at her in surprise, and then quickly away, for fear she'd withdraw it. The whole way down the beach and back, she kept her narrow fingers entwined with his own. Until a dried horseshoe crab caught her eye and she bent to examine it. He'd kneeled with her in the sand, trying to listen as she spoke, but already missing the warm press of her small hand in his. She described a large crab her father had found years ago and how they'd set it free, dragging it gently back into the waves. It was a good story, but he felt a ripple of sadness when she dashed ahead to catch up with her sisters. Eventually they turned back for home and were halfway down the beach when the thud of footsteps in wet sand came up behind him. It was Wren. She handed him a razor clam shell before slipping her hand back in his. She held it all the way home. When Hank's eyes filled with tears, he'd blamed the wind. Wren glanced briefly at him knowingly. Just as she did now, when he rose from the table.

"I appreciate that," he said, pushing his chair

99

in gently. "But I'll be in the den if anyone needs me."

Hank closed the door behind him and leaned against it, exhaling. It was the day they had all known might happen. From the beginning, Lindy had warned that Caleb Bailey was a wild card. Ever since, Hank had tried to conduct himself carefully, walking that narrow line between being a father figure but never daring to lay claim to the title.

When he first met Lindy, she was newly divorced, having proved to the court that her husband was in absentia as both parent and spouse. Lindy had never held her husband accountable for child support, a fact that perplexed Hank. After all, she certainly could've used the money. And the kids deserved to know where he was. "What's the point?" she'd asked when Hank questioned her decision. "I know him. I know him better than anyone. There is no money, and if there ever is he'll be drinking it. He's not fit to be in the girls' lives. I didn't want to remain tied to him any longer. Can you understand that?"

He'd come to. Lindy could not afford to fight the past; she had three girls who needed her in the present. And it took everything she had. Her greatest gift to him had been to let him into their lives, to share those beautiful complicated headstrong girls with him. Father or not, he'd fallen in love with them all.

But, now, he realized how careless he'd gotten, how cavalier. With each passing year that Caleb stayed away, the likelihood of his returning floated further away from the safe shore they had created. Hank couldn't help it: over the course of all that time, he'd let himself love these girls like his own. Taking Piper's picture when she dressed up as a lobster for her first-grade school play. Holding newborn Lucy in those early morning hours after Wren delivered her at Cape Cod Hospital. Walking Shannon down the aisle in her white gown at the Wequassett Resort. With each year, each milestone, each breath taken, he'd believed it to be true.

Outside, in the dining room, came the rise and fall of female voices. A melody of the backdrop of his life.

Hank winced. What a goddamned fool he'd been.

Eight

Wren

*S*he's standing at the top of the steps at Lighthouse Beach. It is a summer day of splendor, the dune grass shifting gently in the salty breeze, the sun high over the channel. Chatham Harbor is a liquid sky, so blue is the water. The Rosa rugosa blooms on either side of the trailhead. Wren looks down to the sandy beach below. She shields her eyes from the sun. Somewhere down there is her family.

But as she begins the steep descent to the sand, a fog rolls in. A charcoal swirl that coils its way along the shore spreads like a cloud of smoke up the beach. She turns to Chatham Lighthouse behind her, but even its golden beam cannot fracture the dense fog.

From down below, Wren hears a cry. A child's wail reaches her up on the dunes. Something is terribly wrong. She has to get down to the beach to her family. But Wren cannot move. She tries to bend a knee, lift a foot. But her feet are cemented in the sand. Her ears roar with the crash of waves, the voices growing fainter. She opens her mouth and screams, again and again. But no *sound comes out. She cannot stop. Her throat is going to shatter.*

A white flash illuminated the bedroom followed by a crack of thunder, and she jerked upright. Outside, rain pelted her window and she fought to catch her breath, understanding now that it was just a storm. Lucy was sound asleep when she padded into her room barefoot. Wren pressed her lips to her daughter's warm forehead, taking in the visceral scent of faint child sweat and sleep that enveloped Lucy's room at night. She adjusted her blankets and tiptoed out.

The house felt damp but cozy, the echo of driving rain against the walls and windows like a shell. Wren switched on the overhead light of the kitchen stove and put on the teapot. She couldn't go back to sleep on nights like these.

It had been a long time since she'd had the dream, so many that she couldn't count. In the earlier years she'd awake twisted in her bedding, gasping for breath as if the cotton sheets were pulling her under. Shannon was having them, too, though she never wanted to talk about hers. When Lindy realized that she'd taken them all to a child psychologist, a woman the girls called Miss Anne.

Every Saturday they went, first as a family in their newfound number of four, and later individually because Miss Anne believed one-on-one sessions might allow the girls to open up more. Wren recalled the defensive look on her mother's face. "That's ridiculous. My girls know they can speak freely in front of me. We have no secrets."

Wren felt embarrassed, both by her mother's strong words against Miss Anne, who was younger and softer spoken than their mother, and by the realization that, in fact, her mother was wrong. There were things Wren could not say in front of her mother. And here was an outsider telling Lindy what Wren wished her mother knew instinctively. Yes, the Baileys were close. But they were also close in their pain, bound in that net so snugly that it precluded full disclosure, lest it fray the thin ropes that held them together.

Shannon refused to talk to Miss Anne. Wren recalled the four of them sitting on the hall bench in the waiting area just outside the therapist's door, like a lineup at a police station. When her turn was called, Shannon would not budge. After some cajoling, and eventual mild threatening, she would begrudgingly stomp into the office and park herself roughly in the wingback chair that faced Miss Anne's desk. There she remained, arms crossed staring straight ahead, as the grandfather clock ticked through the twenty wordless minutes of their session.

Wren, however, found freedom in hers. Initially

there had been some wariness about the intimacy of the situation. Miss Anne did not know them, and yet they were expected to discuss their most private, most awful experience with this woman. It went against all of her instincts. But when she found herself seated across from the friendly young woman, whose lipstick was the prettiest shade of red, something her own mother would never wear, Wren felt a flood of relief. Unlike in her own crowded and loquacious home, Wren could speak without interruption and Miss Anne listened. In her braver moments Wren shared her sixth-grade crush on John Waltham, at which Miss Anne smiled. In a darker moment she wondered aloud if it were her mother's fault that their father had left them. As soon as that awful thing was said, Wren had reeled from an instantaneous fit of guilt, bending over at the waist and bursting into tears. How could she say such a thing about their dutiful mother? The same mother who was shrinking before their eyes under the weight of it all. Surely her mother missed Caleb Bailey as much as they did. After all, *she* had been left, too.

Wren wished in that moment that Miss Anne would say something, chastise her, correct her mean spirit. The silence that stretched out between them was agony enough. In the end, Wren realized that Miss Anne's role was not to placate or judge. This was on Wren's shoulders, and with it came a burden the kind of which she had never borne. She was not alone, not exactly, but this was up to her.

In the end, loading the three of them up in the car and dragging them all to the little cottage on the town green every Saturday morning ended up being the greatest gift Lindy could have given her daughters.

Now, sitting at the kitchen table with teacup in hand, Wren considered the last few hours. The dinner party had not ended well. Lindy refused to read the letter. She held it up in her hand, seated at the head of the table, staring at it. As if she could see through the paper folds and overlapped lines of handwriting to decipher it. It didn't matter what it said, she claimed. She knew what it meant. He was coming back. All she wanted to know now was what that spelled for each of them. Her grace and calm extended only to her three children; she, herself, had no interest in ever seeing Caleb Bailey again. But what did the three of them want?

Wren already knew these answers. Piper was determined to see him, and Wren couldn't blame her. She'd been so young.

Predictably, Shannon had maintained her post. Shannon was not pliable like Piper; when a door closed, it remained so. Wren imagined the hinges rusting off, the door handle falling away. The wood that remained petrified, turning what once was a doorway to a wall of stone. Even Caleb Bailey could not penetrate it.

As for Wren, she held a middle ground not unlike her position as middle child. Like Shannon, there was anger that their father had not succeeded in finding treatment. It often felt like he had chosen alcohol over them. But over the years it had petered out, its concentration no longer as coppery on the tongue. Like Piper, she was curious. She wanted to see what this man looked like. Hear what he had to say to them all. She would listen. And that was the only promise she was capable of making right now.

But there was one more reason behind Wren's decision to let Caleb Bailey back into her life. There was the matter of Lucy. Lucy, who did not know this grandfather. And more importantly, Lucy, who did not know her own father. Wren, who'd once been so firm in her belief that Lucy did not need a father (just as she had survived without one herself), had questions of her own. She found herself thinking back to James more and more. A man she had pushed out of her mind just as certainly as she'd pushed him out of her life the summer she found out she was carrying his child. Perhaps in trying to be nothing like her father she had, in fact, become just like him. Because the truth was Caleb Bailey wasn't the only one who had done something unforgivable.

So had she, and to the person she once loved most: James.

Wren had not cut James out of her life because he was a bad person. Quite the opposite, he had brought a peace and richness to her life during the time he was in it. He knew the lyrics to all of the songs of his namesake, James Taylor. He owned a slobbery sweet-natured yellow lab, Beatrice, who went everywhere with him and whom Wren couldn't help but think summed up all the things she loved James for best: easygoing, gregarious, and always up for anything. James was a roll-up-your-sleeves kind of guy. Handy, good with tools, and happy to help anyone out. James had gone to Providence College, and she appreciated that he was as comfortable slipping on a dinner jacket for a four-course meal in the Stars dining room at Chatham Bars Inn as he was pulling on his rubber fishing coveralls and heading out on the boat for a twelve-hour day. He wore his thick dark hair cropped short. She loved that his blue eyes were framed between that and a couple days' worth of stubble, which she sometimes scratched under his chin just as she did Beatrice. "Who's a good dog?" she'd joke.

Despite her determination to stay away from the pitfalls of falling in love, she'd fallen deeply. They met at the Hooker's Ball one summer and not a day went by that they didn't see each other after.

But over the couple of years they were together, Wren learned that there was something inside James that longed for more beyond the cozy borders of their life together in Chatham. Like the distant spark he got in his eyes when he talked about the future. A spark that Wren recognized with dread from her childhood. It was independent of their love, something within him that she could not touch and therefore could not alter. What worried her was that it seemed to take him away from her.

It flickered when he was heading out on the boat each morning at the Chatham Fish Pier. When he talked about being out on the water, offshore and free from the land. His work intoxicated him on the good days, causing him to wonder aloud about traveling and fishing more distant waters for different catch. She tried to tell herself to ignore the nagging fear that came when this wanderlust surfaced. When the New England seasons changed and the fishing grew harder—the cold, the wind, the days of small catches—his zest for being out on the water dimmed somewhat. And during the harshest winter months, it halted. But that was where she came in, reminding him of their cozy life together in Chatham in the little apartment they eventually moved into together on Main Street over the storefronts. When it was quiet off season they could wander across the street to the Squire for French onion soup and pints of beer before dancing the rest of the night away in the tavern with the other locals, then stumbling across the street to their bed where they made love and fell asleep tangled together. They had everything they needed right there, she reminded him. The proximity to her family, whom he genuinely liked, and their shared friends. Their work. The town that reminded him of his own childhood town, Westerly, Rhode Island. When she turned his face toward hers and reminded him of all of these things, his eyes would brighten, and she would feel him return to her again.

About two years into their relationship, James began talking of moving to the Pacific Northwest. To work on the bigger commercial ships, the ones that went out for months at a time for catch like sockeye salmon and king crab. "The work would be hell, but there's nothing like being out in open water like that," he told her. "And the money, Wren! Think of it."

She tried to point out the differences. These were not day boats; he would be gone for months at a time. There were weather considerations. Bleak conditions. Dangers.

"It's not that different," he'd argue. "Different catch and longer trips, sure. Sometimes harsher conditions, depending. But also more money!" He'd grabbed her hands in his, his expression alive in ways she'd not seen. It was alluring. And also terrifying. "Look, I've fished all of my adult life on the Cape. I've worked the different boats. I could do that out there, too." Wren waited when James flew out to Washington and spent a week interviewing with ship captains. When he called to tell her he was offered a job on a commercial boat out of Gig Harbor, James's voice boomed with new life. "You should see this place, babe. It's the quintessential coastal town." Wren didn't say, "But we already live in that town."

James spoke fast. "I've already scouted out a few apartments, and I found one I think you'll love. It's small, but it's down by the harbor and there's this great little coffee shop around the corner. I'll send you the links."

At first James's enthusiasm was contagious. She allowed herself to picture the two of them moving out to Gig Harbor. When she was nine years old, Caleb had taken the family to Olympic National Park. It was one of those rare occasions the whole family had packed up and followed him on an assignment, and she remembered the striking landscape. At one point during the trip they'd taken a boat trip on the Puget Sound and she recalled thinking how different it was from the East Coast: the light, the color, the sharp contrast between land and sea. Unlike the low-lying East Coast dunes dotted with posh residences that rolled gently into the Atlantic, the Pacific was so dramatic. It seemed wilder out there, the contrasts more jagged, the terrain less touched. The effect left her feeling both awed and vulnerable.

Listening to James, she tried to get on board. She tried to picture what kind of work she'd do, what kind of harbor town they'd live in. And then she imagined the reality of the long months while he was gone at sea. Living in a foggy, gray fishing village. Adjusting to life alone, his side of the bed cold for months at a time. And then there was the danger involved. Men got caught in lines or tangled in gear without warning. Hooks went through hands. Lines wrapped around legs. In a breath a man could be whisked over the side and into the black arctic waters so fast that sometimes no one realized. There was so much that she knew could go wrong.

But it was the not knowing that scared her most. Not knowing where he was out there in the middle of the dark sea, not being able to reach him with any regularity. Waiting for his boat to come in like some colonial whaling wife. Until the soft parts of her that missed his touch would harden, and she'd adjust to his absence. And just when she'd adjusted he'd come home, for a couple months. The reunion would be sweet and heady, and they'd not be able to get enough of each other. But then they'd have to learn how to coexist again. How to navigate their living space as well as their temperaments, relearning the rhythms of their moods until they became in sync with one another. And life would be good again. Except there would always be the next trip hanging over their heads. The countdown to the next stretch of time without. Until the days dwindled to his departure and they'd be raw and hungry for one another, tiptoeing around the looming separation. It would grow old, or it would cause her to. Wren was okay being on her own. What she was not okay with was letting someone in, and then letting someone go. Over and over.

She'd done it as a child with her own father, and she'd seen the toll it took on Lindy. More than once she'd wave goodbye to her father in the driveway and return tearfully to the kitchen to find her mother dry-eyed and subdued, washing a pot in the sink with grim, purposeful strokes. It was how her mother handled it, but it made her distant each time he left. As much as she tried to keep it from her daughters, it was always a few weeks before Lindy softened and came back to them as herself. No, Wren would not sign herself up for that kind of partnership.

The problem was Wren loved James on a cellular level. Her body responded to his touch, even in the rare moments she did not want it to. She bent to the sound of his voice, his breath in her ear. The way his eyes crinkled with laughter at something she said. She could not imagine life without him, just as she could not imagine asking him to stop doing what he loved. Who was she to ask him to set aside these desires to move out west and find a crew? To someday work his own boat. He would do it for her, she knew, but it would change him. Just as it would change her to follow him out there and spend her life always having to say goodbye. She wrestled with this notion all throughout their relationship. Until the morning she found out she was expecting Lucy. What began as a burst of love for what they'd created together filled her with dread. This was not the life she wanted for her child.

When James returned home to pack for their move out west, Wren steeled herself and broke a small part of the news: she didn't think she could move with him. She needed time to think. James was floored. "But this is what we want! How can you just let it go? How can you let *us* go?"

"Baby, it's what *you* want."

"I can't give everything up I've worked for," he said. It tore her apart. She stood in the doorway watching him empty his side of their shared closet into an old brown suitcase. James left the watercolor of Chatham Harbor that hung over their bed. "You can bring this out when you come," he said. "When you're ready." When he couldn't find his leather slippers it was she who crawled under the bed to retrieve them. "Wrenny. Please. Just give it a try. Come for the summer and stay till Christmas. If you hate it, we can rethink."

She wanted to believe him, and she knew his words were sincere. But she also knew the look in his eyes: the same look her father had when he slung his camera bag over his shoulder and packed the car. James couldn't stay in Chatham, and she couldn't make him. They'd resent one another if she tried. It would be the end of them, either way.

Now, as the rain pelted her dark windows, Wren left her mug of tea untouched and went to the desk in the living room. In the drawer was the pack of monogrammed letterhead that Shannon had given her for Christmas. Too formal. She paged through a stack of blank cards. That didn't feel right either. Thinking better of it, she put all of it back in the drawer. Instead, she went to the notebook she kept in the kitchen for jotting down grocery and to-do lists. She tore a page out, grabbed the first pen she could find, and sat down.

Without greetings or niceties, she scrawled what came to her mind first. The irony was not lost on her: it was the one question they'd been wondering all these years.

Hi Dad,
When will you be coming back?
Wren

Nine

Piper

The Mid-Cape Highway was a snail trail. Piper rolled down the windows of her Prius in the hopes of a remnant of salt air. But all she got were the fumes of the hulking Suburban in front of her. The car had Connecticut plates, a luggage container on top, and a rack of bikes strapped to its tailgate. It figured. *Vacationers.* She peered up at the merry row of stick-figure family decals across its rear window: a father, a mother (what happened to *ladies first?*), three kids, a baby, a dog. By the look of it they all appeared to be crammed in there. Piper shuddered. *This* she did not yearn for.

She glanced at her phone on the passenger seat. Derek had not left any new messages. Before leaving Boston, she'd texted him to say that she was going away for a couple nights, purposely leaving out her destination. She imagined his surprise over her impromptu getaway: Where did she go? Who was she with? She promised herself she wouldn't contact him further until she heard from him. To her dismay his only reply was a stupid thumbs-up emoji. What did that even mean?

It reminded her of an article she'd read in *GQ* magazine about grown men who used emojis. Some of her girlfriends said they'd never date a man who did. It was a death sentence. She had to agree, there was something emasculating about it. But the sad truth was she'd be clicking her heels together if Derek sent her a heart.

The line of traffic resumed its slow roll. It was almost as bad as a Saturday when all the vacation rentals let out and both sides of the highway filled with renters funneling on and off the Cape. Piper was neither of those—she was a true-blue Cape Codder, but only because of her family's preceding generations that had lived in Chatham year round. Even her childhood friends who'd grown up on the Cape and gone to the same schools were still considered wash-ashores if their family history didn't extend beyond at least three generations of Cape residents. Real Cape Codders were fiercely protective of their stomping ground.

Of them all, her mother had been most sorry to see her leaving that morning. "But you just got here."

"I know, but I have to get back. I've got an interview." It was a lie. But she did have to go.

There was no way Lindy was about to let Piper out of her sight once she arrived for Sunday dinner, and so she'd spent the night in her old bedroom. It wasn't so bad. After the others had left, she and her mother stood on either side of the bed and made it together. There was something to be said for climbing into your childhood bed, she realized later, sliding beneath the crisp sheets and delighting in the brush of cold cotton against her bare legs. Dinners cooked at home always tasted better. Beds made by your mother always felt snugger. This she could not argue.

When she'd awakened, the first light dappling the honey floorboards in her bedroom, she'd experienced one of those moments you feel only as a child. The ones where you are not quite sure how old you are, or what day it is, but you know you are safe and sound and the world feels right, if just for a breath. She'd stretched lazily, willing the feeling to stay, trying to trick her mind to fall back to slumber, to block out the pressing worries that crowded the foot of her bed in wait: rent money, finding a job, Derek. Heading back to Boston had actually been hard. Lindy handed her a bagged lunch like she was still a school-girl, and stood on the porch steps hugging her goodbye.

"Good luck at your interview, honey. Promise to call me tonight and tell me how it went?" The pride in Lindy's eyes stung.

"Thanks, Mom. I'm sure the interview will be fine," Piper had lied.

There *had* been an interview scheduled for that Monday afternoon, but Piper had called the school secretary before her drive down Friday afternoon and canceled it.

"Would you like to reschedule?" the secretary had asked. After all, Piper's résumé and application had landed her in the top ten candidates of a pool she knew was well into the hundreds. A rather desirable pool to be in, as everyone knew there were more applicants than positions available in the metro area. Piper should have leapt at the chance.

Without hesitation, Piper had replied, "No, I do not wish to reschedule." The truth was she had no intention of going to that interview, or any other.

She'd lied to them all the night before at dinner. She knew it was crazy: Who completed a master's degree in education and suddenly decided teaching was no longer for her? She could just imagine the look on her sisters' faces if they knew the truth. What she could not imagine was herself, closing the classroom door and standing up in front of twenty-five kids every day, and the tick of the wall clock blurring into the backdrop of children's voices. It was a paralyzing thought.

Piper liked kids. And she had loved going back to school. Her master's degree had allowed her to study across the board: science, art, psychology. For a girl who was notorious among her family for being indecisive, the degree was an all-you-can-eat buffet of liberal arts course work. But with her student teaching completed, what had seemed like a good idea was in fact a terrible one. How could she possibly be responsible for the education of all those small beings in her charge? To teach them to read? To problem-solve? To be good little people, period. Unlike Hillary, who had completed applications en masse all spring and was now fielding job offers, who *could not wait* to set up her very own classroom and hang up the *WELCOME!* sign on the first day of school, Piper was rendered sick by the thought. Those kids would depend on her. Their parents would demand things of her. Her colleagues would expect things from her. She knew because she'd suffered it all during her student-teaching internship in Arlington. The school had matched her with a lovely veteran teacher, Mary McAllister, in a fourth-grade classroom— Piper's first choice. The children had welcomed her eagerly, and the staff could not have been more accommodating during her twelve-week internship. But with each after-school meeting they had, each lesson plan they reviewed, and with each book Mary pulled from her shelf and placed in Piper's hands, she felt the walls close in.

The kids didn't help. The more she grew to really know them, the worse it got. They were no longer nameless beings that trotted through her imagination with chapter books tucked neatly under their arms. They were complex but mostly lovable beings. Like Thatcher, whose parents were going through a volatile divorce, or Rich who had Asperger's. And shy Haley who barely peeked out from under her row of thick blonde bangs and still read at a first-grade level.

Piper left work thinking about those kids every day. They infiltrated her car ride home and her sleep at night. Sitting at the bar with friends for Friday night happy hour she found her mind wandering back to them, wondering if things were okay that night at Thatcher's house. Or if Rich had made it home unscathed by the sixth-grade bully on the bus. Piper had not expected her insides to shift in the way that they did. Her carefree equilibrium was gone. As was her time. The correcting of student work and planning of lessons at home each night. The required professional development workshops outside of school hours. Forget those lavish summer vacation weeks that friends in other career fields loved to wag their fingers at—those were mental-health days largely filled with curriculum work. As for the day-to-day grind, Piper had learned the hard way that once the classroom door shut, you were in a sort of child-induced incarceration. The students were both your jailers and your cell-mates. No phone calls, no emails, no grabbing a cup of coffee. At least not until the bell rang for lunch, some three hours later! She couldn't even leave the classroom if she had to pee. No, teaching was not a good match for her. There had to be something else. But she had to find it soon; she was living off her student loans, which at this point had grown into an amount akin to a mortgage payment, only with no house to show for it.

When she finally turned the key to her apartment two hours later, her nerves were shot. Piper threw her tote on the sagging couch in the tiny living area and glanced around. It was Monday: her roommates were at work and the only sound in the apartment was the hum of the air-conditioning unit in the window. The fridge was empty, save for a bottle of wine (not hers) and some yogurt (also not hers). She pulled the tub of Greek yogurt out and stood at the counter eating. She needed groceries, which made her wonder idly about her dwindling bank-account balance. Hank had given her a one-hundred-dollar bill before she left, tucking it in her palm when she said goodbye. "Don't tell your mother," he'd said with a wink. "Treat yourself." If only he knew that she was already a month behind on her share of the electric bill and gas.

She reached for her purse and it was then she saw the rectangular pink candy box. Yesterday, on the way to their mother's for dinner, she'd visited the Candy Manor with Wren and Lucy. Wren had wanted to pick up some chocolate fudge, a family favorite. The moment Piper stepped through the shop's pink door she'd been hit by the smell of sugar. It was intoxicating. Behind the old-fashioned glass counter, a woman stood at a large copper pot with an equally large wooden spoon. "Look!" Lucy had cried, tugging Piper by the wrist. "She's making fudge."

Piper had witnessed this countless times during her own childhood, but it never failed to mesmerize her. The pink store teemed with confections, glittering sugar-covered lollipops, and display cases of handmade chocolates and truffles. There was an entire wall of jelly bean bins. Piper had purchased some coconut clusters that she and Lucy had devoured in the car. And one other delectable thing: a box of chocolate covered cherries. Derek's favorite. She'd completely forgotten about it until now.

She checked her watch. Derek's Intro to English Lit lecture would be ending in half an hour. If she caught the Green Line on Commonwealth, she might make it. Smiling, she grabbed her phone. She'd figure out groceries later.

An hour later, Piper leaned against the wall outside Professor Jenkins's door jiggling the pink box of chocolate-covered cherries. Jenkins was one door down from Derek. The department secretary's desk was stationed in the hallway within sight, and Piper didn't want to raise eyebrows.

"Be discreet," Derek had warned when they first got together. It was his only request of her, and as such, she remained determined to prove herself. But it was getting harder.

She was about to give up when she heard voices coming down the hall. It was Derek. And someone else. Piper let her eyes travel over the brunette's face briefly, before feigning disinterest. She was dressed preppy, like him (therefore, decidedly not his type), and was talking about an assignment. Piper was pleased to see Derek was having trouble listening.

But her rib cage fluttered when he noticed her. Showing up like this was something they had agreed she would not do.

The two stopped outside his office door as Derek unlocked it, but his eyes were already on Piper. "My apologies, Miss Bailey—it seems I forgot our appointment."

Piper lifted one shoulder, ignoring the brunette's curious gaze. "No problem. I can wait."

"As you were saying, Margaret . . ." He held the door for the student, leaving it ajar.

A few moments and several questions later, Margaret exited the office holding a book. Piper peered over her shoulder to better see the cover: *Collected Poems of Dylan Thomas. Novice,* she thought.

"I think you'll find that helpful," Derek said, following her to the threshold.

He watched her walk down the hall before turning to Piper. She struggled to read his expression. "Come in." There was no joy in his tone, and Piper deflated.

"I'm sorry," she began, as soon as she was inside. This time Derek closed the door. "Are you mad that I . . ."

Before she could finish Derek was upon her, his lips against hers, his arms encircling her waist before she could get the words out. Piper inhaled sharply as he pushed her against the edge of his desk.

He pulled away, cupping her face. "What were you thinking?" But his voice was tender.

"I just got back," was all she could say. Proximity to him always had an effect on her, and her body arched involuntarily toward his. She closed her eyes. "Did you miss me?"

"You never told me any details. I didn't know when you'd be back."

She smiled, tipping her head back. He *had* missed her.

"It's not like you tried to reach me."

He kissed a trail down the side of her neck, whispering as he went. "I wanted to, but the weekend was crazy. My in-laws were visiting, and the kids had a birthday party." He reached her collarbone and his lips lingered.

Piper tugged at the collar of her shirt, and Derek's mouth followed. She groaned, her hands traveling across his back and down his spine.

It was always like this with Derek. Unlike any other boy or man she'd known, his hands had a way of reading her body, responding to every shift and breath. Piper relented, and as she did she felt the coiled spring within her loosen and give. When Derek lifted her up she wrapped her legs around his waist. But there were things she wanted to ask him, things she needed to say. "Derek, I went home to the Cape. Remember how we talked about going away together?"

He nuzzled her cheek. "I don't care where you went, as long as you're back."

As he lifted her up the roiling questions in her mind faltered in their haste, and her worries flickered and snuffed out like a candle. "I'm back," she said.

Afterward, as they lay together on the small leather couch in his office, Piper felt the rush of satisfaction give way to the creeping return of questions. It was a constant push and pull. She didn't want to ruin these private moments, rare as they were. But there were things they needed to discuss. Like *what* they were doing. *Where* this thing between them was going.

Piper watched as Derek buttoned his shirt and smoothed his hair. "I've got my mother's seventy-fifth birthday this week," he said. "What do you think I should get her?"

She smiled to herself as she gathered her

things. She liked hearing the ordinary details of his life, of being asked to weigh in on things like his mother's birthday. "She liked the art print you bought for their anniversary, right?" They'd picked it out together at a small gallery while walking around the South End one rainy afternoon, a gold-leaf framed watercolor of a meadow of violets. It was a rare outing for them, and Piper knew it was only because it was New Year's Day and the city streets were empty for the holiday. And because his wife and kids were still in upstate Vermont at her parents' place, having extended their Christmas visit.

He turned to her. "You remembered that?"

She wanted to say, "Are you kidding? It was one of the best afternoons of my life." They'd had Irish coffees and scones at a bakery, strolled through the streets holding hands beneath the safety of their umbrella, and gone back to her place to make love. Her roommates had both gone home for the break, and it was the longest uninterrupted stretch of time they'd had together. Derek had insisted she stay in bed and had made a dinner of fried eggs and green peppers on the hot plate in her tiny apartment kitchen. Instead, she said, "Yeah, wasn't it that little gallery on Tremont?"

He held her gaze, a slow smile spreading across his face. Piper wasn't sure if he was pleased by the memory, or the fact she remembered that his mother liked watercolors, but the way he looked at her made her insides flip-flop. "I don't know what it is about you, Piper Bailey. But you always surprise me."

He was happy, and she decided to run with it. "So, the summer classes are over at the end of the month, right?" It was a lame question to an answer she already knew; the four-week course ended the last week of June.

"And . . . ?"

"And I seem to recall the mention of a little getaway. Just the two of us?"

"Pipe." She loved this. He was the only person outside her family who ever called her that. "You know I'd love to do that, but I just don't see how we can. We can't even go to a restaurant together here in the city." He buckled his belt and sat down beside her.

"We've talked about this. It's just the Cape."

Derek laughed. "Just the Cape? That's the summer extension of Boston. Everyone from the university heads out to the Cape. You know that."

"Not everyone. Besides, Chatham is my hometown; there are places I can take you that are off the beaten path. Places we could actually be together." She'd planned the trip one thousand times in her mind. It was what they'd spent the winter talking about when lying together during a stolen hour in her apartment bedroom. It was what had sustained her, the promise that they would find some meaningful time together, and soon. That time was here.

"I don't know. I'll have to look at my calendar. Melody is talking about going to Nantucket for a couple weeks . . ."

Melody. Derek's wife.

Piper sat up and tugged her shirt over her head, feeling suddenly exposed. "Don't worry about it," she said quietly. Hillary and Claire had warned her this would happen—they'd told Piper not to expect anything from him. "Has he shown any signs of leaving her?" they'd ask. And Piper would always have to shake her head no.

Piper had never planned to get involved with a married man. It was so cliché. But having spent every Tuesday and Thursday listening to him lecture, watching the way he sat on the edge of his desk, ran his hand roughly through his hair when an idea excited him, it did something to her. After the poem recitation in his office, she knew it wasn't just her. It started innocently with a coffee in the student center to discuss a paper she'd written. Which led to a discussion about where he'd gone to school (University of Colorado at Boulder) and his major and the music scene and his favorite band. The Samples, did she know them? She did not. But she went home that night and downloaded the album, *No Room*, and listened to it until the sun rose. After the next class, she lingered in the doorway. "My favorite track is 'When it's Raining.' "

Derek lifted one eyebrow. "Try 'Outpost.' 'Did you ever look so nice.' "

A week later they went to see a band downtown, though not together. She went with Claire and a couple girlfriends. Derek met them there. They danced and laughed and drank too many beers in cheap plastic cups. He was careful; he went home alone. But only after a furtive kiss in a dark corner by the ladies' room.

It was like that for a while. Attending events separately, but finding seats next to each other where Derek would run his hands up and down her skirt during the show, causing her skin to buzz until the stage began to blur before her eyes and it was all she could do to make it to the intermission, where they'd make out in an alley pressed against the side of a cold brick building. Until he'd pull away, with a look of remorse and sadness that made him look younger and truer than she felt she had ever been.

"I can't," he'd say, lifting up his palms in surrender.

She'd cup his face in her hands and press her forehead to his. "It's okay," she'd whisper. "We don't have to." As if she could impart a moral pass to either of them for having come to their senses in time.

But it grew old. Later when the same act

130

repeated itself, she'd hang onto his shirt, crying, "It's just *us*. It's you and me, Derek." As if they could occupy this fervent sliver of space and time. Like it was something they could harness between them, and any obligations outside of the two of them did not exist. To that point, their relationship had been clandestine and furtive, and it seemed like enough. They talked, endlessly and about everything. There were late nights sitting in dark out-of-town pubs talking politics and childhoods and their favorite Middle Eastern restaurants in the city. Derek made her feel safe. And savored. He always shared a cab home with her, delivering her to her apartment where he waited until she closed the lobby door safely behind her. He asked about her courses in the education department, and the other professors. "Watch out for Delaney," he warned. "He'll take one look at you and be done." She'd delighted in the jealousy that sparked in his eye, and the feeling that she was his, in some small way.

But the trouble was, she had fallen in love. She had not told him this; she did not dare. But the words pressed at the corners of her mouth each time she saw him, especially when they parted. The truth was, she needed more. Their secret relationship was not enough. It made her feel lonely, and, worse, cheap.

Piper dressed quickly. "Maybe we should just take a break for the summer." She did not want that, in fact she feared it might actually kill her, but she could not face a summer without seeing him either.

Derek reached for her. "Honey, please. I want all this as much as you do. Just give me some time."

She resisted, but the look in his eyes and that boyish flop of dark hair that fell across his forehead got her. "Do you?"

He nodded emphatically.

"Then make it happen this time. By the end of the month, let's have a date on the calendar." It was a bold move for her, this ultimatum. But if she weren't mistaken, it didn't cause annoyance to flush his cheeks. If anything, he was looking at her with what she might go so far as to call respect.

He pulled her close. "I promise."

When she left his office, Piper kept her eyes trained on the carpeted floor as she passed the assistant's desk. It was when she got to the stairwell she realized with regret that she'd forgotten to give Derek the chocolate-covered cherries. When she found them at the bottom of her purse, the pretty pink box was crumpled, the bow crushed.

Ten

Wren

What was it about middle children? Wren stood in the mirror studying her reflection. She was thirty-four years old, and a single mother, something she prided herself in, but had begun to doubt. Until now, she'd taken the safe route of career choice managing other businesses' money working as a bookkeeper. Compared to her sisters, Wren wasn't just the middle child in the family: she was also the middle achiever. Shannon had created the perfect family nest, something she painstakingly crafted like a flawless little fortress, copper whale weathervane and all. As for Piper, who routinely overdrafted checks and whose only profession thus far was as a debt-ridden student, at least when she screwed up, she did so royally. That took commitment. Despite their very different tracks, both of her sisters leaned into the wind. What did that say about Wren?

Wren was not a risk-taker. Unlike Piper who seemed to thrive in precariousness, who even cultivated it, Wren did not like change. Shannon may have been the sister that others might call the safest; after all she, too, had stayed in Chatham. She'd long operated on sensibility: marrying her college sweetheart, working at his agency, starting a family. But even within the confines of those "safe" choices, Shannon pushed the envelope. She pushed *herself.* She didn't just have kids, she had the most well-rounded high-achieving kids: chess players, sailors, cellists, debate team! Her house was not just a house. Five thousand square feet, exclusive Stage Harbor neighborhood, direct waterfront. Shannon didn't just live in Chatham, Shannon was leading Chatham. Fundraisers. Boards. Committees. Wren was exhausted just trying to list them all.

Which is what finally led her to open the Fisherman's Daughter. Wren created a business plan and ran the numbers. She figured she could survive at least a year trying to break even. And then perhaps another year after that. If her business plan tanked, she could always go back to bookkeeping. There was plenty of business in town, and as a local she had contacts up and down the Cape. The Fisherman's Daughter was no longer just a dream; it was brick and mortar and fingers crossed behind her back. If it went under, Wren could live with that. What she couldn't live with was straddling the fence any longer.

Her phone dinged. "Where are you?"

"Crap." She raced for the closet. Shannon

had invited her to lunch with Lindy at her golf club, and now she was late. She plucked a pale-blue shirtdress off a hanger, prayed it wasn't too wrinkled, and slipped it over her head. As a last-ditch effort, she grabbed a bright orange Lucite cuff bracelet from the silver tray on her bedside table. She'd snagged it the day before from a jewelry order that had come in at the shop and was glad she had. The pop of color on her wrist made her smile. She was halfway out the door when the house phone rang. She hesitated, then checked: it could be Lucy's school. But the caller ID showed an unfamiliar Arizona number. Without answering, Wren set it back in its cradle.

It was the perfect beach day, clear and hot, so she hoped the main drag into the village would be quiet. The Jeep top was still down from the glorious weather of the day before, and the wind whipped at her hair. She turned on the radio.

When they were little, Caleb used to take them into town for breakfast on weekend mornings, letting Lindy sleep in back at the house. He'd pile the three girls into the wood-paneled station wagon and drive up Route 28 to Larry's PX for blueberry pancakes and whipped cream. Wren remembered sitting in the back seat beside Piper, still in her footy-pajamas with her blankey wrapped around her neck like a scarf, as their dad cranked up the car radio. It was always classic rock: Cat Stevens, Neil Young, James Taylor.

Caleb's voice was rich and raspy, and when a good song came on he threw his head back and belted out the lyrics. He knew all the words to all the good ones, and she learned them, too, listening to him and singing along. Her favorite was Harry Chapin's "Cat's in the Cradle." Caleb would roll the station wagon windows all the way down and their long hair would blow across the back seat, a sea of blonde rivulets, until there was no discerning one child's hair from the other. "My little birds," he called them.

They'd all sing together, *"When you coming home, Dad? I don't know when. But we'll get together then. You know we'll have a good time then."*

Wren had the latest correspondence from her father tucked in her purse.

I'll be there the twenty-third, he wrote. *I'll be taking the Cape Regional Transit Authority in Harwich. I won't be any trouble. I booked a room at the Chatham Motel.* Wren pulled into the club parking lot and grabbed the letter from the glove box.

"The bus?" Shannon said, sitting on the back deck of the club. "He's taking a bus home?"

A breeze came up over the green, and the Nantucket Sound sparkled behind her under the midday sun. She'd waited until they ordered before sharing the news. They'd ordered salads

136

and oysters, toasting the start of summer vacation with Bloody Marys. But despite the high sun and clear skies, a somber mood soon blanketed their table.

Lindy was sitting back in her chair, hands in her lap, listening quietly, her face as placid as the water. Since the disclosure of the first letter's arrival, Lindy had remained stalwart in her post: the sudden return of their father into her daughters' lives was for them to decide how to navigate. She would impose no outward opinion one way or the other. But Wren could tell that this odd piece of news poked at her curiosity.

"Does he not have a car?" she wondered aloud.

Which gave further rise to the many questions that had been swirling in Wren's mind about their father's present situation, and what was drawing him back to them after all these years.

"I'll bet he lost his license." Shannon tipped an oyster back without pleasure.

"I'll bet he's broke."

"Shannon." Lindy's voice was firm, but not upset. "You are under no obligation to anyone other than yourself and your family, honey. None of us are. But let's not jump to dire conclusions just yet."

Shannon shrugged. "Try telling Piper that. In her world he's coming home so we can all be a big happy family again." She dabbed her mouth with her napkin and stared out at the sound. Wren could feel the ire emanating across the table.

"Piper just finished grad school. She can barely afford to live in the city, Shan. She's in no position to offer your dad handouts even if she wanted to."

"Has that ever stopped her before?"

Wren sighed. It was true; Piper may have been the one with the least amount of resources to give, but she was also the first to offer more than she had. Whether it was running up credit card bills or giving away too much of herself to men who weren't good for her. It had landed her in trouble before; trouble that she often confided in Wren in phone calls late at night, or in Lindy when asking for a small loan "just to get me through" on her rare visits home.

"That's all I know," Wren told them both. "He arrives this weekend." She helped herself to an oyster and tried to concentrate on its briny sweetness.

Her mother, she noticed, had not touched her lunch. She crossed her arms and leaned forward between them. "There's something you two need to remember. After the boat accident, I'm the one who told your father he couldn't stay with us, at least not until he got some help. That was me. You didn't do anything to make him leave. And you don't have to do anything now that he's coming back."

Shannon reached for her Bloody Mary, and

Wren realized with surprise that the glass was empty already. "I'm still not sure I want to see him, period."

Wren had hoped differently; she knew Shannon harbored the most anger and reservation about the whole idea, but she needed her older sister in this. She wasn't sure she could do it alone.

"You don't have to," Lindy said. "You're a grown woman."

Wren shifted uncomfortably in her seat. It didn't matter that they were grown women, as she'd called them. Wren had felt the flutter of those hard childhood years since the realization of Caleb's return. She didn't like the division she was starting to sense between them.

The server arrived, scanning the mostly full plates. "Would you ladies like me to wrap these?"

Shannon held up her empty glass.

"Another drink?" the server asked.

Before Wren could object, Shannon nodded. She had to get back to the store, and surely Shannon had had enough.

But Shannon leaned back luxuriously in her seat. "Lunch is on Reid and me! Take your time. Mom, do you want dessert? They have a sublime blueberry tart. Local." Her voice was a bit too loud. She thrust the menu across the table, nearly knocking over Wren's water glass. Wren glanced at the nearby tables of diners.

Lindy, too, was eyeing the empty glass in front

of Shannon. "I'm going to finish my salad. You should, too, honey."

But Shannon wasn't listening. She was scrolling through her phone, her neatly plucked brows furrowed. "I want to show you both my latest listing, but I can't seem to find it . . . Oh, wait. Here it is! Reid landed the old house on Oyster Pond I was telling you about at dinner. We're listing it at one-point-six." She handed her mother her phone.

Lindy shaded the screen with her hand before passing it to Wren. "Good lord, I remember when that house was built. Couldn't have cost more than fifty thousand back then."

Shannon beamed. "We beat out two other agencies!"

Wren watched her out of the corner of her eye, as she leaned over her mother's shoulder and pretended to look at the photos on the screen. To the naked eye, Shannon was the picture of poise. Her blonde hair was pulled back, her Linda Farrow cat-eye sunglasses perched neatly atop her head. Wren would never have known the brand and certainly not the cost, except for the fact Piper had swiped them off Shannon's head the second she walked in the kitchen the other night at Lindy's. "Fancy pants. These would've cost a pretty penny," she'd exclaimed to the kitchen as a whole.

Reid had winced. "Don't remind me."

"Hey," Shannon had said, snatching them back. She polished the lens with the corner of her shirt. "Don't be rude, Pipes."

Piper had whispered in Wren's ear, her breath hot and accusatory, just like she used to when they were little. "Twelve hundred dollars."

Wren had nearly choked on her wine.

She knew that their older sister didn't like to talk about money, that she considered it déclassé, but twelve hundred dollars would've covered the entire accent lighting budget in her new store and probably the new toilet in the back bathroom, too. Wren knew Reid and Shannon were well off, likely more so than all of the rest of them combined, and to her credit Shannon never once boasted about it. But the excess worried Wren at times. It wasn't just the house, the cars, the hired help for the property. Even the kids had state-of-the-art sports equipment, the most expensive shoes, the very best instructors: all things they would outgrow. It just seemed so lavish.

"Congratulations," Wren told her, handing her back the phone. Shannon's appearance was crisp and manicured, like the other women outside. But Wren could detect the chinks in her older sister's armor; small things no one else would notice. It was in the way Shannon fiddled with her watch while they were talking, turning it to and fro on her slender wrist. And how she'd glanced around for the server throughout the entire meal, well before the level of her Bloody Mary reached its halfway mark. And there was more: behind the erect posture there was that glazed fatigue in her eyes Wren had been noticing in recent months, the red rims of her eyelids. Wren felt for her; she knew that the sometimes annoyingly high standards Shannon may have expected of the rest of them were nowhere as stringent as the ones she expected of herself. Shannon was not just Type A. She was Type A+. How tiring it must be listening to that endless voice inside her head: *"Sold a house? Get another listing! Avery won her tennis match? Now teach George to sail!"* For all her admirable accomplishments, Wren was pretty certain Shannon never slowed down enough to enjoy any one of them. It was a rat race she'd signed herself up for, a circuitous route that went round and round like a hamster wheel, with no finish line in sight.

Now, with their father coming back, Wren worried how she would handle this, too. Shannon had always been so buttoned up in her emotions. Unlike Piper, who would flee, either down the street as a child or back to the city these days, hiccupping back tears as she went. Or like Wren, who knew she retreated into her home and work, avoiding everyone in the family but Lucy. But not Shannon Bailey. No—Shannon got her hair done and took everyone to lunch. Now, as the sun slipped behind the only cloud in the sky, she waved down the server and asked for two blueberry tarts to go. She turned to Lindy and Wren, smiling tightly. "You'll love them, I promise."

Wren tried not to notice the way her hand shook when she signed the check. *Onward!* she imagined the tinny voice inside her sister's head shouting.

Eleven

Caleb

He could sense the coast even before he could see it. The pitch pines, the scrub brush, the wild rose hedges along the road. He'd drifted off sometime after leaving South Station Terminal in Boston, and although he wasn't sure how long he'd been out, he suddenly was quite sure of where they were.

Outside the window the low beach scrub rolled away, dry and scraggly. The bus lurched and hissed slowing behind a line of cars as it pressed up Route 6. Up ahead the exit for Sandwich loomed on his right. Caleb rested his head against the smudged window pane and closed his eyes. His grandfather, Owen Livingston Bailey, had grown up in Sandwich, had found work as a builder, and eventually put up his own house and raised his family there. He'd been the one to first put a fishing rod in Caleb's hands. From the age of five or six on, whenever he visited his grandfather, they'd pull out the dented dinghy from behind the shed and carry it down to the kettle pond just across the road. All afternoon, rain or shine, they would sit and cast their lines for perch and bluegill. Caleb was patient and quiet, his grandfather said. The two things that made a good fisherman. As their lures bobbed and floated atop the pond surface, Caleb would study his grandfather's knobby fingers, thick and gnarled with age like tree branches. It was hard for the older man to hold a pencil or work beneath the hood of his Ford pickup, his fingers fumbling to grip the tools he needed. But somehow he could still thread a line and spool a reel despite the trembling in his hands. It didn't bother Caleb; rather, he liked to watch the old man's hands work. They were slow and familiar, and in familiarity was comfort. The languid afternoon stretched itself across the pond as the two hunched together on the wooden seat of the dinghy staring at their red-and-white bobbers.

Sometimes they spoke, of boyhood stuff like school and siblings. And about girls—how the ones in his class were a strange and chatty bunch who followed him around—what not to say to them even if they were bothersome. And later, especially if he liked them, what he should say. His Grampa Owen was the man who taught Caleb how to fish—to bait a hook, spool a reel, cast a line. All with few words: a nod here, a grunt of agreement there. He taught him to feel the line—how to know when to let the spool spin, when to reel it in. Lessons that took him from kettle pond to college, and eventually out into the world at large. Lessons in how to be a man.

Caleb knew he had not become that man. As much as he'd wanted to. He'd been given a talent for capturing images and a woman whom he loved with a fierceness that he could never seem to capture. And he'd lost it all.

Twelve

Shannon

It was the fourth day of summer vacation and the kids were flopped across the living room furniture in various states of repose, still luxuriating in the freedom of their school-free mornings. In that vein, the kitchen countertops looked like the beach after high tide had washed in and out, detritus scattered across their surfaces.

"Who made toast?" Shannon called out in the direction of the living room. No one answered.

She grabbed a dishtowel and swept the crumbs into her hand, polishing the countertop as she made her way to the garbage. There was an open jar of peanut butter with the knife still stuck in it, and what looked to be raspberry jam smeared on the marble surface. Someone had left a burned bagel in the toaster oven. Shannon sighed. It didn't matter that she'd risen before each of them and offered to make an egg frittata for breakfast. They'd each rolled out of bed and straggled downstairs only to collapse on the couch and flick on their various devices, grumbling that it was too early to eat.

"How about bacon?"

Silence, except for the fingers tapping on screens.

So she'd retreated to her office upstairs to download photos and work on images for the agency's latest listings. Now, an hour later, Winnie was still hunched over her phone on the couch. George was sprawled belly-up on the leather ottoman watching the Disney Channel upside down. The only difference was the evidence, strewn across the kitchen, that they had indeed eaten.

Shannon scooped up the empty juice glasses and plates and loaded the dishwasher. "George, Hermit Crab school starts in thirty minutes. Run upstairs and get dressed." It was the morning she'd been dreading, the same morning she'd dreaded with Winnie and Avery, a few summers earlier. George was starting his first day at sailing camp.

George appeared at the kitchen island. "Do I get my own Opti?"

Shannon regarded him over the counter: his cherubic face, still filled out with childhood plush. The mop of blond hair that he swept aside each time he spoke. She forced a smile. "Yes."

"Not true," Winnie called out authoritatively from the couch. "Not until you're a Sprite. And that's with an instructor. You can't go on your own until you're a Seaman." Winnie had been in the Seamen last summer.

George's face fell. "You'll get to try out all

kinds of boats," Shannon assured him. "Including an Opti. Now go get ready. And don't forget your water shoes."

George glared at his sister, who had already returned her focus to her phone, whooped loudly and took off. The second she heard his footsteps on the stairs Shannon leaned over the countertop and put her head in her hands.

"Breathe." Reid came into the kitchen and poured himself a cup of coffee.

"Easy for you to say. Your family grew up on the water."

He came over and put a hand on her back. "So did yours, honey."

Shannon shook her head. It wasn't the same. Reid's family had long belonged to the yacht club. He learned to sail before he learned to ride a bike. It was true that she and her sisters had also learned those things. But in local waters and in humble watercraft. Caleb had first taken them out fishing in the family's dinghy on Oyster Pond. As for sailing, they'd had an old wooden Beetle Cat that he was forever working on, that they stored on blocks in the backyard of their Ridgevale Beach home before taking it over to Lighthouse Beach. It was the first watercraft she'd ever sailed in alone, and the very same one her mother decided to sell, years later, after she told the girls that their father would not be coming home.

· · ·

It had been a late fall day, beginning in a silvery frost as the girls waited for the school bus outside Beverly's house. The sisters were waiting by the mailbox, shivering and huddling together as they tried to stay warm. Piper had discovered a puddle laced with ice and was dragging a stick through it, etching its frosty surface. Shannon stood back, not wanting to get splashed.

Behind them, Lindy waited on the front porch cupping a steaming mug of tea, as usual. What was not usual was the weighty dread that had settled in Shannon's stomach ever since her father's leaving. It had happened before—these "trips" he'd take—sometimes for weeks. Sometimes for a month. But Caleb had always called or sent word in the form of a postcard from some place the girls considered exotic: the red desert from the Arizona badlands or the white peaks of Denali. They were used to his coming and going, the ebb and flow of missing him and then reuniting, listening intently to the grand stories of his travels as he splayed the photographs across the dining-room table for their eager consumption. With great animation he'd tell them about the places he had been to and the people he had seen. It was a small way of bringing them along for the journey. The homecomings were celebrations, a balm to his absences that would sustain them until he went off on another assignment. But that was before what had happened that morning on Lighthouse Beach. He'd been gone for over a month by that time.

From the end of the sandy lane there came a crunch of tires, and Shannon glanced up to see a strange white pickup truck pull into her grandmother's driveway. Lindy came down the front steps and Shannon noted the lack of surprise on her mother's face. Whoever he was, she was expecting him. The man got out of his truck and waved. "Good morning," he said.

Lindy invited the man down the driveway to the shed in the backyard. Wren and Piper were still busy dragging sticks through the frozen puddle; Shannon strained to hear what the adults were saying. They stopped outside the shed where their boats were stored. The man circled the boats and lifted the edge of one of the covers, pulling it back slowly. It was the Beetle Cat. Shannon watched as he ran his hands down the wooden sides: she'd made it a point not to look at the boat after that morning. It didn't matter that Lindy had asked the neighbor to help collect the boat from the beach that day and bring it back to the house, even though Shannon would have preferred to leave it in the sand. To let the sea drag it out into the surf and have its way with it. What mattered was that it was hauled to the far corner of the yard and covered over, like a dead body at the site of an accident. It was a signal to an end. She would not climb into its wooden hull again, she would not sail into the wind and out to the sandbars.

After a few moments the man covered the Beetle Cat back over and turned to Lindy. They exchanged words, and he pulled his wallet out of his jeans pocket. Suddenly Shannon understood.

At that moment, the school bus came heaving up the lane and halted in front of them. Shannon looked to her mother, unable to speak, her tongue twisting with questions. "Mom?"

Even from a distance Lindy's eyes were set with resolve. And something else: apology. She mouthed, "It's okay."

But it wasn't. Shannon had not wanted to lay eyes on that boat again. It was hers to ignore and hers to hate. But getting rid of it was not something she'd considered. This was not up to her mother. Lindy had not been there on the beach that morning.

The school bus doors flipped open and her sisters turned to wave goodbye to their mother. "What's Mom doing?"

Shannon did not answer. "Mom!" she called out.

The man was still talking, but Lindy glanced over at them. That was one thing Shannon knew about their mother—no matter what was going on around her, Lindy had one eye and ear always open to them.

She waved and blew them a kiss. "Have a good day at school!"

Wren turned to her sister. "What's happening?"

"Nothing," Shannon had said, stalking down the driveway toward their mother. The man was still talking as she approached. Something about a grandson who loved to sail. She didn't care. She marched right up to her mother and cut him off.

"That's our boat."

Lindy glanced at the man. "This is my daughter." Then to Shannon, "The bus is waiting!"

Shannon didn't budge. "I won't let you sell the Beetle."

Lindy took her hand and pulled her aside. "Excuse me," she said to the man, her smile fading.

Shannon didn't wait for her mother to start in with whatever lame reasons she had. Lindy had not been there that day on Lighthouse Beach. It had been Shannon, Piper, and their father. And now he was gone.

"I won't let you," Shannon said. Tears were beginning to sting the corners of her eyes, and she didn't know why. She hated this boat. She hated everything about it. Which was exactly why she should let her mother sell it that day. But suddenly all that mattered to her was that it stayed. That was its rightful place, by the shed and under the tarp. It didn't matter if they never let it touch salt water again; it had to stay.

"Honey, please try to understand. It's just sitting here, and this boat is worth a lot of money."

"Then I'll get a job."

Lindy's face softened. "No, baby, it's not just about the money."

"Then why sell it?"

Behind them the bus driver honked. Lindy glanced up the drive and then at the man, who was shifting now from one foot to the other.

"Come on!" Wren called.

Shannon turned. Wren was standing on the bottom step, her face full of worry. And there was Piper, her little face pressed against the window watching them. Even from where she stood, she could see Piper's eyes were pressed tight, her mouth ajar. "See, Mom? Piper's crying."

Lindy's face fell, and Shannon's chest ached at the site of it. But if that was what it took . . .

"Excuse me." It was the man. Shannon stared at his hands, at the folded bills in his palm. "I can see you have your hands full here, so how about I settle up and come back later for the boat?"

Shannon glared at her mother.

"I'm sorry, sir. But the boat's not for sale any-more."

"Excuse me?"

But Lindy was already walking down the driveway. "I've made a mistake. I'm sorry to have taken your time." She broke into a run and grabbed Wren's mittened hand, and gently pulled her down the bus steps. Shannon listened as her mother apologized to the driver, too. So many apologies.

Then she flew up the bus steps, ignoring the driver's objections that parents were not allowed to board the bus, and down the aisle where Shannon could see her stop at Piper's seat and scoop her up. A moment later the four of them stood in the driveway in a cloud of bus exhaust, Piper's legs wrapped around Lindy's waist, her face buried in her mother's hair. Wren looped her pinky finger uncertainly through Shannon's.

The man had already climbed back into his truck. "I'm sorry," Lindy called, again.

Shannon remembered they'd gone back into the house, where Lindy piled them under blankets on the couch and put a kettle on for hot cocoa. They'd gone to school late. The boat remained in the backyard all fall, under the tarp. Shannon was true to her word: she'd never stepped in that boat again.

But Lindy had stayed true, too. Every few years Shannon would find herself in their grandmother's carriage house, now Lindy and Hank's, searching for a gardening tool for her mother or retrieving a bike for one of the kids. She'd glance at the hulking vessel in the corner with relief. There was something about it being there that she counted on.

Now, Reid squeezed her shoulder and lowered his face to where hers still rested in her arms on the kitchen island. "George is going to be fine, honey. The instructors will take good care of him. Just like they did with Avery and Winnie." He kissed the side of her head and waited until she nodded. He knew this was hard for her.

Today she would drop her youngest, her baby, George off at the Stage Harbor Yacht Club. George was a strong swimmer and had taken to the ocean just as eagerly and naturally as his sisters had. Shannon struggled not to interfere with their attachment to the water, no matter how much it rattled her. She knew she was the only woman on the Cape who dreaded a perfect summer day at the beach with her family. She'd already taken one of the small yellow pills Dr. Weber had prescribed her for occasions like this. Usually she took half. But that morning she'd gazed at the tiny yellow tablet in her hand wondering how something so small could handle worries so big. She'd popped the whole thing in her mouth.

Reid was dressed in his taupe summer suit, looking crisp and relaxed. "You're not coming?" she asked.

He tipped back the rest of his coffee. "I have an appointment with those buyers from New York, remember?"

"The retired couple?"

Reid nodded.

"But don't you want to talk to the instructors?" She tried to keep her voice even. She didn't want to worry Reid with her own worries. But she couldn't help it. If they had ten more children, it would still be hard for her to let them go out in a boat. He understood that.

Reid glanced at the wall clock then at her. "Do you need me to? Because I'll have to push back their appointment if I go." His blue eyes were empathetic, but also serious. This was work, and he didn't like messing around with other people's time once he committed.

Shannon hedged as a wave of anxiety washed cold up and down her arms. Aside from a slight fuzziness, the pill wasn't making a dent. She did need Reid, but she also knew what that would mean. Reid would come, but he'd be tense. He'd want to get going right away, but she hadn't even packed George's lunch yet. It would require they take separate cars to the yacht club where they likely couldn't find two parking spots in the small lot, resulting in him getting blustery with frustration. And then she'd spend the morning worrying not only about George on the water but also her husband being annoyed with her. "No," she said abruptly. "No, I've got this."

Reid looked surprised. And if she wasn't mistaken, impressed. "You sure?"

Yes, this was the way to go. Let him leave for work feeling confident in her. She nodded.

"Okay then." He pulled her in for a kiss. "I'll call you later to see how it went."

Shannon held on to him tightly, barely able to listen. Her skin prickled. "Sounds good," she managed.

She waited until the garage doors opened and his BMW backed out of the drive. Then she packed George's lunch with shaking hands and sent Winnie upstairs to get dressed. When the kitchen was finally all hers she went to the stand-alone freezer. The bottle of Grey Goose was like ice in her clammy hand. It sloshed against the sides of the juice glass as she poured: just an ounce, she told herself. Just to stop the trembling. She stood at the kitchen island and tipped it back, staring through the living room and out at the ocean through the giant picture window they'd installed. Nothing. Not the usual liquid warmth in her throat, not the subsequent unspooling in her limbs.

Maybe one more? This morning was different, after all. Reid knew what sailing did to her; he should've been the one taking George, just as he had with the girls. Shannon thought he understood—he was usually so supportive—but on mornings like this, when her heart pounded against her rib cage and he just stood there in their gleaming marble-and-stainless-steel kitchen looking serenely back at her, she realized he did not. He did not see the coursing adrenaline, the pinprick of sweat at the back of her neck. She realized that she'd become so good at it, even her own husband saw what everyone else did: the sleek hair, the designer jumper, the composed features. Shannon let out a caustic laugh.

She poured one more shot and tried to focus on the horizon. The light streamed in with the promise of a new summer day. What a wonderful decision it had been to open up the kitchen wall so they could see straight out to the water. The water. She tipped the glass back and dropped it in the farmhouse sink with a clatter. "George!" she called. "It's time."

Thirteen

Piper

"He's coming back," she said, glancing up from her coffee to gauge his response.

"Your father?"

So, he *was* listening. They were grabbing a quick breakfast at Pavement Coffee House, near the university. All morning Derek had seemed distant and distracted, and while her father's looming return should've been her focus, it had been interrupted by her growing concern over the distance she was now certain she was not imagining between them. Derek had yet to commit to a date to come see her on the Cape. Worse, since school had ended they'd seen less of each other. Was this how it was going to be now that she was done with her course work at BU? What would happen to their relationship when she got a full-time job? Piper had always prided herself on the fact that she didn't need anyone. But she needed Derek.

"How long has it been since you've seen him?" he asked. He'd been reading this morning's *Globe*, and he gazed at her across the folded top of the Regional section.

Piper sipped her mocha latte and held it on her tongue, willing the sweetness to squelch the sadness of the truth. "Almost twenty-three years. I was just four at the time."

"Jesus." Now she had his attention. "I remember you talking about him leaving when you were young, but somehow I don't think I got the crux of it. Twenty-three years." His faced filled with empathy and something even more dear to her these days: interest.

Finally. This was what she needed.

"What do you think will come of this reunion?"

Instinctively, Piper put a hand to the scar on her forehead. Since childhood there had been allusions made to her father's absence. It depended on who was speaking about him: she'd once heard a local artist refer to his traveling spirit and creative hunger. Piper wondered at a hunger that could not be contained by the elbow of the Cape any more than it could be contained by the love of a family. Her mother called it a sickness, his "drinking," something he could not be entirely blamed for, yet something he was ultimately responsible for addressing. Piper had always found the duality of that confusing. Shannon likened it to bare-boned selfishness. As she got older, Piper began to connect the blurry dots like a constellation. Caleb Bailey was as bright and luminous as his talent suggested, but between those starry rays was darkness. And it had seemed the darkness had swallowed him up in the end.

"I don't know what to expect," she admitted. "My sisters are older, and they have stronger feelings about him leaving. Let's just say, we don't talk about it much."

"Weren't you curious about him though?"

"Sure. But I also knew it would cause ripples within the family. I've always thought I'd look him up someday. I just never had the guts to go through with it." She picked at her croissant and thought a moment. "You know how you hear all those references about 'Daddy's little girls'? Little princesses who want ponies and all things that sparkle?"

Derek nodded. "Like the lyrics, *'Papa's gonna buy you a mockingbird'*?"

She smiled softly. "I've never been that kind of kid. Maybe it was because I didn't have a dad, and therefore it wasn't an option. But I don't feel like I missed out on any of that stuff. What I did miss out on was simply having him around."

"As in a male role model?"

Piper shrugged. She wasn't sure that she believed that, necessarily—the Freudian thinking that daughters needed to attach to their fathers, just as sons turned to their mothers. She'd certainly had strong role models in both Lindy and their grandmother Beverly. And later, Hank. Besides, in today's modern society, little of that traditional nuclear family was the norm. "Let's just say the women in my family aren't shrinking violets. As far as my mother and grandmother went, I received more than my fair dose of strong role models."

Derek smiled appreciatively. "So no fatherly expectations, then?"

Piper shrugged. "It's too late for the pony. But who knows, maybe we can just start with a friendship."

Derek's gaze was solemn, but he smiled at her stab at humor. "You're pretty amazing, you know that?"

Piper felt herself flush, something that wasn't an easy thing to make her do. Derek had surprised her early that morning with a text: *I've got two hours. Are you free?* She'd flushed then, too.

But who could blame her? It had been a week since they'd seen each other, and her limbs were aching with missing him. She hated that her response to him was so physical: Piper prided herself on appreciating his mind, his humor, which were so much more sophisticated than the guys her age. But there was no denying the visceral connection they shared, and it left her wanting during their separations. As soon as she'd gotten his message, she'd sat up and texted him straight back: *Come over. Come get in bed.* And he had.

It wasn't as if he'd interrupted anything. She'd

been lingering under the covers, not wanting to get up and face the day. Not the yellow utility and gas bills that were thumbtacked at an angry angle to the bulletin board by the apartment door. Not the lengthy grocery list Claire had taped to her bedroom: it was her turn to buy the shared household supplies. They were out of toilet paper, and her roommates were *tired of using Kleenex to wipe their butts, for Christ's sake.* All compelling reasons to hide in bed until she heard the front door close and knew they'd left.

Things were getting dire. Piper was out of money, and she hadn't found a job. She'd already used the money Hank had given her to pay back Claire for last month's rent contribution. She did not want to have to ask Shannon for financial assistance, but she was on the verge of having to do so. Reid wouldn't mind, and although she knew Shannon would never turn her away, help always came with a medicinal dose of unwanted advice. Hoping to avoid that, she'd inquired again with the Brookline Arts Center, only to learn that the job had been taken. The campus career services office had called back to tell her that all the educational outreach positions she'd inquired about had long ago been filled. They suggested an internship with Boston Children's Museum, but Piper didn't need intern experience. She needed money. And fast. Though the thought of bussing tables in a restaurant depressed her as much as the thought of folding clothes at the Gap. She had a damn master's degree, after all.

None of this had been shared with Derek, however. Being a graduate student had meant she was enrolled in an educational institution—it implied intellectual prowess and a course of study. A plan. But now that she had completed her program, it didn't feel like she was done with school, so much as school was done with her. Losing the title of student reduced her to a terrifying new title: unemployed.

It wasn't just panic for herself she felt. It was panic about what this would mean for her relationship with Derek. They no longer shared a campus. Or roles they had happily filled to this point. The bond that had brought them together was severed: Piper wasn't the student to his professor. Now she was supposed to be part of a productive workforce, as Derek already was. A real adult. As such, her current jobless state wasn't going to do anything to cultivate his interest in her as a partner. Or whatever she was to him. Which was another thing she didn't want to think about.

"When does he arrive?" Derek asked, puncturing her thoughts.

"This weekend. I'm driving back to the Cape the night before, so I can be there."

Derek was staring thoughtfully at his plate. "Listen, I wanted to talk to you about that."

Here it was. He was about to tell her that he could not get away with her to the Cape, after all. She could already list the excuses: His family or his wife's family was coming to Boston to visit. Or maybe both! She braced herself.

"So, it looks like I'll be in Chatham after all."

Piper leaped out of her chair and shrieked. "Really? You're coming with me?" She noticed the couple at the table next to them staring, and she threw the woman a withering look. But when she turned back to Derek, he, too, was holding up his hands to calm her down. "Pipe, please. Sit."

She didn't care if people stared. Never before had they been able to spend any real time together, let alone out of town. It was always a stolen moment, last minute, in her cramped apartment, where she had to worry about roommates coming and going. Derek didn't want to risk anyone from campus seeing him, even though she'd assured him again and again that her roommates didn't know him and therefore wouldn't recognize him. And even if they did, they were cool; they were her friends. But that did little to allay his concerns, and between his teaching schedule and his family commitments, they'd been forced to live on what she not so fondly referred to as a "bread and water" relationship diet. There could be no sleepovers or romantic weekends. No restaurants or dates in public. A trip together still seemed out of the question. She was starving.

"I know the first place I'm going to take you," she cried, grabbing his hand across the table. "There's this great spot on Oyster Pond where we can kayak. We'll pack a picnic and some wine, and we can sit on the dock when the sun sets—"

"Piper."

Derek's expression held none of the excitement she felt. She swallowed hard.

"When did you say you're coming?"

"I didn't. I haven't had a chance."

Piper let go of his hand. "Sorry. I'm just excited. We can finally be *alone.*"

Derek winced. "That's what I'm trying to tell you. I'm coming to Chatham. But not in the way you think." He glanced around the café and lowered his voice. "It's a family vacation. Melody planned it with her sister this week. I had no idea they'd chosen Chatham."

Piper stiffened. "How long?"

"How long for? I think we'll be there for a week."

"No." Piper's mouth felt like sandpaper. She cleared her throat. "How long have you known?"

"I don't know . . . maybe two days. I wanted to wait until I saw you."

The hope that had been fluttering through her chest grew heavy and landed square in her middle. "You saw me this morning. You saw a whole lot of me, in fact."

Derek pressed his lips together in embarrassment as the server came to clear their plates and bring the check. Piper waited, but she wasn't done. Not nearly.

She leaned across the table, the words hissing from her lips. "Remember? When you came over and climbed into my bed and we made love?" They'd laid limbs entangled all morning. And yet he'd said nothing.

"Piper, please hear me out. We were supposed to go to Nantucket, but the rental fell through. Something about the house being for sale and suddenly securing a buyer. So, it was a last-minute change. I had no idea they'd settled on Chatham."

There was nothing she could say. "So you're going to the Cape. And you're going to stay in my hometown. But you'll be with your wife." She stood and tried to untangle her purse from the back of her chair. Derek stood with her and reached for the check.

"You know what, Derek? You've been making promises to me for a long time now. And time after time you break them." She wrenched her bag free from the chair and fumbled inside for her wallet. "Give me the check," she demanded.

"What?"

"Give me the goddamn check." She was getting the hell out of there. But before she did, she certainly wasn't going to let him pay for her.

He handed her the check, warily, and stood by

168

as she fumbled through her wallet. Receipts and coins spilled out onto the table, but all she could find was a one-dollar bill. "Fuck." The tears had already started to spill down her freckled cheeks. It was a matter of seconds before her nose turned bright red.

"Piper, please." Derek took the check gently from her hand. He set a twenty-dollar bill on the table and began to scoop up the stray change that had fallen from her bag.

"Leave it," she barked. Derek looked distraught, but did as he was told, and she took the smallest pang of pleasure from it. "Have fun on the Cape," she said, and then she lurched for the exit. The door swung shut behind her, and without thinking she turned left, the wrong direction, she realized too late, from her T-stop. But she wasn't about to turn around now.

Piper did not look back as she stormed down Commonwealth, but she listened. Her ears strained against the city noise. There was no patter of hurried footsteps behind her, and no one called out her name. Derek wasn't going to come after her.

Fourteen

Wren

"There are things we can do for ourselves." How many times had Lindy said that over the years?

Wren had a distinct childhood memory of her mother standing on a small blue stepladder in the middle of the kitchen. She'd been balancing on the top step, and she'd asked Wren to hold the ladder for her even though it was clear to her that that wasn't necessary. Later, Wren understood that Lindy hadn't needed her help; what she'd needed was to illustrate her self-reliance.

"See this broken bulb?" Lindy asked, as she unscrewed it overhead. "It's been flickering for months. Driving me crazy."

Wren had heard her mother comment on the flickering light numerous times, always to her father. He would nod distractedly and shuffle back downstairs to the basement where he kept his office. Where the girls knew not to bother him. Where a trash can of bottles filled quickly each week, especially when he was working on a deadline for an assignment. Meanwhile the rest of them would continue on with life, as if he weren't there, flickering light bulbs and all.

"I asked your dad more times than I can count to change it, but heaven knows why, when I could've just done it myself."

Wren gazed up at her mother's long fingers as they gripped the fragile bulb, turning it until it secured. "Now, go turn it on and let's see." Wren had hurried to the switch and flicked it. Lindy's smile standing up there beneath its yellow glow was triumphant. "How about that, Wren Bailey? Two girls and a set mind." Wren had smiled awkwardly; it was just a light bulb. But she understood. Lindy would not burden her daughters by complaining about their father's shortcomings; instead she would teach her daughters how to navigate them, filling the cavities with competence and spackling the hurts with love.

Fourth grade was the year when it all came to a head. Her father had landed a coveted shoot in Kathmandu. "I'm going to the Himalayas, girls! The tallest mountains in the world." For the first time in a long while, their father was excited. Ecstatic. There was special equipment he'd need for the weather conditions, and the altitude. He drove to Hyannis to outfit himself. An expensive new lens was purchased for his old Nikon. "It'll more than pay for itself," he assured their mother. Suddenly there were travel books on the coffee table in the living room.

Caleb joined them in their bedroom at night, clambering across Shannon's bed and pulling them all in close where he paged through books, showing them pictures of icy mountain peaks, Nepalese festivals, and Buddhists. "Just look at the colors," he'd whisper as the girls took turns flipping the pages. What Wren remembered most was that her father seemed to be back. Ebullient and available and hers, once more.

His trip began in the first week of school, and the girls marked off the days on the kitchen calendar until he'd return. It would be the last week of September, but Wren was used to that. Her father would come home happy and bearing gifts, and there'd be photos spilled across the dining-room table of the places he'd been. Glossy waves of images that told the story.

One week later, their father came back. There was no celebration, no photographs printed. Caleb went up to her parents' room and stayed there. Lindy's mouth was set in a grim line thereafter. "What happened?" Shannon asked.

"They hired another photographer."

"A poser!" her father shouted from upstairs. "A goddamned novice poser who probably never developed chemical film in his life."

There was no further explanation, but Wren knew it was because something bad must have happened. And she feared it had more to do with her father than the novice photographer.

If Caleb's work thinned out, his drinking did not. More and more often his office door remained closed, or they'd find him sitting at the kitchen table poring over stacks of black-and-white photos from his earlier shoots when they came home from school. Always the sweet yeasty smell of beer on his lips when he kissed them hello. At night she would overhear their parents arguing in hushed but urgent tones. "You need to address this, we can't keep going on like this," her mother would plead.

"You don't understand," her father replied. "That assignment was mine. They stole it from me."

It always came back to Kathmandu. An unseen place Wren now hated. "How do we cover the bills this month? Have you seen the pile on the kitchen counter?"

"Are you questioning my career, Lindy? Do you want me to quit what I love and get a job in some closed-off corporate office?" her father would hiss. "Is that what you want?"

"We can't pay the electric bill on talent!"

There would be the thunder of feet on stairs, the slam of the front door. Followed by the gentle whimper of her mother through the wall. Wren would pull the pillow up over her head. Wren ached for her mother, but she was wrong. Her father was talented. Everyone in Chatham knew that. Her teachers at school said so, whenever she brought in magazines featuring his work for show-and-tell. As did Mr. Gregg, who owned the Chatham Market, and who always asked Caleb what location he was off to next. "You've got the best of both worlds!" he'd gush as he bagged their vegetables and milk. "Traveling the world and raising a family here on the Cape. You're a lucky man, Caleb."

Wren's father would smile and shake his head and tell Mr. Gregg he was too kind, it was just honest work.

And when he was short on cash for the groceries, Mr. Gregg would wave a hand. "No problem. Next time. I'll put it on your tab!" Only Mr. Gregg didn't smile the next few times it happened. He'd glance nervously at Wren and her sisters and lower his voice. "I'm sorry, Caleb, but you need to take care of the account." Wren tried to conceal the deep wave of shame that rose as her father replaced the apples to the bin, the bread on the shelf.

That fall a *FOR SALE* sign went up in the front yard of their Ridgevale cottage, and Lindy packed them all up and moved the family to her mother's house. This time Caleb did not mention Kathmandu.

Beverly lived in town on School Street in a cozy neighborhood Lindy fondly referred to as the rabbit warren, a tangle of narrow lanes that looped around shingled cottages and tended

174

gardens that bordered Mill Pond. It was nestled between the busy Main Street shops on one side and Chatham Lighthouse on the other. Wren loved it. There was an energy in town she had not felt on the sandy lane by the beach, and it appealed to her growing teenage need to be close to things happening. Each Saturday she held Piper's hand and walked her south to Eldredge Library for the children's program, enticing her little sister to come along with a promise of a stop at the pink front door of the Candy Manor on the way back if she behaved. On the warmer weekday afternoons, they hopped on their bikes and turned north, passing the Cranberry Inn until they reached Bar Cliff Road. There they turned right to the lighthouse, and finding the lot empty, they lined their bikes up against the beach fence at the top of the stairs and raced down the steps that ran through the steep dunes, down, down, down, until they hit the cool sand of Lighthouse Beach where they shed their sneakers and streaked across the sand to the water's edge. Living in town fit.

In the old house, the Bailey girls had all shared one room. At their grandmother's they had two bright airy rooms to choose from upstairs, both wallpapered in navy-and-white chintz and out-fitted with antique brass beds. The rooms felt a bit formal for a trio of girls who wore their long hair in loose ponytails and fancied Converse sneakers and jeans over the dresses their grandmother bought them each Christmas.

Beverly had married her high-school sweetheart, Lindy's father, Bert, who passed away in his fifties of a heart attack on a cod-fishing boat, leaving her with a broken heart and young Lindy to care for. Beverly possessed a bachelor's in philosophy, course work she'd once found fascinating in college, but which was largely impractical to a widowed mother in a fishing community.

After Bert's death she collected the life insurance, paid off the house, and headed straight through the doors of the Cape Cod Community College, *"the oldest student in my class—oh, how they stared!"*—to earn her degree in library sciences. For the next twenty-five years she worked as the head of the children's department at Eldredge Library. Beverly was well versed in single parenting and in living alone. But she was not a homebody. She played bridge with her Chatham neighbors and attended fund-raisers and art gallery openings. She was an active member of First United Methodist and volunteered at the Atwood House, organizing their visiting lecture series. Wren had wondered how she felt about the five of them stomping through her quiet front door. Her grandmother did not allow the girls to hang up posters of boy bands with thumbtacks in her good walls and did not tolerate them leaving their laundry strewn across the hardwood floors, but she understood the importance of having a room of one's own. In that vein she welcomed the Bailey granddaughters with a flourish, accepting that this generation twice removed was of an energy and mind-set of their own. Which she encouraged. She assigned Shannon, then fourteen, to the smaller room overlooking the garden, and Wren and Piper to the one across from it. There were fluffy down comforters on the beds, and lovingly chosen hardcover books on their bedside tables. New holiday dresses hung in each of their closets. "This is your home now, too," she told them. Though there were a couple of rules. "You may decorate your rooms any way you choose, as long as you keep them clean. No boys upstairs, as your great-grandfather used to say. Dinner will be served at six each night. And if you're going to play loud music, you best make sure it's the Beatles." She ran her hand through her sleek silver bob. "That Paul McCartney does things to a girl."

Later that year, after the accident on the beach and when their father had gone, snow came to Chatham in amounts the seaside community was not used to. The girls donned hats and mittens and grabbed shovels. Even little Piper, who stood in the drifts with a sand scooper. Cape winters were usually mild, long stretches of gray and wind and drizzle. But that first winter their father left, all Wren remembered was white snow that piled and drifted across the sandy beaches, covered the rooftops, buried the cars. The Bailey girls shoveled and dug until they had to strip off their hats and unzip their coats to cool off.

The work was slow going. "We'll make cocoa when we're done," Lindy promised when someone fussed or grew tired. Soon they'd cleared a pathway down the front steps and up the walkway to the car. And all around the car itself. The car was snow-laden and largely stuck.

Lindy climbed in and started it, the engine clicking irritably in the cold. "All clear?" she'd shouted out the driver's window. Shannon had pushed Piper and Wren aside and given her the thumbs-up. The car rolled back a few inches and then commenced a swift spinning of tires in the newly packed snow. Piper shrieked as it sprayed them in white. It was no use.

Wren's arms were tired, her back sore. At that moment there were words on the tip of her tongue—foul colorful choices—that she could have so easily spat into the frozen air. Her father's name sharpest among them. Piper was starting to fall apart, and Shannon looked put upon. But it was the look on her mother's face that kept her frozen to the spot. If Lindy had ferried them through the last few months unshaken, she looked soon to shatter that morning. Standing beside the car, the exhaust fumes thicker than their frozen breath, their mother's gaze swung back and forth between her rumpled children, the deep snow, and the frozen car. Wren saw it: the tremor in her chin as she pressed her cracked lips together.

But she did not cry. "Sand!" her mother said, suddenly.

Shannon and Wren fetched the sand bucket from the porch. It was so heavy that they staggered down the walkway like two drunks, the metal handle biting their fingers through their mittens. Together they sprinkled sand behind the tires, packing it with their mittened hands. The next time Lindy rolled the car back, it caught and then surged back across the sand-strewn tracks they'd made, leaving a car-shaped spot of exposed gravel where it had been. They'd cheered, jumping up and down in their snowsuits, then collapsed on their backs in the fluffy white drifts, exhausted. Wren stared up at the open sky and a chunk of the worry that had been burdening her shoulders fell way. She imagined it hitting the frozen ground and melting, spreading around her silhouette like a snow angel. Her mother was right. It was hard, and sometimes cold work, but there were things they could do for themselves.

Still, there was their father's absence. Wren had overheard her mother talking to Beverly one rainy afternoon at the dining room table. "I don't think he's coming back," said her mother.

Wren had been on her way downstairs to find a

book she was writing a report on for school when she'd heard her father's name. She sat down on the staircase, barely breathing as she listened. Beverly had been worrying aloud that perhaps talking about him would be harder on the girls.

But Lindy had felt otherwise. "Mom, no matter what happens he's still their father. What kind of message does it send to them if I silence anything to do with his memory? It's like telling them that half of who they are isn't worth mentioning."

Sitting on the stairwell and staring out at the rivulets of rain coming down the front windows, Wren let her mother's words wash over her. They were as powerful as they were painful. It was true their father had done an awful thing, just as it was true he would always be a part of them in spite of it. And although she didn't want to talk about him—not yet, anyway—it was a relief to know that she could when she was ready. And that her mother would listen.

The first few months he was away, Caleb sent money. It was irregular, and often from a different return address. But it was never enough. Their mother would have to go back to work. She enrolled in the community college to update her teacher's certification.

Still, Wren was fortunate in her upbringing: it was a childhood strong on female influence and long on love, even if she did miss her father and their little cottage by the beach. It was also why she had not hesitated when it came to raising Lucy on her own. Not that she had intended to be a single mother, but as Lindy had ingrained in them, she could do this herself if she had to.

Now, as she sat waiting in the Stop & Shop parking lot for the Cape community bus to arrive with her estranged father, she wondered about this decision. When Lucy was a baby it had seemed easier. She didn't know any different than it being just the two of them, and Lucy seemed content with their little life in Chatham. There were sand dunes to climb and hermit crabs to collect, and Wren could show her all of the best spots to do both. She loved the diverse mix that the hardworking fishing community and the vacationing summer destination provided; there was balance in that, she felt. Yes, she had managed to carve out a nice little life for them in their cottage on Queen Anne, and there was something safe and solid about raising her only child in the very place she'd grown up.

But as Lucy grew older, she began to notice that they were different. Other families had moms and dads, or in the case of a set of twins in Lucy's kindergarten class, two dads.

"Who is my dad?" she began asking in nursery school, when they drew pictures of their family. Then there was the father-daughter Daisy Scout dance at Valentine's Day. Wren had panicked and sent Hank to the dance. Bless him, the man had shown up in a suit with a rose corsage for his little date, and Lindy clamored over both and snapped pictures of Lucy in her pink tulle dress. But none of this satisfied Lucy for long. *Where did her daddy live? What was his favorite color? When would she see him?*

Wren had hot-footed it to an LCSW in town, who explained that honesty, in a developmental way, was the way go. "It's kind of like the birds and bees talk," the therapist had said. "Answer only what she asks. Don't go overboard with details, as she may not be ready for them all." She'd also recommended some children's literature for talking points.

After a quick stop at Where the Sidewalk Ends bookstore, she picked up some parenting books, and by that night she was tucked in with Lucy reading aloud. But the questions still came.

Wren had been so sure they did not need James, but she was beginning to realize that that may have only been true for herself. Lindy had taught her girls that they could live without their father; but she'd also honored the fact that he was half of each of them, and she'd tread carefully to respect that half, always. This was something Wren had not done for Lucy. And as she sat waiting for Caleb Bailey's bus, it occurred to her she may have made a terrible mistake. As a fatherless child, herself, she'd imposed the same fate on her daughter.

Just then came the industrial hiss of bus brakes, jolting her back to the moment. He was here. She took a deep breath as the doors swung open. The driver exited first and went around to the luggage area on the side of the bus. Down came the passengers, and Wren could feel the thudding grow in her chest. A young woman with pink hair. An elderly couple who emerged blinking in the bright sun like lost birds. Wren studied the faces: a middle-aged man, a family of four, a group of college kids in baseball jerseys, who must've come in for the Chatham A's league. Suddenly she went from the dread of what she was going to say to Caleb Bailey to the thought that maybe he had not come: a far worse thought. An old thought that turned her stomach sour in the way it had when she was eleven years old.

She opened the door and got out, shielding her eyes in the bright sun. No, there was no one who resembled her father. No tall men with broad shoulders. No red hair. Had he missed the bus? Changed his mind? At that thought, she strode toward the bus.

The driver was still dragging all of the luggage out of its compartment as passengers encircled him, reuniting with their belongings. Others, like herself, had joined the small crowd of arrivals. There were greetings and hugs. The boys in baseball jerseys headed toward a red van parked nearby. Wren looked left and right. She waited while the driver pulled another suitcase out. "Excuse me?" she said, her voice cracking. "Do you have a Caleb Bailey on the bus?"

He turned to her and ran a handkerchief across his brow. "Hang on, Miss. I'll have to check my roster." She waited for what seemed like forever as he lined up the last of the luggage. Finally he grabbed a clipboard and started flipping through its pages. "Who are you looking for?"

Wren glanced up at the dark bus windows. It appeared empty, but she couldn't be sure. "Caleb Bailey," she said, uncertainly.

"Here," said a voice behind her. A voice that was softer and drier than she remembered, but as familiar as the smell of Lucy's head, the sound of the surf at Ridgevale Beach, the salt in the Cape Cod air. She turned and looked up into the hazel eyes she had struggled all these years to evoke. "I'm right here," he said, smiling softly.

Something inside her gave. The laugh lines around his eyes were grooves now, and he wore a neat beard and mustache, still red but tinged with gray. He was thin, a ladder of the man she remembered, and yet he was also the same. The almond eyes. The easy smile. The large warm hands, one of which he extended to her now and rested on her shoulder. He squeezed it gently. "Wren."

She swiveled away from him, his hand sliding away from her shoulder, and feigned focus on the assemblage of remaining luggage. "How many bags did you bring?"

If her father expected a different greeting, he did not push for it. But when she risked a backward glance she saw his eyes cloud sadly, if only a little. "I just brought one," he said, reaching past her for a large green suitcase.

Wren straightened. "All right then. Let's go."

Fifteen

Shannon

She'd picked him out of the small group of passengers right away. There was no doubt in her mind when he appeared in the bus doorway, the last one to do so, that it was her father.

Shannon sucked in her breath and squinted for a better look. Caleb Bailey had aged. Gone was the strong set of his shoulders, filled out from a lifetime of swimming in the Sound and outdoor living. Gone, too, was his crown of strawberry blond hair. It was still there, but it had faded in both thickness and pigment to a thin cap of sandy-colored down.

Shannon had not planned to be there at all. But as the day of his arrival grew closer, something that had been nestled hard and deep within her resolve began to shift. It began one night at dinner when Reid asked her what she thought he looked like, and it took her by surprise. All this time she'd spent hating the father who'd left them—that broad-shouldered young man who'd driven away in a blue Chevy all those years ago. But Caleb Bailey was almost seventy now. He was old, and it was hard to keep hating someone whose appearance she couldn't pin down.

Dr. Weber had been the one to posit the question most firmly. She'd gone to her usual session earlier that week, the focus of which she'd imagined would be George's sailing lessons and the pressure she was feeling over the Ridgevale house listing. She'd been especially on edge lately, and she was eager to hear Dr. Weber's thoughts on the matters. But he didn't want to talk about any of those things. "Tell me," he said, as soon as Shannon sunk into the upholstered recesses of his armchair by the window. She loved Dr. Weber's office. It was such a calming place. "How are you managing your feelings about your estranged father?"

Shannon blinked. She'd only mentioned to the doctor once that her father was coming back to town. He had not been a focus of their meetings, and honestly, she did not want to spend any one of her forty precious minutes on him. "There's nothing to manage. As I mentioned last time, I don't plan to see him."

Dr. Weber had cocked his head and looked back at her. When she thought she could not stand the silence for another moment he scribbled something on the yellow legal pad he always kept open on his lap. Shannon wondered what it was.

"Yes, I know that is your plan. But I wonder if you've considered something beyond that."

Shannon glanced at the wall clock, then back at

her doctor. She really wanted to move on to her work concerns. Bitsy was driving her crazy as of late. "Have I considered . . . ?"

The doctor smiled. "You've mentioned some undesirable things that could happen if you do see your father. Wasted energy. Exposing yourself to old hurts. Conflict."

Shannon nodded impatiently.

"Those are understandable, of course. But I wonder about something. Have you considered what will happen if you don't?"

The question had stayed with her all week. No, she had *not* wondered what might happen if she didn't see him. Because that was exactly how her life was now. She hadn't seen Caleb Bailey in years. And she was perfectly fine as it was.

But when the eve of her father's return came in a cool and starry late June night, Shannon found herself pacing the upstairs of her Stage Harbor home in her bathrobe. Maybe she should call Wren in the morning and offer to go with her. It didn't matter that Wren said she could handle this alone. Wren was tough, but she wasn't steel.

By three a.m. Shannon gave in and went to the small drawer in her bathroom vanity. There she retrieved her orange prescription bottle. She'd split an Ativan in half and chased it with the half-drained vodka tonic on her bedside table—no big deal—it was just melted ice at that point. When the alarm went off at seven for Reid, she'd lain in bed feeling like there was sand beneath her eyelids. Morning light blasted the room. She would not call Wren, she decided. But she could also not stay away. And so here she was, parked halfway across the lot in her sunglasses and a baseball hat, watching for her estranged father like some kind of stalker.

When he emerged, she knew him immediately. "There he is!" Shannon wanted to shout to her sister who was off to the side talking to the driver. What was she doing? Shannon had to fight the urge to get out of her car and push them toward one another.

At that moment the minivan parked in front of her beeped, and a woman rolled her shopping cart up to it directly in her line of vision. "Shit." Shannon strained to see past her tailgate as she slowly loaded groceries into the back. Desperate, she rolled down her window and stuck her head out, craning her neck.

She could tell the moment Caleb Bailey recognized Wren. Something in his posture gave just a little, and Shannon felt herself exhale. When he walked up to Wren, Shannon could not help herself any longer. "Turn around!" she shouted out the car window. They were too far away to hear, but the woman by the minivan startled. She dropped a grocery bag, its contents rolling across the pavement. "What the hell?" she cried, glaring at Shannon.

Shannon was about to get out and help, but the nasty snarl on the woman's face caused her to instead roll up her window. "What the hell is wrong with you?" she mouthed through the glass. Why were people so tightly wound these days?

Shaken, she returned her attention to the scene unfolding by the bus. Wren was standing ramrod straight. Shannon knew what it meant. It was the same way she'd stood in the high school cafeteria as a freshman, eyes darting uncertainly around in search of a place to sit. And even though she didn't want to, something protective had come over her, and Shannon had elbowed a friend aside and waved her little sister over. The same feeling rose up in her now as Shannon watched them. She watched her father reach for Wren, his arm hesitating in the air between them before it settled softly on her shoulder. Shannon was genuinely surprised when Wren did not hug him, and more so when she turned away. So she wasn't the only daughter who harbored angry feelings.

They headed for her Jeep, shoulder to shoulder but apart. There was something familiar about the way they moved, and Shannon leaned forward to get a better look. There it was: the same purposeful bounce to their gait. Shannon had known her sister's peculiar gait all her life. It had allowed her to pick Wren out of a crowd on the soccer field or walking up Main Street. She'd never realized she'd gotten it from their father.

As she watched the two climb into the Jeep, Shannon slid lower in her seat, feeling suddenly like some kind of voyeur. She stayed there until the Jeep exited the parking lot and veered left to Chatham village. She remained until it was out of sight.

Something was in her eye, and she reached behind her sunglasses to try to wipe it away. She realized it was tears.

Sixteen

Hank

L indy was beside herself. "He's been through a lot. He's going to need a lot of help," she told Hank as she darted around the house that morning.

On the Cape there were what they called beach days and what they called town days. A beach day was of the hot and humid variety, necessitating an escape to the cold surf and salty breeze. A town day was a softer sun-filled day that allowed you to stroll comfortably down Main Street, a gentle breeze rolling along the sidewalk reminding you that you were still at the shore, but you could take a break from the sand and hit the shops or go out to eat. Today was the deliciously rare combination of both, and Hank had risen hoping they could go for a bike ride and enjoy it. He'd been mistaken.

"I know that, honey," he tried to assure her. "We'll make him as comfortable as we can." He set the newspaper down on the kitchen island and watched her bustle between the sink and the fridge, stopping to scoop up the breakfast dishes with a flurry. "What time do we pick him up?"

"In ten minutes." She stopped and faced him. "Can you drive? I'm too nervous."

Hank was just grateful she was talking about Bowser and not her ex-husband, who was also due in town that day. Bowser had had his hip surgery two days earlier and had been recovering at the animal hospital since. They were releasing him this morning.

Hank had gone to the hardware store and picked up a wide sheath of plywood to put over the top of the two back steps so Bowser could get down to the grass to relieve himself. Lindy had set up water bowls and made up dog beds all over the house. Bowser would not be allowed to use the stairs for the rest of the summer, so she'd set up a rest area in the screened-in porch. "He likes the salt air," she'd said. Hank nodded. She set another up in the kitchen. "You know how he likes to be a part of everything," she explained, as she dragged it to the corner by the sink, then changed her mind and relocated it by the fridge. "Pack animal mentality." Hank nodded again.

However, when he rounded the corner to the living room and tripped over yet another bed ("I ran to Big Lots and got a few more. Don't worry—they were inexpensive!"), he was not as accommodating. "Lindy," he said. "We'll likely have grandkids coming and going all week, what with Caleb's return. I don't think it's a good idea to try to open a canine convalescent home at the same time."

She'd appeared in the doorway, arms crossed. "It's going to be a trying week," she'd allowed. "I'm just trying to make him comfortable."

What Hank had wanted to say, at that point, was, "How about me?"

When he'd first met Lindy, he'd known Caleb only through the factual wreckage she slowly entrusted him with. And through the memories of the girls, sometimes wistful, sometimes pained. Initially he'd pegged the man as a coward. A selfish individual. A fool in the greatest sense. What kind of man walks away from four remarkable young women?

But then, after marrying Lindy and moving to Chatham full-time, he came to know Caleb Bailey through the town's eyes. He knew him from his work, acclaimed work that was displayed proudly in the downtown storefront windows and galleries. His bestselling print to the summertime crowd: a sailboat moored off Monomoy Island. And one Hank had to admit was powerful: a Nigerian boy seated on a stoop holding a red clay pot hung in one of the gallery windows. He knew Caleb Bailey in the framed aerial photograph hanging in the entry of the bank, a reminder he didn't particularly enjoy seeing every time he went in to cash a check or make a deposit, but one he grew used to over the years, so that these days he would come and go without even noticing it when he walked past. In the early years there were the conversations at cocktail parties or informal gatherings among Lindy's friends who, eventually, also became his. Caleb's departure was still a curiosity in the small community and worrisome among her friends. *Brilliant* was a word often used by those in the know. *Talented. Charming.* Especially by the women. But there were other words. Hank was never sure if they tacked these on for his benefit, out of deference to his new station in life as husband and stepfather. But they fleshed out the man who, up to that point, was largely myth and memory. *Impulsive. Restless. Alcoholic.* And the one that meshed most with what the Bailey girls had shared to that point: *wanderlust.* Having never met the man, Hank couldn't say for sure if any were accurate. But he trusted that they were, given the credibility of the people who uttered them in these intimate gatherings over martinis and crudités. History spoke volumes, and Caleb Bailey had left more than just a history behind. He'd left behind his greatest works.

What was hardest for Hank was the unpredictability of his return. Of course they could look him up. With the advent of the Internet and social media, the world shrank to a mere neighborhood, and it didn't usually take more than a few strokes of a keyboard to find out about someone. Hank knew; a few times, in his newspaper days, he'd used his contacts to do just that. But to his surprise, it had been tricky to track down Caleb Bailey. He wasn't regularly employed, and he had stopped having gallery showings altogether. His work, when evidence of it showed up, seemed infrequent. Eventually, Hank made a few calls to an old friend at the *Globe*. Within two weeks he received a manila envelope in the mail. Caleb Bailey was living in Arizona. He made some calls to local businesses who were likely to know the man's whereabouts: a few art galleries, the local library, a framing and printing business outside of town. Whether people were not inclined to speak openly to a stranger with a Boston accent or honestly did not know who or where Caleb Bailey was, Hank couldn't say. The one account with any reliable information was the business Hank took a stab at: the owner of the Whistle Creek Tavern, one of two pubs in town. Loud music crackled in the background. Hank had to press the receiver to his ear to hear the man. "Caleb? Yeah, I know Caleb. But he ain't here now. Who wants to know?"

"An old friend," Hank lied. "Just trying to reach him."

"Well come on down, he's here most nights."

Hank had felt guilty looking him up without telling Lindy first. But he hadn't been sure he could find him to begin with, so he argued with himself that he'd wait until he had something to share. When he did finally, Lindy wanted no part of it. "I'm the one who asked him to leave," she reminded him. "I told him that he was not to come back into the girls' lives until he'd gotten help. That never happened."

"So we should keep this from the girls?" After all, it may not have been his place, but Hank still didn't like the fact that the children didn't know the whereabouts of their own father.

In the end, Lindy had told them. That very day, they sat down in the living room together. Each girl had responded differently. Shannon shrugged. "Why should we care?" But Hank saw the flicker in her eye that suggested otherwise. Wren had listened quietly, before asking, "Was it 'Dad who looked for us or did you look for him?" Lindy had glanced at Hank. "It was me," he admitted, softly. "I have a friend who finds people. It's his job."

"So Dad isn't the one who sent the letter."

"No," Hank said. "The letter was from my friend to me." He felt like he owed her an apology at that moment. He shouldn't have meddled.

Piper took her cues from her sisters, but was more concrete. "So is he coming?"

All eyes landed on Hank at that point, and it was more than he could bear. "No, honey. We just know where he lives."

"Are we going to visit him?"

"No," Lindy said, scooping her up. "When you get older, if you want to visit him someday, you can, honey. But we live here, in Chatham, and this is our family. And we have so much love." She looked around at her girls' faces. "You know that, right?"

It was an unhappy discussion, and Hank was immediately ashamed and angry at himself for having even introduced their father's whereabouts back into the girls' lives, if only for a conversation. "You did it with good intentions," Lindy told him, later that night. "And you're right. Caleb is out there somewhere, and if the girls decide to look him up, someday, I'm going to have to deal with that. I guess it's good to remind them that they can if they want."

If the man himself did not return, his work occasionally haunted them. One winter afternoon the whole family had gone to the dentist for cleanings. Piper grew tired of the worn coloring books in the children's corner of the waiting room and so she imitated her older sisters and began flipping through magazines.

"Mommy look!" she'd cried and run to show Lindy a full-page spread of a zebra racing through the Serengeti. Lindy, engrossed in a novel, had glanced at it briefly. Piper had moved on to show Wren, who let out a gasp and shoved the magazine back under her mother's nose.

"Mom."

Hank had just finished his turn in the dentist's chair and stood in the doorway of the waiting room as all three girls surrounded their mother. "What is it?" he'd asked.

Lindy held up the copy of *National Geographic* for him to see.

"Nice zebra," he'd said.

"It's Caleb's," Lindy said.

The magazine had come home with them, tucked tightly under Piper's arm. From then on it hung over her bed. No one said a darn thing about the thumbtacks securing the photo to the good wallpaper.

There were other incidents that showed Caleb was indeed out there, somewhere. Sometimes a photo credit was given in a catalog. Once, he shot the cover of *Time*. Back then, Hank wondered if he'd ever get over the feeling that he had stepped inadvertently into someone else's shoes, like an imposter. Most of all, Hank worried he might come back someday and want all those things back.

But as the years passed and life normalized, the fears he'd harbored began to fade. Lindy was the biggest reason. The way she'd suddenly stop what she was doing in an ordinary moment and take his face in her hands, urgently. "Do you know how much I love you?" she'd ask, her voice a whisper.

And there were the girls, who tiptoed politely

about him only for so long. Who later stormed past him, so comfortable were they around him by that point, that there was never hesitation to slam a door or throw him a baleful look. He received the full treatment as a parent, and that was just as welcome to him as was the slipping of a small hand in his own when crossing the street or the coming to wake him in the middle of the night after a bad dream. They needed him. And they'd grow to love him and be embarrassed by him and loathe him at any given moment, just as any child of his own would. By then Hank no longer felt that he was wearing another man's shoes. These were his now. And he would fight to the death before he stepped out of them.

Now, however, the old fear prickled him like one of those hair-thin slivers in your fingertip. The kind you cannot see and don't even realize is there, until you bump it just the right way. That's how Hank felt about Caleb's return. And he wished Lindy would stop fussing about the dog and take notice. He didn't care if that made him sound like a big baby, he wanted her to fuss over him for a change.

When the vet tech led Bowser out from the back, even Hank had to admit the poor dog looked pathetic. His big head was ensconced in an even bigger cone, his tail between his legs as he slunk out into the waiting room.

The look on the dog's face was pretty much how Hank felt. "Here comes my sixty-fifth birthday trip!" he said.

Lindy was on her knees. "My big brave little man," she said, stroking his face.

Bowser's left flank was shaved, and a dark arc of sutures ran down it. Hank flinched. He'd never been good with that kind of stuff.

Lindy stood and squeezed his arm. "Don't worry, I'll be the one to take care of it."

Getting the dog in the car was a whole other story. Hank had made sure to drive the "dog car," and they'd laid blankets across the back seat. Two vet techs escorted them out and demonstrated how to lift him gently by twisting a thick towel under Bowser's belly. Bowser didn't look pleased, but he didn't complain. "There you go, buddy." Hank closed the back door and winked at his wife. "Better get him home and settled. Isn't Wren picking up her father about now?"

Lindy slid her sunglasses on. "Indeed. Seems there's no shortage of needy males today."

He was about to get in the car when one of the receptionists ran outside waving. "Mr. McWilliams! You almost forgot your receipt."

Hank folded it and slid it in his coat pocket. "Couldn't forget it if I tried."

She smiled. "It's really wonderful what you and your wife did for Bowser. Not everyone would spend that kind of money. They might just put their dog down." Just before she went back inside she spun around. "Oh, and I heard you mention it in the office—happy birthday, sir!"

Seventeen

Piper

Damn Derek. Her father was on his way home now. And she wasn't there.

She passed a Massachusetts state trooper along Interstate 90, and pumped the brakes. She couldn't afford a ticket. She couldn't afford anything. When she'd gotten back from the awful fallout at the coffee shop the afternoon before, she'd been planning on hopping in the car and heading straight to Chatham before her father arrived. But when she got to her apartment, Claire was waiting for her cross-legged on the couch. There were two shot glasses and a bottle of Fireball on the coffee table. Claire looked pained. "Sit down."

All Piper could do was drop her bag on the floor. "Well, fuck. Why not?"

"You know I love you, right?" Claire ran a hand through her sensible short hair and let out a long breath. "Which is why I'm going to say this. You have to move out."

Piper was not surprised. She had it coming. "I know. I'm sorry I've gotten so behind on rent and bills. I'll find a way to pay you back, I promise."

Claire studied her. "What's going on? You're one of the smartest people I know. But it's like you aren't even trying to get a teaching job."

"I was thinking that if I took a few more classes in business, then maybe I could find a way to use my education degree to consult . . ."

Claire flopped back against the cushions in exasperation. "More classes? Piper. You don't want a degree in business any more than you wanted one in education."

Piper covered her face with her hands. "I think I need to go home." She'd failed. Failed to find a job. Failed to get her shit together. She and Derek were clearly done. "I need to figure things out."

Claire handed her a shot glass. "I'll toast to that."

They sat like that on the couch for the rest of the night, passing the Fireball bottle back and forth between them, reminiscing. Then it was the tissue box. Later they ordered Thai food and stood in Piper's tiny room packing up her things until they could barely keep their eyes open. "I'm going to miss you," Piper said, stuffing the last of her sweaters into a duffel bag.

Claire sat on the edge of the bed and smiled sadly. "Yeah. You really suck."

That's how she found herself climbing into her Prius a hangover and a day late in going home. But really, what difference did a day make? Now she was going home for good.

Wren had left her two messages, neither of which she'd been able to bring herself to listen to. They'd be wondering where the hell she was. By the time she approached the rotary on Main Street, it was past one o'clock, and Piper wasn't sure whose house to go to first.

Shannon picked up on the first ring, sounding indignant. "Where *are* you?"

Piper directed her car straight up Main. Decision made: she'd go to her mother's. "I'm in town. Where are *you?*"

"Where I'm supposed be. At home."

"You're not with Dad?"

"No." That was it. No explanation. "I thought you were coming home last night?"

"Change of plans. So, where is he?"

"Wren picked him up a little while ago. I thought you were planning to be here to see him."

"Says the sister who is in town but chooses not to?"

"Come on, Piper."

She didn't need this. What she needed was to concentrate. The sidewalks were bottlenecked as she approached the middle of the village by the Wayside Inn. She stopped to let a throng of people cross the street, half listening to Shannon go on about what a bad idea this was for all of them. She was just about to proceed when, without warning, one of those pastel preppy-collared families stepped out on the pedestrian walk. Piper hit the brakes. "Jesus." Then, "Not you. Tourists. Listen, I have to go."

There was a pause. "I saw him."

"God, Shannon. Why didn't you start with that? How is he?"

"I didn't talk to him. I saw Wrenny pick him up at the bus stop. We took separate cars."

So, she hadn't been able to stay away. "And?"

Piper had to press the phone tight against her ear to hear Shannon. "From what I could see, he's pretty much the same. Older, thinner. But definitely him."

This was where her sisters always forgot: Piper didn't have the same benchmarks they did. Their memories, both visual and actual, stretched miles beyond her own. She'd barely been four when he left. All she had to go on over the years were photographs and family stories. "How'd it feel to see him?"

Here, any indication of sentiment evaporated. Shannon cleared her throat. "I didn't really feel anything."

Piper sighed. "I'm heading to Mom's. I'll call later, okay?"

"Okay. By the way, how long are you in town for?"

Piper didn't want to tell Shannon that she was home indefinitely. She hadn't even told their mother yet. Her thoughts flashed back to Derek, whom she had gotten only one text from since leaving the coffee shop. *I'm sorry.* It was clear to her that he wasn't going to chase her down or ask her to come back. Which only stung harder. In another week he'd be coming to Chatham, and even though he'd be staying in town, he'd be further away than ever.

Piper pushed the thought from her mind. It was time to focus. Their father was back in town and back in their lives, and that thought filled her with a rush of hope as blinding as the sun outside. "I'm here as long as you need me," she told Shannon.

Both cars were in the driveway when Piper pulled up. The muffler on her Prius had to have announced her arrival, but no one came to the door. Not even Bowser.

"Hello?" Piper called. She pulled her duffel bag and purse from the back seat, then thought better of it. Best to tell them first, before dragging all her crap up the porch steps and dumping it at the front door.

Lindy appeared at the screen door. "Honey! I was wondering where you were." She hurried out and hugged Piper tightly, then held her firmly at arm's length studying her expression. "Have you seen him?"

"Not yet."

"Come in then and see Bowser. Hank's holding on to him so he won't try to hobble out here and overexert himself. We just picked him up from the vet."

Piper followed her mother inside. "I totally forgot he was having his operation." She stepped over a dog bed and found Bowser and Hank in the kitchen. Toys and bones were everywhere.

"Welcome to the rehab center," Hank said.

Piper gave Hank a quick hug and knelt by Bowser. "Poor thing." He was wearing one of those pathetic cones and every time he moved his head it clunked against her knees.

"Don't get him excited," Lindy warned. She was stirring a big pot of something on the stove that smelled intoxicating. "Lunch?" Piper asked hopefully.

"For Bowser," Lindy explained. "Chicken and rice. His tummy is sensitive from the painkillers."

Piper glanced at Hank sideways. "Want me to make you something?" he offered.

"Thanks, I'll do it." She went to the fridge and examined its contents. Piper pulled out a bowl of homemade chicken salad and sat down on the kitchen island. "This is really good! What's in it? Raisins?"

"Cranberries." Hank appeared at her side with a plate and a spoon, eyebrows raised.

Piper licked the fork and set it down. "Sorry," she said, again. Her head ached and she was tired. Why was everyone so tense?

"So how're the interviews going? Any leads on

a teaching job?" The pot on the stove was at full boil and a cloud of steam enveloped her mother.

"Not yet," she said, standing. "I think I'll go upstairs for a nap."

Hank followed her to the landing. "Let me help you, honey. Is this all you brought?"

There was a loud clatter from the kitchen and they both turned to see Lindy bending over. "Damn it!" She'd dropped the big metal spoon and soup had splattered the floor. Bowser stretched his head from the safety of his bed to lick it. Hank grimaced.

Now would also not be a good time to tell them that everything she owned was parked in their driveway. Piper pointed to her lonely duffel bag. "Yep, that's all."

Eighteen

Wren

She let herself in the locked door of the Fisherman's Daughter and closed it quickly behind her before leaning against it. The store was dark and quiet. This was her safe place. This was the place she felt she had everything under control.

The shoppers and vacationers had arrived en masse, but she kept the front door shade pulled down and had hung a sign that Lucy had helped her to paint that read GRAND OPENING COMING SOON! in bright red letters. Lucy had painted little blue fish around the edges. The display window was fully decorated. There was a vintage mannequin wearing a stretchy blue-and-white-striped dress beside a table with jewelry. A wooden trunk holding carefully arranged linens and scarves was open like a treasure chest. Wren took pleasure in the mix of elements: wood, linen, metal. She was almost ready to open her doors to the town. Something she'd worked all year to prepare for and something she'd been looking forward to for so long. But all of that paled in light of that morning.

Her father was back. She'd dropped him off at the motel with the only belongings he carried: a leather suitcase that she could tell used to be nice but was now held together with a strip of duct tape. And a black battered portfolio she recognized immediately; he'd stored and carried his work in it back in their Ridgevale beach home.

When she'd turned around to face him at the bus stop, she'd not been ready for what came. Leading up to this day, there had been so many scenarios she'd let play out. As a girl, she'd imagined it as a reunion of strong embraces and a child's face buried against her father's neck, breathing his familiar scent in again. As an adult, she felt a wave of protectiveness for that little girl who never had the opportunity. What came to her was that this man was a stranger. There was no pull in either direction of joy or anger. He was her father, but he was reduced. And she could not be sure if Caleb Bailey had been reduced by time and circumstance, or simply reduced in her eyes. It didn't matter. He had once been the most important man in her life, but when he stood in front of her under the hot sun she'd felt nothing at all.

"Thank you for picking me up," he'd said, as he buckled his seatbelt.

She didn't know how to begin, and she was terrible at small talk. Suddenly she wished she'd brought Lucy. Lucy could talk to anyone about anything. Wren ached for her little girl. "How was the trip?"

"Long."

She glanced over at him. "About three days," he added. "Though I switched buses a couple times and stayed with a friend in Indiana."

It seemed an eternity to sit on a bus. "You came from Tubac?"

He nodded. "That's right."

What was he doing in Tubac, Arizona? She'd gone so far as to Google it—an artist's colony, population of about one thousand. But if Caleb Bailey was going to tell her that or anything else about himself, it would not be then. He pointed out the window. "Will you look at that. The old Kream n' Kone is still there." He turned to her. "Your mother and I used to take you girls there for fried clams and ice cream."

The mention of her mother—of them all as a family—jolted her. Suddenly she was sitting at one of the outdoor tables, swinging her legs back and forth happily. There was a plastic tray of fried seafood. Piper was a baby, nestled on her mother's lap. A trail of chocolate ice cream was running down her arm.

Wren turned sharply into the Chatham Motel parking lot. "It's been redone," she said. They pulled up in front of one of the units. Wren kept her eyes trained straight ahead.

"Very good," he said. "I guess I'll check in."

Wren started to open her door to retrieve his luggage. He put his hand on hers, and she froze. "Thank you," he said. "I know this is all very strange."

Wren felt suddenly very small and strange, indeed.

He removed his hand. "Can I call you after I have a nap?"

"Okay. Let me help you." She hopped out of the Jeep and pulled his bag and portfolio from the back. The suitcase was heavy, but she managed to slide it out.

"I've got it," he said, reaching for the handle. But when Wren let go the full weight of the bag jerked Caleb forward and it hit the ground with a sickening smack.

"Sorry! Are you okay?"

Caleb winced, but nodded. "I'm fine," he said, righting himself, even though she could tell he was in pain. "I'm fine, really."

"You have my number?"

"Yes, right here." He reached in his shirt pocket and pulled out a folded square of paper. It was the letter she'd sent. Only it had been folded into a small square, the edges worn and soiled, as if it had been carried and read many times.

He saw her looking at it oddly. "It was a long ride home."

Home. She wasn't sure she could agree.

"Do you need help?" she called after him. What

she really wanted was to go, but she didn't want to just leave him there either.

Caleb paused. "No, but there is something I need from you."

Wren hesitated. She'd already agreed to see him. She'd just picked him up and driven him here. Small things, but it was still a lot.

"I'd like to take you to dinner. You and your sisters. Is the Squire still open?"

Wren nodded, but this was a terrible idea. Shannon would never go for it. Besides, the Squire was a bustling family restaurant in the heart of the village. Wren wasn't sure she was ready for dinner. She wanted to suggest instead that they go somewhere to talk, like for a walk on the beach or her front porch. Places where they could get up and walk away if they needed to. But the way he was looking at her interrupted her thoughts.

"What's wrong?" she asked.

Caleb Bailey shook his head wistfully. "You look just like her."

"Who?"

"Your mother."

Wren fumbled in her pocket for her keys and turned for the Jeep.

"I'll phone you later about dinner," he called after her.

Now, in the safety of her store, she flicked on all the lights but then changed her mind and turned

214

them off again. She went to the cash register and stood behind the counter, running her hands over the polished wooden surface. Her eyes moved slowly around the store, taking in the lush collection of wares she'd curated and the artful displays she and Ari had carefully arranged. She was finally ready to open on Monday. There were email blasts to share and social-media reminders to post. In another hour Lucy would have to be picked up from her playdate. In the meantime, she should call her mother. Lindy would be worrying, probably watching the clock and waiting by the phone at this very moment. But she couldn't bring herself to do any of those things.

Instead, Wren lay her head on the cool surface of the counter in her empty shop and let the tears spill. Caleb Bailey had said so, himself. He was home.

Nineteen

Shannon

"Port is right and starboard is left!"

Shannon smiled. "Other way around, buddy."

George loved sailing. Of course, he did—all of their children enjoyed learning to sail. But George *loved* it. "Next time you have to stay," he told Shannon when she'd picked him up. "I want you to watch me. It was a-ma-zing!"

Seeing his joy in the rearview mirror made her stomach sink.

"This is good for both of you," Reid said. "I wish I could take the morning off and watch him myself."

Their house was just a few streets over from the Yacht Club, and they'd been members since the summer they moved into the neighborhood. It was a unique place, small and rustic, in an old building on the corner of Stage Harbor Road by the marina. The club was attended by an intimate group of longtime family members, many of whom were represented by several generations summer after summer. All of the children were enrolled in sailing lessons and regattas. There were seasonal social events like clambakes and barbecues under a tent along the small strip of beach in the harbor. There was no stately club-house with a ballroom and lavish locker rooms. It was a place of like-minded members who loved the sea, to sail, and to socialize.

Shannon hated anything to do with the water, but what made the club palatable for her was the small bay location. It was quiet and comparably calm. You could see directly out to Monomoy Island, whose barrier protected Stage Harbor from the open waters. If she had any affection for a body of water, it was the lack of surf and relative shallowness that got her. She knew, of course, statistically speaking, that a child could drown in four inches of bathtub water. But residing on the Cape meant raising children along a coast bookended by the wild surf of the National Seashore and the open waters of Nantucket Sound, so in this realm Stage Harbor's quiet waters were as close as she could get to feeling relatively safe.

She pulled into the tiny lot of the club. Not far off the beach she could see a tight cluster of Optis. That had to be George's class. She walked down for a better look and found another mother, Sherry Briggs, doing the same.

"How's he doing?" Sherry asked. "Caitlin loves their instructor, Sam. She's so good with the kids."

Shannon nodded blankly. She'd met Sam the first morning she'd brought George for Hermit Crab class. The handoff had been hard. She'd stood at the edge of the parking lot longer than all the other parents, her stomach sloshy with nerves when she watched George join his group and they sat in a circle on the sand and listened to the rules and routines. When they stood up and walked to the water crafts she'd made haste to her car. Like Reid said, George was in good hands, and most importantly, he seemed happy. But she could not bring herself to watch as they headed down to the boats.

Now she shielded her eyes and nodded politely as Sherry Briggs went on about a ladies' luncheon and other upcoming social events. Shannon spotted a bright orange rash guard in the distance. That had to be George.

"So, are you going to walk in it?"

"I'm sorry, walk what?"

Sherry looked at her funny. "The fashion show."

"Oh, yes. Sorry. I was trying to locate George." Shannon pointed and waved. "Yes, I hope to. Are you chairing the event again? You did such a lovely job last year."

This remark returned Sherry's smile promptly to her face. "As a matter of fact, I am. Do you have any interest in helping again this year? I'm always looking for volunteers."

The class was heading back in, and after a few crisscrossed paths and jumbled turns, George ended among the front boats. Shannon's tummy flip-flopped as she watched him head for the beach. "Hi, honey!" she called when he was within earshot. "I would love to, I really would," she told Sherry as she edged her way toward the beach. "But things are so busy at the office right now, and I have family visiting from out of town." She couldn't believe she'd tossed her father right in there with her list of reasons to avoid taking on yet another commitment she couldn't see managing. The fashion show was a lot of fun, Shannon knew, and there really wasn't a reason she couldn't squeeze it in, but lately she just felt so tired. What she wanted right then was to pluck George out of the boat and hug him. She just wanted to go home.

Sherry didn't miss a beat. "Yes, I suppose summer is busy for us all. But I'll keep you in mind as we get closer! Who knows, maybe your load will lighten?"

"Who knows?" Shannon said brightly over her shoulder.

George climbed out of the boat and helped his instructor pull it up on the sand before racing to his mother. "Did you see me? Did you?"

Shannon picked him up. He was so big now, and almost too heavy to lift, but she did it anyway and breathed him in. "You smell like sunscreen and sun," she told him, planting a kiss on his head. "Go finish your lesson and I'll meet you in the car."

There were two messages on her phone. One from Shirley asking about an open-house date. And another from her mother-in-law, Bitsy. Bitsy's curt formality cut through the sunshine of the afternoon.

"Shannon, I would like you to please call me. Soon. It's about Nantucket Drive."

Shannon had downloaded, edited, and emailed the photos she'd taken the other day to all concerned. Since then, she'd avoided asking about the listing. If Bitsy had seen to it to hire a film and media crew to best capture the essence of the property, then that was her detail.

But it appeared something was wrong. Reluctantly she dialed Bitsy's personal number.

"Yes?" Shannon hated the way her mother-in-law answered her calls. Obviously, she could see it was Shannon. Would it kill her to say hello? She decided to try Bitsy's MO on for size.

"Bitsy, it's Shannon."

"Shannon. Finally."

Shannon rolled her eyes. Bitsy had left the message not five minutes ago. "What can I help you with?"

"The seller of the Nantucket Drive property has a vision." Shannon had heard enough about the man's vision. If Bitsy paid any real attention to her daughter-in-law's work, she might have realized Shannon had a vision of her own. "At his request, we secured a crew to come out and photograph the house. We allowed extra time for all of this because such vision takes time, of course, but that did set us back a week in both online and print marketing. That said, here we are on the proposed date of filming and it seems the crew had us listed for this date next month."

Shannon couldn't believe it. "Next month?"

"As in July."

"How unfortunate. I'm sorry to hear that." Shannon did not feel bad for Bitsy, though she genuinely did for Reid. She knew the chaos this would've created.

"Unfortunate doesn't begin to describe it. Which has led me to you."

Shannon held her breath. This was indeed a mess, but it was not her mess, and she sure hoped Bitsy wasn't going to heave any of this explaining to the seller on to her. Bitsy was famous in the office for delegating distasteful tasks she deemed beneath her to those who actually worked beneath her.

"I need you to photograph the property. And soon. Will you do it?"

George was coming up the club driveway with what looked like a fistful of sand. He opened his mouth, but she couldn't hear what he was saying.

"Uh, I would like to help the agency in any way I can, as I originally offered," Shannon reminded her, "but what's the time frame?" Shannon already had the Hooker's Ball coming up and the chamber of commerce was holding its lobster bake in a few weekends.

"The owner wants to meet you first. To discuss that vision of his that I mentioned. I'll call you later with a date."

"Meet me first?" Shannon had assumed Bitsy was asking for emergency help. Now she had another hoop to jump through?

"Yes. This is a very important listing. And we are already behind."

George pressed his face against the car window. "Look what I found!" he mouthed.

Shannon put her finger up to her lips and rolled down the window. It was a fiddler crab. "Wow!" she mouthed, then pointed to the phone. "Grandma!" she mouthed.

"All right, Bitsy. I'll do my best." Shannon did not say what she wanted to, which was that she would've had the place photographed by now and would be already designing marketing layouts in both print and online if the job had been hers to start with. "I think I'm free later this week, between camp and sailing."

Bitsy cleared her throat. "Yes, well, I'll let you know when the owner is available."

George stuck the crab in the window. "Is this

alive?" Shannon turned her head as a rancid smell filled the car. It was dead.

Bitsy was not quite done. "This shoot needs to be different, dear. This one needs to be really good."

Shannon would ignore this. She would ignore it and focus on the bright face of her boy in the window, and even the droopy crab in his hands. "Bitsy, I've got your grandson here. Would you like to say hello?"

There was a pause. "Give George a kiss." Then the line clicked.

Shannon pushed George's hand gently back through the window. "That guy needs to go back down to the beach."

George cocked his head and stared at the fiddler crab. "Yeah, he's dead. Must've been a real old crab."

Shannon watched him trudge down to the water. "Yep. Just like the one Mommy was talking to on the phone."

Twenty

Piper

S he awoke with a start, thinking for a moment she was back in her Boston apartment. But the late-afternoon light was too golden, the lofty ceilings too bright and airy in her childhood bedroom, and she collapsed back on the sheets with the realization that she was home on the Cape. The room had grown stuffy. She'd tugged off her T-shirt and napped in just a tank, and now she rose and went to the window to let in some fresh air. Her grandmother's house (she would forever think of it as such) was an older home, and the windows upstairs swelled with humidity and salt air and stuck sometimes in the summer months. Piper stuck her head out and looked down. The little eyebrow colonial across the way had been smartly redone in the last year, and the cedar shingle siding was a coppery hue in the sun. Beverly's house was a two-story Cape which allowed Piper to gaze over the neighbor's' rooftop, past its little cupola and whale weathervane, in the direction of Chatham Lighthouse. She could smell the salt on the humid air, and she gulped once, then again, like she was hungry.

She turned her phone on and her heart did that little thing where it seized whenever a message chimed, as it did now. But it was only Wren. She scrolled back to Derek's messages, whom she'd listed as DW. There it was: *I'm sorry.* Piper oscillated between feeling sorry for herself and wanting to make him sorry. But she'd realized the hard way long ago that there was no way to make someone whose head was already turned away from you regret your absence. Even if the realization had taken you by surprise, it had already happened on their end. They had moved on. And the quicker you did, too, the better. But Derek was different. She had risked so much of herself in getting involved with him. Her principles to start: she would never before have considered getting involved with a married man. She was not that kind of girl. But it had turned out she did. And she was. And the sorry of it all extended so far beyond their apparent breakup that it blanketed her senses like the cold sting of a freshly fallen snow.

She returned to Wren's message, determined to focus on the here and now. "I dropped Dad off at the motel for a rest. Said he'd call later. We are all invited to join him for dinner."

"Where?" Piper wondered aloud. This would be good. The four of them sitting down together, face-to-face, finally. She wanted to know the things other children completely took for granted, and were often even annoyed by, in their own fathers. The sound of his laugh. Whether his brow furrowed liked hers and her sisters' did when they concentrated on something. How he twirled his spaghetti around a fork. Small things. Small things that would fill the big holes she'd been carrying around her whole life.

Downstairs the house was quiet. Hank's car was gone from the driveway. Out back she found Bowser sleeping on the screened-in porch. Her mother sat in one of the wicker chairs beside him, clutching a mason jar of iced tea and staring out absently at her garden. Piper paused in the doorway, studying her. Lindy was in her mid-sixties, but silhouetted against the outdoor light her profile could have been that of a thirty-year-old. Her elegant neck, the high cheekbones she'd inherited from Beverly. Over the years of single parenting, she'd been tired. She'd lost her temper and made mistakes. Looking at her now, Piper marveled at how strong she must've had to be raising the three of them alone; but she'd not let those years erode her, wearing her down to a softer, sadder version of herself. Piper had seen it happen to other women. Strong, beautiful women like Lindy who were undone by loss or deceit. They seemed to age overnight, fading into the background. But not Lindy. If anything, those years had sharpened her features, her voice, her will.

She turned suddenly and saw Piper. "Goodness, you startled me."

"Sorry, Mama. I just woke up." She sat down on the lounge beside her.

Lindy swiped at her eyes quickly with the back of her hand as she turned to face her.

"Are you crying?" Piper leaned closer.

"No, no. What's up?"

"There's something I need to tell you."

Lindy brightened. "Oh? Good, because I've got something to share with you, too."

Piper was still thinking about her mother's red-rimmed eyes. "You first."

Lindy pressed her lips together. "I've been thinking about your father coming back. And how to best handle this for you girls."

This was the only thing that had worried her about her father's return. How it would impact their mother. "Mama, you already did—for all those years you raised us alone. You handled it better than anyone could have."

Lindy let out a sad little laugh. "Well, I don't know about that. You're leaving out a lot of ugly mistakes."

Piper felt like an imposter sitting there talking with her mother so openly like this, all the while clutching her own invisible basket of mistakes.

"So," Lindy said, "after thinking about this, I've decided there's one thing I need to do. I need to be there when you see your father."

"Really?" Piper was an adult; she squelched the childish hope that burst momentarily in her chest at the thought of her parents being together, if only in the same room.

"Wren called. She told me he wants to take you out for dinner in town."

"So, you're going to join us?"

Lindy shook her head. "No. I'm going to hold the dinner here."

"Here?" Piper glanced around. This was the last place she had pictured them reuniting. Bowser in his cone with dog beds spread all over the house. On her mother's turf. And with Hank? "But Mom."

The look on Lindy's face silenced her. "Don't give me too much credit, kiddo. This may be self-interest."

"Won't that be hard for you? And what about Hank? Even if you host it here, I still don't think Shannon will come."

"That's okay. I respect her decision." Her mother set down her iced tea and rested her elbows on her knees. "Look, I couldn't change the fact your father stayed away. But I've always felt guilt about telling him to go."

Piper pressed a finger to her scar. They never talked liked this. "You were trying to protect us."

"Still. I was there the day he left, and I've been there every day since, haven't I?"

Piper nodded.

"Then honor that. Let me be there the day he comes back."

"If you're sure. Do the others know about this plan?"

"I called Wren while you were napping. She called your dad, and Shannon, too. Dinner is at seven."

"So Dad is coming here?"

Lindy nodded. Piper couldn't imagine what he must be thinking about that. "And Hank?"

Lindy smiled. "Is a saint. He's at Chatham Market picking up some things for dinner right now."

Piper stood, the people and facts roiling around in her head. "I guess I better shower and pull myself together."

"Wait," Lindy said. "What were you going to tell me?"

Piper paused in the doorway. "Oh, nothing important. Nothing that can't wait."

Twenty-One

Hank

There was no line at Shop Ahoy Liquor, but Hank was creating quite the holdup standing at the counter considering his wine options. "What are you pairing the wine with?" the owner asked, trying to be helpful.

Hank sighed. Damned if he knew. Could he recommend a dry white for estrangement? Perhaps something full bodied and red for family angst? In the end he chose a Semillon and two Malbecs. Then pointed to his old standby, a bottle of Maker's Mark, on the shelf behind the cash register. It was going to be a long night.

He had nobody to blame except himself, however. Lindy had been fretting about all week. Fretting about the girls and the dog. Fretting over how the grandkids might best be introduced to Caleb, if indeed Shannon would allow her kids to be introduced to him at all. They were big decisions, decisions that involved a number of players over a number of years of heartache. That week Hank had watched Lindy cook, garden, talk, and pace into a state until he could watch no more. And so last night, as they went for their evening walk around the neighborhood, he proposed his idea. It was an idea he did not relish. But it was the only one that gave him some sense of control in a situation that was clearly beyond any of their control: they would invite Caleb Bailey over for dinner.

Lindy had halted in the middle of the road, and at first, he was afraid she'd smack him. "Brilliant!" she said, wrapping her arms around his neck. He'd stood there staring up past the shingled rooftops at the pink sunset, feeling the fierceness of her love, and right then something deep and knotted he had not realized was tied up inside him had loosened. Like a tangled spool of thread unwinding.

"You're right. This is the only way to do it," she gushed, as he quickened his pace to keep up with her on the way home. Her stride was swifter, lighter, which was more her usual self, but already he lamented her getting away from him so quickly. He could've stayed there in the middle of the road holding on to her all night. "We will face him head on, together. And on our own turf." She'd paused, as if trying to catch her own thoughts. "It's good it's not the old Ridgevale house, but the home we've since made without him. I think it's emotionally safer that way." Hank listened carefully for any hint of ire in her voice, for some sense of raking Caleb Bailey over the coals as she invited him right up her front steps, but there was none. He wasn't sure how he felt about this.

There had been plenty, back in the early days. Resentment. Lament for the loss of his role in their lives. Girls needed their fathers, she said, and he did not disagree. But although he initially wished she'd be more upset now with Caleb, he realized maybe this way was better. Anger was passion. And as far as Hank could tell, the only passion Lindy reserved these days was in relation to her children and himself. And how she could make this sudden reunion easier on all of them.

With the setting decided upon, next up was the matter of the guests. It was determined that it would be just the Bailey women for this first meeting. As expected, Shannon would not commit, but Lindy held out hope. The last item was the menu.

"It will be yours and the girls' favorites," Lindy told him that afternoon as she bent over the kitchen island, twirling a pencil thoughtfully in her hand. Piper was upstairs napping, and they were speaking softly so as not to wake her. She hadn't looked good to Hank, and she was another question mark on his mind.

"Don't worry about me," he'd said. "Depending how things go, I may end up drinking my dinner anyway."

Lindy began listing. "Grilled salmon. Strawberry spinach salad. Oh, and let's grill some of those little fingerling potatoes with fresh rosemary." Here she'd rushed out to the garden with a pair of scissors and returned with sprigs of herbs which she quickly dipped into mason jars and filled with water on the windowsill. Then she tore the list off the pad of paper with a flourish and held it out to him. "Got all that?"

He did now, in four different bags across the back seat. He thought of the last thing Lindy had said as he walked out the door, keys in hand.

"You do a lot," she'd allowed. "For all your girls."

It was a phrase Lindy did not use often, but it still had the same effect on him since the first time she'd uttered the words. They'd been married about a year when she'd had quite a row with Shannon over a missed curfew and a subsequent grounding. Hank had seen more than his fair share of temper tantrums and tears before. There had been some good sisterly spats thrown in there, too. But he'd not seen the likes of this, the kind of digging in of heels and stubbornness, as if to the death. There had been screaming accusations and slamming of doors and finally a standoff in the form of a silent streak that went on for two days. He couldn't remember all the details now, but Wren had sided with her sister out of solidarity and Piper had cried on and off because no one would play with her, and Lindy was unreachable, so entrenched was she in her attempts to get her daughters to concede.

Finally, he had been the one to make the rounds. To knock on doors and sit on the edges of beds, to withstand the cross looks and dramatic sighs. It did not go smoothly. He'd appealed to Wren and soothed Piper, and finally, endured the floodgates of tears as Shannon poured out her heart. At one point, he'd looked up to see Lindy standing in the cracked doorway as he sat still as a statue while Shannon howled and cried and blew her nose into his tear-stained sweater.

He wasn't sure if any of it had done a damn bit of good until he came downstairs a couple hours later to a sound that had become foreign in the house. *Laughter.* He peeked around the corner and there they were, the four of them. Lined up on the couch, passing a tub of ice cream back and forth between them watching *Little House on the Prairie*. It was a miracle what a tub of ice cream and Melissa Gilbert could do for four warring women.

Later that night, in the privacy of their bed, Lindy rolled over and propped herself up on one elbow. He'd steeled himself, at first. This posture usually preceded a "concern" that required discussing. Hank was not up for this. He was tired, and his book was particularly good, and frankly he just wanted to be left alone.

"I learned something today," she'd said. "It's important that you know it, too."

He drew in a breath, thinking back to Shannon's outpouring. Piper's tears. "Did I do something wrong?" he asked, warily.

Lindy shook her head. "It's about the girls."

He waited.

"They're not just mine anymore. It seems they're your girls, too."

That was all. She'd leaned in then and kissed his forehead, before rolling over. Soon her breathing evened out into the soft snore of slumber. But Hank had sat awake a long time, the page of his particularly good book left unturned, replaying his wife's message. *They were his, too.* Those three stubborn, unpredictable, beautiful girls. It was the greatest gift she had ever given him: permission to love them like his own.

Which is how Hank had ended up driving to Shop Ahoy Liquor and then pushing a grocery cart around Chatham Market, a stepfather buying dinner for an estranged father. He'd checked everything off the list that Lindy had requested. There was one important item not on the list that Hank had made sure to add to the cart: two tubs of ice cream—the good kind. Vanilla for Wren and chocolate for the other three. What Lindy failed to realize is that she, too, was one of his girls.

He hoped this idea of his would not backfire. What, exactly, he wished for he could not say. Hank did not want Caleb Bailey in his life. And

235

he worried what this meant to his wife, how it might change her. Or, ultimately, change them. But he also wanted peace for the girls, which he knew would ultimately give Lindy peace, too. Maybe the stars would align, and it could be a success. It could also be a spectacular disaster.

Back at the house, Piper greeted him at the door in a pretty white sundress, her long wet hair smelling of lavender. She took the grocery bags from his arms and he followed her into the kitchen where Lindy stood at the island chopping greens from the garden. Wren was there, too, sitting on a stool with a glass of wine. Her expression was somber but when he walked in, she looked up and smiled.

Lindy did, too. "There he is."

Twenty-Two

Wren

When she'd dropped him off at the Chatham Motel, her father had the rumpled and unslept look about him that comes with riding a bus across the country over several days. Now, as he stepped out of the car at the foot of her mother's front porch, he was a different man.

Caleb paid the Uber driver and turned to face her. He'd dressed casually for dinner in a short-sleeved button-down shirt and Bermuda shorts, his standard summer look that flashed with bright familiarity from her childhood. His hair was neatly combed, and he carried a small bouquet of flowers. Anyone walking by with their dog on this lovely summer evening would have guessed he was just another dinner guest, not a man who'd been missing for twenty-three years, about to climb the steps of his estranged ex-wife's house to meet with two of his three daughters.

"Beverly's house," he said, appraisingly. He raised his eyebrows. "She here?"

Wren had to smile. "No. Not yet, anyway. It's Mom's and Hank's now. Beverly still comes up every July."

He looked slightly relieved to hear that as he started up the steps. "Everyone's inside," Wren told him.

He brightened. "Shannon?"

Wren shook her head. She wouldn't make an apology for her sister; Shannon wouldn't have it.

Caleb ran a hand through his hair and smoothed his shirt. He didn't try to give her a peck on the cheek or a hug in greeting, though he looked like he could have used either one of those things himself.

"All right," he said.

Wren held the door open for him.

Before, if someone had asked her to imagine how a dinner like this would have gone, she might've guessed it would be painful. There was so much to consider. Like the long-held questions finally able to be asked and released into the air. The hard truths of the answers, assuming any were given. She might've predicted Piper's nervous enthusiasm, her vast and uneasy attempts to pull everyone together in conversation. She would've surely predicted the set of her mother's jaw, her abiding silence at the table. Hank was a wild card. On the one hand he was as predictable in his disposition as the local tide charts, but the man loved her mother in a manner so singular that Wren could imagine some kind of confrontation. How wrong she would have been on all counts.

Caleb entered the kitchen ahead of her, where the others had taken their places like a well-rehearsed play. Lindy went to him first. There was a moment—an intake of breath—as she allowed herself to get a good look at the man. But there was no demonstration of emotion as to how she felt about what she saw.

"You're back," she said. Before he could answer, she extended her hand like he was a stranger, and he shook it.

If Caleb was disappointed by this reception, he did not show it. He held her hand a moment longer than he might have, but that was all. "Lindy," he said softly. "You look well."

At this point Piper proved unable to contain herself any longer. She edged up beside them, her face open and expectant as a child's, and Wren had a hard time looking at all the hope it revealed. "Dad? It's me, Piper."

He smiled almost shyly, shaking his head all the while in wonder, and she stepped into his arms and wrapped her own tightly around him. Here Caleb faltered. Wren felt the tears prick her eyes as he tipped his head, as if the sun itself were shining on his face. "Look at you," he said, stepping back. "A thing of beauty."

Wren glanced over at her mother, who was standing at the ready. Lindy looked prepared to jump in at any moment.

When the two parted, Caleb ran the back of his

239

hand roughly across his cheeks and then turned to Hank. "I'm Caleb Bailey. It's nice to meet you."

Wren was proud of Hank. He did not puff up his chest, nor did he linger in the background. Instead he shook his hand and clapped Caleb on the back gently. "Welcome. What can I get you to drink? Wine? Bourbon?"

At the same time, both Lindy and Caleb answered.

"Just water, please."

"Oh, he doesn't drink."

Hank looked uncomfortably between the two for a beat, then recovered. "Water it is."

An awkwardness hung over the kitchen. It wasn't just the calling out that their father didn't drink; it was how quickly her mother had spoken for their father, and Wren could tell it surprised Hank, too. Was it possible to fall back into old habits after so much time?

Wren went to the sideboard and pulled down a wineglass. Her father may not drink, but right now she needed one.

It was no secret to Wren and Shannon that Caleb Bailey had had a drinking problem. But, it was not something they'd ever discussed, especially in front of Piper. Lindy had always answered any questions they'd had—she'd encouraged it even—but there was something too hard about saying his name out loud, and though Piper would sometimes ask wistful questions or wonder aloud over the years, there was no real danger in it coming from her. She didn't recall the facts, and for whatever reason the rest of them had done very little to fill the holes in her memory.

Wren filled a glass with Malbec. While she was at it, Wren poured Piper a glass of white wine and filled a tumbler with ice. "What's that?" Hank asked.

She poured two golden fingers of bourbon over the ice and handed it to him. "Fortitude."

After that the evening progressed at a quiet, if formal, pace. They sat on the screened-in porch while Hank stood nearby grilling salmon. Caleb asked after Beverly's health, about the where-abouts of friends from the old neighborhood, what line of work Hank was in. The polite veil of manners followed them into the dining room, where there was a moment's hesitation as every-one stood awkwardly around the table, unsure of which seat to take. Lindy took her place at one head and nodded at Hank to do the same. Seemingly relieved, Caleb took a seat in the middle, across from Piper and Wren.

"I do wish Shannon had joined us," he said.

Lindy did not reply.

Luckily the food filled the lull. There was grilled fish and fingerling potatoes, a bowl of garden salad and fresh-baked cornbread. Platters were passed and served, plates filled and emptied.

The clink of silverware was the only thing interrupting the conversation, most of which came from Piper. She had questions, so many questions, but their father took it all in stride. He spoke about his work and Arizona. About some of the places he hoped to see while he was back on the Cape. The weather. Everything except what Wren was certain was most on everyone's mind.

But Caleb spoke with such ease beneath the flickering candlelit chandelier, seemingly relaxed even in Beverly's Chippendale chairs, that the evening took on a soothing cadence. Wren found she was finally able to let out some of the breath she realized she'd been holding. The topics were safe, and she was perfectly fine dancing around them this first night. When the meal was finally over and Wren began to believe they might actually end this first meeting unscathed, Piper set her fork down. "So are you moving home for good?"

All eyes swiveled to Caleb, who seemed to sink a little beneath their weight. "Well, I haven't thought that far ahead. There are some things I need to take care of, so I guess that will determine my time here."

It was an instant disruption to the quietude Wren had been almost able to enjoy up to this moment.

Lindy, however, had apparently been waiting for it. "Then you'll be returning to Arizona?"

Caleb hesitated, but in the end, said yes.

"And what is it like there?"

It was a small artist's colony, he explained, and he'd been there for many years. He had a little house, one bedroom. No bigger than a Chatham boathouse, he joked, though no one really laughed. He cleared his throat. "I travel when I get assignments, but those are few and far between these days."

Wren wondered why that was, as she listened. It seemed to her that he lived simply. He went on to make a point of saying he lived alone, at which Lindy did not blink.

Hank stood to clear the plates, something Wren was sure he was aching to do, if for the first and last time in his life. She half wanted to join him. But something held her at the table. Whether it was curiosity or wanting to protect her mother and sister, she couldn't say. Her father rested his chin in his hands and looked directly across the table at her. She almost blushed. "So you've got yourself a store in town."

"I do." He knew this, of course. His first letter had found her there. She still wanted to know how.

"Wren's grand opening is this week, actually," Lindy said, proudly. "She's worked very hard to get the shop up and going."

Caleb nodded approvingly. "I have no doubt. What kinds of things do you sell?"

243

Wren told him about the local artists she'd made relationships with, and how she'd had an aesthetic in mind from the start. "But I wanted it to be local and I wanted it to be eco-conscious," she explained. "So I've had to handpick items carefully. Which takes time."

Caleb was listening intently, his green eyes shining for the first time since landing on Piper. She couldn't help it; Wren felt the pleasure of her father's approval, just as she had as a child.

"I'd really like to see it sometime," he said.

She could feel her mother's gaze, and she imagined Lindy taking her temperature on this. Her store was a piece of her, after all. The most important thing she'd created, after Lucy. She hadn't even opened its doors to the world, let alone to a man who was for the first time walking back into her life. He must've sensed her reservation, because he quickly added, "If that's okay with you, of course. I understand if it isn't."

It occurred to her in that moment that she'd come wanting something from her father that night. Perhaps some kind of answer or apology, neither of which had been offered to any of them yet. She'd had no intention of sharing herself with him in any meaningful way. How could she? But now she surprised herself with her answer. "There's something more important than the shop you might be interested to know."

She reached for her phone and held it up to him.

Caleb took it gently and peered at the screen. "I'll be damned."

"Her name is Lucy. She's six years old."

Lindy's eyes blazed, and in reply Wren reached under the table and rested a hand on her mother's knee. For a long time, he stared at the photo on the screen, and then he set the phone down on the table between them. "Thank you," was all he could manage.

Lindy's chair scraped abruptly across the floor. "I'm going to see about coffee," she said. They sat in silence, the hushed murmur of voices and the clink of dishware coming from the kitchen.

"This is hard for her," Piper said.

Wren stood, too. "I'll be right back."

Wren was glad for the spotlight to be off of her. Her father's gaze was warm and without want, but it was also familiar in a way that made her ache, and she needed to step out from under the light it cast. She left Piper filling their father in on her course work and job search.

Hank was alone in the kitchen, standing at the sink. He wore yellow gloves and the tap was running. But he was just staring at the dishes in the basin.

"Where'd Mom go?"

He pointed a gloved finger to the sun porch. "Give her a minute," he mouthed.

"What about you? Hiding in here with the cutlery?"

"Guilty. I figured I'd get a head start so your mother doesn't have to face the full sink at the end of the night. And I suppose I wanted to give all of you a few minutes alone." He turned off the tap. "How are you doing?"

Wren shrugged. "It's all very strange, to be honest."

Hank nodded sympathetically.

"I mean, here we all are. And there's so much ground to cover. And yet we're not really going anywhere." She stopped, suddenly, and a lump rose in her throat. "I only just told him about Lucy. He didn't even know he was a grand-father."

Hank pulled his gloves off and went to her.

Wren didn't cry, but she wished she could. There was something inside her that she needed to expel. "I feel off-balance," she said, finally.

Bowser, who'd been sniffing around the kitchen for handouts, clunked his cone against the kitchen island, startling all of them. It was a good excuse to laugh. "Speaking of balance, how do you think he feels?" Hank joked. Then, more seriously, "Listen, this is strange for all of us. None of us knows what he wants, but I have a feeling we'll find out soon."

Wren nodded. "Okay. But can you come back out there?" she asked.

"I will. As soon as your mom is ready."

Wren went to the bathroom where she splashed cold water on her face. When she opened the door, Piper was standing right there.

"Oh, sorry. It's all yours."

"I don't have to go."

Wren pulled her into the small bathroom and they shut the door behind them. The childishness of it made them both giggle. "How are you doing?" Wren whispered.

Piper was animated. "Did you know he worked as a photojournalist in Syria?"

"No. I did not." Crammed together in the marble bathroom under the stairs she couldn't begin to imagine his experience in the war-torn country.

"Shannon should be here. He has a bunch of work he brought with him, back at the motel. He said he'd be happy to share it."

Wren thought of the black portfolio he'd carried off the bus that afternoon. She could understand Piper's interest, something she felt, too. But she wasn't sure she wanted to open that portfolio, no matter how compelling the stories it contained. While it may have explained what he'd been doing and where he'd been, it could never justify why he'd stayed away. Why should she care to view the collection of places and people who'd taken up all those years, years he should have been spending with them?

But looking at her expression, Wren could tell Piper wasn't thinking along those lines. And she wasn't sure which one of them was better off as a result.

"You're coming back out, right?" Piper asked. "I don't want him to leave yet."

Wren followed Piper out of the bathroom and through the kitchen. She was pleased to see Hank had abandoned his post at the sink. It was still full. They found him back at the table with Lindy making small talk.

Seeing them, Caleb stood. "I think I'm going to have to call it a night," he said.

"Wait. You're going already?" Piper glanced quickly around the table, trying to determine what she'd missed. But there was no apparent ill will. The evening was just over.

"Yes, I'm afraid the trip out here was a long one and I'm pretty worn out. Nothing a couple good nights' sleep won't fix. But I want to thank you all for a wonderful dinner." He looked at Lindy. "Thank you for having me."

He pulled a phone from his back pocket, an older model iPhone with a cracked screen, Wren noticed. "Excuse me a moment, while I call for a ride?"

"I can drive you," Piper offered. "It's no trouble."

Caleb looked surprised. "All right. That's very kind."

Hank and Lindy walked them to the door. Unsure of what to do, Wren followed.

Caleb stopped at the top of the porch steps and looked up at the swollen moon. "Do you think we could drive along Chatham Harbor on the way to the motel?" he asked Piper. "It's a clear night."

Piper liked the idea. It meant the night was not over yet. "We could go for a walk down there if you'd like."

"A drive by is all I can manage tonight, I'm afraid." He looked at Wren. "I look forward to seeing that store of yours some time."

"I'll be there tomorrow," she said.

"Tomorrow," he said. It sounded like a promise coming from his lips.

As Piper backed out of the driveway Lindy and Wren remained on the porch watching them go.

"What a long weird night."

Wren wrapped an arm around her mother. "So, what did you think?"

"No one knows better than we do how much time has passed. Just look at the years—you girls grew up. But I have to say, I was completely taken aback when that gray-haired man walked into my kitchen tonight. It's like I still expected him to be young, somehow."

"I know. How do you think he's doing? He didn't drink."

"I noticed."

"But still, he seemed so different than I remembered. Sober or not."

Lindy wrapped her arms around herself in the cool night air. "He's aged quite a bit, honey. Living project to project and traveling as much as he did is lonely. It may sound adventurous when you're young. But I imagine the older you get, the more you want a warm bed and a pot of something cooking on the stove to come home to. It doesn't sound like he's had that."

Wren wondered if there was sympathy in her tone or if it was just her own sense of it that she attached to Lindy's words. Either way, she'd gotten the same feeling. Caleb Bailey was an articulate man who'd led an interesting life doing the work he loved. All over the world, in fact. But he seemed empty sitting at their family table that night. And he seemed tired beyond the long bus trip to get there.

Inside, the kettle whistled from the kitchen. Hank was making tea. Wren glanced up at the sky. The same night sky he used to point to before he went away on a big trip. She never liked it when he left; she used to cry that she couldn't fall asleep until he came back.

"See those stars?" he'd ask, pointing skyward with one hand and holding her against his side with the other. "When you miss me at bedtime, I want you to look up at them. Because no matter where I go, we will always be under the same sky. And then I won't seem so far away any-more." He'd taught her the constellations, the Big and Little Dippers. And her favorite, Orion. "Start with his belt," her father would remind her. "Those three stars are the most prominent. Can't miss 'em."

Now, standing on her mother's porch, she found Orion's belt overhead and followed the line of stars up to the tip of his sword.

"I'm glad it's over with, but I'm also glad we did it. Thanks, Mom."

Lindy leaned her head against Wren's. "Don't thank me yet. I just hope you and your sisters get what you need from this."

Wren thought about this. About Shannon's absence, and her own uncertainty. "Well, if Piper's behavior tonight is any indication, I'm a little worried about her. You know how she is; she opens herself up too easily. She wants too much."

Lindy held the porch door open. "Go easy on Piper," she said. "That's the one thing I worry about with all three of you. What you want isn't necessarily what you need."

Twenty-Three

Caleb

Moonlight illuminated the motel room in soft-blue light, spilling over the white bedding. He rolled over to face it. It was quiet, save for the reassuring thrum of peepers in the woods outside, and even they were only interrupted by the occasional car passing on Route 28. It was warm, and he slept bare-chested, his arms free from the sheets. He stared at his hand resting by his pillow as if it belonged to someone else. In the glow of the moonlight, it was just a silhouette, transformed. Gone were the ropy lines of veins and the age spots, the crepey skin that gave acknowledgment to the years behind him. He made a fist and held it up in the light. Anger had found him. It was not meant for the girls or Lindy. Or the fact he'd made it back here. His grip softened, and he let his arm fall back onto the bed. Already he could feel himself losing strength.

They had passed two liquor stores when Piper drove him back to the motel, and it had been hard to avert his gaze. It had been three years that he had been truly sober. There had been many times before that he'd tried, stretches where he made his AA meetings and stayed the course religiously. In the beginning the attempt to get sober was all about the family he'd left behind. He owed it to them. He would not let go of the vision he had for their future. But as the years passed and his attempts failed, he turned back to the bottle. At times because he'd given up on that future; at others because he was afraid to remember the past.

Though he'd decided that his family was better served by his absence, there was still his work. The singular hunger he had, stronger than his desire to drink. He didn't care about paying rent or putting food in the fridge; but he needed to work. Luckily, he'd kept some contacts over the years. Some who were loyal friends, some who simply appreciated his work. In the beginning, he learned how to pull himself together for short stretches when he landed an assignment. But it grew harder. There were times when he lost assignments for showing up hungover or worse, like the time he staggered onto the set of a documentary project he'd been brought on board for in Santa Fe. They were shooting in the Native Nation reservation west of the city documenting a Navajo man who was a revered silversmith. Caleb had no memory of the drive from his hotel to the reservation that day. He arrived late and more than a few days unshowered. The thing was, he was excited about this project. It had been some time since he'd had real work, something substantial like this. What was more, he liked the man, Josef Nez. He'd spent the day before at the artist's home, talking to his wife and three of his grown children, following Josef around his small workshop in a shed behind the house. Josef was seventy-nine, the father of seven children, and had supported the family with his silverwork his whole life. He showed them his creations: thick cuff bracelets set with turquoise, women's Concho belts, sterling-silver bolo ties. As Caleb watched the old man cut and hammer, turning sheets of metal between his gnarled fingers, he had felt inside him a stirring, a hunger that began in his gut and moved into his fingers. Josef did not speak much to the crew, so much as he invited them into his process. There was artistry in the quietude of his work, and in the warmth in his dark eyes when he placed a silver ring in Caleb's palm. This was the job Caleb had been waiting for.

But the night before shooting began, the crew had met in an adobe-style café for dinner that turned into drinks. Caleb had been dry if not sober for a few months. He did not turn down the occasional beer, and on this night with dust in his shoes and the desert heat permeating the crowded bistro, he was alive and hot and thirsty. He had a beer. Then another. He remembered turning down a round of shots of tequila at some point in the night, but he must not have later, for he awoke late in his motel the next morning, his mouth as chalky as the red landscape outside. When he stumbled into Josef Nez's living room, it was not the looks of the crew, or Dennis, the producer, that got to him. It was Josef Nez. He did not speak to Caleb but stared through him. As Caleb stood in the middle of the room, struggling with the zipper on his lens bag that would not open, aware suddenly of the acrid smell permeating from his cotton shirt and the brightly colored rug that would not stop swirling, he looked up. He didn't hear Dennis muttering under his breath, ordering him outside. He didn't notice the other members of the crew fiddling with their equipment, stepping in where he should have been setting up. All he saw was Josef Nez staring at him with his hooded watery eyes. Josef shook his head. In that moment the room came into focus.

Caleb left the reservation and bought a packet of cigarettes and a liter of soda. He got in his car and drove straight through to Arizona, the radio off, his head humming with static. He'd given up his family and his life in the Northeast. If he gave up on his work, too, he was a dead man.

That was the last time Caleb touched a drink. As dark as the journey out had been, he had tools. He had his meetings. He had his sponsor, Alice.

255

He had God. But being here, in Chatham, he felt the old itch crawling to life under his skin. He felt it in his fingertips that had drummed on the dining room table tonight under Lindy's gaze. It coursed through his muscles, causing him to want to get up and away, any place, as if he could put distance between himself and this growing urge that was spreading within him.

Caleb got up and went to the bathroom. He poured himself a cup of water and took a pill for the pain. When he slid back into bed he did not worry about how he might feel in the morning or what effect his pain might have on the things he hoped to do with the girls. It was enough that he had tomorrow. That he was here in Chatham with his girls.

As he lay in the motel room waiting for sleep to find him, he pictured each of them tucked into their own beds. Wren to the north on Queen Anne Road, Piper and Lindy to the east in town, and Shannon to his west in Stage Harbor. All the bright points of his life spanning out like points of a constellation, with him at its center.

Twenty-Four

Wren

Lucy did not understand. "Where has your daddy been?"

Wren ran the brush through her daughter's baby-fine hair. "Ponytail or braid?" she asked.

Lucy looked up at her mother in the mirror. "Ponytail. But where *was* he?"

It was the question that had shadowed the Bailey women their whole lives. Every Christmas in that moment where you found yourself sitting by the tree, the whole room illuminated in light and laughter, your loved ones close—there would be that sinking pause when you remembered someone wasn't here. It was the same with Wren's eighth-grade graduation ceremony at school, the first major milestone she celebrated (though endured might've better described it) after Caleb left. It happened every year, though the traditional holidays became easier. It was the odd ones that caught you off guard—like when she lost her first molar. Their dad had always risen first and tucked a seashell under their pillow from the tooth fairy. It would be a unique one—pearly pink or golden. A special shape. That first time she sat up in bed and slipped her hand under the pillow out of habit, her fingers searching against the cool cotton underside and finding nothing. Those were the things that surprised you.

"My father has been living in Arizona," Wren said, carefully. "But now he's here to visit." She'd read in a parenting article some time ago that when children ask difficult questions, honesty was best, but there was no need to go overboard with details. The article had advised that you start with the simple bites of information and see if that satisfied the child. As Lucy contemplated this answer, Wren swept her hair up and secured it with a pink elastic. "How's that?" she asked.

Lucy turned her head to and fro, her ponytail swishing in the mirror. "Good, Mama." She turned and looked up at Wren. "So, is he my grampa now?"

Wren studied her daughter's tiny upturned nose. The curiosity in her wide brown eyes. "Yes, I suppose he is." She held her breath, waiting for the sensible follow up: "What about *my* dad?" But this time Lucy didn't ask. Satisfied, she marched to her bed and grabbed her stuffed elephant. "I'm hungry. Can we eat breakfast now?" That was all.

As Wren stirred pancake mix in a bowl, she thought about the complications of her family.

Beverly was on her way up to the Cape for her annual visit now. She was taking the train from South Carolina, stopping in Delaware to see friends in Rehoboth, then again in New York, before arriving in Chatham. Lucy had spent part of every summer with her great-grandmother since birth. After Beverly, all Lucy had in the grandparents department were Hank and Lindy. Technically Hank was a step-grandparent, though Wren had certainly never thought of him as such. For a man with no children of his own, he excelled at this whole family thing. And let's face it, her family was a lot.

But a family unit was important to a child's sense of self. Wren had always been sensitive to the fact that Lucy was not only without a father, but there was also the loss of what a father could bring into her life. Another set of grandparents! Uncles and aunts! Cousins! James had all of those things. Lately Wren was left with the sense that she'd provided her child with only half of a family.

Her mind wandered to the last week she'd had with James. They were living in the little apartment over Main Street, and his bags were packed for Washington. Late-night conversations that turned into arguments. James was set in a way she had not seen before. It left her feeling alone, alone with a growing baby between them. Several times she almost told him, especially when she

259

was angry. But she couldn't share the news. Not in that spirit.

She pictured her mother and sisters, and then she pictured herself with the new baby so far away from all of them. And James out at sea. It wasn't fair, since he didn't know about the baby, but she grew angry. "I don't see where I fit in," she said. "I need time."

By the end of the week she was packing her own bags. "What are you doing?" James asked when she filled a duffel bag with some of her things.

"I'm going to stay with my sister Shannon. I don't want to fight anymore. I can't think clearly."

James scoffed, and a sneer flickered across his face. "Your sisters. I have never understood this bond you three have. It's like none of you can make a decision without checking with the others. Is she the one who's telling you to stay home?"

Wren grabbed her bag. "How dare you talk about my family that way?"

"I thought I was your family!" It was the one time she'd ever seen him completely lose his temper. James swung away from her, his face full of disgust, and punched the wall. There was a sickening thud of flesh against Sheetrock as his hand sunk into the wall. Gray Sheetrock splintered, falling to the floor with a puff.

"Stop it!" Wren cried.

James tucked his hand against his stomach, but Wren could already see the trail of blood running down to his elbow.

"Fuck," he muttered.

"Let me see." Wren was crying, but she reached for his hand. "James, please."

"Just go," he said, turning away. He went to the sink and ran the tap. Wren watched as the water washed red into the basin. His knuckles were split, and a large gash ran down the center of his hand.

"You need stitches," she cried.

James spun around. "I said, 'Go!'"

She grabbed her duffel and walked around him, flinging the door open. Head down, she raced down the back stairs until she burst outside to the alley behind Main Street. The sun was impossibly bright, and the street was clogged with the happy hum of tourists. Wren blinked in the brightness of it all. As she rounded the corner a woman pushed a baby stroller past with twin girls. One smiled up at her. Wren slung her bag over her shoulder and walked head down toward School Street. James never called. Though she knew this was probably best for both of them, she spent the rest of the week crying herself to sleep at night, the phone tucked beneath her pillow just in case.

The others had firm thoughts on all of it, and

as usual none hesitated to dispense them. "He's selfish," Shannon said. "This is his dream, not yours."

Their mother struggled to make sense of it, and Wren shied out from under the umbrella of her scrutiny. "This doesn't sound like you and James," she said. "Are you sure nothing else is going on?"

"He called us codependent," Wren shared. The words felt unkind coming out of her mouth, as if she were betraying James's confidence. She knew he'd said it in a moment of anger, and she could also see he might have a point. But as she predicted, it was the nail in the coffin for Shannon.

"Screw him. He doesn't know anything about us."

"You're too young to hitch your wagon to one guy," Piper allowed. "Let him go out there. I don't think he'll like it as much as he thinks. Who knows? Maybe he'll come back."

But Lindy seemed to consider this. "I disagree," she said, finally. "But he may have a point about staying in Chatham." She looked around the table at her daughters' faces. "Have I ever made any of you feel like I expect or want you to stick around here?"

Piper actually laughed. "Hello? Boston dweller, who doesn't plan to ever move back."

Shannon threw her a look. "No, Mom. Reid and

I were both very happy to make a life here. It's a wonderful place to raise the kids."

"Only you can afford it," Piper added.

Shannon ignored the slight, but this was one thing that worried Wren. Chatham was a resort town, and the taxes were high. How long would her little apartment suffice? She couldn't imagine lugging a baby stroller up and down the narrow back stairs. Where would the baby sleep? These were considerations that had begun to distract her from James. With each passing day, they became more real concerns.

"I love Chatham," Wren assured her mother. "But it's also because all of you are here. I want my kids to be close to family." They all looked at her. "Someday," she added quickly.

Morning sickness found her almost immediately. The smell of eggs in her mother's kitchen made her stomach roil. The sight of meat on the grill caused her to flee from the room. But she still hadn't told them yet. At night she soothed herself reading *What to Expect* in her bed. She'd borrowed it from the Eldredge Library and kept it tucked beneath her mattress like the worry dolls her father had brought back from an assignment in South Dakota when she was little. They were tiny wire dolls dressed in Southwestern prints, their miniature mouths painted red. Her father told her to place a worry doll under the mattress to ward off bad dreams. Now, she kept the pregnancy book there. Only the more she read, the less worried she was. As she paged through she was fascinated by the growth of the fetus, even in the first few weeks. She couldn't believe it when she read that the baby's brain and spinal cord were already forming!

Wren knew James was leaving town the day after the Hooker's Ball. That whole week, neither had broken down and reached out to the other. It filled her with as much anger as it did sadness. They were both as stubborn as the other, only James didn't know what was at stake. Wren knew she had to cut him loose. James was too young, too full of wanderlust to settle down and start a family. And she knew more than anyone what that was like for a child.

She also knew what it would do to James. If he learned she was pregnant, he would want to do the right thing and stay in Chatham, even if it went against every grain of who he was. The thought of him giving up on his dreams would be the death of all of them. Her way was better: it would set all of them free. Even if it broke her heart pulling the trigger.

Wren's plan was simple if brutal. The day before the Ball she reached out to her old flame, Darby Vale, who she'd dated on and off during college summers. She'd run into Darby a couple times over the years, and she knew that he still came up from New York to visit his parents on summer weekends. James had never liked Darby. He'd found him pompous and pampered, both of which were reasons Wren had broken up with him years ago. But she needed Darby for what was to follow.

To her surprise, Darby was quick to reply to her voice mail. Yes, he was on the Cape. Yes, he was free for the Hooker's Ball. If she weren't feeling so poorly about what she was doing, she might actually have enjoyed the ease with which her plans were rapidly unfolding.

That night Wren stole one of Piper's dresses from her closet. A bright-colored, snug-fitting pink number that showed off her long legs and tanned shoulders. She spent extra time curling her long hair, not because she liked it that way, but because it would look so different. James loved her long hair worn down and straight, her face clean and natural. Fussing over her appearance with makeup and hair would send a message that things were different, that *she* was different.

When she walked under the twinkling lights of the white tent on Darby's arm, she felt like an imposter. Beverly had taken one look at her outfit, and her brow had knit in silent disapproval. But she graciously kissed her granddaughter's cheek in greeting. Shannon was not as demure. "What are you wearing?"

Wren had tugged self-consciously at the short hem. "What? It's Piper's."

265

"I can see that. What's it doing on you?"

Wren ignored her, reintroducing her family to Darby. This part seemed to please Beverly, even if it raised an eyebrow from Lindy. Now more than ever, Wren could've used a drink. A double pour of gin with lime. Anything to fuel her falsity. Instead she'd have to stick to club sodas, but she'd do her best to make sure she gave the illusion she was drinking. She ran a hand over her still-flat tummy and scanned the crowd for James.

Darby was oblivious to her nerves and her wiles. He was his usual self, leading her around the crowd and blathering on about his work in New York, the renovations his family was doing to their Barn Hill house, his squash game. This worked for her even if it drove her crazy, and she indulged him, running her hand up and down his arm encouragingly at each cringe-worthy joke he told. Tossing her head back along with his friends in laughter. Others turned to look at them. Her choice of date had been masterful.

Just as the band started up, she spotted James. He was standing to the side with friends. Friends she knew and adored and would've given her left arm to join on any other night. He was dressed up in a taupe linen suit, his only good summer suit, and he'd just had his hair cut. The vulnerable sun-kissed nape of his neck was visible over his collared shirt, and she felt the urge to go to him and place her hand on it.

As if feeling the weight of her eyes on his back, James turned. At the sight of her, he forgot himself. He smiled. Wren almost smiled back. But the initial spark of joy vanished from his expression as he understood. The garish dress. Darby's arm around her waist. His mouth opened as if he was going to say something across the wide grassy expanse between them. She would hate herself for the rest of her life for what she did next. She squeezed Darby's arm hard. When he turned she grabbed his face between her hands and kissed him full on the mouth. She could feel his surprise, as their lips didn't quite match up and he'd been midsentence. But then he pulled her closer and stuck his tongue in her mouth.

When they parted Darby licked his lips playfully. The couple with them chuckled and Wren forced a smile, even though she felt sick to her stomach. When she dared a look back, James was gone. Darby brought her a gin and tonic, which she promptly dumped in a flower arrangement when he wasn't looking. It didn't matter what she ate or drank; for the rest of the night she couldn't get the coppery taste of deceit out of her mouth.

At the end of the week she learned that James had moved to Washington. She'd continued to see Darby on occasion to keep up the pretense that they were together, though to his frustration she'd kept it strictly platonic. Luckily for her he was tied up most of the summer in New York, and though he invited her to come down several times, she never did. She was almost certain he was dating other women, which was fine with her. They were not together, despite his efforts. By summer's end he grew tired of her chasteness. If Darby ever found out she was pregnant, she didn't know. There was no reason for him to think it was theirs.

James reached out to her only once. From time to time she might run into his friends around town. This time, she was shopping at Chatham Market and bumped into Murphy, his buddy from the Pier. He noted her protruding belly with unchecked surprise. They exchanged quick pleasantries. The next day James called. His voice was soft, and if she wasn't mistaken, hopeful. "How are things?"

Wren saved them both from strained niceties. "I'm pregnant," she said.

James paused. "Is it . . . ?"

"No," she lied. "No, it's not yours."

Was she making the biggest mistake of her life? Of his?

But while she lay wiping tears off her cheeks and questioning her motives, the baby kicked. Wren placed both hands on her burgeoning belly. She decided she could do this. Whether she was ready or not, she would do it for both of them.

"Is breakfast ready?" Lucy raced up behind her and threw her arms around her mother's waist.

"Ready as ever," Wren said wryly. She had to stop second-guessing herself. Lucy was fine, and so was she. And there were other important matters that needed her attention. "Let's eat. We're late for the shop."

The phone rang, and Lucy picked it up and studied the screen. "It says Arizona," she said, holding it out to her mother.

Wren looked. Was it the same Arizona number that had called before? But her father was here, now. And it wasn't his cell phone, which he'd given her. "Wrong number," she said, putting it down. "Let's get going."

When they pulled into the lot behind the store, Wren noticed someone standing outside the front door. It wasn't Ari.

Piper stood outside, her arms wrapped around herself even though the day was already promising to be a hot one. "Hey Lucy, girl!" she said, scooping her up for a big hug. But the look she gave Wren over her niece's tiny shoulders spelled something else entirely. "Can I come in?" she asked.

Knowing that they'd be spending a good deal of time in the shop, Wren had organized provisions to keep Lucy happily entertained. Wren reached under the counter and handed the basket of goods to her daughter. Lucy's face lit up. There was an assortment of craft supplies, including a box of newly sharpened colored pencils, a green kitty cat journal, a spool of sparkly thread, and a tiny mason jar full of seashells. Lucy shrieked with delight and disappeared into one of the dressing rooms, pulling the curtain tightly closed behind her.

Piper raised her eyebrows.

"That's her 'office,'" Wren explained. She flicked on the lights, turned on some light music and pushed the stool toward Piper. "So, what's going on?" she asked, keeping her voice low.

"I'm home for good," Piper said.

"Because of Dad?"

Piper shook her head gravely. "Because I fucked up."

Wren threw a cautionary look over her shoulder toward the dressing room and turned the radio up. "Jesus, Piper. Come on."

"Sorry. See what I mean?" she put her head in her hands.

Wren wanted to understand, but she didn't have time for theatrics or, honestly, any more trouble. She thought about Piper at dinner the night before. She had seemed edgy, especially when asked about her work and school life. But Wren had expected that, with their father being there and all. "It can't be that bad. You just finished school, you'll find a job soon enough."

"Everything I own is crammed into the back of my car. But Mom and Hank haven't even noticed, there's so much going on. And I don't have the heart to tell them—partly because there's so much going on."

"You left Boston?"

Piper nodded. "I haven't been able to make rent in three months. Hank helped out, and Shannon wrote me a check the first month. I didn't want to ask you, since you haven't even opened the shop yet. Claire couldn't float me anymore."

Wren let her breath out. Frankly, she couldn't imagine floating anyone that long. "What happened to finding a teaching job?"

Piper shrugged like it was a matter of deciding between dinner options. "I'm not feeling it."

"Piper." Wren had seen her like this before. She was famous for starting things she did not finish, and equally famous for her inability to commit. It drove Shannon nuts, and she was surprised to hear Shannon had actually lent Piper money to begin with. She'd never said a word about it to Wren. "You've got more degrees than the rest of us put together. It's time to figure this stuff out."

"I know, and I tried. I applied for jobs and I even got a couple interviews. But when they called me to come in I just sort of freaked out. I don't want to teach. I can't imagine being responsible for a whole classroom of kids."

271

Wren glanced back at the dressing room. "But you love kids. And they love you right back."

Piper's eyes welled up. "I know. Which is why I just can't. All those kids belong to someone, and those parents would be relying on me . . . and the kids would need so much from me. And that guy I was dating?"

Wren braced herself. Piper's track record with guys was well established in the family. She picked the worst ones, and the worse the guy the longer she held on to him. "What about him?"

Piper's shoulders started to shake. Wren pushed a tissue box in front of her.

"He's married."

"Jesus, Piper!"

"I know. I lied to all of you about him getting out of a relationship. He's in it for the long haul, and he's not ever going to leave her. What's worse, he's coming here this week. With his family."

"He has kids?" Wren pushed her chair back. This was too much, even for her little sister.

"I know. I told you I fucked up." She was crying in full now, but Wren couldn't stand to hear another word. This was low. Piper was better than this, and yet her behavior said otherwise. Lindy would flip if she knew.

Wren ran her hands through her hair. "Does Mom know?"

Piper shook her head.

The shop door opened, and Ari breezed through

with two iced coffees. "Good morning! One more day until . . ." She took one look at the two sisters and stopped in the middle of the floor. "Sorry. Want me to come back in a few?"

"No, no! Please come in." Wren waved her in and took the coffees. She was grateful for the interruption. "Ari, you remember Piper."

"I'm so sorry to interrupt. I can come back," Ari whispered.

"Don't you dare."

Ari glanced back at Piper who was still sitting at the counter. "Everything okay?"

"Just as it should be." Wren forced a smile. "The usual joy of family."

"Did you see the sculpture came in last night?"

"What? Where?" It was the one specialty piece Wren had ordered for the shop. A huge splurge. She'd been expecting it all week.

"In the back. I'll show you."

Together they positioned themselves on opposite sides of the oversized box.

Piper stood back as they passed her, moving carefully through the store. "What's in the box?" she asked. She didn't seem to be taking the hint that Wren was done listening. She had work to get to. Important work.

"It's a splurge," Wren admitted, setting the box down. She opened the top delicately and began pulling back the layers of tissue to reveal a mountain of foam packing.

Gingerly, Wren sifted through the Styrofoam peanuts. Piper and Lucy crowded around.

"Is that the glass wave?" Lucy asked excitedly.

"It is," Wren said. "And we can't touch it, okay baby?"

Curiosity got the better of her, and Piper joined them. All four leaned over the box as Wren scooped the last of the packing away to reveal a sparkling crest of green-and-blue glass. "Oh, man." Wren ran a finger tentatively over the top of it. "She did it for us. She really did it."

A crest of clear glass bubbles seemed to float atop the wave like crystal beads, and Wren took Lucy's hand. "Very gentle now," she instructed her, and she ran her small index finger over the bubbles. Lucy giggled.

"It's so smooth mommy."

It was the most beautiful piece she'd ever seen, and any regrets about the cost or doubts about the choice evaporated in the morning air. She thought of what the artist had told her when she described her vision in her studio in Provincetown. "Art is memory." As Wren ran her daughter's hand over each tendril of hand-blown wave, she felt it. There would be a discerning buyer who would see it for what it was and want it. A piece of the Cape to take home with them and display in their own home.

"It's stunning," Ari breathed. She stepped closer for a better look. "Where are we going to put it?"

"Because it's so delicate, we need to put it somewhere up high. I don't want shoppers to bump into it."

"Or kids to touch it!" Lucy said, proprietorially, as she headed back to the dressing room.

At that moment, there was a knock from the front door. The bell overhead jingled. "Oh, sorry! I forgot to lock it when I came in," Ari said.

Just what Wren needed. Their first customer, who she'd have to turn away. "I'll take care of it." She headed to the front of the store, prepared to apologize. "I'm sorry but we aren't open for business yet . . ." she began.

Caleb Bailey stood in the middle of the shop. "Should I come back?"

"No. I mean, please come in." Piper, hearing his voice, followed her to the front.

"What do you think? Isn't this place great?" She whisked past Wren and grabbed their father's arm, pulling him in.

But Wren couldn't stay. She didn't stay to see the look of wonder on her father's face as Piper led him around, pointing out the handmade jewelry and picking up a fisherman's sweater. She didn't even want to bring her father back to the rear of the shop to show him the glass sculpture. Instead she went to the dressing room behind the counter and kneeled down.

"Knock knock," she said.

The curtain swung open. "Yes?" Lucy asked.

She had a smudge of purple marker on her nose. "There's someone here I want you to meet."

Lucy looked over her mother's shoulder. "That man?"

Wren nodded. She realized that even though they'd discussed her father's return that morning, Lucy wasn't connecting the dots. They hadn't been expecting him so soon—Wren had thought he'd call first.

"Okay. But I'm working on a picture," Lucy said.

Wren would normally tell her to pause what she was doing, to come out and say a proper hello. But she decided to let things unfold. "All right. Can you come out in a minute, though?"

Lucy nodded and swept the curtain closed.

Wren returned to the front of the shop. Her father was standing with his hands on his hips staring up at an antique map on the wall. "Monomoy Island?" he asked. She nodded, taking pleasure in the attention he was giving every piece.

He regarded it another moment, then moved on to a watercolor hanging nearby. "The fish pier," he said, approvingly. "Before they added on."

Piper came to stand beside her. "He likes it," she whispered. "He likes everything you have in here." She turned to their father. "You haven't seen the best one yet."

Without waiting for permission, Piper glided

276

into the back of the store. "Wait!" Wren inter-rupted.

"Relax, sis. I've got it." Wren tried not to grind her teeth as Piper slid the box to the middle of the floor.

"That's incredibly fragile!" she warned.

Piper ignored this and pulled open the lid. "I've got it."

Wren stood back as her father bent over the box. He reached his hand in and carefully pushed back the packaging. Finally, he looked back at her. "Why this piece?" he asked. This time he wasn't smiling.

Wren felt the back of her neck prickle. "Because I liked it."

Caleb considered this and reached inside the box.

She wanted to say, "Be careful!" But she was taken aback by what he'd just said. He regarded the piece more carefully and settled it slowly back into its nest of wrapping. "What do you like about it?"

Piper looked perplexed, too.

"Look," Wren said, trying to keep her voice light. "I spent a lot of time considering the kind of items and art I wanted to carry. I know art is subjective . . ."

"Don't be offended," their father said. "I'm just curious. Why this one?"

But she was offended. A minute ago, he'd been

277

poring over every item in her shop with seeming approval, and now he'd picked her favorite piece and was criticizing her choice. A choice that she took very personally. Who was he to walk in here and question her like this?

"I liked the artist," she said, scrambling. "I liked the way the blown glass tapered at the tips of the wave, the way it was so solid and powerful at the base, but so fragile at the top."

Caleb shrugged.

"You don't like it?"

"I didn't say that."

Wren prickled. What was wrong with her? This was her store, and everything in it was so her. If he didn't appreciate that, well then . . . She couldn't help it. "Then what *are* you saying?"

Piper threw her a look. But she didn't care.

"You have a strong aesthetic in here," he began. "There seems to be a connection to each piece. So I just wondered why this one."

"Because it tells a story." There, she'd blurted it out in a voice that was too strong, perhaps defensive. But it was all she had. Suddenly she felt like crying.

Watching their father move through her store, running his hands over the things she'd picked with such care had an effect on her she hadn't anticipated. When he turned to look at her, his face was so full of awe and tenderness that she felt she might cry. She hadn't known how much this would matter to her. And now he just stood there, staring back at her.

"What?" she asked. "What is it?"

He smiled. "I wanted you to defend your aesthetic. You have a good eye, Wren. Don't be afraid if someone challenges that."

Something else had caught his attention.

"Now what?"

Caleb peered around her. "Now, I think I need to introduce myself," he said.

It was then Wren realized that Lucy had come out of the changing room. She was right there, at her elbow.

"Mama," she said, shyly. "I finished my picture."

Lucy held up a drawing of a boat. There were two stick figures on it. Both had big eyes, one with long lashes. The round orange sun was smiling.

"Baby. It's beautiful."

"May I?" Caleb asked softly, holding out his hand.

Lucy leaned shyly against her mother, and Wren felt that sudden maternal pull, the need to keep her there, pressed safely at her side. What if he said something about Lucy's drawing like he had about her sculpture? But Lucy held the picture out for him to take.

"Do you know who I am?" he asked.

"Lucy," Wren said, wanting to take control

of the introduction. "I'd like you to meet your grandpa."

Lucy regarded him seriously. "I knew you were coming." She pointed to one of the stick figures in the picture. "That's you."

Wren sucked in her breath.

After a long moment Caleb glanced up at her. "Looks just like me," he said. "And who is this pretty one?" He pointed to the other stick figure, the one with long eyelashes.

Lucy laughed. "Don't be silly. That's me."

Twenty-Five

Piper

Why had she come home? Wren was her only hope at a sympathetic ear, but she hadn't given it. Piper knew her relationship with Derek was wrong. She'd never thought otherwise. But she'd fallen in love, and now everything was a mess. Wren was the one person in her family she'd been counting on to set judgment aside.

And then there was her father. Piper had been excited to show him around Wren's store and showcase her sister's hard work. Wren certainly wasn't doing it. Caleb loved everything in that damn shop, and Piper could see how pleased it made her sister. It was all going so well until she pulled out the glass sculpture. Wren hadn't wanted her to touch it. God, she was so uptight these days, more and more like Shannon. But it all seemed to go off the tracks when he asked questions about the sculpture. It had started out as genuine interest, Piper thought. He was an artist. Visuals were his life's work. But Wren had bristled, becoming suddenly defensive. And that was when Lucy appeared.

Good Lord—the way her father had looked at her little face when she'd stepped out of the dressing room and handed him that drawing. Piper had had to walk away. Caleb was smitten, and why wouldn't he be? But in that moment, it occurred to Piper that Wren had so much to show. So much to show for herself and her life. Her new business. The love she'd stocked it with. And most of all, little Lucy. What did Piper have to show for her life?

She'd really been hoping they could get lunch together afterward, but then her dad said he wanted to get back to the motel. It was as if his curiosity had been sated, and he'd seen all there was to see. She was about to offer to buy the two of them a cup at Monomoy Coffee, but then she remembered her nearly empty wallet. She was twenty-six years old, living in her mother's house, and down to her last ten dollars.

The drive home the night before had been the only time she'd been alone with her father. He seemed pulled between the fatigue of his journey and his desire to see more of his old hometown. "Let's drive along Shore Road," he suggested. And so they did, looping up and around the edge of the harbor. He asked about the new cottages by Chatham Bars Inn. He wanted to see the Chatham Fish Pier. She'd been happy to drive him around, slowing while he rolled down the window to look. Answering his questions about old houses that had gone missing, replaced by new big construction. The once-wild stretches of shoreline that had been built up. *It must be so strange,* she thought, *to come home and find that your memory no longer matched the land.*

When she finally returned to her mother's, Hank and Lindy were sitting at the kitchen island with cups of tea. "Want one, darling?" her mother asked.

"I think I'm going to turn in," she said, feeling suddenly worn out.

"Are you all right?" Lindy wanted to know. She could tell her mother didn't want to pry, but that she was concerned.

"I am," Piper said. She told them how she'd driven him through town and past all the places he'd asked to see. How surprised he'd been at how Chatham had changed.

"Time waits for no man," her mother said, rising and putting her cup in the sink.

"Was it hard having him here tonight?"

Lindy rinsed out her cup and set it in the dishwasher with all the other dishes and glassware they'd gone through at dinner. The top carriage sagged beneath the weight of it all. "It stirred up some dust from the past," she said, finally. "He's different, of course. We all are." She turned around suddenly, her eyes on Hank. "What was it you said earlier? About coming back to a place you'd been away from."

Hank was staring out the window past them all. He looked startled from his quietude. Piper didn't blame him. It must've been an exhausting evening for him, too. "Oh, you mean the Frost quote?"

"Yes," that was it.

Hank cleared his throat. "Home is the place where, when you have to go there, they have to take you in."

Lindy turned to Piper, an indignant look on her face.

Piper was confused. "We took him in, Mom."

"We did. But the question remains." She set the dishtowel on the rack and straightened it, taking her time, before finishing her thought. "Is this still his home?"

Lindy strode past her, stopping to peck her quickly on the cheek. "I'm glad you're home," she said. She went upstairs to bed.

Piper looked at Hank. She felt guilty, suddenly. She'd wanted them to do this, she'd been the one to push the hardest. "Is this too much for her?"

Hank sipped the last of his tea. "Don't you worry about your mother. She'll let us know when it is."

Now, with no plans for the rest of the day, she found herself wandering aimlessly up Main Street caught in the sidewalk flow of the tourists. All morning she'd kept her phone turned off. The only text she'd gotten since arriving on Cape was from Adam. "You didn't say goodbye." What a mistake it had been to go home with him. He was a good guy, and she'd acted like a jerk.

The noise in her head was as bad as the crowd on the sidewalk. She needed some peace and quiet, so she crossed the street and headed up to Where the Sidewalk Ends. Piper knew the bookstore owner, Caitlin. She was one of Shannon's good friends, and she'd opened the shop several years ago with her mother. Piper waited impatiently behind a couple of young women in bright-printed dresses, who were sipping iced coffees and blocking the door.

"I can't believe he did that. So what did you tell him?" one of the women said.

"I told him it was over. I have my whole life ahead of me." She flipped her long brown hair over her shoulder emphatically.

Piper eyed the woman who had her whole life ahead of her. She couldn't have been more than twenty, and even she was not settling for some guy's nonsense. She groaned and ducked past them.

Every time she walked in, she had the same feeling. The shop was a book lover's haven: post and beam construction of honey-hued wood, vaulted ceilings with sweeping picture windows that let the sky inside, and a reading corner by the fireplace in the rear. The main floor housed everything from new fiction releases to local Cape Cod history. Display tables dotted the hardwood floors with breezy summer releases, coastal cookbooks, and lifestyle titles. Up the winding wooden staircase was a loft filled with children's literature. Just outside and across the porch was a children's annex ripe with picture books and colorful toys connected to the main building. Piper poured herself a cup of coffee, grabbed a new summer title off the first display table she passed, and made a beeline for the overstuffed armchair tucked away in the back. *Heaven,* she thought, falling into its cushioned recess.

Beside her, an older woman was checking out the display of knitting books, picking one up and running her hand over its smooth cover. Then putting it down and doing the same to the next. Piper didn't blame her. It was hard not to do that to every single one.

She examined the book she'd picked. It featured a summer cottage surrounded by hydrangea, a soothing palette of blues and lavenders. According to the jacket it was about a family coming together for a reunion at the shore, which made her snort. She determined to stay put and read a few pages, to soak in the needed peace and quiet of the bookstore, but no sooner had she opened the cover than her phone dinged. It was him.

On Cape, Derek texted. *Can't stop thinking of*

you. Piper fell back into her chair with a surge of glee. Followed by shame. How was it that he could undo her so easily with a scant offering of seven words after days of silence. Oh, but those words!

She glanced around the shop, suddenly on edge. Derek's family could be among any of these people.

She'd never laid eyes on his children. They were a subject he did not often broach, and the limited responses he'd given when asked were clear indication that they were a part of his life he did not wish to include her in. In the beginning she'd asked about them with the same keenness one has to learn anything and everything about your new lover, trying to scrounge up the pieces that made up who this person was and what fit them together. Derek had loosened up since then, remarking on one story or another about the kids from time to time: something funny that Ryder said when he'd driven him to school that morning, or a proud comment about Lydia reading the entire Little House series over one summer. On those occasions she felt it was an invitation of sorts. She tread carefully though, limiting her questions about them lest the mention of the children stir up feelings of guilt about what he was doing. Away from his family. Away with *her.*

There were times she'd screwed up royally.

Like the Saturday they planned to meet for coffee last spring. He'd warned her in advance that it would be a quick visit because his daughter Lydia was having her eighth birthday party that afternoon. Things had been going well between them, and Piper found herself caught up in the break of winter weather, the excitement she had for Derek and how hard he seemed to be working to get together with her more often. She hadn't planned to do it, but on the way to the coffee shop she passed a toy store. The excitement she'd felt picking out a gift for Lydia was tangible. Derek had said she liked to draw, that horses were her favorite animal. She'd found the cutest dapple gray plush pony on a shelf in the window. It was perfect. It only made sense to pick up the metal tin of artist colored pencils, as well. They were a splurge, but she could picture the appreciation on Derek's face when he saw them. It was a gift to him, too. And it showed that she listened when he talked about the children, that she cared. In that spirit she'd grabbed a large sketchbook, too. The woman at the cash register tucked each item lovingly into a striped bag. When she walked into the coffee shop and set gift bag with the frilly pink bow on the table between them, Derek had looked confused. "What's this?" he'd asked.

Piper beamed. "Just a little something I picked out for Lydia."

He did not peek into the bag. So she opened it

for him. "Look! I found the sweetest little pony. I hope she likes it. Oh, and I remember you said she likes to draw." She'd reached inside the tissue-paper depths to pull out the stuffed animal.

The look on his face was not what she'd expected. "What's wrong?"

Derek was staring at the bag. He ran his hands through his hair. "Piper. What am I supposed to do with this?"

Her excitement drained. "Give it to her?"

"And who am I supposed to tell her it's from when she asks?" He sounded angry now.

"I don't know. I guess I didn't think about that part."

Derek was shaking his head. "That's right. You didn't think."

Now it was her turn to get angry. "What I was thinking was that she'd like the pony. You said she likes drawing and coloring." She grabbed the bag and shoved it under the table. "Never mind."

Derek leaned across the table, his expression softening. "I'm sorry. You're right, she would like all of those things. What little girl wouldn't? But Piper, this would confuse her. She doesn't know you. And I don't want to have to lie about who it's from."

Piper concentrated on the space over Derek's head, on the sign above the coffee counter that listed the menu. *Mocha latte. Spiced chai latte.* Tears pressed at the corner of her eyes. She'd humiliated herself enough already, she would not let him see her cry. "I'll return it," she said under her breath.

Derek apologized. He explained his point, which now that he said it did make sense to her. It had been a sweet gesture, and he was sorry he couldn't accept the gift, but what would he tell Lydia? Or his wife?

Somehow, they'd recovered. She tried to listen as he switched the subject. She tried to taste the sweet vanilla in her coffee that he brought her moments later. But all through their visit, the gift bag hummed beneath the table like a vacuum. She'd been unable to focus on their conversation the rest of the meeting, so aware was she of it. It was as if the very absence of his children had somehow created an awkward presence between them. A part she was not permitted to address, and one that she was denied access to. She understood, of course. There was something sacrilegious about the names of his children coming out of the mouth of his mistress. But it had left her feeling excluded. And stupid. Just another unseen boundary she'd tripped over and fallen on her face in front of him. They were everywhere, these emotional minefields.

Now, she looked around the store at all the faces coming and going. What would she do if she bumped into Derek and his family? A few days ago, he'd let her walk out on him without even trying to come after her. Her roommates had declared she couldn't stay there anymore, and she'd packed everything she had and driven home. She'd spent every night since crying herself to sleep, too stubborn to contact him but simultaneously wondering if this meant they were really through. Now Derek was on the Cape. And texting her that he couldn't stop thinking about her.

She hopped up and hurried to the front of the store, returning the book to its table before ducking out the bookstore door. It didn't matter that she was minding her own business. Or that she was surrounded by tourists who knew nothing about her. Piper suddenly felt like she was hiding out in her own hometown. She pulled her baseball hat low over her eyes. All she was missing was a scarlet letter on the front.

Twenty-Six

Shannon

"Are you excited for the Hooker's Ball?" Lindy asked.

Shannon had called ahead before stopping by. It was one thing to say that you didn't want to see your estranged father when he came back. It was another to make that happen. Since her mother had lost her mind and agreed to host a "welcome home!" dinner party, she wasn't sure what to expect anymore. For all she knew, if she pulled in unannounced she'd find Caleb kicking back on the porch swing with a couple of beers. But Lindy had assured her neither was true. Shannon did not ask how Caleb was. But she did inquire about how her mother felt. It was not every day you hosted a dinner for your missing husband with your new husband and two of your three offspring.

The dinner had been *fine,* Lindy said. *Though, of course, she was missed. Was Shannon having second thoughts about seeing her father?*

No, Shannon *was not.*

Shannon sat on the front steps watching her mother weed the garden beds on either side. She

292

knew she should offer to help, but she was in a blush-colored blouse and her white AG cigarette pants for the office. There was no way she was getting into the dirt. "Bitsy bought two tables this year for the agency. You and Hank should come and sit with us."

"Don't forget your grandmother."

Beverly was arriving the next day. Lindy tossed a soil-clodded root into the basket and wiped the back of a gloved hand across her forehead. "I believe her exact words were, 'You need to dance through this. Or at the very least, drink.'"

Shannon laughed. "The Ball? Or Caleb's visit?"

"You know your grandmother. Both."

Beverly's arrival each year was something the three Bailey sisters looked forward to. It was one of the rare times Piper would agree to come home, though she usually timed it for the day their grandmother arrived and left the same day she did. "What's going on with Piper?" Shannon asked. "She came early and she's still here."

"I wish I knew," Lindy said. Shannon watched as she dug her trowel deep into the soil. "She seems to have a lot on her plate. Her father, her mysterious new relationship, her job."

"She has a job?"

Lindy looked sideways at her. "She will. You forget how hard it was when you graduated from school."

"Mom. Please."

"Please what?"

"I graduated in four years. Then did two-years' worth of grad school in half the time. Then landed a job before I walked for graduation. Piper has been in school for eight years on and off. With three unrelated degrees to show for it and not a single job to put on her résumé."

"As we are well aware, Shannon."

Shannon didn't mean to badger her mother with it all. They all knew, they were all concerned. But they also seemed to forget how hard she had worked to acquire just as many degrees in half the time. All while working some odd job or other as she put herself through. She couldn't begin to imagine the tens of thousands of dollars of student-loan debt Piper had accrued. "She's coasting, and everybody acts like it's all well and good."

"Maybe you should talk to her, then," Lindy replied. She was bent over the flowerbed; her face was shaded by her floppy straw hat, but Shannon knew the look that was on it.

There was a growing rattling sound, and they both looked up as Piper swerved into the gravel driveway. "Speak of the devil," Lindy said. The brakes on the ancient Prius squeaked.

"You need to get that thing fixed," Shannon said, as Piper stepped out.

She had a foul look on her face. "It's just the muffler."

"Just the muffler? You sound like a motorcycle gang coming up School Street." Shannon looked at her mother to echo the sentiment, but Lindy was distracted by something else.

"What's wrong, honey?" she asked.

Piper slammed the car door and trudged up the walkway. "Nothing."

"We were just talking about the Hooker's Ball. Shannon said we can all sit at the Whitcomb Group table."

Shannon threw her mother a look. "Well, hang on—I'll have to check with Bitsy first. I mean, she buys a group table each year. But I don't think she intends for me to fill it with every member of my family."

Piper halted on the walkway. "Relax, Shan. I don't have any intention of taking up space at your royal family table."

This was disappointing news to Lindy, however. "And why not?"

"Mom." Shannon interjected. "You heard her. She doesn't want to go."

Piper stopped on the bottom step and waited for Shannon to scoot over so she could pass. "I didn't say that."

"Well, do you want to go?"

"I'm undecided."

Shannon gazed back at her little sister. Her strawberry-blonde hair was springing out at all directions from beneath a worn baseball hat. Her denim shorts were too short. Shannon probably would've mustered sympathy for her if only she weren't so infuriating. "Please decide soon." She inched over and let her by. "On something," she added.

The screen door creaked then slapped shut behind Piper. "I heard that."

Lindy was watching Shannon with a mix of maternal impatience and concern. "How about you inquire about the table and let me know?"

"I'm heading to the office now. I'll ask. But you know Bitsy. This is a work event for her, and I'm not sure a Bailey family table will go over well."

Lindy pulled her gloves off and took a long drink of water. "We can always get another table, I suppose."

Shannon didn't want that either. It would certainly be preferable to sit with her mother and Hank than Bitsy alone. They were good at keeping the conversation light and fun. Even if it meant Piper coming along. Though she'd have to check in on her dress choice. The last time the family had all gone, Piper had shown up in a figure-hugging off-the-shoulder number that her derriere practically hung out of, causing almost every man to do a double take and every woman to wince. The fact that she'd done shots at the open bar with the guest speaker before he addressed the attendees had not improved the evening. "I'll let you know. I have to get to work. You know that Ridgevale listing that Bitsy handed off to a professional film crew?"

"The one you'd wanted?"

"Yes. Well, it turns out they didn't even show up at their scheduled time. The owner is not happy. We have a meeting with him this afternoon."

"So, who's going to photograph the property?"

"Funny thing. Bitsy is dumping it in my lap now."

Lindy set down her trowel. "Honey, I'm glad for you! You wanted this, right?"

"Mom, I'm runner-up. Second choice. Who now has to save the day."

Lindy shook her head. "Who now has an opportunity. Grab it. Shake it up and put your stamp on it."

Her mother was right, but Shannon just couldn't see it that way. It felt like no matter how hard she worked or how reliable she proved herself to be, she was forever swooping in and doing damage control. "I've got to run. I want to work on some concept ideas. We've got little time and a demanding seller." Shannon hurried down the steps to her car.

"Shannon?" Lindy called to her.

She turned around.

"You know, you can always change your mind. It might be a good thing."

Shannon hesitated. Her mother wasn't talking about work or the Hookers Ball. "I've spent my whole life doing what's good. For everybody else."

Lindy's face softened. "I know that, honey. I meant for you."

Lindy's words stayed with Shannon as she turned right on Main and then on to Shore Road. Traffic was heavy, and she scooted along the back roads past the golf course on her way to the agency. She'd been so rattled she'd forgotten to stop for coffee.

Reid took one look at her when she walked through the office door and motioned for her to follow him into the back. There was little privacy in the old building, but he shut the door to his small office and pulled her against him. "Talk to me."

Shannon inhaled deeply. Her husband smelled of aftershave and home. "Beverly arrives tomorrow. The dinner party apparently went just fine, without me. And my mother has grand ideas of the whole family coming to the Hooker's Ball and sitting together at your mother's table."

"Wow. You had quite the visit."

She pulled away and tossed her purse in his chair, but she was smiling. "And your mother has yet to reply to my email concerning the photo shoot for the Ridgevale property."

"About that! I have news. Banks wants to meet you."

"When?" Finally some progress.

"Today. At two. My mother asked me to pass on the message."

Shannon tsked. "She couldn't email me, herself? What if I wasn't free at two?" This was typical Bitsy.

Reid crossed him arms. "Well, she originally asked for noon. But I told her you were busy."

Shannon glanced at her watch. It was only eleven thirty. "Why would you do that? I'm free now. I can still make it if I get back to her." She pulled out her phone, but Reid gently took it from her hand.

"Because you're not free. You have a lunch date. With me."

Lunch was not such a terrible idea, after all. Reid had made a reservation at Impudent Oyster, something they used to do all the time but hadn't in ages. Afterward, he walked her to her car and held open the driver door. He'd taken her in his arms and pressed his chest against hers, holding on for a moment. "What are you doing? I can't be late."

He pulled tighter. "Just breathe."

There they were in the middle of town, in the rear lot by Kate Gould Park. But Shannon did as she was told. She felt the warmth of her husband's chest, the tightness of his arms around her. "I'm proud of you," he said. "I know this week has asked a lot of you."

Her mind ticked through it all. "George started sailing camp. Our baby is now out on the water."

"And doing great," Reid whispered in her hair.

"And your mother gave that job to some outside crew who didn't even show up."

"But now it's yours," he reminded her.

"Yes, but now I need to get over there. I need to kill this shoot. The seller is a notorious pain in the ass." She thought a minute. "And Piper's home, and Wren has her grand opening coming. And now my grandmother's coming home." She let out all her breath and let the full weight of her body lean into Reid.

"As did your father."

She stiffened. "That doesn't change anything."

Reid pulled back and looked at her. "Doesn't it? Shannon, maybe we need to think more about this. Do you want to at least see him once before he leaves? Do we want the kids to meet him?"

Shannon blinked in the bright afternoon sun. She wished she hadn't left her sunglasses in the car. She really needed to get over to the Ridgevale House. And she really did not want to talk about her father. She felt the tightness in her shoulders creeping back. Another mimosa would have really done the trick.

"I've got to get over to the house," she said,

shielding her eyes. She kissed Reid quickly on the lips.

"Shannon." The look of longing in his eyes had vanished.

"I'll be home by four. Scallops for dinner?"

As she watched Reid walk back to his car, she couldn't help but feel empty. Her husband had surprised her and taken her to a lovely lunch. She was heading to a photo gig she should've been excited about. Piper was home, and Beverly was soon to be. That should've been enough. Why did everything have to circle back to her father? Every time she interacted with any one of her family, she seemed to say or do the wrong thing. Despite how hard she worked, here she was disappointing everyone anyway. She threw the car in drive.

Everett Banks let them in with a curt nod. Bitsy followed his brisk lead through the foyer, but Shannon lingered. Light greeted her immediately in the living area, streaming from the rear of the house, which overlooked the water. Her heels clicked on the hardwood floors, and she paused in the center of the living room, taking it all in. The furniture was an unassuming beach palate of contrasts: white upholstery, dark wood accents, jute rugs. The back of the house showcased the home's best feature: an endless stretch of dune and water and sky.

"Let's review the contract in the kitchen,"

he said, and Shannon had to pull her attention away from the view to follow. The kitchen was modern and sleek, featuring a celadon-painted kitchen island with a white marble surface. The appliances were stainless steel, chef grade. Off the kitchen was a small breakfast nook with an oak pedestal table surrounded by caned chairs. Simple, tasteful. They sat and Bitsy went through the vision they'd put together for the print.

"If I go with your agency, I want high-quality full-size brochures," he said. "Card-stock-like material."

Bitsy assured him they would provide as such. He turned to Shannon abruptly. "You've seen the house. So?"

Shannon cleared her throat. She'd planned her sell for days. "Your best selling point is your view."

Everett gazed out the window at it now. "Damn right. But that's obvious."

This was not going the way she'd hoped. "With the view in mind, I want to photograph the house in a way that lets the ocean inside."

Everett Banks stared through her.

She stood and moved toward the large sliders against the far wall. "From what I can tell, every room in this house has some sort of vantage point to the beach. If I shoot the rooms with the view from the windows highlighted, it's going to drive home the notion of your prime location. And the natural light will make the space large and bright."

"That's well and good. But it's not just location. What about the custom touches?" He jabbed a finger in the direction of the living room. "The vaulted ceiling? The beams and built-ins? Brazilian cherry. Hand-hewn."

Bitsy had been studying Everett as Shannon spoke, but now she turned to Shannon. "Give him an example."

Shannon groaned inwardly. That was the thing about visions—you couldn't explain them until they were formed, and although she knew this would be a hard sell, Shannon hadn't seen enough of the house yet to get this specific.

"Go on," Bitsy said, her lips pressed together. "We're all ears."

"Right, of course." Shannon stood and headed for the living room, just off the kitchen. To her dismay they followed. She scanned the room for an obvious feature, her eyes roaming over the custom floor-to-ceiling built-ins flanking the fieldstone fireplace.

She was about to mention the contrast of materials used, and how effectively that would show in the photographs, when Everett interrupted. "What I was thinking you should do is . . ."

Relieved to have bought some time, Shannon feigned an interested expression, while glancing surreptitiously around the room. Custom book-shelves. Fieldstone fireplace. Wide plank hard-woods. But then her eyes landed on the framed print over the mantle.

She strode up to it, her heart in her throat. It was an original. Unlike the photographs Caleb had printed in both limited and mass editions, this was the only copy. The photograph was of a red sunset taken at the foot of Ridgevale Beach bridge. The wooden railings arched out and away, seemingly leading the viewer over the wooden bridge to the expanse of sand on the other side. Overhead the sky slashed the sea with fiery strokes. It was the lone figure midway across the bridge that made her breath catch. A little girl in a white smock dress, her back to the lens. One arm raised as she pointed to the burning sky.

Bitsy and Everett had stopped talking, and Shannon became aware that they were watching her with curiosity.

"Is everything all right, dear?" There was nothing *dear* about Bitsy's tone. She was annoyed that she'd strayed from the conversation.

Everett Banks came to stand beside her. "He's a local. At least he was," he informed her. "I bought that off him when we first moved here."

Bitsy joined them reluctantly. Shannon could feel her impatient energy behind her. "How nice." Clearly, she hadn't looked at the artist's name.

Everett wasn't done, however. "My wife had a fit when she heard what I paid for it. But that little girl. She reminded me of my own."

Shannon nodded. "The little girl in that photo is seven years old."

"No, I'm pretty sure the photographer said six."

It was one thing to walk away from a conversation with a client. It was another entirely to correct him, in his own home no less. "I'm sure you're right," Bitsy said to Everett, glaring at Shannon out of the corner of her eye.

Shannon stepped closer to the picture. She remembered the day. The sky had gone blood-orange as they were grocery shopping in town, and her father had driven too fast down Main Street, trying to make it in time. She hadn't been wearing a seatbelt and she'd slid off the seat of the VW Bug as he turned down Ridgevale. When he came to a halt at the lot, she'd leapt out of the car and followed him to the beach. It seemed like forever that he stood, turning this way and that, his camera clicking again and again. She'd grown bored and walked down beneath the bridge to search for fiddler crabs. That was where she'd found the stick.

"I wouldn't have bought it if she weren't six. That was the point. It was a gift to my wife on our daughter's sixth birthday."

Shannon didn't care about Everett Banks's wife, or what he thought he'd been told. Caleb wouldn't have said otherwise just to make a sale.

"That's a lovely story," she said turning to face him now. "I hope it doesn't change the joy you've had in the piece; but with all due respect, I happen to know the little girl in that photograph is seven."

"Excuse me," Bitsy interrupted, her cheeks flushed. "But we should really sit down and review the contract."

Everett Banks was not used to having people disagree with him. Although he was clearly annoyed, he was also intrigued by this woman standing in his house telling him about his art-work. "You speak quite confidently about a piece of work I purchased directly from the artist himself. May I ask how you are so sure of yourself?"

"Simple," Shannon said. "That little girl is me."

Twenty-Seven

Wren

The grand opening was tomorrow night, but instead of putting finishing touches on the shop, she was home in her kitchen. "I'm so sorry. Potato pancakes seemed like such a good idea at the time."

Ari peered between two mounds of grated potatoes and peels from her station at the kitchen island. She plunked the grater down and paused to shake out her hand.

"But it looks like you're almost done?" Wren asked hopefully.

Ari blew a lock of hair off her forehead out of the corner of her mouth and nodded toward the floor. There was still a large bag of potatoes to go.

"Crap."

"Yeah," Ari said.

Wren looked doubtfully at the colander of fresh scallops in the sink. She'd run to the Chatham Fish Pier first thing that morning, but despite their early start she still had to pat them dry, slice them, and dredge them in flour, before combining them with the potatoes and eggs to fry them. All that was just for one recipe. There were three others to go. "We need more help."

She'd tried to keep the menu simple. Fried scallop and leek potato pancakes with sour cream dipping sauce, tiny paper cups of clam chowder, baked pita chips with red onion jam, and an assortment of artisanal cheeses and crackers from Chatham Cheese Company. She'd even dug up a recipe for a frothy Cape Cod cranberry champagne punch that Lindy used to serve on New Year's Eve. In line with her store motto she'd stayed true to local food. What she needed now was local help.

"Is there someone you can call?" Wren had never seen the girl balk at any shop task, but right now Ari looked desperate. The kitchen was filled with steam and heat from simmering pans on the stove top, and her hair was stuck to her head. Both of their eyes were rimmed red from slicing three pounds of onions for the jam recipe. Two pans of it simmered on the stove. The whole place positively reeked of balsamic vinegar.

"God. I'm turning this into a sweatshop, aren't I?" Wren left the fishy-smelling scallops in the sink and surveyed the damage. The onion jam needed to be reduced, cooled, and jarred for transport. Someone had to pick up the cheese platters at Chatham Cheese. Leeks needed to be cut, and potatoes grated. She couldn't even locate the ingredients for the dipping sauce. "We need backup."

The back door opened, and Lucy came in with her favorite Buff Orpington chicken tucked in her arms. Badger followed.

It wasn't the help Ari had in mind. "Wow. A chicken? In the kitchen?"

If Ari didn't think she was nuts already, Wren figured she did now. "Lucy honey, we can't have a chicken in the house. We're making food for the opening."

"I know." To Ari's dismay, Lucy marched up to the island to inspect her work. "Henrietta loves potatoes. Got extra?"

Ari blinked. Henrietta let out a soft purring noise.

Wren didn't have time for this. "Not now, Luce. Please put the chicken back."

"Can I help?" Lucy asked.

"I would love that, but we're grating and cutting. I don't want you to hurt yourself."

Lucy scowled. "I know how to cut. Hey, we could do a cooking show like we used to!"

Wren felt bad, but this wasn't a day for pulling out mixing bowls and making a good mess together in the kitchen. Lucy's favorite was baking. She'd push a chair right up to the counter and climb up on it. In an authoritative voice, imitating the Food Network stars, she'd explain the recipe to Badger. Wren and Lucy used to cook together all the time. Though to be honest, Wren couldn't remember the last time they had. This year she'd bought a cake for Lucy's birthday, in April, and last Christmas Lindy had taken over the gingerbread house and invited Lucy to her place, because Wren was away at a jewelry show. She knelt down. "How about you come back in an hour and you can help me package the potato pancakes?"

"An hour?" Lucy's shoulders slumped. "What do I do until then?"

Wren mustered the last of her patience. "How about you and the chickens do a cooking show outside? You can invent a bug-and-flower recipe. The girls will go wild!"

"No, I already played school with them. They're bored." Lucy let out an exasperated breath and headed back outdoors with her chicken.

Wren noticed Ari had retrieved ice from the freezer and was wrapping her hand in a dish-towel. "Oh no. It hurts that badly?"

She shrugged. "Just need a break from the grater. It'll be fine."

Who could she call? Lindy had been cleaning the house for days. She always got overwhelmed and went underground before Beverly's visits, and the timing couldn't have been worse this summer. Shannon had mentioned a photo shoot she was doing for a listing. Piper!

Lucy tromped back inside, chicken-free but

this time with Badger. "Wash your hands," Wren reminded. She took the onion pan off the stove, gave it a stir, and set it aside to cool. "I'm going to call my sister."

Ari brightened. "Is she a good cook, too?"

Wren appreciated that Ari seemed to think she possessed kitchen skills, but she couldn't say the same for Piper. "She doesn't really cook," she admitted (*or take directions,* she thought to herself), "but we'll put her to work."

Hell, she'd offer to pay her if that's what it took. If she could only find her damn phone. She began shoving the piles of produce and spice jars aside. "Where's my phone?"

Ari cleared her throat politely and pointed. There in the living room was Lucy playing on it.

"Luce, honey. I need my phone to call Auntie Piper."

"You told me to do something else. So, I'm playing *Mermaid Salon.*"

"Lucy. Now!" Wren hadn't meant to snap. Lucy popped up off the couch and stalked into the kitchen, a sour look on her face. "You can use it when I'm done. This is for . . ."

Lucy turned on her heel. "For the shop. I know, I know."

Badger glanced worriedly at Wren. "What, you too?" As if in reply he turned and trotted upstairs after Lucy.

To further dismay, Piper didn't answer. Wren

tried texting her, but she didn't reply to that either.

"No luck?" Ari asked.

"Not giving up yet." Wren went out to the front of the house where a light breeze was coming through the screen door. She tried her sister's number again. This time she left a message. "Pipe, it's me. Please call back. It's an emergency."

"What's the emergency?"

Wren looked up. There, at the bottom of the porch steps, was Piper. And their father.

Her dad held up a bag. "Bagel?"

Soon the downstairs of Wren's house had turned into a commercial kitchen. Piper took over the potatoes and Ari went to work on the sauces. Wren mixed the pancakes.

"Got an apron?" her dad asked.

Wren eyed him curiously as she retrieved one from the closet.

"I used to make some mean pancakes, if you recall."

It was a strange feeling watching her father man the stove, spooning small circles of the mix onto the pans.

"You want to keep them small," Wren said peering over his shoulder. "And get them good and brown before flipping, or they'll break."

"Oh, and don't forget to use vegetable oil," Ari

said, placing the wrinkled recipe on the counter next to him. "The butter burns."

Caleb fielded the directives good-naturedly; in fact, if Wren had to bet, he was rather enjoying himself. Piper did not fare as well: she nicked her knuckles several times. Wren pretended not to hear when she held out her bowl of grated potatoes and announced, "Don't worry. I pulled the bloody bits out."

They worked their way through the menu list, taking turns at the stations. The kitchen island was designated for cutting and prepping. The stove became the fry station. At one point, Caleb suggested it would go faster if they had more pans. "Does your mom still have that oversized iron skillet?"

Wren winced. The casual reference to both her mom and the once-shared skillet made her flinch, but she decided it was no more crazy than the hodgepodge of people filling her kitchen. Ari made the sauces and jarred the onion jam for transport.

Curious about the new voices in the kitchen, Lucy reappeared downstairs.

"Well, well," Caleb said from his post at the stove. He waved the spatula in greeting, which elicited a giggle. "Want to help?"

"Mom doesn't want me to."

Wren sighed. "Honey, that's not what I meant."

"I know how to cook," Lucy said, crossing her arms.

"Is that so?" Caleb glanced between the two. "Well, Mom knows best. But now that she's put me to work, maybe you can help me out?"

Lucy glanced at her mother. "She said it was dangerous."

"Dangerous?" Caleb bellowed playfully. "The only thing dangerous is that dog." He pointed at Badger, who thumped his tail. "Looks like a fierce beggar."

This delighted Lucy. "Oh, he is! The fiercest of them all."

Before Wren could blink, the chair was pushed up along the stove and Lucy was leaning against her grandfather, helping to spoon out the mix. "This okay?" Caleb mouthed.

While they worked pouring and flipping, Lucy talked nonstop. About school and cooking and the beach and Badger and the little boy next door who spit too much but was okay to ride bikes with. Caleb took it all in with great attention, and Wren marveled at the instant bond. Here was her usually shy girl completely at ease with a man who until yesterday was a stranger. It was the only natural thing that had happened since Caleb Bailey's return. Before Wren headed out to the Chatham Cheese company to pick up platters, the last thing she heard Lucy say was, "I don't have a dad." Followed by, "Do you like chickens?"

By late afternoon, when everything was prepped, they organized the food into aluminum containers and trays. By four o'clock even the sink was empty, and the dishes put away. Lucy took Caleb by the hand and led him out to the backyard to introduce him to the chickens.

Wren pulled her greasy flour-covered apron over her head and tossed it on the counter.

"So, are we . . .?" Ari asked.

"Done," Wren assured her. "I can't thank you enough." The store had already been set up yesterday. They'd strung white lights around the front window and hung paper lanterns throughout the store. A small table in the back was set up with platters that would later be filled with all the food they'd made.

Ari pulled her patchwork messenger bag over her shoulder. "See you tomorrow, then."

Wren poured two glasses of iced tea and collapsed into one of the kitchen chairs opposite Piper. "You guys showed up at exactly the right time. You saved me."

"It was fine." Piper held up her knuckles. "Band-Aids and all. I think this is the most fun Dad has had since he came back."

Wren glanced out the window. They were standing by the coop, and Lucy was trying to hand Caleb their silver-laced Wyandotte, Clementine. Clementine wasn't having it. She flapped her wings and flew out of his reach. "Yeah, how about that?" she said.

"Dad and I wanted to come by the shop with breakfast. But when you weren't there, I figured we'd pop over here. Hope that was okay?"

If someone had asked her if having Caleb pop over to cook for her open house was a good idea, Wren would've put the kibosh on the idea immediately. Piper was famous in the family for her ill-thought-out ideas, and it was something they usually gave her a hard time about. But today Wren felt suddenly grateful to her little sister. Sometimes spontaneity was just what you needed. "Listen, I know you're looking for work. I want to pay you for your help today."

Piper sipped her tea thoughtfully. "I have a better idea."

"Oh?"

"Give me a job."

Wren laughed. "At the shop? Pipe, it hasn't even opened yet. And I've already got Ari."

"Just hear me out. I'm not going back to Boston for a while. And I'll do whatever you need. Sales. Cleaning. Advertising. Babysitting. Think of the time it would give you with Lucy."

Wren felt Piper's dilemma, but this was not something she could rescue her from. "I'd love to help you out, but I don't have extra funds. Everything I have I put into the shop. God, I don't even know if I can afford Ari yet." A loud shriek of laughter came through the window and Wren glanced outside at Lucy. She'd been so happy to be included in the kitchen work that afternoon. God, she couldn't remember the last time she'd done anything just the two of them.

"I hear you," Piper said. "It was just a thought."

"Piper, what you need is a real job. As in a career. Not babysitting or filling in for me."

Piper nodded, slowly. "I know. I've got to figure my shit out." She pressed her fingers to the pink line on her forehead as she spoke.

It was an absentminded gesture of anxiety, something she'd done since she was a little girl, but seeing her worry the scar touched Wren. She looked outside again, at her father and Lucy. "But maybe we can figure something out for now. Just while I get the shop up and running."

Piper slapped the table. "Really?"

"Don't go getting all excited just yet. But what you said is true: I do need more time with Lucy. Let me think about it, okay?"

As it was, the schedule being shared just between the two of them required Wren to be there almost every day. And what if she or Ari was sick? She couldn't close the shop, especially during the summer tourist season. They were scheduled to be opened six days a week as it was. It would be a huge relief to have someone else on board. The question was, could she afford to hire her?

• • •

No sooner had the door shut behind Piper and Caleb, and she'd wiped down the countertops one last time, did the phone ring. All Wren wanted to do was collapse on the couch with Lucy.

Wren picked it up. "Hello?"

"Ah, finally. Hello, this is Alice."

Wren paused. She didn't know any Alice.

"Your father's friend in Arizona?"

"Oh." A strange feeling rose in Wren's throat. She did not know who Alice was, but she did not want to find out.

"I'm just calling to see how my boy is doing. You girls treating him all right up there?" Alice's voice was melodious, velvety. And assuming. Wren prickled. Who did this woman think she was?

"We're treating him just *fine.*"

Alice hesitated. "I was worried about him. There are some things you should probably know . . ."

Wren interrupted. She did not need to be told anything about her father from this strange woman. "Well you needn't be. He's home now. With us." Before Alice could say anything more, Wren thanked her and hung up.

The phone rang again, startling her, but to her relief it was Shannon. "Tomorrow's the big day! How're we feeling?"

She decided not to mention the nosy woman from Arizona. Whatever life Caleb led down there without them, Wren really did not want to know about it. But Shannon was already plowing on. "I know you said you want to do this by yourself, but these kinds of events can quickly become overwhelming. I've got that great caterer that Reid and I use for our parties. Remember our midsummer night party last year? It's last minute, but I could call her if you need food supplements or serving ideas."

"Thanks, but the menu is done. Ari came by today, and then Piper surprised me with Dad. It took forever, but I think we're good to go."

"Did you say Dad came over?"

Wren knew the news would not be welcome, but she was not about to tiptoe or lie. "I didn't know they were coming, but it turned out they were a big help. You should've seen it. Dad made the potato cakes with Lucy at the stove."

Shannon was quiet for a moment. "Well, that must've been interesting."

"It was. I wish you'd been here, too."

"Yeah, well. I guess that leads me to my next question. Is he going to be there tomorrow at the opening?"

Wren sucked in her breath. "Good question." *This* was what she'd been most worried about. It wasn't the event itself. It wasn't the business anxiety that had trickled through her mind all winter as she rounded up store inventory: *What if no one likes this stuff? What if it doesn't sell?* Those all would've been worry enough for any entrepreneurial businesswoman and single mom. Instead, her family was the ever-present wild card.

As she'd learned over the years within a family of mostly women, no amount of preparation could fortify the best-laid plans against one curveball comment from a relative. No matter how close you were or how hard you loved, family drama could dismantle your biggest day in the shortest time. And now, with her father home, Beverly on the way, and all three sisters back in town again, the air was ripe for a storm. What better time for it to break than on her grand opening?

"He wants to come, and I would like him to be there. The only question mark is you."

Shannon scoffed. "Oh, so now I'm the question mark?"

Wren closed her eyes and leaned against the fridge. They were all entitled to handle this in their own way, but now lines were being drawn in the sand. Lines that put family members on one side or the other. "So you'd miss my grand opening just to avoid seeing Dad?"

"What choice do I have? You know how I feel, and yet you're inviting him."

That wasn't exactly true. Wren hadn't planned this. Just as she hadn't planned his return, or his showing up in her kitchen and acting like a grandparent. She hadn't been sure if she was comfortable with any of it, but now that things were unfolding, she had to admit she was kind of liking it. "Shannon, I don't want to choose, but if you're going to boycott the show because of his presence, then I'll tell him to stay home. It's more important to me that you're there." Wren didn't want this, but she wanted her sister there. After all, Shannon had been there for her all along.

"I'm a big girl, Wren. You don't have to un-invite him on my account."

"No, I want you there. I just didn't want him to feel excluded."

Shannon's voice was as steady as a talk-show host, but Wren heard the anger. She might have been able to mask her feelings from everyone else, but she wasn't fooling her sister. "Listen to what you're saying. He chose to exclude himself from us for twenty-three years. During which, may I remind you, I was there for every need you and Piper had."

Wren felt her throat tighten. "I know! I was there, too, Shannon. Which you seem to forget."

The line went dead, and Wren chucked the phone across the kitchen. It hit the floor with a crack and skidded into the living area, stopping at Lucy's feet. She looked down at it, then up at Wren, her eyes wide. "Mama?"

Lucy pointed to the broken phone. The batteries had come out of the back and were rolling across the floor. "You dropped it?"

Wren went to her and scooped her up into a hug. "No honey. I lost my temper, and I'm sorry."

Lucy pulled back and examined her mother's face warily. Staring back at her big brown eyes, it was all Wren could do not to cry. "It's okay, Mama."

Forget the shop, forget her father and Shannon and all the rest of them. In that moment Wren hated herself. She hated her temper. She hated all the hours she'd been spending away from Lucy, who needed her, and yet whom she was failing right here right now on this rare afternoon she was actually home.

"Are you mad?" Lucy asked.

"Not anymore, and certainly not at you. Mommy is just tired from work these days. But don't worry, because you know what?"

"What?"

"The store opens tomorrow, and then we'll have the whole summer together. You can come to work with me any day you want. And we'll spend our afternoons at the beach together, just us."

All she'd wanted was to show her daughter that she could do this: she could start a business and run it and be a good mother. Even if it meant doing it all by herself. But instead she was showing her that it was stressful and hard and that it took you away from the ones you loved.

Lucy leaned against her. "Can we go to Ridgevale Beach? I want to bring my net."

"Because you like catching all those hermit crabs don't you? We need to get you a new bucket."

"And a shovel, so I can build a tall wall so they don't escape."

Wren laughed sadly. She had no idea how she could make any of what she'd just promised happen. The truth was she was only going to get busier, if the shop was successful at all. But how many more summers did she have left with her little girl? How could she, as a single mom, say no when her child asked her to take her to the beach and catch hermit crabs? She did not want Lucy to have the regrets she did as a child. She'd have to find a way to balance better. There was no other choice.

Twenty-Eight

Hank

Beverly was one of his most favorite people. She was elegant and articulate. She was meticulously put together, one of the only people he knew who still carried a monogrammed hand-kerchief. And she was a battle ax.

No sooner had she arrived at the house did she have a recommendation. Beverly was noted for her recommendations. "Why don't you let that poor dog be a dog?"

Lindy was leaning over Bowser's dog bed on the floor, gently rotating his hind leg in a circular motion. "Mother, he just had major surgery. Part of his physical therapy is to manipulate his muscles and tendons."

"Physical therapy for pets. What will they think of next?"

Lindy forced a smile and moved on to the next leg. "It's good for him. This exercise is called 'bicycling.' I have to do it to him three times a day."

Beverly set her teacup down. "Hank, dear. When was the last time she 'bicycled' you?"

Hank leapt to his feet, his cheeks flushed

deeply. "Anybody need me to run out and pick something up?" He'd already been to the grocery store and the fish market. He'd asked about picking up more wine. Surely someone needed some obscure prescription filled. He'd be delighted to drive all the way to Hyannis for it.

Thankfully Piper picked that moment to walk through the front door. She'd been the only Bailey girl to have seen Beverly yet, and Hank was thinking now would be a great time for the others to follow her in. She threw her purse on the kitchen island. "I got a job!"

Beverly beamed. "Do tell."

Despite his opportunity for a clear exit from the kitchen, he lingered. Hank had been wondering about this very matter. He did not like to pry. The girls got enough of that from their mother, whom he did not blame, but he'd learned that the less he asked any of them the more they shared. Still, Piper was home with every box of stuff she'd taken out of the house three summers earlier when she went to Boston for grad school, and then some. He knew because he'd helped her unload her car a couple of days earlier. She'd been parking over to the side of the house since returning, and he hadn't understood why until he happened to walk by. Piper's things filled the back seat all the way up to the ceiling, and his first thought had been *How does she see anything out the back?* Until his second thought clicked with realization. He'd found Piper sunning herself in the backyard with a copy of *Vogue* and a beer.

"Have you told your mother?" he'd asked.

"About?"

He motioned for her to follow him out to the front. When they paused in front of her car she slumped. "I'm going to, but things have been a little crazy around here lately."

Hank did not agree or disagree with her assessment. What he did do was offer to help her carry the stuff in. "It's dangerous to drive like that," he said. Piper consented, with what seemed to be a good deal of relief. It didn't hurt that Lindy was also out in town. Together they made at least six trips up and down the stairs to her room. With each one, Piper spilled her guts. "I can't teach, Hank. I just can't do it." Followed by, "My roommates kicked me out. Nicely. But still." And, "Don't worry! I only plan on staying for the summer. I think."

Box after box he lifted and listened, until the last trip up the stairs when it was his turn. "Listen, kiddo. You're right, things have been rather busy here lately."

"Crazy."

Hank blinked. "That, too. But there will be even *more crazy* if your mother finds out from someone other than you."

Piper hugged him. "I know. I will soon."

He certainly hoped so. This was a complication

for him. Hank did not keep secrets from his wife, though there were occasions he was privy to information before she was. If battle lines were drawn, he always backed up his wife. But Piper wasn't a sixteen-year-old caught sneaking a boy up to her room on a summer night. He would give her until the end of the week before he brought it up again.

With this sudden announcement of employment, they gathered around the kitchen table. "Did you hear back from one of the schools in Boston?" Lindy asked.

"Not exactly. It's closer than that."

Lindy looked confused for a moment, then suddenly clapped her hands. "Honey! Did you apply to one of the Cape school districts?"

"It's not for a school."

"Not a teaching position?"

Beverly reached across the table and clasped Piper's hand. "Go on, dear. I haven't many years left."

Piper looked around the table bashfully. "I'm working for Wren! I'm going to help her out at the Fisherman's Daughter."

Hank glanced around the table, taking the temperature of each expression. Lindy looked confused. Beverly was nodding. He wasn't sure what to think.

"But what about teaching? You just finished your degree. You are going to keep looking for a teaching job, right?"

Piper lifted one shoulder. "I don't know, Mom. I'm having second thoughts."

Lindy sat down. "Second thoughts." She glanced suddenly at Hank. "Did you know anything about this?"

"I didn't." He looked at Piper meaningfully.

"No Mom, he only knew about the apartment. And I was waiting to tell you until I figured something out."

Lindy's head swiveled between the two. "What about the apartment?"

"I kind of lost it."

"You lost your apartment?"

"Well, my student loans ran out. And Boston is so expensive. I can't make rent without a job, which I planned to apply for, but I realized this spring during student teaching that it just wasn't for me."

Lindy's voice was almost a whisper. "You realized this spring."

"Yeah. It just seemed easier to come home and get back on my feet. Just for a while!" she added quickly.

Lindy stood abruptly, then sat back down. "Huh."

Hank approached her like one does a wounded animal. "Honey, I'm not sure if you noticed Piper's car when she came home, but after I took one look at it, it occurred to me she might be prolonging her visit. I suggested she discuss this with you."

But she was already moving past him, as if floating. "Three years of graduate school and teaching is not for her." She headed for the front door.

"Sweetheart? Are you all right?"

"Just taking a little walk," she said.

This was not a good sign. Lindy was a woman of colossal contradiction. The more she wanted to yell the quieter she became. She walked when she wanted to slam doors. When livid, her expression went blank.

Hank shadowed her, keeping a slight distance. "I could keep you company on your walk?"

"Best not."

"For just a bit?"

"I wouldn't."

The screen door hushed closed behind her and Hank stood on the other side, watching her sail down the front steps and out onto the street. He had a feeling she'd be gone a while.

When he returned to the kitchen, Piper had made herself scarce. Beverly remained at the table, gazing out the window contentedly. She lifted her teacup to her red lips. "It's so good to be home with the family. Such energy with the young ones under the roof, don't you think?"

Hank managed a small nod.

She sipped her tea. "Now, when do I get to lay eyes on that father of theirs?"

Twenty-Nine

Piper

The proverbial cat was out of the bag. It brought her little relief. Piper checked the text from Derek again. It had come yesterday, but she'd still not replied.

It wasn't that she didn't want to. Her fingers positively ached every time she held the phone and read the message. But what to say?

The truth was there was too much she wanted to say. At first, she felt empowered by the fact that he'd reached out. The ball was in her court: she imagined him checking his own phone, wondering when she'd reply. Missing her. The initial rush of power fueled her to hold out longer.

But that faded, replaced with the simple fact: she missed him. She missed him, and she wanted him back. And here he was, saying the same! But it was impossible. Derek was not available to her. He'd given no indication he would ever leave his wife, and replying to him now would only prolong the hurt. She needed to move on. Regardless of what she said or how she said it, communication was communication. It kept them connected. And the kind of connection she wanted—no, needed—from Derek was not something he could deliver on. Wren's response to her admission had driven home what she already knew to be true. He was married. He had children. The whole thing was wrong. Before she could change her mind, she deleted the message with a swipe and shoved her phone back in her purse. It was time to go to the opening.

She found Hank in the kitchen dressed smartly in Nantucket red chinos and a blue-and-white-checkered shirt. He checked his watch. "We'd better get going," he said to no one in particular.

Beverly and Lindy descended the stairs as one flowy patterned unit. Piper noticed that her grandmother held her mother's hand and Lindy kept the other firmly wrapped around her for support as they made their way slowly down. But despite her cautious progress, Beverly looked anything but frail.

"Grammy, you look gorgeous!"

Beverly fluttered her eyelashes. "This old thing?" For a woman who'd favored tailored clothes in subdued earth tones in her younger years, Beverly had embraced color and movement in what she referred to as her "wiser years." She wore a white buttoned blouse over the turquoise maxi skirt. The effect was fluid and summery, giving her grandmother a watery, Mother Earth feel.

"Is that skirt from the Fisherman's Daughter?"

331

Beverly reached the bottom and ran her hands down the soft folds of fabric. "Wren sent it over for me this morning. Isn't it something?"

Hank could not take his eyes off of Lindy, who was wearing a vintage Pucci shirtdress that all three Bailey girls coveted. It was a hand-me-down from Beverly's closet years ago that she only pulled out for very special summer occasions, and it was a not-so-funny family joke that they would fight each other for it when she tired of it or couldn't fit into it, whichever happened first. So far neither had.

"Are we walking?"

Parking was always a problem downtown, so the location of the house was lucky—they could walk right up to Main. It had been a cooler day and there was a light breeze, making it a beautiful night to walk.

"We're taking Grandma in a car. But you go ahead and we'll meet you. Wren must be frantic with last-minute details."

Crap. Lindy was right, Wren would be frantic and she should be there. Piper grabbed her handbag and took off. She turned left on to Main Street and trotted up the sidewalk, only to find that the rest of the way was bottlenecked. At day's end, people streamed off of the beaches and into town. Downtown Chatham was not the place to be on foot when you were in a rush. "Excuse me," she said, dodging a family coming toward her. She then got stuck behind a young woman with a double stroller who kept stopping to gaze at store windows, *Move over!* A man coming toward her hopped off the sidewalk to let her pass. "Sorry! Thank you!" Wren's shop was just up ahead across the way. Piper had just crossed the street, and was walking head down as she rummaged through her purse for a tube of lip gloss, when she smacked into a man standing outside a shop. Her bag fell to the ground, its contents scattering on the sidewalk. "Oh God. Sorry!" she cried. She popped down and began collecting her things.

The man bent to help her, as did his friend. "Are you all right?"

"Yes, it's my own fault." Her stuff was everywhere. Wallet. Pens. Pieces of paper and receipts. There was the damn lip gloss! She gathered it all up in her hands and stood. "Thank you so much." He handed her bag back to her and it was then she finally looked up at him. Thirtysomething, dark hair, collared shirt. But it was his friend she could feel staring at her who almost made her drop her bag again.

"Piper."

"Derek?"

The man glanced between the two. "You two know each other?"

Derek spoke first. "This is one of my students, Piper Bailey." He looked both surprised and uncomfortable, and the introduction ended there.

"I'm Chad."

"My brother-in-law," Derek added quickly.

Piper shook his hand firmly, trying to keep her own from shaking. "Nice to meet you." She snuck a look at Derek. He looked so handsome in a blue button-down shirt, his face already kissed with a day by the shore. "Enjoying your stay?" she asked.

He was staring at her, and she was relieved to be wearing her pretty white sundress. She stood up a little straighter.

"Uh, yeah. Yeah, Chatham's great." He turned to Chad. "Right?"

"We spent the day at the beach," Chad offered. "What was it . . . Ridgewood?"

"Ridgevale," Piper said. "Best beach for little kids." She looked at Derek as she said this.

"It was! The kids loved those tidal pools under the bridge. Tons of hermit crabs."

"Piper lives here," Derek said.

"Really? Lucky you. Say, where can we find a sandwich shop? Someone said it was down here somewhere?"

She pointed up the road. "Yeah, just ahead on your left. Jo Mamas."

Chad was gazing down the street looking around, and Derek risked a smile at her. A sweet boyish smile. Piper felt that if she stayed on the sidewalk a second longer she might lose her composure. "Or try the Wicked Codder," she said, turning back to Chad. "Was nice to meet you, but I've got to run. Late for a party!"

Derek sputtered back to life. "Okay. Yes! Take care."

She didn't dare look back, but somehow she knew if she turned around Derek would be watching her go.

The Fisherman's Daughter's front door was covered in plain brown wrapping paper. There were blue-and-green starfish drawn all over it in crayon: Lucy's work, Piper was sure. On the sidewalk was a chalkboard sign covered in white lights: *Grand Opening Party! 6:00 today!* Seashells had been glued around the chalk lettering. It was rustic and festive and the stuff of mermaids. Wren had done it.

The door was locked so she knocked. Wren poked her head out. "Thank God! Where were you? I need you."

"I'm here, I'm here!" Piper followed her in. Paper lanterns hung from the ceiling, bathing the shop in warm light. In the back, an old-fashioned drink cart was set up with a punch bowl. A wooden table was laden with their hard work from the day before. Piper snagged a potato scallop cake.

"Hey now," Wren warned. But she was all smiles, dressed in a soft white tank and a green flowing skirt, much like the one Beverly wore. "You turned Grandma into a hot ticket," Piper told her.

Wren's face lit up. "Did she like it?"

"Like it? She may take over the shop when she gets here." Piper glanced around "Where's Luce?"

The dressing room curtain whipped aside. "Ta da!" Lucy popped out in the cutest blue-and-green smock dress. Her arms were covered in bracelets, from her tiny wrists right up to her elbows. "Baby, those are for sale. You need to put those back!" Wren told her.

Lucy twirled over to Piper, tipped her head against her in a quick hug, and twirled away to a display table where she extended one skinny arm and then the other dramatically. *Clink, clink, clink* went the bangle bracelets as they slid back into their silver tray.

Now was not the time to fill Wren in with news of her sidewalk run-in with Derek, but Piper's heart was still pounding. That smile he'd laid on her.

"Shannon isn't coming," Wren said.

"What do you mean she's not coming? This is your big night."

Wren shook her head.

"She'd better be sick. Like bubonic plague sick."

"It's because of Dad."

Piper couldn't believe it. She knew Shannon was stubborn, but this. This was too much. "It's because she's an ass."

"No, don't," Wren said. "I admit, I did feel that way yesterday when she called and told me. But this is heavy stuff for her."

Piper looked at the closed front door. In thirty minutes they'd be opening it to the town and customers would be filing in. In thirty minutes their father would be one of them. He'd insisted on coming on his own, not wanting to take time away from anyone having to pick him up. "Do you want me take him home early? Then she can join for the party."

"No, I'm going to let it go." She glanced around the store and rolled her shoulders back. "This is what I have to focus on."

Piper pulled her in for a hug. "Good girl." Resting her chin on her sister's shoulder she couldn't help but laugh. "If you want me to drive over to Stage Harbor and smack her, I will."

In spite of herself, Wren laughed, too. "Stop! You're a horrible person."

"We both are."

Moments later there was another knock. Hank escorted Beverly in on his arm, Lindy following. "My my!" Beverly exclaimed. She opened her arms wide to the shop and to Lucy and Wren who hurried over to greet her. Lucy gave her great-grandmother the grand tour of "all the sparkly things," as Hank held on to her arm. Lindy dipped into the punch and circled wagons with her daughters.

"Shannon's a no-show," Piper announced.

"What?"

"Piper, please. Let's not get into it now," Wren pleaded.

Piper glared at Lindy. "Can you believe her?"

Lindy seemed more concerned about how Wren felt about it. "What happened?"

Wren began fussing with plates of food, picking them up and rearranging them. "She doesn't want to see Dad."

There was no hiding the surprise on Lindy's face. "Oh. I didn't realize he was coming."

Wren groaned. "Does that upset you?"

"No, no, sweetheart. You invite whomever you want. This is your night."

Wren glanced around her shop, exasperated. "If only that were true."

At five minutes to six, Wren unlocked the front door and they all stepped out onto the sidewalk, where to Piper's surprise quite a few people waited. Ari gathered both ends of a giant Tiffany-blue ribbon that had been secured to either side of the doorway, and tied a neat bow in the middle. She handed Wren a pair of scissors. Already people had gathered on the sidewalk, some lining up for the opening, some stopping out of curiosity. Lindy appeared in the doorway carrying a tray of champagne-filled flutes and passed it over the ribbon to Ari before ducking under herself.

"What's this?" Wren asked.

Lindy was already getting choked up as she passed around the flutes to those closest. "You didn't think we'd let you open your doors without a proper toast, did you?"

Piper watched teary-eyed as Wren glanced around the growing crowd with a shy smile. Wren was strong in quiet ways. She was so proud of her big sister. What an amazing mother she was to Lucy, and what a huge accomplishment to envision and then open her own place. All on her own.

"Speech!" Hank shouted, raising a glass.

Reluctantly, Wren took her place in front of the door. "I want to thank you all for coming tonight. There have been more than a few nights that I passed here in the shop, redoing the floors and painting. Or working from my home. One hundred seventy-eight nights, to be exact." Her voice cracked slightly, and Piper felt a lump grow in her own throat.

Beside her, the photographer from the *Cape Cod Chronicle* began snapping pictures. It was then Piper noticed Caleb standing a few heads behind him, among the crowd. "Dad," she called, and he made his way to her. Piper pointed excitedly to him the second Wren looked over.

Wren cleared her throat. "Chatham is my hometown, and my goal was to bring to Main Street something unique and something we can all feel

339

good about. All of the merchandise carried here is sourced from local artists and designers, and is eco-conscious. It's about quality, and it's about time." Here she looked down at Lucy. "Lucy, I hope you know that Mommy did all of this with you in her heart. Will you help me open the store for all these lovely people?"

Lucy stepped out tentatively in front of the crowd, glancing over her shoulder at all the strange faces. With Wren's hands on her own they held the scissors up to the bow and sliced in one clean sweep. The blue ribbon fell away and a burst of applause erupted on the sidewalk. "Welcome to the Fisherman's Daughter!"

It turned out to be quite a party. The shop could barely contain all the visitors who streamed in and out. Jack Johnson played on the speakers and plates of food were passed. Customers sipped punch as they inspected the shelves of artwork, *oohed* and *aahed* over the jewelry, and waited in line to try on clothes in one of the two dressing areas. Ari stood sentinel at the cash register and Lindy sat alongside her, tucking purchases into the monogrammed recycled-paper bags with ocean-blue tissue paper. From time to time Beverly's ebullient voice sailed over the crowd: "This shop belongs to my granddaughter!"

Piper tried to keep an eye on her father. She was wary of him bumping in to Beverly. Each knew the other was there, but in all the excitement and with his late arrival they had not, to her knowledge, crossed paths yet. Caleb stood protectively by the wave sculpture, which had been placed by the front window. He seemed to have memorized the sculptor's information, and he shared it with anyone who came within earshot. She'd have to tell Wren about it later.

Wren was busy greeting customers as they came in the door. She answered questions about the designer who made the seaweed scarves and the jeweler who created the antique button necklaces. Already the racks of clothes were thinning out and there were a few bare spots on the wall where artwork had been taken down and purchased. With everyone focused on the front of the store, Piper had positioned herself by the dressing rooms, making suggestions and finding sizes for shoppers. Midway through the night a cute blonde woman emerged from the dressing room in a stretchy navy-and-white-striped dress that hit midthigh. She stood in front of the mirror, looking sheepishly at her reflection. "I don't know. This is way more fitted than what I usually wear." With her was a little girl with braids who was making silly faces in the mirror.

Piper came up to stand beside her. "Are you kidding? You look like a million bucks." She meant it. The dress hugged her flat stomach and showed off her strong legs.

"Are you sure?"

Piper winked at her in the mirror. "If I looked like you do in that dress, I'd be wearing it right now. And to bed. And again tomorrow."

The woman laughed. "You're sweet."

Her daughter tugged on the hem of the dress. "Mommy, can I go play with that girl?"

Piper followed her gaze to where Lucy was sitting behind the counter stacking a sleeve of plastic cups she must've snagged from the refreshment table. Piper knelt down beside her. "You know who that is? That's my niece, Lucy. She's six."

The little girl smiled. She was missing both front teeth. "I'm six!"

"Six? Wow!" Piper said. "You can go say hi to her if you want. She's really nice. Her mommy owns this store."

"Is that all right?" the woman asked. "I hadn't planned on bringing her in here with me, but when I walked by and saw the sign I had to come check it out."

"Of course you did. It's no trouble, I'll keep an eye on them while you're changing."

"Thanks! This is the best customer service I've ever had. Usually people see me coming with the kids and beat it." She returned to the dressing room with two more things. When she came out she looked pleased.

"Make a decision?" Piper asked.

"I'm getting this cute top." She held up a white

tunic. "And this skirt. But I'm going to think about the dress." She called to her daughter who was busy with Lucy. The two had built quite the tower. "Thanks, again, for all your help!"

Piper grinned back at her. "It's my job." She was enjoying this retail thing. She loved clothes, even if Wren's style was slightly more subdued than her own. And she loved talking to people.

By nine-thirty they were half an hour past closing time and still ferrying the last of the shoppers out the door. All the shops on Chatham closed early, and yet there were still people lingering among the display areas and straggling out the door. Ari counted the money in the till and whispered something to Wren.

When the last shopper left, Wren closed the front door and turned the *OPEN* sign to *CLOSED*. She flopped against the door. "I think I may collapse. But good news: we cleared one thousand and sixty-two dollars tonight."

"And forty-three cents!" Ari called from behind the counter.

Beverly started clapping, and they followed suit. "Bravo."

Wren looked exhausted, but in that drenched enduring way of a new mother who's just given birth. "Now, it's time to kick you all out," she said, half-joking.

Piper, who hadn't had a second to eat a thing,

surveyed the food table. It had been ransacked, and only the crumbs of pita chips remained on a platter; a spoonful of red onion jam was left in its ramekin. She scooped it out and popped it in her mouth. "Any champagne left?"

Lindy shook her head. "Gone. Just like my stamina."

Her family was spread out around the shop in various states of fatigue. Beverly had long ago been seated in a cushioned chair in the corner. Lindy was perched on a settee by the dressing room with Lucy, who was curled up fast asleep on her lap. Hank leaned against one of the mirrors, a dazed look on his face. Caleb came to stand by Piper, inspecting the table for scraps. "Looks like the buzzards got it all."

"Yeah, and I'm starving." She turned to look at him. "Did you eat anything tonight? You look a little pale."

"Just tired." He dabbed at his forehead, which she could see under the lantern had a few beads of perspiration. But it had been hot and stuffy in the store all night with the crowds, and she realized she, too, was feeling it.

"I do say, I think we'll all sleep well tonight," Beverly said. Everyone murmured consent, but no one stirred.

"I guess we should bring the car around for Mom," Lindy said, looking to Hank.

"I'll get it."

Beverly began to rise from her chair, but it was deeply cushioned, and she faltered.

"Allow me." Caleb hurried to her side and offered his hand. She stared at it like it was something that might bite her, then up at him.

Piper felt her insides chill, but she couldn't tear her eyes away.

Here it was. They had been separated from the bustling crowd all night, but now they were face to face.

Hank had straightened and seemed on the verge of going over; for whatever reason, Beverly had been his charge all night and he did not seem ready to be relieved of his position. But he was also a gentleman.

"May I?" Caleb asked again, a little louder.

Beverly looked to Wren. Then Piper. Lindy spoke. "It's okay, Mom." And with that she extended her hand.

"Thank you," she allowed.

Hank excused himself to pull the car around to the front. Wren scooped Lucy off her mother's lap, so Lindy could follow.

"What time do you open in the morning?" Lindy asked.

Wren seemed dazed. "Ten o'clock. We get to do this all over again."

Ari had begun cleaning up platters, and Piper joined in. "Go on home," she told Wren. "Let us finish up."

"I couldn't possibly." But the look on her face said otherwise.

"Your sister's right," Lindy insisted. "We're taking grandma home, and you should do the same with Lucy. It's been a long wonderful night. Go rest."

Wren looked prepared to argue, but her mouth opened and shut. "All right," she agreed. "It's time for all of us to call it a night."

Caleb had just gotten to the door with Beverly when something happened. It happened so fast, Piper could not say if Beverly lost her balance or if he tripped, but suddenly there was a shout and a flurry of motion. When she turned, Hank was in the doorway clutching Beverly, who had not fallen but was sagging in his arms. But Caleb was crumpled on the floor, his limbs askew.

Piper froze. She felt the wind of her mother come up behind her and pass over her. She watched Wren swing Lucy into Ari's arms before running after her mother to the doorway. Both women knelt beside Caleb, Lindy feeling his chest, Wren cradling his head. The walls pressed in against her temples and Piper couldn't make sense of anything they were saying. Her grandmother seemed all right. But then, why wasn't Caleb getting up?

When Wren spun around to face Piper, her voice was urgent, her words jagged. "Piper! Call an ambulance. Now!"

346

Thirty

Shannon

She was still awake when the call came just before midnight. Reid was snoring softly on his side, but that wasn't what had been keeping Shannon up. All night she'd felt guilty.

"What do you mean we aren't going to Aunty Wren's opening?" Avery had asked at dinner. Shannon had been working in her office on the photos she'd taken of the Ridgevale place. The work had to get done, but really she was trying to distract herself from the anger she'd felt at Wren and her father. Surprisingly the photos had come out well. Far better than she'd thought. She'd opted to use her wide angle 17-millimeter lens, a risk because it could result in a little distortion in the images. As she scanned the photos, she was happily surprised. The home's open-concept space had translated beautifully, appearing generous both in light and square footage, just as she'd hoped. She found a few living room shots that needed tweaking. And one taken from the dining area looking into the kitchen. Nothing she couldn't fix in Adobe Photoshop. As she worked, she felt an ease of contentment swell within her. The same ease she'd felt in college when she minored in fine art and photography, and she'd had her first show on campus. There was something about being in the studio, alone with your work and your thoughts. The images you produced became your thoughts. It was a satisfaction she had not felt in a very long time, something familiar and sweet that caused an ache akin to nostalgia and yet created an energy to do more. To create. To capture. To share. But it was how she felt afterward that hit her most. More than the two vodka tonics she'd had at her desk, more than the prescriptions her doctor had given her, working like this gave her a profound sense of peace. Something she realized she'd been chasing.

When she was done editing she compiled the best shots in a folder marked *Ridgevale*. She couldn't wait to show Bitsy. In more ways than one. Though she was still a little nervous. Upon learning that she was Caleb Bailey's daughter, Everett Banks had been intrigued. It was the only time Shannon had seen the man exhibit any interest or faith. "If you've inherited any of your father's talent, I believe we'll have a winner. I look forward to seeing your work." Bitsy, of course, had seized upon this. The same man she'd once referred to as a "hippie picture-taker" was suddenly exalted to artist. Shannon had felt a stab of defensiveness, if not on his part then at least for the work and the family name. There was no denying the man's brilliance, even if it had caused his ruin, in her opinion. Now the question was: Did she possess any of it? It was a question that had caused a nervous flutter in her rib cage. A flutter that went well beyond the scope of this demanding client and her mother-in-law's agency.

As a result, she'd gotten so absorbed in her work that she hadn't realized it was already six-thirty. The empty drink glasses on her desk hadn't helped. Avery and George had found her at her laptop, claiming they were starving. Shannon hadn't even given dinner a thought. Reluctantly, she'd trailed them into the kitchen.

"Did Aunt Wren cancel the party or something?" Avery wanted to know.

"Not exactly. She's still opening the store tonight, but as I've been trying to explain it's not a family party. It's for the customers. I can only imagine how hot and crowded it's going to be in there. We'll pop by tomorrow."

"Is Grandma going?"

"I think so."

"So Hank and Piper will be there."

"Probably."

"What about Great-Grandma Bev?" She was the kids' favorite, and frankly Shannon was especially bummed not to be seeing her at the party. Knowing her, she'd get all dressed up and work the crowd, charming everyone who came through the door into buying some of her granddaughter's wares.

"I don't know. I guess Grandma Bev will go, too."

Avery scowled as she set one of the last napkins down. "It sure *sounds* like a family party."

"Avery, please. We'll go tomorrow."

"Will the whole family be there tomorrow?"

Shannon did not answer.

Reid came inside from the back patio carrying a platter of burgers and grilled salmon. He was still in his work clothes, his shirtsleeves rolled up. He, too, had apparently been surprised to arrive home to a dark kitchen and empty table "What, am I a short order cook and waitress?" Shannon had asked them all as they gathered around the island like stray cats. "It's not like there's no food in the house. Let me introduce you to the fridge! Meet the pantry! Knock yourselves out."

This concerned George. "You want us to make our own dinner?"

This was not how their house worked. Their mother had dinner on the table by five o'clock every night. One serving of protein, two of vegetables, at least a whole grain and a glass of cold milk. Hell, there were usually fresh-cut hydrangeas in a crystal vase. *What was wrong with her?* she imagined them thinking as they wandered through the dark kitchen while her desk light hummed beneath the closed office door.

At least Reid was trying. "I would cook once in a while," Reid had calmly chimed in. "If only you communicated such wishes." Now, as he set the grilled meat platter beside the salad she was dressing, he gave her a look. Dinner may have been salvaged, but he was not in agreement with her unilateral decision to skip Wren's opening. She could perhaps count on him to respect her rationale, but explaining that to the kids—well, that was all on her.

Avery was setting the table. Since she was "starving," she'd taken it upon herself to get up off the couch and get things moving without Shannon having to nag her. George was pouring glasses of milk. As Shannon mixed herself another vodka tonic she looked around at all her family members pitching in. This "forgetting about dinner" thing was working out very nicely, after all. She'd have to do it more often.

"Drink?" she asked Reid.

"No, thanks." He loosened his collar. "I've been running around with the Pearsons all after-noon looking at building lots. Think I need a water instead."

Shannon sliced a lime, dropped two wedges in her glass. She was okay drinking alone.

Avery was not letting the opening party go, however. Winnie came in from playing basketball in the driveway. "What time are we leaving?" she asked, plopping down in her chair.

"Wash hands," Shannon said.

She groaned but went to the sink.

"Never," Avery informed her. "Mom said we're not going."

"What?"

Shannon had just speared a piece of salmon. It was lightly grilled with a golden crust, just the way she liked it. She'd meant to thank Reid, to offer up a smile to show her appreciation and perhaps a little apology. She *had* been distracted lately. Distracted and irritable. But now she set her fork down. "Everyone, please. I did not cancel on Aunt Wren. We're just going tomorrow, instead."

"What about our new grandfather?" Winnie asked. Then quickly correcting herself, "I mean, your dad."

She'd asked the children not to call Caleb that. "He's never been a grandpa," she'd said simply, when she first told them the news of his arrival. "Hank and Grampy Whitcomb are your grandpas."

"We have no plans to see him either," she said.

"Does he want to see us?"

This was what she had warned Wren about. Inviting Caleb Bailey back into their lives was not singular to them. Now there was another generation involved. A wonderful, thriving, curious, sensitive generation that all this time he had neglected to know and were doing just fine without him. Having him back was too complicated. The children would have questions. They would likely get attached. And who knew how he would disappoint them next? No, she was not opening her family up to that.

"You are all wonderful grandchildren to your real grandparents. But he's not family."

She gauged their faces for confusion. For hurt. For anything of that nature. They'd been over this before, and she would keep going over it as long as they needed her to.

Avery poked at her food. "But we're still going to miss the party. I had a great outfit picked out, too."

So it was the party they were most concerned with. What started as relief turned to annoyance. What about "Because I said so," like her mother used to say when she and her sisters were kids. Shannon looked to Reid for support, but he was concentrating on his plate. She pushed her chair back. "You know, I should get back to work. Mommy has a project she's trying to finish. A very important project."

"But you didn't eat," George said.

"I'm not hungry." She picked up her plate and set it in the sink, still full. Looking down at the roasted fingerling potatoes and the perfectly cooked salmon made her sad. She was ruining a dinner she hadn't even made. So much for showing Reid some appreciation. So much for family time.

She stalked back to the table. The kids looked up at her in various stages of stunned concern. Reid didn't even bother. "You're not going to eat with us?" Avery asked.

Shannon plucked her vodka tonic off her placemat. "Not tonight."

When the phone rang before midnight, she was almost relieved. Let it be Wren calling to chew her out. She deserved as much. Or Lindy, calling to fill her in on all the details of the evening that she'd missed out on: who came, what they said, what they wore. She bet the food was delicious; Wren had put together a unique menu of summer bites. A menu their father had somehow become involved in helping to bring to fruition. What good fortune for all of them that he'd decided to show up just in time to fry Wren's potato pancakes! Christ—Shannon bet his appetizers tasted the best. She'd have to ask her mother if she'd tried any.

She rolled over and pressed the phone to her ear, ready for all of it. *Bring it on,* she thought. Tell me all about the happy family reunion you had without me. But it was not Lindy.

"Shannon?" It was Wren. She sounded very far away.

"I'm sorry . . ." Shannon began. She didn't mean to act like such an ass to her sisters. She really didn't, but she also didn't know how to stop, and so the only thing she seemed capable of doing these days was to keep on being one. It wasn't like she was particularly discriminating in her asshole-ness. After all, Reid and the kids got a fair dose of it tonight, too. Maybe Wren would forgive her if she told her that. Maybe they'd even laugh together about it, like they used to.

"It's Dad," Wren interrupted.

"What about him?"

"We're at Cape Cod Hospital. He collapsed at the opening tonight. They've done some tests and he's resting now. But he looks pretty bad."

Shannon pressed the phone harder to her ear.

"You should probably come," Wren said.

"Was it a heart attack?"

"We don't know yet. They're still waiting for results."

Shannon glanced at the clock. She could be in Hyannis within an hour. She could wake Reid and go right now. "Is he dying?"

"What? No, I don't think so. But we still don't know what's going on."

"Thanks for letting me know," Shannon said.

"Aren't you coming?"

"Sorry you have to deal with this on your special night. I'll call you tomorrow."

Before Wren could reply she set the phone back

in its cradle and lay back down. If she fell asleep soon, she could probably get a decent night's rest before the kids got up. They had a busy weekend ahead. She wanted to look good for the Hooker's Ball.

Thirty-One

Wren

The male attending physician in the emergency room, Dr. Verelli, looked to be ten years younger than Wren. Under the glare of the fluorescent lighting and after the night she'd had, Wren was pretty sure she was sporting another twenty.

It was just her and Piper in the waiting room. Hank had taken Beverly home, and Lindy had gone home with Lucy, who never woke even during all the chaos.

So far, Dr. Verelli had come out to speak with them twice. First to let them know their father was stable and that as far as they could tell it did not appear to be some kind of cardiac episode, and then again to run through some lab tests they were administering. But that had seemed like forever ago.

"At least the coffee is good." Piper had been up and down out of her seat, pacing and offering to make Wren tea or coffee or fetch her water. Wren had finally agreed to a cup of tea just to get her to stop. It had gone cold, but she sipped it now, thinking. She hadn't told Piper yet that

Shannon wasn't coming. Piper was distracted, texting the whole time, and Wren was afraid to ask to whom. At one point her phone rang, and Wren caught a glimpse of the illuminated screen. *Derek.* She'd watched her sister hurry outside, the phone pressed to her ear, and then as she paced back and forth on the sidewalk outside the glass emergency-room doors. So Piper was still talking to him, after all. A plume of anger rose inside her. Not just because Piper was falling back in to her old nonsense, but because she had no one, herself. There was no one else to leave Lucy with at a time like this. Just as there was no one else for her to call, or to comfort her. She was exhausted and alone, and frankly she didn't feel like putting on her brave face or "handling it" anymore. Damn it, didn't she deserve to have someone, too? Though she had no one but herself to blame for that.

When Piper came back inside, she seemed lightened. "So, if it wasn't his heart, then it must just be exhaustion." She plopped onto the seat beside Wren. "He did travel on that awful bus for almost a week, and what with all the stops and detours he probably didn't eat or sleep a bit."

Wren tried to shift gears and focus on their dad. She had wondered the same, but there was something in the back of her mind that refused to let her relax her fears with Piper's hopeful outlook. She'd have to hear it from the baby-faced doctor before she'd allow herself to believe it. "Did you call Hank? He's probably wondering." She would not ask her sister who she'd been on the phone with, but she'd sure as hell remind her who she should have called first.

Piper nodded. "Done. I called Mom, too. She said not to worry, she'd sleep over at your place with Lucy." Piper looked so young, hugging her knees on the chair and looking at her with such hope that Wren couldn't stay mad at her. She didn't have the energy for it.

"Hopefully we'll be out of here soon," Wren managed.

Piper turned suddenly to Wren, and her smile crumpled on her face. "We just got him back." Tears sprang to her eyes.

"I know, Pipe. I know." Wren draped an arm around her. She could feel Piper's back heave against her, her narrow spine rising and falling with each tearful hiccup.

"I can't lose him. Not again."

Wren tugged her closer. "We're not going to. No one said anything about that."

But how were any of them to know? Even if this incident turned out to be mere exhaustion, there were other ways to lose the man. As Shannon had warned, did any of them really know their father better now?

Wren wanted to say she did. She knew him in the way he'd stood at the oven with Lucy, making the pancakes for her opening. In the way he'd challenged her to rethink the ocean sculpture in terms of art and placement. The laugh at Lindy's table, where after twenty-three years, he was still allowed back if not entirely welcomed by the woman he'd left.

Sitting in the overly air-conditioned waiting room with Piper tucked up against her like some kind of broken bird, Wren wished she could tell Shannon those very things right now. She wanted to yell them at the top of her lungs. Shannon should've been there. At the very least for Wren and Piper, if not for Caleb Bailey.

The double doors swung open and the young doctor strode through, his expression neutral.

Piper popped up and began blotting her nose. "How is he?"

"He's doing better, but we'd like to keep him overnight."

"You're sure it wasn't his heart?"

The doctor glanced at Wren. "We're sure. You can see him and talk to him before you go tonight."

"Was it just him overdoing it?"

He seemed to be hesitating. "Yes, that is always part of it. We've gotten him pretty well hydrated, and we're working to control his pain."

"Pain?" Piper asked.

But Wren had seen it. The way he sometimes halted in the middle of a room and grabbed his lower back. How he rubbed his knees when he sat down, and the slow way he sometimes rose from a chair. She'd wondered if it might have been arthritis, but if he caught her watching him curiously, each time he'd seemed to downplay it, and she hadn't wanted to pry.

Having heard what she hoped to, Piper rallied. "Can we see him now?"

"Yes, you can." He turned to Wren. "Assuming he rests and his numbers continue to rise, your father can expect to be discharged in the morning. Did you provide all your contact information at registration so we can call you when he's ready?"

Wren nodded. "I did, but I'll confirm they have the correct information."

Piper grew impatient. "Can you meet me in there, Wren? I'm going to go back and see him."

"Yeah, sure." She began to gather her things, aware of the doctor's presence. There seemed to be more he wanted to say. "So he's really okay?"

Dr. Verelli ran his hand through his hair. "I had a long talk with him. He's going to have to take it easier."

She'd make sure he did. First thing, she was going to check him out of the motel and invite him to stay at her place. He'd have access to her car if he needed it, and she'd be able to make sure he was eating regularly. But there was something about what the doctor wasn't saying that caught her attention.

"Thank you for all your help," she said. "Is there anything else?"

The doctor shook his head. "Take good care of him. Rest is imperative." He paused before adding, "Talk to your dad."

She found Piper standing by their father's bed. Wren was taken aback by how small he suddenly seemed in the bed. As if he had somehow shrunk on the ambulance ride over. "How're you feeling?"

He was awake, but his eyelids fluttered with effort. "Okay for an old coot."

"You're not old." Piper adjusted his blankets, mindful of the IV tubes.

The doctor had said he could be discharged in the morning, but Wren couldn't help but wonder how.

"I'm sorry," he said. "I seem to have ruined your party tonight."

Wren forced a smile and waved a dismissive hand playfully. "That party was already over. It just extended the excitement."

This seemed to amuse him, and he laughed softly. "Well, all right then. Out with a bang."

The night nurse came in and explained that they'd be moving him upstairs to a private room.

"Can we come?" Piper wanted to know.

"No, sweetie. Your dad needs some rest, and it

may be awhile before they get his paperwork and transition him upstairs. We're a little slower at night."

This was not what she wanted to hear, but Piper relented. "Well, Dad. I guess we'll see you in the morning."

He turned to her. "You will."

Wren watched as Piper bent down and kissed his forehead goodnight, wondering at the tender irony of it.

"Hey Pipe, can you grab the car and bring it around?" Wren asked.

"Aren't we walking out together?"

Wren needed a minute alone. She wasn't sure why, but she couldn't leave just yet. "I want to say goodnight."

Piper glanced between the two like she was missing something, but shrugged. "Okay, I'll meet you out front. Goodnight, Dad."

Caleb lifted a tired hand and turned to Wren. "I don't want you girls worrying. I won't be any trouble; I'll be good as new tomorrow."

She put a tentative hand on his. It was rough and calloused. But warm. "Dad. What did the doctor say?"

Caleb shrugged and his gown shifted, falling off one shoulder. He had trouble pulling it back up.

"Here. Let me."

When she met his eyes, they were gray and

watery. A weight pressed in her middle. "Tell me, Dad."

"Ah, Wren. My curious little bird." He did not try to lie to her. "I'm sick, kiddo."

As soon as he said the words, Wren realized she'd known. She'd known it in the way he stepped off the bus stairs. The way he tired so quickly and easily each time he came to the shop or stopped by the house. It had been right in front of her all week. "How sick?"

Caleb stared at his blanketed feet. "It's cancer. Pancreatic cancer."

Wren stared out the glass windows of his room to the nurse's station. A middle-aged nurse was sitting at the desk, head tipped back as she laughed at something her young male coworker said. The area hummed with incessant activity: flickering screens, monitors that beeped, the buzz of fluorescent lights. She squeezed her father's hand. Lindy's neighbor, their dear friend Mrs. Pruitt, had lost her husband to pancreatic cancer when Wren was a teenager. She remembered hearing her mother bringing them food. What she recalled most was the speed of his decline. The swift shock followed so soon by his death.

"How long do we have?" she asked.

"Not very. A couple months maybe."

Wren cleared her throat. "Okay then." Tomorrow she would bring him home. She would make up Lucy's room and get a list of all the foods he could eat, the foods he wanted to eat. When she picked him up she would do it alone, and she would find the doctor. She would collect all the information he had: his medications, his lab work. She put a hand to her head, her mind racing against her fatigue with newfound urgency.

But Caleb wasn't finished. "There's a reason I didn't tell you girls. I thought I could come back and see you again, and then go home before you knew." He paused. "This isn't what I wanted." Her father lay on his back staring up at the ceiling with such hopelessness that Wren did what Piper had done. She leaned over his bed and kissed her father's head. Once, then again. "Sleep," she whispered. "We'll talk more in the morning. Just get some sleep, Dad."

She was halfway through the door when she heard him. His voice was a whisper. "Promise me something, Wren?"

She hesitated. "Whatever you want."

"Please. Don't tell the others."

It was a promise she was not sure she could keep. But as Wren looked at her father, fighting the sleep he needed, she gave. "I promise."

Thirty-Two

Piper

She never should have called him. But the next afternoon when he made his way toward her across the decking at the Chatham Bars Inn Beach House Grill, Piper almost slipped off her barstool. Derek slid onto the seat next to hers, glancing around. "Are you all right?"

Piper squeezed her beer, willing her hands to stay on the icy cold bottle. "I didn't know who else to call last night."

"It's okay. Luckily I was up watching the *Late Show*." He looked at her carefully for the first time. "It was risky though, Piper."

She deflated a little. "I know. I'm sorry."

The bartender came over. "What can I get you, sir?" For a moment Piper worried Derek would go. But when he picked up the beer list and studied it, her insides stilled.

He ordered an IPA and turned to her. "You look good."

She'd picked out her red tank and white shorts with some thought, much as she hated to admit it. But she reminded herself that her father was the reason she'd reached out to Derek. As she'd followed behind the ambulance all the way to Hyannis the night before, she'd realized that there was only one person she wanted to call. Risky or not.

"Tell me more about your father. Has he been released?"

Piper gave Derek the whole story as they sipped their beers together. At one point when she started to tear up, he reached over and wiped the corner of her eye gently with his thumb. He paused, but he didn't withdraw his hand. And she'd pressed her own atop his.

"Piper, we can't." He looked away. "God, I wish we could. Being up here I keep expecting to run into you at every corner I turn. I look for you at the beach. I look for you in crowded restaurants . . ."

Piper exhaled. "You do? Because I do, too! All the time."

"And now—seeing you. The way you look, knowing what you're going through." He let out his breath. "You're killing me."

Piper didn't wish any suffering on him, but she accepted this news with more hope than she knew was wise. If neither one of them could stand being apart, maybe Derek would realize that he wanted more of her. That he needed her, the way she often felt she needed him.

"Can we go somewhere?" she asked. Then, quickly, before he could disagree, "Just for a few minutes to be alone. To talk. Because I know a place."

Derek tipped back his beer and looked around the deck. The beach club was halfway full mid-day, but the kind of people he would know, if any of them were indeed here, would be vacationers like himself, and they'd all likely be on the beaches or in town with their kids.

"Piper. Stop." His voice was a low growl, but there was something playful in it.

Whether it was the courage from the cold beer on the hot day, or the lack of sleep she'd gotten the night before, Piper seized upon it. "Please, Derek. Just once." Then, as she ran her hand over his knee, her fingers brushing beneath the hem of his khaki shorts and squeezing, she said what always got him. "It's just *us*."

Derek stared out at the water. He didn't answer. She waited and swigged the last of her beer as she did, willing him to say the words. When he still said nothing, Piper grabbed a ten-dollar bill from her purse and pushed it across the bar and stood. Derek reached for her hand.

"Where?"

Feeling light-headed, she snatched a paper napkin off the bar and wrote down the address. She pushed it over to him.

"What is this place?"

"Don't worry. My family owns it. Park in the rear lot and come in the back door."

Derek was shaking his head as if changing his mind. "When?"

Her heart flip-flopped and she hopped off the barstool. "Ten minutes." She'd given Derek the address of the Fisherman's Daughter. Wren was picking up their father at the hospital. She'd arranged for Ari to cover the morning, and Piper was supposed to relieve her for the afternoon. It would be just her, alone in the shop, and before she could think about her exhausted sister or her sick father or what a sacrilege Wren would consider this selfish move, Piper hopped in her car. The sand and gravel spewed beneath her tires as she turned toward town.

The shop was empty when she blew in the door, and Piper peered past Ari to the back. "Oh my gosh, how's your father? How's Wren? How are you?"

"He's going to be okay, thanks. Wren is bringing him home now. So, no customers?"

"We've had light traffic so far, but it's a good beach day so I'm sure it'll pick up this afternoon." Ari pointed to the MacBook screen by the register. "We sold a print and a sweater though. That was good."

"Great, great." Piper shoved her purse under the counter, her eye on the front door. "So, I'll take over now and let you go. You must be hungry for lunch."

Ari seemed in no rush to leave. "I brought a

369

salad, actually. Wren asked me to show you how we're recording inventory as it sells. Do you want to go over that now?"

A couple of women had paused at the front window and looked to be about to come in. "No, that's okay. I think I've got it."

"So Wren showed you?"

The door opened, and the women came in. Piper exhaled in frustration. "What?"

Ari was frowning at her curiously. "The inventory program?"

"Thanks, Ari. I've got it." Piper needed Ari to get going. Now. And she needed to sell something to these women, fast. She sailed over to them. "Welcome to the Fisherman's Daughter. Can I help you with anything?"

Both women were a little older than Lindy, and smartly dressed. They were looking at the necklaces together. "No, thank you," one said, with a bright smile. "We're just browsing. So when did you open?"

Ugh. Conversationalists. Piper needed buyers. Or get-out-ers. But guilt flashed like a reminder. This was Wren's first day open. And this was her job. If she was going to risk everything, she could at least sell a scarf first.

"Just last night. Is there anything special I can show you?"

She directed the pair to the rack of clothing that had already been fattened up from last night's stream of sales. Ari was good, she'd have to give the girl that.

As the women perused, Piper was relieved to see Ari collecting her things. "So, I can come back later if Wren needs me," she was saying. "Or I can stay now, for a bit more."

"No, no!" The words came out louder than she meant. "I mean, you've done so much. Last night was crazy, and you could probably use the rest. I'll let Wren know when she comes in."

Ari glanced around but finally headed for the door. "Okeydokey. Good luck!"

"Thanks!"

It seemed like forever that the women puttered around the shop. Finally, one selected a linen shirt. "What do you think?"

It was a lovely color, but it was a bit large. Piper glanced at the clock again. "Let me find a smaller size."

In the end she made the sale, and no sooner had the pair exited the shop door than Piper flipped the *OPEN* sign in the window over. Then, thinking better of it, she hurried back to the counter where she ripped a piece of paper off a yellow legal pad and scrawled a note in marker. *Back in TEN MINUTES.* She raced back out and taped it below the closed sign. Then she flipped the lock, turned out the lights, and was heading to the rear of the store just as she heard a faint knock. Her chest rapped in response.

Piper opened the door. Derek stood on the back steps, looking over his shoulder nervously. "Where are we?"

She grabbed his hand and pulled him in. "My sister's shop."

It was dark, and they were in the back by the storage closet. "What? Are you crazy?"

Piper placed a hand firmly over his mouth and reached around and pulled him against her with the other. "No talking."

For a moment she feared he would pull away and leave. That his common sense or a scrap of decency would get the better of him. But as she kissed his mouth, running her tongue along his lips she felt him respond. First his mouth, then his body. Without warning he wrapped both arms around her waist and lifted her up, kissing her roughly all the while. Piper let him, encircling his waist with her legs. Wrapped together they stumbled forward.

"The dressing room." She pointed.

Crowded together in the small space, Piper coursed with energy as she fumbled with his belt and he with her button. They peeled the shorts off of each other, each one stepping out of them. Again Derek lifted her up, and Piper wrapped herself around him as he pressed her against the wall. She cried out. All summer she'd waited, not knowing if they were on or off. Loving him and loathing what they were doing simultaneously.

Praying he'd choose her but knowing all the while the impossibility of it all. She tipped her head back and surrendered to it, the wave of all of it.

After, they bent to retrieve their things, laughing nervously, bumping into one another. The rush of elation ebbed, and she looked around at what they'd done. Their clothing tangled together on the floor. The twisted curtain half drawn around them. Through the opening she looked into the store. Her yellow note was affixed crookedly to the door like a tawdry warning sign. A girl in a dress was reading it.

Derek tugged his clothes on. Piper slumped on the small ledge in the dressing room and watched him dress, feeling the exhilaration flow from her veins like she was being drained. "When can I see you again?"

Derek was looking for a shoe, his face obscured by the thick flop of brown hair. Her fingers ached to touch it. "Piper, that was—I don't know . . . amazing. You are amazing." He squeezed her bare knee.

He was leaving her already.

"Derek, I think I've fallen in love with you." She had never said it before, not to any boy or man in her whole life. And she'd never planned to say it to Derek either. Not until he showed some form of real commitment. Not until he'd proved himself worthy. But the words tumbled out of her mouth, and instead of feeling regret she felt free. There. He knew all her secrets now.

"Jesus, Pipe." Derek reached for her hand and pulled her toward him. She resisted, her eyes on his, waiting for him to say it back. "Come here."

He hugged her. She could feel his heart against hers, hear his breath in her ear. She held her own, waiting.

"Can I see you tomorrow?" he asked.

Piper nodded, her cheek raw against his stubble. As the tears spilled onto his shoulder, Piper stared gloomily across the shop floor. The girl at the front door walked away. The shop was dark and still.

He could still grow to love her. She felt it happening in moments like the one they just shared. Right now, this was all he had to give her, and a part of her hated herself for taking it. But she was hungry. If she could just hang on a little bit longer.

Thirty-Three

Shannon

The Hooker's Ball was held annually at the VFW grounds under a big white tent, and it was a bit of a family tradition for the Bailey women to go. It all began the evening of the ball twenty-five years ago, when someone manning the shellfish table left their post to assist the refreshment table, whose punch bowl had overturned. Beverly, who had been waiting at the front of the line in a powder-blue chiffon dress with a hankering for fresh-off-the-boat littlenecks, soon found herself standing behind the counter handing out mussels and steamers to hungry guests. She'd had such a good time that she manned the table all night, leaving only for a quick spin on the dance floor when the band started up with Frankie Valli and the Four Seasons's "Big Girls Don't Cry." From there it just seemed natural to join the board of directors. For fifteen years she worked alongside the local fishermen and -women, as well as local businesses, championing the non-profit Fisherman's Alliance's goals of fisheries management and ecosystem protection. It was a passion she'd handed down to each of her grand-daughters, who growing up in the community had a sound respect for the hard work and the science behind Chatham's commercial fishing fleet. Lindy had served on the Hooker's Ball committee, as did Shannon. Piper had helped pass out educational coloring books to the visiting families on the Chatham Fish Pier. For her part, Wren had fallen in love with one of their fishermen.

Each year at the ball, Shannon couldn't help but be reminded of James. She was sure Wren was, too, which was probably why she hadn't gone in any of the years since she showed up in that awful pink dress with Darby Vale and broke James's heart wide open in front of half his fishing fleet. It was unlike her. And it stung Shannon that Wren had kept them all in the dark over something so important.

When the sisters were younger, they'd shared everything. Late at night they'd whisper across the dark expanse between their twin beds: secrets, confessions, fears. Who Wren prayed she'd get a Valentine card from in sixth grade. Which boy Shannon danced with at the middle school holiday soiree. Shannon showed Wren her first training bra and didn't tease her when she caught her trying it on in the bathroom one day. All of that seemed to change after their father left, though Shannon wasn't quite sure why. Just as she wasn't sure what had happened between Wren and James that night of the ball.

For two years the two were inseparable. Wren was working in town as a bookkeeper and James worked on dayboats out of Rock Harbor in Orleans and Chatham. During their two years together, Shannon couldn't think of a summer night that the two weren't together. They went to bonfires at Harding Beach, headed over to Wellfleet for a drive-in movie, or drove up the arm of the Cape to Provincetown for some nightlife. Or they hung out on the front porch, sipping beers and watching the sun set over Chatham Light. James was a staple at Lindy's Sunday Something-Rather Dinner Party, the one who brought fresh bay scallops or bluefish, striped bass or mussels fresh off of his boat or a boat of his fellow fleet. Along with a six-pack of beer. As far as the family was concerned, they were holding their breath for an announcement of engagement.

Instead Wren had shocked them in a dry-eyed moment one summer night when she'd ended the relationship. A week later she attended the Hooker's Ball with Darby Vale. Wren proceeded to laugh too loudly and carry on too obviously, making a bit of a spectacle of herself on the dance floor. Shannon couldn't help but wonder if it was in large part for James's benefit. James had arrived late and alone, looking solemn as he stood on the edge of the crowd with fellow fishermen. More than once Shannon caught him staring sadly at Wren as Darby spun her around or led her from table to table, holding court as if the party were their own. At one point, Beverly had directed Shannon to retrieve her from the refreshment table: "Your sister is partaking in more than her fair share of the celebrations. It's time to collect her glass slippers and summon the pumpkin."

When Shannon asked Wren about it the next morning, Wren was tightlipped and sullen. "Aren't I allowed to have a little fun?" she'd asked.

A few weeks later, after James had moved away, Wren announced her pregnancy. They all knew it was James's baby. It drove Lindy mad. There were long debates about women's rights and bodies, largely from Wren and Piper. Followed by reminders of paternal rights from Lindy. And strong suggestions to seek legal counsel. What about child support? Did she understand the lifetime financial commitment of raising a child? Could she really manage that alone? And worse, as far as Shannon was concerned, what if he changed his mind down the road and wanted to be a part of the child's life? What if he wanted custody?

The one thing they agreed on and that kept them circling back to one another was their support of Wren: she would not hear of anything except having the baby. As her belly stretched and swelled over the coming months, the women's focus shifted from father to baby. Wren had made her wishes known, and if she said she'd handle it and raise the baby alone, they'd step in line and close their lips on the matter. In the end it was Lindy who reminded them all that there were things they could do alone if that was their choice.

Shannon had never agreed with her sister's decision to keep the news from James, and she'd spent plenty of time trying to convince her to reach out to him. But in the end, it was her sister's life to lead.

Tonight, as she walked under the white tent, Shannon reminded herself to try to be in the moment, as Dr. Weber routinely advised her. Something that had been harder to do since her father had returned. She pushed back at the memory of James and the worries about Caleb Bailey. Tonight was hers to enjoy. Her grandmother was in town, her friend Ellis was joining her, and for the first time in many years, her whole family would be at the ball. Best of all was the news she'd gotten from her mother-in-law that morning.

"Mr. Banks liked your work. The photo coverage is yours," Bitsy said.

Shannon did a little dance in the middle of her

kitchen. Did she detect joy in Bitsy's voice, or was it her imagination?

"I think your family connection went a long way," Bitsy added. "But let's keep our private lives separate from work, all right?"

It was just her imagination. So what if Shannon's connection to the famed Caleb Bailey had played a role in her getting the job? It was also true that Everett Banks hadn't agreed to work with her until he'd seen the photos. Couldn't Bitsy throw her a bone?

Feeling celebratory, Shannon had taken her time getting ready for the ball. She'd selected a sleek white jumpsuit from her closet. Her blonde hair was slicked back, revealing the vintage gold drop earrings Beverly had given her on her wedding day. As they walked hand in hand beneath the tent, Reid leaned in and whispered, "I'm the envy of every man here tonight, honey."

While Reid went to get drinks, Shannon perused the silent auction tables. Their old friends from Stage Harbor, Ellis and Sam, arrived, and Shannon waved them over. "Thank God," she told them. "You beat my family and my mother-in-law."

Ellis was a regular at the ball and used to this. "Which table are you sitting at this year?"

Between Bitsy and Beverly, Shannon had felt a silent tug of war, so each year she and Reid tried to appease both matriarchs by taking turns at their tables, as divorced couples do with Thanksgiving. It was ridiculous, but the only way she knew to manage it. "I can't believe I'm saying this, but I'm actually glad to be at Bitsy's this year."

Reid arrived with drinks and promptly handed one over to Ellis.

"How's your father doing?" she asked. Shannon had not shared any of the news of her father with Ellis, but apparently word got around.

Shannon shrugged. "How should I know?" Then, when she saw the look on Ellis's face, "Wren said he's out of the hospital. But let's focus on fun tonight, okay?"

They spent the evening mingling, and Shannon was reminded why she so enjoyed this event each summer. Unlike the Yacht Club events where she knew every man, woman, and child, let alone dog, the ball was an interesting mix of attendees. There were the fishermen and -women, of course. And the local business people. There were sponsors from the bank and some of the restaurants. But there were the board of directors and staff, whom she found most interesting. The Fisherman's Alliance comprised an eclectic and necessary group of scientists, ecosystem advocates, financial advisors, and commercial fishing industry people all focused on the same cause. It created a camaraderie and bridge between people who might not otherwise cross paths. Having grown up in Chatham, this fascinated her.

Shannon made her way to the bar for another drink. Her family had still not arrived, and for a worried moment she wondered if something else had happened with her father. Not that she would've changed her mind about seeing him. She'd told Wren as much the night before on the phone. And she'd steeled herself for their response to her absence when she saw them tonight. But they were late, and Beverly was never late to the ball. This raised a small flag of worry on her very small island of concern.

Ellis and Sam had taken their seats with friends from the neighborhood, and Reid found her now. "You're having another?"

"Why do you ask?" She looked back at him levelly. Was he keeping count?

"I could've gotten it for you."

The president of the board of directors was standing on the stage in front of the band, and he tapped the microphone. There was a murmuring and shuffling as people made their way under the tent to their respective tables. Shannon and Reid took their seats.

"I would like to welcome you all to the twenty-sixth annual Hooker's Ball," the president began. A round of applause echoed through the crowd, and it was then Shannon spotted her family seated across the way. She was relieved. Hank and Lindy looked happy, sitting closely. Beverly sat regally beside them, followed by Piper. It was Wren's presence that caught Shannon by surprise. She'd come! They all looked lovely, a perfectly normal family dressed in their summer whites and pastels, the picture of functionality from a distance. Shannon took a deep sip of her vodka tonic. The night was young.

Once the speeches were made, and the guests were urged to "bid and bid healthily!" for the auction items, the music started up again. Everyone rose to mingle. Drinks were poured, the food tables opened, and the evening suddenly took on a cheerful energy. Shannon found herself swaying to the music in her seat. Where had Reid gone? She wanted to dance!

She found him across the tent, leaning over her family's table chatting. Shannon drew in her breath and approached.

Wren looked up first. The second she saw Shannon coming, her expression changed.

"Honey! Don't you look nice." Lindy popped up and pecked her on the cheek. As did Hank. There seemed to be no ill will there. Shannon bent down and kissed her grandmother. "My earrings!" Beverly exclaimed. "How nice."

That's what all of it felt like to Shannon. Niceties. Except for Wren, of course.

"I hear last night was rather eventful." She looked at Wren. "But also successful."

"Oh, yes." Lindy was shaking her head, as if she still couldn't believe it. "We weren't sure we were going to make it tonight, but we haven't missed one yet. I figured it'd be good to get everyone out."

"Blow the stink off us," Beverly added.

"Though it was a huge success for the Fisherman's Daughter," Hank added. Here he raised his glass, and everyone followed suit. Shannon, too, though her glass was suddenly empty, it seemed.

"Well, I was sorry to miss it," she admitted. Wren was fiddling with her purse, but Shannon knew she heard. "You deserve all the success."

Wren nodded but managed to look past her at the same time.

"How's he doing?" Reid asked. Shannon gave him a grateful look.

"Well, that's another story," Lindy said, looking somewhat displeased. "Your sister has moved him in with her."

"What?" She'd just talked to Wren last night. How much could her family have possibly stirred up since?

"I'm not leaving him in the motel," Wren said, looking meaningfully at all of them. Apparently, Shannon had missed discussions, as well.

"But the doctor discharged him, honey. Isn't he all right?" Lindy looked concerned.

"He needs to get his strength back."

This sounded to Shannon to be more than a

mere collapse of fatigue, which was what Lindy had described to her that morning. But Wren was the peacemaker, and if she wanted to bring him home and help him out, she couldn't argue.

"As long as it isn't too much for you," Lindy pressed. "You just opened your store last night. Honestly."

There was an extended stretch of silence where everyone stared at their empty plates.

"So, Piper didn't make it?" Reid asked.

"Oh, she's here somewhere." Lindy glanced around the tent. "You know Piper, she's probably sitting at another table chatting, having forgotten the rest of us. Her family . . ." Her thoughts drifted off. Lindy was still wrestling with Piper's announcement that she would not be teaching, after all. She didn't blame her, so much as pity her. Mothers never stopped mothering.

"Well, I'm going to give my best to Bitsy," Beverly announced. It was a welcome change of topic. Reid and Hank rushed to offer her their hands, and she took both. *Clever vixen,* Shannon thought. She made way and watched the two men escort her to the table at a snail's pace, Beverly's kitten heels flashing with each step. Reid was such a gentleman. She really ought to be nicer to him, she decided.

On that note, and feeling the good cheer of her vodka tonic, Shannon sat beside Wren. "Come have some steamers with me?"

Wren rolled her eyes. Everyone in the family knew she hated steamers.

"You know you want to." Shannon poked her sister gently. "Those rubbery little guys. They slip right down your throat so quick you won't even know what hit you. They taste like chicken," she added for good measure.

Wren made a face, but a smile was starting at the corners of her mouth. "Shannon, please."

"Come on, tip some back with me."

"That would be oysters."

"Whatever. Bivalves, all of them." Shannon was feeling punchy. She was getting to her sister, she could tell.

"Oh, fine." Wren stood and dumped her purse on her chair. "Just stop talking."

Shannon felt elated to be walking through the tent with her sister. Wren was talking to her— well, listening to her talk, at least. And it was a gorgeous night, pink and starry as the remains of the sunset stretched across the sky. It had been years since Wren had come with the family to the ball, and for a beat Shannon felt fresh and girlish, like she used to when they walked under the tent together in their summer best, turning heads as people would murmur and stare, whispering, "There go the Bailey girls." Wren was still a beauty, had always been the prettiest of the three. If the quietest. But sometimes Shannon felt her beauty was overlooked, as Piper presented herself so forcefully to the world. And Shannon, well—she knew what she did. She was vocal. And assertive. She didn't present herself, so much as position herself. And so, she and Piper usually got more of the attention, if not for the right reasons.

Now, as they approached the raw bar, she looped her arm through Wren's, playfully. But her tone was serious. "Listen. I really am sorry about last night. I wanted to be there." She picked up a plate and handed it to her.

Wren took it. "Then you should have been."

"Hey. We talked about this."

"And you definitely should've been there at the hospital. How could you just hang up like that? Do you have any idea what that was like for me and Piper?"

Shannon hadn't expected her to be this mad. It was their turn in line. The older woman serving the oysters pointed to the sign. "Wellfleet, Duxbury, or WiAnno?" she asked.

"Which are more briny?" Shannon asked, feeling flustered.

"The Duxbury are quite buttery," the woman said. "But if you like salt, the Wellfleet are perfect."

They took their oysters to a stand-up table to sample. Wren tipped hers back in silence.

"Look, I don't think it's fair of you to drag this out. You know how I feel about Dad. I'm sorry he's sick, and I worry about how this impacts you, but it doesn't change how I feel about him."

Wren was shaking her head, in disgust or frustration, Shannon couldn't say. Damn Caleb Bailey. He was back, and he was dividing them even when he wasn't present. And he was taking advantage of Wren and moving in, at the worst possible time of all, as she opened her new shop!

"What can I do to help at the shop?" Shannon asked. Maybe this was something she could take off Wren's plate. The photography for the Ridgevale house was done, and the listing confirmed. Bitsy was off her case. "Can I take over a shift for you? How about I take Lucy to the club with the kids one afternoon? Or three?" She was trying.

Wren looked exhausted. "Shannon, last night was pretty bad. I know Mom said he's going to be fine . . . but it's not that simple." She stopped, as if unsure what to say.

Shannon draped an arm around Wren's bare shoulders. "I know. It's all complicated. I want to help, but I can't help with Dad. Tell me what I can do to help you. Will you let me do that at least?" She was losing patience.

"Shannon, if you'd just come see him. I think you'd understand if you saw him."

Shannon slammed her drink down. "Enough." She spun around looking for Reid, but the tent was spinning, and the flickering lights got to her. She reached for the edge of another table but grabbed the tablecloth instead. It yanked out from under the food plates and glassware that were on it, sweeping it all away from the couple who'd been eating there and onto the ground. The woman gasped, and the man bent to help Shannon. "Oh, God. Sorry! I'm so sorry." She was already on her knees picking up the strewn plates, collecting pieces of shrimp and chunks of fish from the blades of grass. When she stood the woman looked at her open-mouthed. Streaks of cocktail sauce smeared the front of her white top. "Shit," she muttered.

Wren appeared at her side with napkins. "Shannon," she hissed.

Shannon took the whole wad and began swiping at her top, but it only resulted in smearing the red stain further across her chest. She wished the man would stop staring at her—couldn't he see this was embarrassing enough already? "What about seltzer?" he suggested warily.

Shannon held up her hand. "Don't worry about it. Really." But her words sounded slow and sticky, even to her. What was happening? She'd only had three drinks. Well, four, if she counted the wine at the house getting ready. Actually, she'd had two wines.

"Where's Reid?" she said, spinning around to Wren. "I want to go home."

Wren had been helping the woman pick up the glassware, and she glared at Shannon. "I'm so, so sorry," she told them again. Though they seemed more concerned about Shannon than their spilled dinners. She grabbed Shannon by the wrist.

"Ow!" she said.

Wren moved awfully fast for a woman in heels. The crowd whipped by, faces blurring, the lights twinkling overhead. The band sounded good. She should find out who they were. She was always looking for a good band for her and Reid's Labor Day party. Oh, there was the president of the Fisherman's Alliance. "Darrel!" she called out happily. She tried to wave but Wren was gripping her wrist and she still clutched the wad of red napkins in the other. Oh, okay, she'd see Darrel next year.

They were heading for the front of the tent when Shannon changed her mind. "Wait. I don't want to go. It's earrrrly." Oh, boy. She sounded so drunk. But she wasn't, really, she wasn't. But she'd put on the brakes and leaned back in her change of heart and Wren had been tugged back with her. Suddenly she felt like she might fall over.

"Shannon?"

She turned her head. "Ellis! Where have you been?"

Suddenly Ellis had her arms around Shannon and she was talking to Wren. Shannon wanted her to talk to her. "Ellis, did I tell you how pretty you look? But those earrings . . . those earrings are not such a good choice. They're so—ugly."

Ellis's face was moving, and Shannon couldn't be sure, but she looked upset. But then everything was so out of focus. "Water." She needed water. Suddenly she was dying of thirst.

More arms. Then voices. Men's voices. It was Reid! "I want to go home!" she cried.

They had left the tent, she was pretty sure, because suddenly it was dark, and the music was distant. Her shoes made clicking noises on the pavement. The parking lot—yes, they were at the car. Someone opened the door and hoisted her up. The leather seat was cold on her bare legs, but she was going home. Yes, home!

"You got this?" It was Wren.

Reid answered. "Yeah, thanks. I'll have her call you in the morning. Sorry about this."

"It's okay. Drive safely."

The last thing Shannon remembered seeing was when Reid swung the car out of the lot, their headlights landed on a woman in an orange dress. She was backed up against a car making out with a man. They squinted into the headlights and quickly turned away.

"Jesus," Reid said.

Shannon dragged herself up for a better look. "Is that—Piper?"

Thirty-Four

Wren

The sweet tobaccoey smell of coffee met her as she rolled over in half slumber, and for a second she forgot all of it. She was in the little apartment on Main Street in the bed tucked under the eaves. Outside on the street below came the voices of shoppers. James had risen early, as he always did before heading to the fish pier at sunrise. There'd be a hot mug of coffee waiting for her on the Formica countertop in the little blue kitchen just outside her bedroom door. And maybe a love note, scrawled in his messy writing on the back of a bill envelope. She stretched out in bed, smiling to herself.

But no—the voices were downstairs, not down on the street. Wren sat up. She was in the Queen Anne house she shared with Lucy. Her father was there.

Wren tossed the covers back and swung her legs over the side of the bed. Her shin had a nice blue bruise blooming where Shannon had accidentally pegged her when she fell down, almost taking a table with her. On her nightstand were the articles she'd printed from the Internet about pancreatic cancer. The different stages, the treatment options. A list of some of the New England–based organizations to reach out to, like Project Purple. Since the night at the hospital, she'd read everything she could find, even after the ball last night, until the computer screen blurred and her head throbbed. But it all seemed to be information for patients at a point Caleb Bailey had long passed. His cancer was advanced stage four, and the only treatments now were pain and symptom management. And eventually, to her consternation, hospice. She'd stopped reading when she got to that.

Lucy and Caleb were already at the table, a plate of toast between them, when she padded into the kitchen barefoot.

"Well, look what the cat dragged in," he said.

"Good morning." She planted a kiss on Lucy's head. The coffee pot was full. She held up a cup to her father. "Want some?"

"Not for me, thanks." Caleb put a hand to his stomach. "Doesn't agree with me these days, I'm afraid."

"Oh, right. Sorry." Wren was still learning what he could and could not eat.

"Look what we made!" Lucy held up the plate of toast. "Smell it!"

Wren sniffed and as she did, a flood of memory came to her. "Hey. Is that cinnamon-sugar toast?" she asked.

Lucy nodded and took a huge bite. "Delicious!"

"That was your mommy's favorite," Caleb told her. "I used to make it for her and your aunties."

It was true. On rainy days or sick days or any kind of day that she and her sisters weren't feeling quite themselves, her father would announce, "I have just the thing!" and disappear into the kitchen. He wasn't much of a cook, but there was just something about that buttery toast sprinkled with a crunch of sugar and whiff of cinnamon. It worked each time. To that day, Wren could not separate the smell of cinnamon from memory of the man.

"So what's the plan today?" he asked, as she joined them at the table.

He looked better. The color had returned to his cheeks, and he seemed stronger. "That depends. How are you feeling?"

Caleb shrugged. "Been better. Been worse. I feel like we need to get out and make the most of this beautiful morning before that changes."

Lucy gazed at her grandpa. "Are you still sick?"

Wren and her father exchanged a glance. "Honey, Grampa is feeling better today. But yes, he is still sick."

"Is it a cold? I had a cold once and I used two boxes of tissues in one day!"

Caleb widened his eyes in amazement. "Two boxes!"

Lucy giggled. In true kid form, she'd already moved on.

Wren tried to conceal her angst. She was going to have to figure out a way to explain this to her without scaring her. Just another worry, on top of what her father's diagnosis meant for all of them. And how to proceed with this new knowledge. Caleb insisted this was not hers to worry herself over, but that was ridiculous. Bullheaded, even. As if she could put down the fact of his terminal illness and set it aside, as if she could just go on with her day and about her business. Not to mention *that*. The shop was barely born and already she was being pulled away from it. It was as if he'd handed her a stick of dynamite wrapped in a patchwork quilt. The outside seemed harmless and reeked of nostalgia from her past. But the contents were dire.

Nothing about this was fair. She'd brought the man into Lucy's life and here she was getting attached, when the truth was at some point in the not-so-distant future she'd have to say goodbye to him. Maybe Shannon was right. Maybe this was the biggest mistake of her life.

"Can we go to the beach?" Lucy asked.

Wren glanced at her dad. "I'm not sure. Is that too much too soon?"

"I think I can manage a trip to the beach. On one condition." He crossed his arms and looked

Lucy straight in the eye. "Can you teach me how to catch a hermit crab?"

Lucy shook her head. "You already know how! Mommy said you lived here."

He threw up his hands. "But maybe I've forgotten. What if I did?"

"Okay, okay. I'll show you." She pushed her chair back excitedly. "Can I get my swimsuit on?" she asked her mother.

Wren nodded over her coffee cup. "Pack some snacks. And a towel."

As they listened to her footfalls on the stairs, Wren waited. "Dad, I've been thinking we could find a doctor for you here, at least for now. What we really need is to form a plan. And I think we should tell the others."

With Lucy's departure, Caleb deflated a little in his chair. The joviality he'd demonstrated moments ago seemed to seep from his limbs, some of the spark from his eye. She did not like this. He was more tired than he was letting on. "Wrenny, there is no 'we' in any of this. This is my struggle that I have unfortunately burdened you with, and I do not wish to do so further. I have doctors, and I have support back at home. It's taken care of. All of that is for when the time comes." He picked at the crust of Lucy's toast. "As for now, I don't want to make plans. I want the time I have left to be unplanned."

Wren could feel herself tearing up, but she wasn't sure if it was because she disagreed with everything he said and thought he should be seeking treatments instead of sitting at her kitchen table, or because she knew he was right and the end was imminent. He had always been stubborn as a bull. But that was when she was the child, he the adult. Sitting across the breakfast table from him now, that was no longer the case. "I understand, but I'm not sure it's that simple. You're here now, far away from your doctors. Beyond our hospital visit and what you've shared since, I still don't know anything about your treatment, your medications. And most of all, you need to think about . . . next steps. I want to know how you want to handle that." She didn't want to say it, but it was something they would have to talk about. What were Caleb's wishes?

He put a gentle hand up. "I already told you, I am not spending my last days—whenever they may come—here on the Cape. This trip is for as long as I can manage it and as long as you'll have me. No more. When the time comes, I've made the arrangements. And that's that."

"But who do you have down there? It can't all be—what's her name—Alice?"

"Alice is my neighbor. We sort of look after one another. She's like a sister, that's all."

Wren hadn't meant it like that. "Dad, please. I

didn't think otherwise, and frankly I don't want to know. I just don't like the idea of you down there." She didn't add, "all alone."

Wren had lost the match, however. Lucy trotted downstairs in her purple rash guard and swim skirt. Her goggles were already affixed to her face. She held a plastic bucket aloft.

Caleb smacked the table lightly. "All right. Beach time!"

They were loaded in the car headed down Route 28 when Lucy asked if they could go to Lighthouse, and Wren was seized with the realization. She'd not been there with her father since the day of the accident.

She kept her eyes trained on the road. "What about Hardings or Ridgevale, honey?"

"But Lighthouse has the waves!"

Wren could feel her father shift uncomfortably in the passenger seat. She glanced at him.

"It's all right."

"Are you sure?"

He shrugged. "No. But I have to go back at some point. Might as well do it together."

As a child, Wren had had no choice but to face Lighthouse Beach. After all, it was around the corner from her grandmother's where they lived. In the days after the accident, they'd stayed close to the house out of necessity. Piper had a neat row of sutures across her four-year-old forehead that caused Lindy's face to crumple each time she looked at them.

But the day Piper had her stitches taken out, Lindy had picked up the big girls at school. Wren remembered Piper had a Minnie Mouse Band-Aid on her head and a lollipop in her hand. "Where are we going?" Wren had asked.

"Some place we have to visit."

Shannon was annoyed. She was missing a test of some kind, and Wren recalled her arguing in the front seat. Lindy had driven past their turn at School Street. When she pulled into the Lighthouse parking lot they all knew something was up.

"What're we doing here?" Shannon had barked.

Lindy had turned to look at Piper and Wren in the back seat, her face full of concern. "It's okay. We're going to the beach."

Wren had felt a stomachache coming on. She hadn't exactly thought about the beach in terms of her father leaving or Piper's head, but being there made her feel instantly sick. "Come on," Lindy had said, opening the car door. She came around to the back and held it open.

Piper hopped out first, and Wren hesitated. "No. No way," Shannon said from the front seat.

"Shannon, my love. You're going to have to trust me."

"This is stupid. I said no."

It was a blustery day, and the wind whipped

at their hair. Wren knew the sand would be biting on the beach. She did not want to go. And Shannon's insistence was causing her to worry.

Lindy scooped Piper up and put an arm around Wren. "Just a quick walk," she said. "We're going down the steps to the sand. That's all. Then we'll go home."

Shannon refused to budge. Lindy started walking, Wren's hand tight in her own; even though she was too old to hold her mother's hand in a parking lot. She followed.

Wren glanced back at Shannon. She stared straight ahead at the Sound, ignoring them.

At the top of the steps, Lindy set Piper down. "Stay here. Watch your sister."

Piper started to whimper.

Lindy trudged back to the car, head down in the wind. Wren watched her yank open the door. She bent down. Wren wondered what she was saying. But it must've been good, because suddenly Shannon was out of the car. She walked a good distance behind her mother, arms crossed, but she was following. "Come along!" Lindy urged her. It was so cold.

When the four of them were finally assembled at the head of the steps, Lindy knelt down. "This is our beach," she said. "This is the beach you learned to fish off of, Shannon. And this is the beach you both learned to swim," she told the girls. "Piper, this is the beach where you will learn to do those things, too. There is nothing here to be afraid of, and so we are going to walk down these stairs together and say hello to the beach." She looked at them, hard. "This is our beach."

Despite the wind, Piper seized hold of the idea they were going to the beach and started down. Lindy scuttled after her.

Wren remembered standing by Shannon, who did not follow. She wasn't going to, Wren knew. She could feel it in her fierce posture, in her short puffs of breath. And she was torn between staying beside her sister and doing what their mother said. She did not want to go down to the beach either. The sound of the surf made her stomach twist, and she closed her eyes, thinking of her father and the boat and Piper bobbing up before disappearing under the water. Why was their mother making them go? It was a terrible idea.

Halfway down, Lindy stopped and looked back. A gust of wind blasted the girls, and Wren had to shield her eyes. When she opened them, Lindy was making her way back to them, Piper on her hip. "Girls, please." She set Piper down, heaving with effort from the climb. Wren felt terrible.

"Okay," she said. She reached for her older sister's hand, but Shannon swatted hers away.

And then Shannon turned for the car. She spun on her heel, her mouth set. But before she could take a step, Lindy had grabbed her.

"What are you doing?" Shannon screamed.

Lindy wrapped both arms around her, and Wren hopped back out of the way as they began to tug and pull in both directions. There was a terrible scraping of feet on the sandy pavement. Shannon was not quite as tall as their mother, but her anger made her strong. She twisted in Lindy's grip.

Their mother had never put a hand on them, not once. And now she was dragging Shannon, her lips pulled back over her teeth in effort. "Mommy!" Wren cried.

"Let go of me," Shannon yelled. "You're crazy!"

Suddenly her sneakers slipped beneath her, and Shannon fell away. Lindy let her go, falling back on her haunches. She watched as her eldest daughter scrambled away from her like a crab. But then she stopped. A strangled sound came from Lindy's throat. Their mother was crying, hot tears streaming from her eyes.

"You have to trust me," she sobbed. "Please, baby. Trust me."

Shannon's face crumpled and she sat down in the middle of the parking lot. Wren watched in horror as her mother crawled on all fours to her sister, cupping her face in her hands. They sat for what seemed like an eternity, and finally Lindy rose. When she extended her hand, Shannon took it.

They walked all the way down to the sand and

kept going. Shannon's corduroy pants were torn at the knee. Lindy's eyes were smeared with tears and mascara. No one spoke, but they put one foot in front of the other, four across as they made their way to the water. As they got close, Piper started to trot ahead. "Stop before the water," Lindy called after her. "We're just looking today."

They stood watching the surf roll in and out, small waves rising up like a cupped hand before opening and crashing onto the sand, the foamy white fingers reaching up toward their feet. After a while Shannon turned back toward the dunes. "I hate this place. And I hate all of you."

Lindy sat down in the sand, her head in her hands. "We had to do it," she said.

They would return, after winter came and went, and the passage of the season somehow made it more palatable. Lindy took them regularly in the summer, and they biked there and hung out with friends as they grew older. Piper learned to swim and boogie board, and Lindy resumed her summer ritual of walking to the beach and taking early morning swims before any of them awoke. Lighthouse normalized for them all, except for Shannon. To this day, Shannon had never swum in the Cape waters, as far as Wren knew. Not on the National Seashore side, though Wren knew she and Reid took the kids up there. Not even in the bay area, along their coveted waterfront neighborhood in Stage Harbor. She'd kept her hate close for twenty-three years.

As they pulled into the crowded lot, now, Wren swallowed hard.

She parked the Jeep in one of the last remaining spots in the rear, and her eyes traveled to the front row of parking spaces. She could almost see the red wood-paneled station wagon parked there, and the three little blonde girls lined up uncertainly outside the car.

They unloaded the beach bag and cooler. Caleb and Wren each took a beach chair, and Lucy plucked her bucket and shovels from the back. At the top of the steps, Wren paused and looked at her father. He placed a shaky hand on the railing and stared over the expanse of the beach blow. His brow was creased, from worry or pain she couldn't say.

"What are we waiting for?" Lucy wanted to know.

Wren studied her father. "You sure this isn't too much?"

He shifted the beach chair on his shoulder and gripped the railing. "Lucy, lead the way."

Thirty-Five

Piper

They were back on. She'd seen Derek every day, sometimes twice, since the day they met at the Beach House Grill. Suddenly he could not get enough of her, and while she found it surprising and confusing given the fact he was on a family vacation and had never before been able to make himself this available to her back in Boston, she did not dare question it. For now, he was hers again.

She'd been at the Hooker's Ball no more than a few minutes when he texted her. *Everyone here is wiped out from the beach and in bed early. I can get away for an hour. Where are you?*

It was not a good time. She was at a ticketed event with her family surrounded by people. And yet it worked. People were dressed up and dancing, mingling and eating. Half of them were knee-deep in cocktail hour. With all the excitement, no one would miss her if she snuck down to the car for a little while. She made sure to show her face and greet those she knew, slugged back a flute of champagne, and scurried through the tent to the parking lot. She'd bumped into Reid on the way.

"Where's the fire?" he joked.

"Oh, I just forgot something in the car."

"Want me to get it for you?" Reid was such a gentleman. But in that moment, she wished he'd be less attentive and get the heck out of there.

"Thanks, but I'm fine." She turned toward the lot.

"One thing," Reid said.

Piper stilled, fearful for a second that he somehow knew what she was up to. Only Wren did, so far, and while her family was completely crazy, as far as she knew none of them had tarnished the family name, so to speak. Least of all Shannon and Reid, with their immaculate house and monogrammed sweaters and perfect family. They were spotless all around.

"I'm worried about Shannon," he said.

Piper let out a breath of relief. "Oh, right. Me, too."

This got his attention. "You are?"

"No, well not really. What I meant to say is things have been kind of strained with my dad back in town, and I know it's been hard on her."

Reid was running his hand thoughtfully over his chin. "Has she said anything to you?"

Piper stole a look at the parking lot, feeling guilty. Her brother-in-law was normally a private guy, and she could tell he was pretty worried. But she didn't have much time. "Not to me," she said. "I'm still hoping she'll agree to see him though."

"Me, too. But it's not just about your father. To be honest I think she's been struggling for a while." He looked her in the eye. "Do you think she drinks too much?"

So, this was not just about their dad. Piper hadn't exactly been spending much time with Shannon since she got back. But come to think of it, when she did see her she seemed to have a drink in hand.

"Has she done anything that worries you?" Piper asked.

Reid shook his head. "Nothing specific, no. The kids are fine, and she's been busy working on that new listing she and my mother landed. I know that was stressful for her. And of course, your father." His voice trailed off as if he'd answered his own question.

"Well, that's probably it then. You know Shannon. She's so put together, always on top of everything. I'm sure she's fine."

Reid brightened a little.

A small black car rolled in and Piper felt a flutter in her tummy as she recognized Derek's Audi. "Well, I better get my thing. From my car," she added quickly, praying Reid wouldn't stick around and wait for her.

"Thanks, Piper. I appreciate what you said." She watched as he headed back up the walkway toward the tent. As soon as he slipped beneath the awning, she hurried down the steps.

She'd worried about how stupid she'd been earlier, blurting out that she loved him in the dressing room. Piper did not fall in love; she certainly did not show her cards to a man, no matter how much she liked him.

But then a terrible thought struck her as she approached his car. What if Derek was calling things off? Maybe she'd said too much; maybe he felt too pressured. His car was running, and she bent down and knocked on the passenger window, bracing herself for the worst.

Derek's face lit up. "God you look hot. Get in here."

They'd made love in the back seat, heaving for breath afterward. "Please stay," he whispered. It couldn't be just about the sex if he were sticking around when she knew he had a family waiting back at his beach rental, just as she had a family waiting for her somewhere up under the tent. "For just a few minutes more," he added, tracing her jaw with his finger.

"People are going to be wondering where I am," she said, secretly pleased to be the one to be begging off for the first time. Before getting out of the car, she glanced around. The band was really going now, and the smell of the fish fry made her stomach growl. If only she could take his hand and lead him back to the party. But still, what a wonderful night this was turning out to be. Derek surprised her by getting out of the car first, and running around to open her door. He took her in his arms once more and kissed her goodbye. It was their only close call, as a car across the lot started and turned their headlights on them. Piper ducked out of the glare, shielding her eyes. "Fuck!" she muttered. But then the car pulled away, and she pulled him in for another kiss, laughing at the danger having passed.

She'd filled her plate and found her family at the table. Wren seemed to be annoyed, saying something about Shannon leaving early, which gave Piper pause. But Lindy and Hank seemed to be making the most of the ball, taking a few turns on the dance floor. Piper ordered herself another champagne and joined them. She ran into a few old friends who gushed when they saw her, one of whom was married with kids. Another engaged, as luck would have it. But she didn't even mind listening as they talked about weddings and first houses. Before the night ended, she got Wren out on the dance floor when the band played "Twist and Shout," and when she fell into bed just before midnight she slept through the night for the first time in months.

First thing the next morning she'd popped into the shower, run over to Monomoy Coffee, and ordered two iced lattes. As she unlocked the Fisherman's Daughter for her shift, she noticed the sky was bluer than she could ever remember seeing it. She'd call her father to see how he was feeling. Maybe that afternoon when she finished work they could take a drive up to Wellfleet.

There wasn't a free moment after she opened, as it turned out. A woman with three boys came in for a gift for her mother-in-law. Piper spent a long time showing her jewelry and housewares, but she couldn't make up her mind. As Piper nervously eyed the boisterous activity level, cringing as they started a shoving match near the wave sculpture, the woman gave in. "Would you please pick something? Anything is fine. I don't care what it costs. I need to get them out of here." In less than five minutes she rang up and gift-wrapped an antique map.

"I can't thank you enough!" the woman said as she plucked a decorative pillow out of one boy's grip and grabbed the hand of the nearest kid and dragged him toward the door.

Then there was a steady flow of lookie-loos, as Lindy called them. A teenager who purchased some earrings. And a phone call from an artist who was confirming an order for pottery. Piper was starving and reaching for her packed lunch when the bell jingled over the door. Could she just get a second to eat?

"Hi again!" It was the cute blonde woman from the opening party who had tried on the striped dress.

"Welcome back," Piper said, shoving her salad aside. "How'd you make out with the white tunic?"

The woman flashed a smile. "Good memory. I love it. But I'm actually here for the dress. Is it okay if I try it on one more time?"

"Sure, come on back." Ari had sold one the other day, and Wren only had a few in stock in mixed sizes. She hoped it was still there. "Size small, right?"

"Right again." Piper liked her style. She was wearing a cute tennis skirt with a denim jacket. Her red Tory Burch bag was a nice pop of color.

"Love the bag," Piper told her, as she flicked through the rack.

"Thanks. Was a birthday present."

To her relief the small dress was still there. "Here you go."

The woman disappeared into the changing room and Piper went back to the counter to steal a bite of her salad. She popped back out. "What do we think? Still a good bet, or should I try something else?"

She examined herself in the mirror, looking over her shoulder as she turned this way and that. If possible, it looked even better in daylight. "It's a winner," Piper said. "Shall I ring it up for you?"

"Yes, please!"

As Piper checked her out, the woman noticed a silver tray of rings on the counter. "Aren't these cute." She tried a few on and set one on top of the dress. "This, too, please."

She was making solid sales today, and it wasn't even noon. Wren was going to be happy.

The door jingled again and a shopper with two little ones came in just as Piper was wrapping the dress. "I'll be right with you!" she called, as she tied a raffia ribbon to the bag and stuck in a sprig of dried lavender.

"Thank you," the woman said. "I'm sure my husband will love this. Won't you, honey?"

The sun was streaming in from the front door creating a glare, and at first to Piper the shoppers were mere silhouettes. But then they took shape. The little girl from the opening night ran up to her mom and threw her arms around her legs. Then a little boy, with a cute mop of dark hair, followed by a man.

"What will I like?" he asked.

Piper looked up and froze.

Derek stared back at her.

"This is the cute little shop I was telling you about the other night. Remember?" The woman held up her bag. "Wait till you see this dress I got. I think we need a date night." She grinned and pecked him on the cheek, completely unaware of the way her husband was looking at Piper, the color draining from his tanned cheeks.

"Thanks, again!" she said.

Piper had to tear her eyes away and force her

mouth to work. "My pleasure," she managed. Piper gripped the edge of the counter as she watched her round up their beautiful children. As Derek turned in her cheerful wake and trailed them all out.

When the door closed behind them, Piper raced from behind the counter to the window where she strained to watch them go. They strolled up the sidewalk toward the bookstore until they were out of her sightline. Then she turned the sign to *CLOSED,* flicked off the lights, and sank to the floor.

Thirty-Six

Caleb

Lucy was the spitting image of her mother, save her dark hair. The turn of her nose, the curious glances. The way she scurried along the tidal pool, pausing and bending to collect, inspect, explore. How much he had missed, staying away.

The thing was, Lighthouse was just a beach. A sandy strip of land that met the sea, connecting up and down the Cape elbow to the other Chatham beaches: Hardings, Cockle Cove, Ridgevale. The water that flowed there was the same that flowed through Nantucket Sound and out into the cold dark stretch of the Atlantic. The shore and water held no memory; there was nothing to say that a single grain of sand deposited here today was ever here before. Let alone on that day.

But stepping off the stairs onto the hot sand, the flicker of surf ahead, Caleb felt himself transported back. The crowds of happy beachgoers could not save him, any more than the blinding sun that contrasted itself in every way from the gray drizzly weather back then could not. Never mind the shrill blow on the lifeguard's whistle when a child on a boogie board floated past the red buoy markers into the swimming section; never mind the purposeful wake of the day boats that chugged past into Nantucket Sound. Lighthouse could not look or sound more different than that day, and yet he was back there again. Knee-deep in roiling gray surf, his fingertips bashed and bleeding from the flipped Beetle Cat whose edges he gripped and tore at, trying in vain to flip it back over. The shouts of the teenage boys nearby tossing a football became the screams he heard coming from the beach in that frozen moment he jerked his head around and saw Wren on the shore, watching as he and Shannon bobbed and sunk. Screaming Piper's name over and over.

When Lucy grabbed his hand, he flinched, squeezed down too hard, raw with the memory of reaching for another. She yelped. Wren spun around, a mother bear. He would enjoy the sight of it, if not for the fact that he caused it.

"I'm sorry," he said, sinking down to meet Lucy's brown-eyed wariness. "I held on too tight, didn't I?"

Lucy nodded, pulling her hand away.

"Gramps just wanted to keep you close, sweetheart. It won't happen again, I promise."

After a moment, she handed him her bucket and pointed to the water. "This way," she said.

His joints ached and his stomach was roiling all

morning. He could feel the sun boring through his skin, bleaching his bones.

"Are you all right?" Wren asked.

But in spite of it all, he was. He cast a backward glance across the sand at the surf. When Lucy slipped her hand back in his, he did not hear the screams in the wind anymore.

Thirty-Seven

Shannon

Her phone lit up with messages when she finally turned it on, around noon. Reid was gone, the note on the counter saying he'd left for the office. He was mad at her. When he was getting ready for work, she'd stumbled from the bed and made it just in time to the toilet before retching up the remains of last night. When she came out, he glanced at her with disgust before heading downstairs to the kitchen.

She scrolled through her messages, wondering if he'd reached out. *Feeling okay?* Ellis texted. *Sorry we missed a spin on the dance floor but don't sweat it. Reid and I had you out of there before anyone really saw.*

The sign of a good friend. Informing you of damage-control efforts, first and foremost.

Another was from Lindy: *You disappeared last night. Did you have fun?* Well, thankfully she seemed to have missed all of her daughter's fun. At least Wren had not informed her of the details.

Wren. She needed to call Wren.

• • •

Downstairs in the kitchen she found the girls standing in front of the open fridge as if they were shoe shopping. "You sure slept late," Avery said. She held a cheese stick between her fingers like a cigarette. Her hair was combed back in a neat ponytail, and she was dressed up in one of her pink Lily skirts.

"Where are you off to?" Shannon asked. Her voice came out like a one-hundred-year-old man. She needed Tylenol.

"Jenny Fromme's birthday party, remember? It's at one o'clock."

"Yes, that's right." Though Shannon did not remember. She didn't even recall having seen an invitation. "Do you need a ride?"

Avery popped the rest of the cheese stick in her mouth, and Shannon's stomach churned. "No. Mrs. Dwight is picking me up."

The Dwights were at the ball last night, sitting at a table from the chamber of commerce. Shannon bet Carol Dwight didn't get carried home by her husband last night.

"What about you?" she asked Winnie.

Winnie was too transfixed to answer. "Your eyes are all smudged in black like a raccoon. What happened to you?"

"Oh." Shannon put a hand to her face. She hadn't washed her face after the ball. "I forgot to take off my makeup last night. I'll shower."

418

"You haven't showered yet?"

"Don't you have practice or something?" She was tiring of the inquisition.

Winnie was still staring. "Tennis was this morning. Dad took me."

So that had happened, too. Shannon popped open the Tylenol bottle and threw back two. "Where's your brother?"

"I don't know. In the office on the computer, I think."

Shannon found him exactly there, playing video games. "Hey, honey."

George didn't look up. "Hi, Mom. Who's taking me to my lesson?"

"You have a lesson?"

"I think so. At the club."

Shannon squinted at the calendar over her desk. Crap. So he did. "It's at two o'clock." It was only twelve-thirty. There was plenty of time. "I'm going to go shower and then I'll make you some lunch before your lesson, okay?"

"You didn't shower yet?"

As soon as Avery was off with Mrs. Dwight (who was the picture of health and non-hangover-ness—Shannon knew because this perky mom actually got out of the car, with her daughter, and knocked on the door to say hello), Shannon fixed the kids sandwiches. Just opening the fridge made her stomach reel. As she folded slices of deli meat onto bread, she felt another wave of nausea. There was no way to get through the day like this. While retrieving the jar of mayonnaise she saw the jar of horseradish. Next to it was a jar of olives. Suddenly the thing she craved more than anything was a zesty Bloody Mary. Did they have a lemon? She found one in the fruit bowl. She'd tried the Tylenol and the water. What was wrong with a little hair of the dog? She juiced the lemon and opened a bottle of fresh tomato juice from the pantry. A tablespoon of horseradish, a dash of Worcester sauce, olive juice. She sprinkled the rim of her glass in Old Bay, filled it with ice and dumped in the ingredients. Grey Goose from the freezer—a few glugs should do it. Shannon never measured. A slice of celery. Nirvana! Who would've thought an acidic and zesty cocktail could be the balm to a ringer of a hangover.

While the kids ate, she tucked the laptop under her arm and went upstairs. But she didn't make it to the shower. Her bed was so alluring, and instead of walking past it she slipped back in. What was ten minutes more? She still had an hour to get George to his sailing lesson. She sipped her Bloody and checked work emails and messages from the office. There was a call from a woman with a British accent to see the Ridgevale place. Finally!

Shannon was about to shut down her computer

and drag herself into the shower when a folder in the bottom corner of her screen caught her eye: *Stock Photos.* It was a folder of saved work taken over the years. Some of it went back to before the kids were born, and were scanned images of nondigital prints she'd done in her darkroom when she and Reid first got married and lived in Orleans. Some was more recent, like the spontaneous photos she'd snap on the way to work when a scene or a sunset forced her car off the road and necessitated she pull her camera bag out of the back. Those were some of her best shots. Chatham Light on a foggy morning as the sun rose. Edith, the grandmotherly waitress at Larry's PX as she handed a chubby-cheeked Avery a hot cocoa with a candy cane in it. Shannon liked that Avery's face peeked out from the corner and that the focus was on Edith's hands, her crinkling smiling eyes. There was a recent shot of a fisherman unloading catch at the Chatham Pier, his yellow coveralls the only pop of color against the gray sea and sky.

Shannon felt good looking at the images, not just because they were personal to her, but because she felt the work was strong. Yet she'd never shown anyone in her family. Caleb Bailey was the artist, not her, and the last thing she wanted was to be compared to a man whose work had come before his family. The office staff had seen some of her work, but that was mostly in the context of real estate images. Still, they were always telling her she should have her own show. That these were pictures people would spend their money on. Shannon wasn't sure if that were true, but lately she'd been thinking it might be time to find out.

She ran the shower and undressed, feeling a pleasing looseness in her limbs. She'd made her Bloody Mary a bit stronger than she intended. But it was so good, and there was only a little left, so she took it in the shower with her. What was the difference? It was mostly tomato juice.

George came in soon after, while she was blow-drying her hair. "You're still in your bathrobe? We're going to be late!"

"It's okay, George. I'll just be a quick minute." Thank God he was dressed.

"Whistle?" she asked, racing past him to her walk-in.

"Got it."

"Sunscreen?"

"Winnie put it on."

"If only Winnie could drive."

"What?"

"Nothing! I'll meet you in the car, honey. Grab a water bottle!"

George was right. She'd taken longer than she meant to in the shower, and there was no time to finish getting ready. She pulled on a pair of soft capri yoga pants and a T-shirt and ran downstairs. "Let's go!" she called.

Winnie was at the kitchen island reading a book. "He's waiting outside. Can we go into town?"

"Maybe when I get back. I've got to get your brother to sailing." She glanced at the clock. "Has your father called?"

"Nope."

She and Reid talked several times a day. It was disconcerting to not have heard anything from him yet, especially after last night. She'd call him on the way.

Poor George. He was already in the car, buckled into his seatbelt. Shannon eyed him in the rearview mirror.

"Hey, buddy. Good job getting ready."

He didn't say anything. It was already two o'clock. They were late.

She backed out of the garage. "I'm sorry. Don't worry, we're just five minutes away."

George stared out the window. Now she'd disappointed another male in the family. She glanced at her phone in her lap. She pressed Reid's number. It went straight to voice mail.

It wasn't fair. For all these years she'd juggled motherhood and working and being a wife and keeping a beautiful family home. She'd tried to appease Bitsy as both an agent and a daughter-in-law. And for all these years she'd kept all her bases covered. Now during summer, her most favorite season of all, she was dropping all her balls. She turned out of her gravel drive and hit the gas.

Shannon's head throbbed. The Ridgevale house was priced high, and Everett Banks refused to hold open houses. She couldn't pop over to Lindy's with the kids or spend any meaningful time with her sisters because they were too busy entertaining their estranged father, acting like tour guides in their own town, taking him into their homes, their new shops, their Sunday night dinners. Leaving her out. At the next stop sign a car cut her off. It was her turn! Shannon laid on the horn.

And Reid—good old Reid who she'd not spent a lick of time with because she was so stressed and strained with the rest of it. The car in front of her slowed to a snail's pace. It was 2:05. "Come on!" Shannon shouted. She glanced at George in the rearview mirror. "Almost there," she assured him.

Now she'd have to run George down to the beach and find a free instructor to help with the boat, as the rest of his class would already be on the water. He'd be upset having to catch up. The car in front of her was clearly on a sightseeing tour, slowing to look out the windows at the houses along the water. They were so close to the Yacht Club, and yet it was taking forever. "This is ridiculous." Shannon accelerated and swerved around the car. The driver threw her a look as she blew past, and it was all she could do not to give him the finger.

"Mommy?"

"It's fine, George."

The Stage Harbor Yacht Club was just up the narrow street on her right. She was about to put her indicator on when she heard the wail of a siren. There in her rearview mirror was a police car. Its blue-and-red lights flashing. "Shit." It was not fine.

There was no place to pull over on the narrow lane, so Shannon had no choice but to slow and pull into the Yacht Club lot. Fantastic. George was not only late, they had arrived with a police escort.

"Mommy, what happened? Are you in trouble?"

She pulled over nearer the marina adjacent, praying it was less conspicuous than the club. Who was she kidding? Everyone could see them.

"It's okay, honey. Just sit still and let Mommy talk."

The officer was a young woman. She knocked on Shannon's window.

"I'm so sorry!" Shannon began. But her window was closed, she was so flustered, and she had to start over again when she rolled it down. "We were running late to a lesson, and that car in front of me kept slowing and stopping.

They were driving rather erratically, actually . . ."

"License and registration, please, ma'am."

The officer did not want to hear about it. She reached across the passenger seat and popped open the glove box. The registration and insurance cards were there, but when she looked around for her purse it was nowhere in the car. "Oh, God. I think I left my purse on the kitchen counter." She turned to the officer. "I was rushing. I'm so sorry!" She handed over the insurance cards, hands shaking.

But the officer remained at the window. "Will you remove your sunglasses?" the officer asked.

"What?"

"Your sunglasses."

"Oh. Okay, sure." Shannon slipped them up on her head. The officer removed her own sunglasses as well, and leaned in her window. "Where did you say you were coming from?"

Shannon blinked. "My home. It's just up the road, not far at all."

"Ma'am, have you been drinking this morning?"

Thirty-Eight

Hank

The first call came from Wren. She wanted to know if they would mind if she and Lucy came over to look at something in the back shed. They were bringing Caleb. Lindy and Beverly were sitting on the sun porch having coffee when Hank brought the phone out. "What do they want from the shed?"

Hank shook his head. Wren had not said, but she was still on the line if Lindy wanted to talk to her.

"Whatever it is, that's fine." She was still distracted from the events of the ball. It had been a lovely night, even if her daughters were not quite themselves. Lindy had complained at bedtime that Piper was so unsettled. "Do you notice how 'all over the place' she is? I'm worried about her."

Hank had, and he was worried, too. But as usual, he predicted there would be many discussions before any action, if any, was taken, and so he'd made an extra-large pot of coffee that morning.

The next call came from Piper. She was

427

working at the shop for Wren, but she sounded funny. Hank handed the phone directly to Lindy. He'd yet to hear what the outcome of that was.

The final call came from Reid. He spoke so quietly that at first Hank didn't think he'd heard him correctly. "You're where?" Hank had asked.

"The police department. Shannon's been arrested. Will you and Lindy please pick up the kids?"

This call he did not hand over to Lindy. He wrote down the details, hung up, and went straight to the sun porch instead. "We have to run over to Shannon's place," he said.

Both women perked up. "Why?" Lindy asked. "Was that her?"

"Not exactly. Reid needs us to pick something up." Hank did not want to say this in front of Beverly. He could've pulled Lindy aside, somewhere in the house, but Lindy was not known for her discretion. And despite her age, Beverly was known for highly attuned hearing.

Both women frowned. "I haven't been to Shannon's house yet, even though she keeps saying she's going to have us for dinner. So busy, these days. So much running around," Beverly sighed. "Maybe I'll fix my hair and come for a ride with you?"

"No!" Hank said. "I mean, it's just a quick drive over to pick something up. We'll be coming right back."

Lindy narrowed her eyes. "What are we picking up?"

For the first time in their marriage, Hank did not answer directly. "Lindy, I'm afraid I'm in a rush. Are you coming or not?"

He'd not spoken to her like that before, and he braced himself for her receipt. To his surprised and great relief, she stood. "Well, all right." Lindy turned to her mother. "It seems we'll be right back. Why don't you hold down the fort for Lucy and Wren?"

Hank did not look back but got the keys. He would drive.

There was no keeping the news from the children. George could not stop talking. Neither could the rest of them.

"The police officer called Daddy, and he had to come to the Yacht Club. But they took Mommy in the police car."

Lindy eyed Hank in the driver's seat. When she was not turning around in her seat reassuring the children in a practiced falsetto, her mouth resumed its position of grim straight line.

They'd met Reid at the house. He was standing in the kitchen, hands on his hips as if at the ready, his shirt unbuttoned, his tie askew. George and Winnie were on the couch on high alert. "I haven't been to the station yet," he said, running his hand roughly through his hair. "I wanted to keep the kids out of it."

"Of course!" Lindy had said. She went straight to the couch, arms open.

"Is Shannon all right?" Hank asked, keeping his voice low.

Reid shook his head. "I wish I knew. I'll call you both when I know more."

Now, all three kids sat in the back, Bowser in the far back. Lindy had insisted on bringing him. "Canine comfort in times of crisis." Hank wasn't about to argue.

"Is Mommy in trouble?" Avery asked, shakily.

"Mommy's going to be okay," Lindy told her. "Sometimes parents make mistakes, too, and we're going to help Mommy make it better. Don't you worry." At the last part her voice cracked, and she turned around to face forward. Hank put a hand on her knee.

"Let's go to our house and see Great Grammy Beverly," he said. "I think there's ice cream in the fridge."

From the back seat came a small voice. "Mommy loves ice cream."

Hank had forgotten all about Wren. Apparently, so had Lindy. "Oh, Good Lord," she said as they pulled into the driveway. Her car was parked to the side. Standing in the middle of their driveway, as if welcoming them home, was Caleb.

"Who's that?" asked Avery.

Lindy looked to Hank, but this time he was out of answers. Shannon did not want the kids anywhere near Caleb Bailey. But Shannon was in jail. Lindy took a deep breath and pushed open the passenger door. "Come on, kids. Let's go meet your Grandpa."

Thirty-Nine

Wren

S he had an idea. Lindy might not like it. Shannon was sure to hate it. Depending on her mood, Piper could go either way. But Wren felt it in her gut, and sometimes you had to listen to your gut, even if it meant not listening to your mother.

There was not much time left, and there was so much still to do. Her phone had rung again, with the same Arizona phone number she'd answered last time. Her father's friend Alice.

"Hello, Wren? It's Alice, again. Do you have a minute, please?" Her voice held a plaintive tone.

"Yes, I'm here."

"Oh, good. How are you all doing?" The familiarity with which this woman spoke to her caught Wren off guard. What did she want?

"We're fine. How can I help you?"

"I'm your dad's friend. And sponsor?"

Of course, his AA sponsor. She let her guard down a little. "Yes, he mentioned you. Hello."

"I'm sorry to interrupt your visit. I just wanted to check on him. How is he doing?"

Wren told Alice about the hospital visit. "Is he

taking his pain meds? If he doesn't stay on top of them, it's harder to regulate."

Alice was not an outsider, Wren realized. Alice was someone her father needed, and someone she realized, with a fluter of relief, that she too might need in the picture. Wren thought of the Fentanyl patches she'd picked up at the pharmacy the day before. "He's been taking the pills, but it's getting worse," she admitted. "His appetite isn't much these days. It comes and goes." She let her breath out. "He was so strong when he first got here."

Alice was a good listener. It gave Wren hope for what was awaiting her father back in Arizona. He did have friends, a home, and people to help look after him. It would make letting him go a little easier. Wren agreed to talk each day, and allowed that there wouldn't be many before she had to get him on a plane back to Arizona.

As they sat on the beach at Lighthouse Beach that morning, it had come to her. The worst day of her life had begun with the boat. What if they were to go back to it?

The house was empty, save for Beverly, who was posted on the front porch as if waiting for them, when they arrived. "Where's Mom?"

"It's a mystery, dear. I'm just along for the show. Grab an iced tea and join me?"

Now, as she stood in front of the shed she wasn't so sure.

"What's the plan?" Caleb asked. She'd not told him but asked him to simply come along on an errand. He was getting tired, she could tell, and she wanted to offer the idea up to him before they went home and he took one of his long afternoon naps. She wanted him to sleep on it.

Wren tugged at the handles, and the shed doors creaked open. They called it the shed, but it was an old carriage house in the rear of the yard under the shade of an oak. Dust motes floated through the air, illuminated by the sunlight that filtered through the side windows. Wren pointed to the far-left corner. Caleb followed.

The canvas tarp was stained and covered in dust, but it peeled back easily. "What do you think?" Wren asked.

Caleb did not speak. He stood a long time staring at the Beetle Cat. Wren watched as he stepped forward and placed his hand on the hull, running it slowly along the sheer oak planks. "After all these years." He turned to her. "Your mother kept it?"

Wren nodded, unsure if this would prove too much. But her father's eyes sparkled. He came to life, lifting the canvas tarp up and away, revealing the whole of the boat.

"She's dusty and old. I'm not sure she's sea-worthy. But I had an idea."

They'd just stepped out of the shed when they heard the car pull in. Caleb went out to the front

434

as Wren tried to decide how to best get the boat out of there. It would take many hands. Her father wasn't strong enough, and it was heavy for two.

She'd half expected Lindy to come fluttering into the back, a suspicious look in her eyes as she sniffed around to see what they were doing in her shed. But the sound of car doors slamming was followed by children's voices coming from the front.

When she rounded the corner, there stood her father in the driveway with Lindy and Hank. The adults were secondary. Lucy was making introductions to George, Avery, and Winnie. Reid and Shannon were nowhere to be seen.

"She what?" Wren could not believe it. She kept one eye on the kids, who were talking shyly to Caleb on the bottom porch step, a tray of lemonade and a bowl of potato chips between them. George blew his sailing whistle, and everyone covered their ears.

Lindy kept her voice low. "Shannon's been arrested. Reid is down there now, posting bail. It seems she'll be free to go after her arraignment."

Wren sat back in her chair, glancing worriedly at Beverly. Her grandmother had her hands over her ears and was shaking her head. "It's too much," she kept saying.

Lindy did not look much better.

"Should I go down there?"

"No." Lindy was firm about this. "Shannon needs us here with the kids."

"What about Dad?" All three women cast their eyes to the bottom step. Caleb was nodding along to something the kids were saying. Avery, the oldest, looked curious but uncertain. Winnie and George were engaged. "She's going to kill us," Wren said. "You know she will."

Beverly lifted both shoulders. "She'll have to get out of jail first."

There was no better or worse time to share her idea, so she just did. Wren gathered the kids up on the porch, and had her father sit down. He was wearing out right before her eyes, and she could tell she needed to get him home. "I have a summer project," she told them, rubbing her hands together. "A sort of family project. But I'm going to need your help."

"What is it?" George asked.

Wren studied each little face, whose attention she had for only a short time. "I can't tell you until you agree to help."

"But we don't know what it is yet," Avery pointed out.

"Trust," Wren told her.

"What if it's gross? Like scooping dog poop?" George burst into giggles and so did Lucy.

Wren put her hands on her hips, in mock outrage. "Would I do that to you?"

"If we agree can we back out?" Winnie asked.

Wren nodded her head. "But I promise you'll like it. And I promise it will be something you'll be really glad you did. Even if it involves hard work."

The girls looked at each other doubtfully. "And fun," she added quickly. "Who's in?"

"I'm in!" George shouted.

"Me, too," Lucy said.

Avery and Winnie looked uncertain.

Caleb cleared his throat. "I can tell this is going to be good, but I can only agree if the girls do, too."

Wren wasn't sure how this would go over. They had only just met him. But to her relief, Winnie was on board. "Okay," she said. She elbowed her sister, who echoed her.

Wren asked Lindy to gather some paper and pens and pencils. She passed them out to each kid and kept one for herself. "Let's brainstorm what we're going to need."

This appealed a bit more to the older girls, who with their sailing experience got to act as the experts for the little kids. Together made lists: clean boat, sand and paint the deck and bottom, check canvas on deck, replace the rigging. To start they would need sandpaper, varnish, primer, and marine enamel. When the list was compiled, Hank went down to the basement to retrieve saw horses. Wren, Lindy, and the kids went out to the shed. The Beetle had been long tucked in the corner, and they had to climb over and around the clutter that had accumulated around it. The kids helped pull things out of the way: old beach chairs, pots, a bike with one wheel.

"Are you a hoarder?" George asked his grandmother.

Lindy smacked him lightly on the head. "Go help Grampa Hank with the saw horses."

Finally the kids stood back in the grass, and the adults surrounded and lifted the Beetle. "On the count of three," Wren said. "Three, two . . ." They set the boat down right side up on the horses. After some shifting and rearranging, everyone stood back. In full sunlight they could see the work that needed to be done.

Wren couldn't help it. Standing around the Beetle Cat like that, all of them quiet in thought, made her think of a funeral. "All right," she said, finally. "Enough work for today. Tomorrow we start bringing this boat back to life."

On the way home, Wren's thoughts whirled. She had to run over to the shop, the very thing that needed her most and that she'd barely set foot in. She needed to get her father to bed, and she needed to go to the market: they were out of oatmeal and bananas, and the green tea he favored. What she really needed was to lie down and be still, without anyone talking to her or touching her or needing one more thing from her. Her sister was at the Chatham Police Department being bailed out by her husband. On top of all that, there was now a boat to restore. It was the single least important thing that any one of them could imagine: and yet restoring the Beetle Cat had suddenly taken on an urgency she could not rationalize.

Lucy was humming along in the back seat, the open window blowing her hair. Next to her, Caleb turned. "Shannon's kids coming over today," he said softly. "How did that come to be?"

Wren looked at him. Up until now Shannon had kept her family away from Caleb. Of course he'd wonder at their sudden turning up in Lindy's yard that afternoon. There was no use keeping it a secret.

"Something happened with Shannon." With one eye on the rearview mirror, Wren quietly explained what she knew. Lucy was getting an education in grown-up life that summer she wouldn't wish on the most well-adjusted adult she knew.

"She was drunk?" Caleb asked.

Wren nodded.

Caleb stared out the window a long time. "Your poor sister. It seems she's inherited both the best and the worst from her father."

Forty

Piper

It was the stupidest thing she'd ever heard. Shannon had placed herself in exile; her kids had been introduced to her father against her will. Wren had started a business she had barely set foot in since the opening party, and Piper herself was unemployed, homeless, and dating a married man. But they were all going to build a boat together.

"Not build," Wren had tried to explain. "Restore."

"Whatever. Who has time for this? Have you not looked around at what's happening to this family?"

But Wren was as stubborn as they came. "Look, I need to get to the shop. And you asked for a job. I'm reassigning you to Mom's driveway for the week. You'll get to spend time with your nieces and nephews, and with Dad before he goes." She shrugged. "Or you can find another job."

Piper hated the idea. Wren was sticking their father right under their mother's nose. And deciding how the kids were going to spend their week, with or without Reid and Shannon's input.

Who knew? Since she'd been bailed out she'd taken exactly one call from Piper, and that was for two minutes. "I fucked up, Pipe. I have to figure this out."

No word since. Reid had been the only one to show his face, arriving to drop off or pick up the kids. He'd been leaving work early to do so, but even still, Lindy's house had turned into a day care of sorts. And a loony bin.

In the end she agreed to Wren's terms for their father. Yes, she needed the money, but she knew enough people in town to get another job if she really wanted to. But Wren was right about one thing: her father wanted to fix up this stupid boat, and he needed help.

For the next several days, Piper found herself in old T-shirts and jeans. They made trips to the hardware store. The kids joked. And argued. They were too hot, too tired, too bored. But they always came around, and just when she figured everyone was about to fall apart, Lindy would show up with ice cream or Winnie would crack a joke. Or her father would call them all around the house in a booming voice and when they rounded the corner, fearfully, they were met with the hose. Piper had never seen Beverly move so fast as when she heard the kids screaming and bustled out to the back to see what was going on. She found them all running around the yard shrieking in joy and dodging the water, Bowser barking and chasing after them. "What on God's green earth?" she yelped, hands on hips. Then to Caleb, "Give me a turn with that."

By the end of the week, the hull was scraped and sanded down. They'd applied marine enamel to the bare spots, and the entire hull had been primed and repainted. Piper had learned more about sandpaper than she ever wanted to know: a 180 grit was good at getting the surface stuff, but a 220 was even better.

After the second day her hands were so raw she had to wear a pair of Lindy's yellow rubber dish gloves. But she didn't care. She needed the work and the distraction; she needed to fall into bed at night with aching muscles, every joint and muscle protesting. She needed to be numb.

Derek had texted the night he'd come into the shop. *I'm so sorry! I had no idea it was your sister's shop. Are you ok?*

Piper had replied. *You were here! Remember the dressing room?* But then it occurred to her that he'd parked and entered the store from the back, that the lights had been off, and they'd never made it past the dressing area. What did any of that matter now? She'd seen his wife. The faceless woman she'd built up in her mind as a needy, naggy wench was flesh and bone. A woman who was not only beautiful but funny and nice. With children. Two innocent children she shared with him.

Piper was dying to see him, but before she could lose her nerve, she texted back, *I can't do this.*

Is this because I didn't say I love you? he replied.

It's because I saw your family. I can't be that other woman.

She'd cried herself to sleep that night, and the following. But as the week went on and she helped take care of the kids and drive her father back and forth to Wren's and work on the boat, she was engrossed and engaged and just plain exhausted enough that she started to sleep through the night. Maybe Wren hadn't been so far off.

By the end of the week, they were done. "She's a little rough," Caleb said, standing back appraisingly, "but she's still a beaut."

"Now what?" the kids wanted to know.

"That's up to your Aunt Wren."

They took a lunch break, as they had each day, spread out on the front porch and around the yard. Avery suggested a game of capture the flag when they finished. Lindy had made grilled cheese for the kids, and sliced watermelon. Piper brought her father's lunch out and handed it to him, a bagged sandwich he brought with him every day from Wren's. "You eat the same thing every day. Aren't you tired of tuna fish sand-wiches?"

"Sometimes, but it's what gives me the least amount of trouble."

She knew he had digestive problems, and he'd been slow to recover from his collapse at the opening. But if she weren't mistaken he seemed thinner to her now than when he had arrived just a couple weeks ago.

"Are you feeling all right?"

"I'm not feeling great," he replied. "But I have to say I'm enjoying all of this. I want to see all of you as much as I can before I go back."

Although there had never been a clear end point for her father's visit, he'd been talking about going back more and more. Something that filled her with anxiety. They were getting on so well, and she was enjoying having him around so much.

"What about you?" he asked. "You've seemed a little down, if you don't mind me saying. Is everything all right?"

Piper took a bite of her grilled cheese. She could not tell him all of it, but she suddenly wanted to. "Someone I've been dating hasn't worked out. It wasn't just him, it was both of us."

"I see. A local guy or someone back in the city?"

"The city. But he's here, actually." She almost added, *"with his family."*

"Have you seen him since he got into town?"

Piper paused. "I shouldn't have. But I did." She had that awful feeling she got in her throat when

444

she was about to cry but she was trying not to. Her father had proved to be a good listener, but she didn't want him to know the truth about what she'd done. Here he was just getting to know her. She didn't want to share the worst of herself. What would he think? And yet she felt like she was lying, sitting here and keeping most of it to herself. "I made some bad choices," she said, finally.

Caleb hadn't eaten much, but he set his sandwich down and stared out across the yard as if he were done. She wondered if perhaps he hadn't heard her, and she was partly relieved; she really did not want to elaborate. But she also needed to confess. At least some of it.

"I am no man to talk to anyone about bad choices," he said. "But one thing I have learned, is people forgive. I don't know whether this young man owes you any forgiveness or not. But either way, you have to forgive yourself."

Piper had not thought of it that way. She hadn't wronged Derek so much as she had his family, and her own values. At least the values she thought she had. All along she'd been worried about what her sisters would think, what Lindy would say if she knew. She had an idea that they knew something unsavory was up, even if they didn't know the details. But she had never thought about forgiving herself. "I never thought of it that way."

"You're a good girl, Piper. I wish I'd been around for you and your sisters more. I wish I'd been able to keep my own problems out of the way so that I could."

Piper had not meant for this; she'd only been speaking of herself. In no way did she want to turn the spotlight on her dad. Not here, and not now. "Dad, I wasn't talking about us."

He looked at her. "I know. But I'd like to, if that's okay." He reached over and pointed to her forehead. "Do you remember how you got this?"

Piper shook her head. "Mom says it was the day we had the boat accident. That I banged my head. But that's all I remember."

Caleb thought about this. "I'm going to tell you something that may change the way you think about me, but I need you to know. You're talking to me about mistakes you've made, and about forgiveness. That morning of the accident, I was drunk."

Piper felt herself exhale. No one had said that to her. In all the years since. "I knew you had a drinking problem. But I never knew it had anything to do with that day." She gasped and put her hand to her scar. "Is that why you left? Because I got hurt?"

"No! No, I was hurting our family before the boat accident. And I had to leave before I hurt anyone else. I have never forgiven myself for that. For the drinking, for taking you kids to the beach that day . . ." He put his hands to his eyes, and broke down in tears.

"Dad, please. I'm okay. You didn't mean to hurt me, and I never blamed you."

"But your mother did, and rightfully so. And I know Shannon did. She won't even look at me. I need to apologize to everyone. That's why I came back." He looked so frail to her.

"Of course I forgive you," she said. She wrapped an arm around his shoulder. Despite the heat, he was wearing a flannel shirt, and she ran a hand across the back of it. "I'm just glad you're here. Now we can get to know each other. Spend more time together."

"There's something more."

The screen door squeaked, and Lindy stepped out on the porch. "The kids are quiet. That's never a good sign."

Caleb sat up and swiped at his nose. "I'd better go see what they're up to."

Piper wanted to tell him to wait. She wished her mother had not chosen that moment to come out. But her father was already standing, at least trying to. "Oh, these legs are old and stiff," he said, reaching for the railing.

Lindy put her hands out. "You okay?"

"Yes, yes," he said, chuckling. "Just not used to chasing all these kids." He turned to look at her. "You've done a marvelous job."

Piper watched him round the corner of the

house, then looked at her mother. Her expression was unreadable.

"What was that all about?" Lindy asked.

"I don't know. He said he came back to say he was sorry."

Lindy waited for her to say more. "How do you feel about that?"

Piper picked up her plate and started up the stairs. Her father's words hung in the air. "I know he just got here, but I feel like he's saying goodbye."

Forty-One

Shannon

It was one thing to be pulled over in front of your yacht club. And yet another to be handcuffed and taken away in a police car. But the moment Shannon could not get from her mind was the look on Reid's face when he picked her up at the Chatham Police Department. She'd been booked and was being held, while outside in the real world a court was determining bail, Reid was scrambling to post it, and someone else had her children. After a promise to appear in court for arraignment, she was released. And that was the worst. They were parked in front of the Chatham Police Department, Reid completely disheveled in his work clothes, his face streaked with perspiration. He had not touched her, would not even look at her. After sitting in the car in silence, she said, "I'm sorry."

Reid exploded. He pounded the steering wheel with both fists, his face a color of red she'd never witnessed. "You drove drunk with our child in the car!"

It was the lowest moment of her life.

When he pulled into the garage, minutes later,

he slammed the door and left her there. Shannon sat in the car alone. When she got up the courage to go inside, she found him in the kitchen, tearing through their cabinets. Doors were ajar at odd angles, the contents spilled across the counter tops. Bottles were in the sink. One by one he raided the liquor: the freezer, the wine fridge, the rack on the countertop. He dumped each bottle down the drain. With every clink of glass or glug of liquid she felt a piece of herself shatter.

When he was done, he turned to her. "I don't know what is going on with you, Shannon. You won't talk to me. You don't want to talk to your family. But today you could've killed yourself and our child. You'd better figure this shit out with your father, Shannon, or I swear to God it will be our undoing. Our whole family's undoing!"

There was not a single thing she could say. He was right about all of it. Only she had no idea how to fix any of it. Pouring all the alcohol down the drain wasn't going to make a dent. She went upstairs to her bed, and she stayed there until the kids came home that evening.

Reid had them take showers and baths, avoiding her in every room of the house. She had no idea what he'd said to them, but she heard Winnie in the hall. "Don't go in there, George. Daddy said she's not feeling well."

George. Her baby, who she'd put in the car

and driven away with under the influence. She wanted to call him in, to call all of them in, but she lay there alone until the sunset streaked her walls in gauzy oranges and yellows. She waited until the showers and baths stopped running, until she heard the kids go downstairs. It was supper time, and when she went down to see about dinner, the kitchen was dark. Reid's car was gone from the garage. Had he taken them out to eat? Was it possible he had taken them away from her for the night? She slammed the door to the garage, a tightening sensation crossing her chest. She climbed the stairs to bed.

That was where she was when someone knocked on her door much later. She rolled over in bed, squinting as it swung open. A head was silhouetted in the hallway light. "Darling?" It was Beverly. Followed by Piper and Lindy and Wren. All four women crowded uncertainly in her doorway.

"May we come in?" Lindy asked. For the first time all day, Shannon burst into tears.

The four of them sat on her bed, watching her as one might a trapped animal. Lindy spoke first. "Honey, I had no idea. I feel like I've let you down."

"I've been so tied up with Dad and the shop, I didn't realize what was going on." Wren scooted over closer. "Are you all right?"

No, she was not all right. But something about

those four women being there—right there—gave her the faintest glimmer that she could be.

"I don't know where Reid is, and he's so mad at me. I could've killed us both. I could've killed someone else. But I didn't think I was drunk. I would never have gotten behind the wheel with George if I did. You know I wouldn't have."

Lindy handed her a box of tissues from Reid's side of the bed. "For years, I watched your father drink. Little bits here and there, but they added up by the day's end. There were times I'd worry, and I'd ask him about how much, how often . . . all of it. And yet he was so highly functioning, so brilliant at his work. I told myself it was the stress of the travel with his job. I told myself it was being away from us, always coming and going. But I could never admit your father had a drinking problem, until the day he took you girls out in the Beetle."

Beverly was sitting very still on the edge of the bed. "It's true. I watched him the same way, and I wondered. But I didn't want to pry. I figured your mother would tell me. Or I'd know for sure. When you're in the thick of it, you start to normalize it."

Shannon sat up. "Do you think I'm an alcoholic like Dad?"

"Do you?" Piper asked.

Shannon didn't know. Yesterday she wouldn't

have said so. She put her head in her hands. "Today was the worst day of my life."

Beverly reached over and rubbed Shannon's foot beneath the sheet. "Let's talk about today. The only thing you did today was embarrass yourself. You did a mighty fine job of it, that's for sure. A for effort! But no one got hurt, thank God. No real damage was done. This may have been the *best* day of your life."

Reid came to bed, but much later. She rolled over and pressed herself against him. "Are you awake?"

At first he didn't answer, and she listened to his breathing. She needed him in this. She could not do it alone.

"I am," he said finally. All the fight was gone from his voice. "But I'm angry, Shannon. I know it's not fair, but I'm so angry at you right now."

She lay quietly behind him. "I know. I'm angry, too."

Slowly Reid turned over, facing her. "When I got that call at work, all I could think was that something awful had happened. That you . . . or George . . ." He couldn't finish.

She pressed her lips to his forehead. "Don't." She kissed him again and again, until he wrapped both arms around her.

"You are going to have to promise me that you're going to figure this out. Whatever it takes.

Therapy. Counseling. I'll support you in all of it. But you're going to have to do this, Shannon. We could've lost everything today."

She knew all of this, and yet it terrified her. Shannon was not sure what was wrong or where to start. But it was something she had been carrying for a very long time. Too long. And Beverly was right; today she got to set it down.

"What do we do?" Reid asked. "Do you want me to call the doctor in the morning?"

"All right. But there's something I need to do first." She sat up in bed.

Wren's house was dark, but the outdoor light was on. She found the key under the potted geraniums on the porch and let herself in. The house was still.

At the bottom of the stairs, she hesitated. What if she woke up Wren and scared her? Or Lucy? Badger appeared at the landing at the top of the stairs, a low growl emanating from his throat. "It's me, buddy. It's okay." To her relief he wagged.

She stopped outside the guest-room door and listened. There was the sound of a light snore within, and for a second, she was taken away. It was summer at the old house in Ridgevale. Shannon had been sleeping in her shared room with her little sister, but it was a humid night and there was no breeze. All night she'd slept fitfully, until one point in the middle of the night she'd had a terrible nightmare. The house was on fire. Her sisters and she were trapped. The fire was everywhere: skittering across the ceiling, climbing up the walls. The whole room glowed in orange light. Shannon sat bolt upright in bed, her nine-year-old chest pounding against her narrow rib cage. With the heat of the room, for a second she feared her dream was true. She cried out and ran to the door. Down the hall she went, to her parents' room. When she raced through the door, her mother's side of the bed was closest. But she did not go to Lindy. She walked around the far side, to her father. She nudged him awake, tears in her eyes. "What is it?" he'd asked, scooping her up onto the bed.

She told him. About the blaze and the fire and being trapped. "I want to sleep with you."

Her father did not tell her to go back to bed. Nor did he chide her. He peeled the covers back very slowly and grabbed his pillow. Down the hall they tiptoed back to her room. "But I don't want to sleep here," she protested.

He helped her back into bed. "Shhh. You are safe."

She watched over the edge of her bed as he rolled out the blanket and set his pillow on the floor. Then he lay down beside her.

She tried to sleep but could not. Each time she closed her eyes the flames licked the back of her lids. "I'm scared," she said.

"My love, you are safe."

Throughout the night Shannon would stir, and each time she peered over the bed he was still there. He did not tell her not to worry. He did not tell her that her fears were silly. When she sat up he could sense her. "You're safe," he'd murmur.

Now, as she stood outside the guest-bedroom door, listening to the gentle vibrato of her father's breath on the other side, she whispered to herself. "You're safe," she said. And then she turned the knob.

Forty-Two

Wren

For the first time all summer it rained. The rain fell in horizontal sheets across the rooftops and shops. It stained the sand on the beaches with watery dapples. It blew and gusted and made the Bailey women wonder if it would ever slow. They spent their days inside, cooped up and edgy. They paced in their respective houses as the Beetle Cat lay on the sawhorses in the driveway. Caleb was growing more tired each day. He did not finish his oatmeal and bananas at breakfast. She knew their time was dwindling. His friend Alice was calling daily now. Wren welcomed the calls, finding comfort in the soft voice on the other line. Knowing she'd also be there on the other side of his trip home. "How is he doing?" she'd ask.

"He's slowing down," Wren said, keeping out of earshot. "I'm worried."

"Honey, I think it's time we book the tickets. Just tell me the date. I'll pick him up. I'll take it from there."

Wren knew Alice was right. Her father needed to get home. Home to die, as he'd made them all promise they would allow him to do. "One more day," Wren would say.

Alice's voice on the other line was thick. "All right, but we can't let many more pass. He needs strength to travel, remember."

"I know," Wren said, trying to keep the tears from her eyes. "We won't keep him much longer."

But the rain did not let up, and Wren knew she had to book Caleb's ticket home. He was ready, he said, when she sat on the couch to tell him she'd spoken to Alice. She called her sisters to tell them, and then she went online. She cried when she chose *One Way*.

On the third day, when she thought the air could not possibly hold another drop of water and that she would lose her mind, she picked up her phone. It had been six years since she had dialed that number; for all she knew it had been changed. She was surprised when he answered on the second ring.

They met at the Red Nun. When she walked in he was already there, seated at the bar, a pint in front of him. She allowed herself to steal the moment, to take him in. His hair was a little longer now, looser around his head. His skin was a little ruddier, from all the time on the water. But when he looked up, his eyes were still the same, crinkling in the corners like they were laughing.

"You came," he said.

"I asked you."

James ordered her a beer and passed it over. They made polite small talk at first. She told him about the shop. He told her about life in Seattle. He'd stayed out there for five years, and he liked it. He'd gotten his master's degree in marine ecology. Working the boats had been harder than he'd thought, but he'd learned a lot. And done all right financially to go back to school.

"Why'd you come back?" she asked.

James shrugged. "I missed the East Coast. It's so beautiful out there, but this is home."

She thought about this. About his wanderlust and how much it had worried her.

"Why did you call?" he asked.

Wren took a deep sip of her beer. "I heard you were back. And I guess I wanted to see how you were."

"Is that all?"

She switched the subject. "What are your plans now?"

"I'm living over in Brewster. I'm working for State, for the Division of Fisheries and Wildlife."

"So you're back to stay?"

"So far. I've been back for a few months now, but the job is going well and I'm closer to my family. My mother is happy about that."

"I'll bet." Wren had always liked James's mother. She'd liked his whole family, in fact.

James's voice had an effect on her that she'd

not been prepared for. It had been so long since she'd seen him. And so long since she'd cared about anyone. Having Lucy absorbed all of her: her time, her energy, her thoughts. But sitting next to him now, hearing the soft gravel in his voice, smelling his scent coming off his wet T-shirt, something in her shifted.

"What about you? You have a child."

Wren reached for her phone but then thought better of it. "I do. She's six. Her name is Lucy."

"That's a great name. I bet you're a great mom, too."

She couldn't help but smile. "It's the hardest job I've ever loved. She's a good kid. Loves animals, nature, reading. I can't keep her out of the water."

James laughed. "Sounds like her mama." A small part of her ached to tell him she was just like her dad, but the larger part remained protective. This was already risky enough.

"You and your husband must be proud."

"Oh, there isn't one. It's just me."

James cocked his head. "Divorced?"

"Never married. Her dad is not in the picture."

Whether it was feeling sorry for her or not, she couldn't say, but James's expression shifted. "I didn't mean to pry."

"You didn't. It's common knowledge. And I'm fine with it. It was my choice, actually." She stole a glance at him to see what he thought about this, but it was hard to read James. He had always been good at keeping his emotions in check.

"How about you?" she asked. "Married? Any kids?"

James shook his head. "No, and no."

"Don't want any?"

"No." He laughed. "I mean, no that's not the case. I do want kids someday."

Wren was surprised to hear this. But she wasn't sure if this was good news or not. If James was back and he was now open to the idea of having children, he might be upset to find out about Lucy. More than upset. As Lindy had warned her back in the beginning, a father could claim parental rights. He might want her.

"I have to get going," she said. She pushed a ten-dollar bill across the bar.

James looked startled. "Already?" Then, "No, please. This is on me."

Wren made a show of glancing at her watch. "Yeah, I have to run back and check on something in the shop. It's been nonstop lately."

"Oh, okay." He started to say more, then decided not to.

Wren slid off the stool. "Well, good luck with the new job. It was good to see you."

"Yeah, you too." James was watching her curiously. He didn't ask to see her again. Nor did he try to get her to stay. "Maybe I'll see you around?"

"Maybe."

Outside in the parking lot, the rain had slowed. Wren ran to her Jeep. This was all a terrible mistake. All she wanted was to get home to Lucy.

After a week of straight rain, the sun finally showed its face. It rose the next morning in a red orb outside her bedroom window, and Wren rolled over to face it. *Red sun at morning, sailors take warning.* They only had a few more days before Caleb would be boarding a plane home to Arizona. She still did not like this decision, but it was his, and he insisted. As the rain had born down on Chatham and the beachgoers filled the shop and crowded the sidewalks beneath their umbrellas, Wren had cursed silently. They needed one day. One clear day with their father before he left. She pulled back the sheets and pulled her curtain aside, tipping her face back in the light. Today was their day.

After a few calls around the neighborhood, she'd found a friend who let them borrow their trailer. It had been years since any of them towed a boat, but as Caleb helped Wren back it up Lindy's driveway, it felt right. They loaded the Beetle Cat. Piper joined them.

Lindy met her outside with a bagged lunch. "Good luck out there."

It was not unlike her mother. To feel one way

about something or someone, and to tuck those sentiments away for the benefit of her girls. Wren could not imagine having invited a man who could not do the same, a man whose demons had kept him away from his family, back into her home and her life for her children. Since becoming a mother she'd made sacrifices, large and small, for Lucy. And there were also times she'd sacrificed her time with her daughter to do the things she hoped would be good for them both. As she hugged her mother goodbye in the driveway she made a decision. This one was for Lucy.

They had chosen Stage Harbor, over near Shannon and Reid's house. There was a boat launch beside the Yacht Club and when they pulled in, Wren was surprised to see her waiting in the lot. She rolled down the Jeep window. "Where are the kids? I thought you were all going to meet us here."

"They'll be here, but I was thinking it'd be fitting that we launch the boat first. Just the four of us."

It was a gesture beyond measure, especially for Shannon. In recent days she'd been coming by here and there to see their father. While she hadn't warmed to him completely, Wren had sensed her need to at least connect. As for him, Caleb seemed more at peace than he'd been since he arrived, and he took her in without question.

Whatever inch she gave, he seemed to measure in miles.

"You coming too?" Wren asked.

Shannon leaned in the window. "Not for me, thanks. But if you don't mind?" She held her camera aloft, shyly.

Caleb smiled, unable to speak at first. "The light is good today," he said.

The protected waters of Stage Harbor were perfect for launching and sailing along the shore, but there were narrow shoals and fast-moving channels farther out. The day was crisp and clear, and there was a good wind coming from the west.

Caleb stood at the water's edge. There was a clear view to Morris Island and the Stage Harbor Lighthouse on the adjacent point.

"What do you think?" Wren asked.

"I think it's time."

Wren backed the trailer down to the water and the three women unloaded the Beetle. Their father hovered on the edge, wanting to help, but unable. Wrapped in a throw blanket, even on this hot morning, he watched from the top of the boat ramp. Once in the water by the dock, it took all three of them to help their father in. He settled on the floorboards of the cockpit. Wren climbed in after him, then Piper. "It's tight in here," Piper said, leaning back against the floorboards.

Caleb's voice was soft against the wind. "You

were much smaller the last time." He looked to Wren. "Why don't you man the tiller today. Shall we cast off?"

The wind was light and the sky clear. Back on the dock, Wren could see Shannon pointing her camera in their direction. She hoisted the sail, one eye on her father as she did. The last time she'd been sailing had been years ago with James, but sitting in the cockpit with Piper and her father today felt natural. The Beetle Cat moved at a hypnotic pace across the water, steady and sure. Across the floorboards, knees to his chest, her father tightened the blanket around himself. "How you doing, Dad?" Piper called.

But Caleb Bailey did not answer. He closed his eyes and tipped his head back against the wind.

Forty-Three

Hank

Twenty years ago when he was a bachelor living in Boston writing for the *Globe*, if anyone had told him if he'd be celebrating his sixty-fifth birthday surrounded by women and children and dogs, he'd have told them they were mistaken. And yet Hank would not have traded a single moment (or canine) for anything.

It was early September, what most considered to be the best time on the Cape. The waters of Nantucket Sound were the warmest they would be after a season of summer sun, and the hours in the day still long and golden. Lindy had reserved a table in the Stars dining room at Chatham Bars Inn, and though Hank had initially wished for a bar seat at the Sacred Cod Tavern, now that he was dressed up and seated by the window overlooking Chatham Harbor and the fishing fleet, he decided not to second-guess his brilliant wife again. Lindy was a vision, seated beside him in a loose flowing dress, her signature bracelets sliding up and down her elegant wrists as she spoke animatedly to the table. Across from her were the girls, cutout silhouettes of their mother, the same long limbs, the same striking strawberry blonde hair. Seated among them were their offspring, bright-eyed and spirited. George had his napkin on his lap, but kept picking it up to blow his nose. Lucy was whispering something in his ear that struck her as so funny she kept breaking down in fits of giggles, unable to finish.

"What?" George would say, then blow his nose. "Lucy, stop talking for a minute. Please."

All around them their mothers and grandmother were doing the same. Hank felt for the kid.

The day before had been a solemn one, and Hank had thought more than once that they should cancel his birthday dinner. But Lindy had insisted. "We need to celebrate," she told him that night, as she fixed his tie for him in their foyer.

"But is it too soon?"

Lindy ran her hand down the red-and-white stripes of the tie, and looked up at him, a flicker in her green eyes. "It's not Tuscany. But it's your day. And that I will always celebrate."

Hank would oblige, even if he still felt moved by the previous day, the day they'd bid goodbye to Caleb.

It was an early morning, well before the sun rose, as the whole family gathered in the dark. Shannon and Reid and their kids. Wren and Lucy. Piper, Lindy, Hank. They had all gathered together at the Chatham Fish Pier, just as Caleb Bailey had asked.

Wren's friend Tony, a young fisherman that James used to work with, had agreed to take them out on his lobster boat. He stood at the stern, hand out, and helped them each aboard. Within moments they were motoring away from the docks across Chatham Harbor, huddled together in the cold morning air.

As the pink glow of dawn crested over Nauset Beach to the east, Hank went to stand in the wheelhouse, leaving the women to themselves. The sight of Wren standing at the stern with the urn in her hands brought unexpected tears to his eyes. He was not sure of his place there that morning. And yet they each had wanted him to come.

They continued south in the harbor, passing Chatham Lighthouse and edging around South Beach. Soon the channel opened up and Nantucket Sound stretched before them. By then the sun had risen, and the Sound glowed like embers. They hugged the shore, past Stage Harbor Lighthouse and Harding Beach. Just off of Ridgevale Tony poked his head out of the wheelhouse. "Is here good?" he shouted.

Wren gave him the thumbs-up, and Tony idled a bit before killing the engine. It was time.

"Okay," Wren said, and they made their way to the starboard side of the trawler. The wind was light, the waters calm. Hank was grateful that the sea seemed to be cooperating.

The children, who moments ago had been excitedly pointing out sights on the shore, huddled by the adults, now unsure of how to behave or conduct themselves. Lucy glanced uncertainly at her mother, and Hank felt for all of them. Caleb had come into their lives for such a short time, and he wondered what sense they could make of saying goodbye so soon.

The three Bailey girls stood together, Wren in the center. Piper went first. "Thank you, Daddy," she said. "For coming home and coming back to us. If only for a while." She reached into the urn and grabbed a handful of ashes, holding them in her hand. Hank had worried about Piper. She had returned home at loose ends, her life blowing about her like tattered ribbons. She'd welcomed Caleb back with childlike earnestness, her hunger for connection visceral. Hank had feared for her the most, but to all of their surprise, she'd borne Caleb's loss the best. She'd spent every day she was not at the shop with him, going out on the water during his last days. It was a childhood summer she'd never had, and Hank hoped it would be enough.

Shannon went next, and Hank's composure began to crumble then. She reached into the urn in one fell motion and retrieved a handful of ash, clutching it against her chest. Shannon, who was so strong and so stubborn, like her mother. Yet as passionate and intense as her father. She was the one who had always seemed so immune to the strains of life, staying the course no matter the weather or the conditions. When she broke down, it came as such a surprise to him, but in a small way as a relief. She finally showed her humanity, acknowledged her limitations. And though she had a distance still to go, Hank had no doubt with her family at hand she would make it. Storm after storm. Mile after nautical mile.

Wren was last, and she held the urn aloft and faced them all, her chin trembling. "We started our lives with our father. A man who loved us and left us, I now realize, because of that love. He thought it was best, and though we cannot get that time back, I like to think that when he finally came home to us, he gave each of us a piece of ourselves back." She paused, her cheeks wet with tears, her voice strained with effort. Piper was crying openly. Shannon kept her eyes trained on the skyline. Wren turned to each of them. "Ready?"

Hank wrapped an arm around Lindy as they watched the girls turn and release the ashes over the side of the boat. Arms outstretched, they let their father go on the wind. The children pressed over the railing, watching in silence. Lucy waved goodbye. Lindy shuddered, just once, and Hank pulled her tight.

Caleb Bailey's ashes floated away from the boat in a sparkling gray cloud, like the mist coming off of the Sound and the waters that lapped at the trawler.

Now, as Hank sat in the formal dining room with his family dressed up and gathered around for his birthday, it hit him. This was his family. Caleb Bailey's return this summer was something he had dreaded. Whether he feared that the man would cause them hurt, or worse, could somehow take them away from him, he realized how ridiculous those notions were. Sure, he had wanted to hit the guy when he walked up their porch steps that first night. Hank had spent the better part of twenty years listening and reaching out and standing in and trying and failing and making a fool of himself in the whole, hard, deep way he had come to love these girls. Caleb's stepping aside had given that to him, for right or wrong, better or worse. They had made the best of the worst of situations, and they had loved. Oh, how they had loved. In the end, Hank was not only thankful to Caleb. He actually liked the guy a little. And he would spend the rest of his life holding on to each hand around this table.

"Grampa, look!" Lucy cried.

The servers approached the table with a huge cake, the most beautiful white iced cake Hank had ever seen. Never mind it was ablaze with the years of his life. As they set it down in the center of the table, the children crowded in and their parents tugged them back. Hank laughed. As they sang "Happy Birthday" to him in a loud, out-of-tune chorus, Hank looked around at each face illuminated in the glow of the candles. These were his people. This family was his.

Hank had come to realize something that summer. They were all flawed, the whole lot of them. Each unique in the ways they carried those flaws. Some fractured along the way, small chips trailing their wake. Some withstood the concussions, one after the other, seemingly impenetrable until they cracked in one ominous split down the center. What mattered was not what broke you, or how you fell to pieces. Because at some point in life, everyone did. What mattered was who you surrounded yourself with when it came to picking up the pieces. It reminded him of something his mother used to tell him when he was a little boy and he was scared: Sometimes bad things happen to good people. When it does, look for the helpers. There are helpers all around, and they will come. They always do.

"Make a wish!" George shouted.

Hank looked up at their faces. They were waiting and watching. Laughing and scolding.

Wiggling in their seats. Reaching for the cake to run a finger through the frosting. Smiling patiently. All of it reflected back at him. What more could he possibly wish for?

Forty-Four

Piper

The traffic off the Cape was still bad, and she honked her horn when a truck cut her off just before the Sagamore. It had been one week since she started her new job, and her heart thundered in her chest when she thought about going back. She was still not sure this was the right choice for her.

It would've been so easy to stay on the Cape. Her bedroom at her mom's was still set up, and Lindy said she could come back any time. To visit. And there was Wren's shop, the Fisherman's Daughter, where she could help out any time. The job had been good for her, the money not great, but it had been a lifesaver during a rough time, and it had been a safe and beautiful space to exist in. A place that she loved working, and she was good at it, but in the end it was a place she came to realize would drive her crazy if she stayed another week more. "Are you sure?" Wren had asked, when she gave her leave. Of course, Piper knew her sister was secretly relieved. Having her there was more of a favor than a help to Wren. But Piper had practically run that store on her own that summer, as Wren popped in and out with Lucy and their father, so overwhelmed by all of it that Piper was glad she'd been able to help out in the end. It was usually them who helped her. It felt good to have it go the other way for once.

Derek had come by, one last time, before his vacation ended. She'd ignored his messages, as much as her fingers ached to text back. *Okay. Come by. I miss you.* But seeing his family had changed everything for her. And she realized she did not love Derek as much as she loved the idea of him. They could never be together. And if they were, it would mean his leaving his family. Piper would never be truly happy with him knowing that. More importantly, she would never be happy with herself. When Derek found her in the shop that last day, Wren had been the one working. Piper wasn't slated to come in until later that afternoon. When she did, Wren pulled her aside. "Someone came by looking for you."

She'd known right away.

"Listen, Piper. You're a big girl. But you descrve better."

"What did you say to him?"

"Nothing. I told him you'd be here at two. What you say to him then, well, that's up to you."

Derek did come back, looking chastened, and sad, but when they stood together on the small back porch behind the shop he reached for her.

"We can't," Piper said. "What we have isn't real. Or right." Then she added, "For me."

She'd kissed him quickly once more, a brief kiss. And when she pulled away she realized that the yearning wasn't there. The pull not as strong. It would take a long time to get over him, but somehow, she would have to. She wanted more.

By early July, Piper understood what she'd been fearing. Her father had indeed come back to say goodbye. If she'd known that in June, when he first returned, the realization might have undone her. She was so lost then, so full of holes. But being home had filled some of them, slowly at first, then more noticeably. It had been a hard, raw summer. But there was beauty in the hard stuff. It was the stuff you used to spackle the holes, one by one. And when you missed a spot, your sisters could point it out to you. Oh, boy could they. But they could also reach the places you couldn't.

They'd sent their dad home on a plane. His friend Alice had flown up to meet him, and on the last night they had a dinner party at Lindy's. One of their Sunday Something-Rather Dinner parties. Everyone brought some hodgepodge dish to contribute. There had been fried fish from the pier and garden vegetables from Lindy's back-yard. Wren showed up with hot dogs—she'd been too busy at the store. Shannon made a cold pesto pasta. Her dad had not been able to eat any of it, except for a little fish he picked at. "I want to remember this taste," he told her. They were sitting on the steps, as they had done so often that summer. The kids were playing in the yard, and there was a squabble between them about whose turn it was. Piper and Caleb had watched, waiting for them to figure it out. But they didn't. So Piper intervened. She'd suggested another game, a game of catch the crab. "I don't know that game," George had said. "You don't?" The girls didn't either. So she taught them.

After, when she came back to the steps her father asked her, "You remembered."

"Sure, I used to play it with Shannon and Wren. When we were little."

He smiled. "I taught them that game," he said. It was a small thing, and yet it connected Piper to her father in a way she had not known she needed but did. The dots of her childhood connected, from her older sisters who had always held so much more memory than she'd had, to their father. It didn't matter that he hadn't taught her himself. The game came from him.

"You're awfully good with kids," he said, struggling to stand up. She rose with him and helped him up the steps. "Too bad you don't think the teaching gig is for you."

She'd made a call the next day, her stomach in her throat. The districts she'd applied to had all filled their teaching positions long ago. But a few days later she got a call from a Brockton elementary school. A first-grade teacher had retired at the last minute, and there was an opening. Would she be available to interview? Two days later, she made the trip. By the week's end she had an offer. Before she could change her mind, she said yes.

Standing before her class that first day was everything she feared. These little people were all depending on her. She who could not pick a major or stick with a job or choose a partner or keep an apartment. All these little feet whose shoelaces came undone, whose hands struggled with penmanship, whose lips tripped over pronunciations as they learned to read. It was perhaps the neediest age she could have possibly taught. And while she felt sick to her stomach walking through her classroom door each day, it got easier. She needed them, too, she was learning. And if she didn't know all the answers, they'd figure them out together.

Her phone dinged on her seat, and she tried to ignore it. On the other side of the bridge the turnaround at Buzzards Bay was clogged. She checked it while sitting in traffic. It was Adam. *Let me know when you're back in town.* She'd reached out to him a few times, but he hadn't responded. It served her right, she knew. But then, one night, they bumped into each other again after Labor Day weekend. Work was good.

He'd been seeing someone over the summer, he said. "Oh, that's great," she lied. She told him about her new job. Her tiny studio that had mice in the wall but one big window with good light. "A new start? Good for you," he'd said.

Two weeks later he'd called. They'd been talking a little here and there since. At first Piper was anxious to see him. She didn't know how to do this thing—the wading in slowly, the taking your time and getting to know a person. It went against everything she'd done up to this point. But Adam was a good guy, and she had not been so good to him. Going slowly was all he seemed willing to offer her, but she reminded herself that he had reached out to her. *Talk would have to be enough for now,* Piper thought. It might even be good for her. But she sure hoped to keep the conversation going.

Forty-Five

Shannon

E verett Banks had not made her job easy. It was nearly impossible to sell a house that the owner refused to show. There were times he was vacationing with his family, and he didn't want to be disturbed. There were occasions when he turned down perfectly good offers—she'd had two!—because something the buyer had requested annoyed him or the way the buyer had worded something offended him. He was temperamental and difficult, and at one point when he said she couldn't show the house because he was in town, she asked him point-blank, "Do you really want to sell this house?"

He'd flinched, as if she'd slapped him. If Bitsy knew Shannon had spoken this way to an important client she'd have taken the listing out from under her and reassigned it. But Everett seemed amused. Delighted, even. "Just get them in and out of here quick," he'd said. "And don't let them track in sand like the last time."

The client was the woman from London who'd first called at the beginning of the summer. She was a business analyst, single, and in her forties, and Shannon couldn't begin to imagine how she'd use the massive place all alone. But Shannon also liked that about her. This was her second showing, and clients didn't fly in for an afternoon for a second showing if they weren't close to pulling the trigger.

The showing went well. But she did not make an offer that day, as Shannon had thought she would. "I'll call you this evening," she told Shannon. "I'll have a number by then."

One thing she'd learned was to not get her hopes up. Good offers were refused. Good deals were broken. She wanted this to work out, and she had a gut feeling it just might, but until she got the call she tried to be patient.

As she went through the house locking up, she went to the rear sliders overlooking the back deck. The weather was poor, not raining but gray and brisk, the scent of colder seasons in the air. It was not an inviting day to walk out the back to the beach, but Shannon found herself sliding the door ajar and stepping outside anyway. She wrapped her arms around herself as a blast of wind met her. Down on the beach, there was real surf. The water came in and out in large, lumbering waves, and the sight of it was disquieting. Nevertheless, she found herself removing her boots, then her socks, and leaving them on the wood decking.

The sand was cold beneath her bare feet, the beach grass sharp, as she followed the path toward the sound of the water. But she kept going. The dunes were beautiful in the green-gray light, the beach grass blowing sideways left, then right. As she emerged from between the dunes, the roaring of the surf intensified, and the beach opened before her. Shannon paused. It was so like that day. The waves. The silver sky. The wind. She shuddered.

Keeping her father away had been necessary, if hard. For too many years she'd fought the hole of his absence, trying in vain to fill it with everything else. Her work. Her house. Her own children and husband. And yet she diminished her joy in all of those things by using them as fillers, seeing them as walls she could raise to surround herself with, rather than doors and windows that let light in. Finally, when she could raise the barriers no more, she crumbled. And so too did the walls. All of her hard work and all of those years fell away around her. It didn't matter what she'd attained or achieved or accrued—at the foundation of it all was hurt. And until she fixed it, she could not build a life atop it. Going back to her father was for her as much as it was for him.

The night she'd crept into the guest room at Wren's, she'd stood at the foot of his bed. In the dark, he was familiar. The outline of his height and breadth matched the one in her memory. But the face on the pillow was drawn, not fleshed out with health or youth as she had recalled.

The vulnerability she saw changed what she had planned to say, and she sat on the edge of his bed and touched his arm.

Caleb had awakened with a start. "Lucy?" he asked.

"No, Dad. It's me."

"Oh, Wren." He'd sat up gingerly, rubbing his eyes. "Is everything all right?"

"It's Shannon."

Caleb sat, and she wondered if he was upset. Or confused. But she heard him exhale in the darkness.

"You're here."

"Yes," she said. "I'm sorry it took me so long."

The days they had were not the stuff of movie endings. She had taken her time to come to him, and she took her time to get closer. If you could call it that. But they talked. In Wren's kitchen, with the everyday chaos of kids and pots and pans on the stove and phones ringing, the awkward spaces were filled. Leaving them room to talk about the real things. His regrets. His struggles with sobriety. Her own.

Shannon couldn't say she accepted his apology. But what she did accept was his coming home. She accepted the gesture of it, as well as the physicality. He was her flesh and blood. Her children should know him if only for a short while. It was all they had.

Caleb's death did not hit her as it did her sisters, at least not in the same way. For years he had been dead to her. His absence had created resentment—a sentiment that did not hurt him, but simmered in her, preventing her from enjoying all she had and built. In the end, his death breathed life into her father. No longer was he the enemy, the one who left. The one who saddled her with adult responsibilities, with grief. Rather, she could remember him now as showing George how to tie a lanyard. Talking to her about her photographs, the ones in the folder she finally sat down and opened after he showed up at her door one afternoon carrying a tattered leather portfolio of his own. Sitting on their back deck looking at images of Africa, of lighthouses, of her children's faces. He was more alive to her in death than he was in life.

As she stepped into the incoming tide, Shannon braced herself. The water was not as cold as the air. Instead, it felt like tub water that had cooled a little, still warm, still womblike. She rolled her pants up over her ankles and took another step in. But it didn't matter; the waves were strong and high, and even at the water's edge the ripples found her. They washed over her toes, splashed up over the cuffs of her pants, soaked her shins. Shannon looked at the horizon. She tipped her head back and laughed.

Forty-Six

Wren

There are two of them out on the water. The little girl has her hair pulled back in a pony-tail, and it whips out behind her like a flag. The wind is strong today, and they change course as they hug the shore, tacking and jibing. The little girl's hand is on the wooden rudder, her father's hand over her own. She is still learning, but he wants her to feel like she is in charge.

She had not known what it would mean to have her father back for the summer, a summer that proved to teem with firsts and lasts. The Fisherman's Daughter had endured its first season, and well. At first, she'd been so strung out, spread so thin with her father's visit and his impending decline of health. The secret he'd asked her to keep, until the others could not help but see and he was forced to share. She worried about Lucy, about what it would mean to gain and lose a grandparent, both in rapid succession. She worried for Piper, whose skin had always been so papery, her vulnerability just under its surface. And for Shannon, who could not and would not feel anything that came her way. Until the feeling came for her. And for their mother, a woman who'd spent her early life loving a man who could not be a parent nor a spouse, but whose heart was still good. Whose love he framed through a lens and developed in a darkroom, if he could seem to capture it in real life. But they had managed, somehow, to let him in and see him through, and let him go again.

Alice kept calling, giving her updates and assuring them that this is what he wanted. When she called one last time, she told Wren that his passing was quick, his mind sharp as a tack to the end. He'd passed with photographs hanging on his wall that Shannon had sent him. With his daughters' names on his lips. The cancer took him, but it did not take his senses. Wren wept on the phone, wondering at how pain could travel the lines and distance straight to her heart from a place she'd never been.

Afterward, as she took Lucy to school and went to the shop each day, she struggled in the quietude. The tourists had left, taking with them the foot traffic, the bustle, and some of the color. It left empty spaces, not only on sidewalks and in restaurants and all across Chatham's beaches but also in her mind. Spaces where she contemplated father-daughter relationships. And what they meant: not to her, but to a little girl. She realized it was not her say or her choice. She'd made mistakes about both of those things. In the end, it was about Lucy. Even if it meant opening herself up to uncertainty. By sharing Lucy and letting some of her go, she was giving something to her daughter.

She knew it was a risk. She knew also that he would be confused, and angry. And that he might never trust her again. But she picked up the phone anyway. She owed it to both of them.

The conditions for sailing are near perfect, and as Caleb would say, the light is just right. They've been out on the bay for a while now. As the Beetle Cat turns toward shore, Wren shouts. She lifts a hand and waves. James and Lucy wave back. It's time to come in for lunch.

Acknowledgments

This is my fourth novel with EBB, and with each new book I not only get to work with the talented team at Simon and Schuster and with MacKenzie Fraser Bub Literary Agency, but I also get to meet and live alongside a new family through the pages. The Bailey women are women of strength and fortitude, who endure not only because they have to, but because they can.

In that vein, I'm grateful for my EBB family, most especially to my editor, Emily Bestler, for her continued expertise and encouragement. I am so fortunate to be a part of your amazing team, and I'm proud of the work we've produced together. Gratitude to my agent, MacKenzie, whose eye and ear remain my navigational instruments for every book and every page. You remain a cherished partner in this literary journey.

Thanks to Ariele Fredman and Rachel Brenner, publicists extraordinaire, who help ferry my books out into the world and get me out there, too. You continue to yield your wands! To Albert Tang, whose covers radiate warmth and heart, and who works so hard to get it right every time. Thank you to the copyediting team who remain my valued safety net. Especially to my dear friend, Amy Caruluzzi, copyeditor and early reader extraordinaire.

Writing is a solitary career, and to this day I remain surprised by the sharp change of gears when I leave my desk and dog and get to dress up, hit the road, and launch a new book. Tremendous gratitude to Elissa Englund and Annie Philbrick of Bank Square Books in Mystic, CT, and Savoy of Westerly, RI, "locally owned and fiercely independent." You ladies know how to launch a book! I'm so thankful to all the indie bookstore owners who invite me and my books through their doors each summer. Thanks also to the many reviewers and bloggers who generously invest so much of themselves into promoting books and connecting readers to authors, especially Jenny O'Regan and Suzanne Leopold. All of you are like book fairy godmothers!

I'm so grateful for the hospitality and generosity of the Chatham Bars Inn Resort and Spa. They graciously hosted me for a portion of the research and writing of this novel, and I cannot recommend a better spot for Chatham Harbor views. A must-visit for cocktails on the Beach House Grill deck after a day at the shore.

Thanks must be given to the picturesque Cape Cod town of Chatham, a slice of Americana seaside heaven. Many of the shops and venues named in these pages are real brick-and-mortar spots, all places I've visited since my own childhood summers in Chatham and all dear to my heart. I consider myself fortunate to bring my own children to this special place every summer to make new memories. Visit Where the Sidewalk Ends for a summer read and stop in at the Squire for the fish and chips. Monomoy Coffee Shop made many iced mocha lattes that fueled the early pages of this book! The Fisherman's Daughter in this book in an imaginary boutique, but there is a real Fisherman's Daughter right on Main Street that inspired Wren's business venture, and it is just as divine.

Finally, thank you to my family and friends. To those who share my books with their own family and friends, and who listen, read, and show up to my events. Who show up, period. To JB, who remains "one of the good ones." Thank you to my McKinney lunch girls, my CC crew, my hometown crowd. I could not and likely would not do this without you. Big love to my parents and brothers, for their continued encouragement and support, and who have been known to drop everything to walk a dog, pick up a child, or tend a chicken. Most of all, to Grace and Finley, my little compasses. You remain my reasons for everything.

Topics & Questions for Discussion

1. The book opens with the story of the Baileys' boat capsizing when the sisters were very young. What did you think about the Baileys in these opening pages? In what ways do their personalities and relationships stay the same as they grow up, and in what ways do they change?

2. *Sailing Lessons* uses five different viewpoints to tell the story of the Bailey family. What do you think the novel would have been like if Hannah McKinnon had told it from the point of view of just one or two of the Baileys? Why do you think she chose not to use Lindy as a narrator? What is the effect of not hearing her narrative voice?

3. While each of the Bailey daughters is very different, they all share elements of their parents, Lindy, Caleb, and Hank. What family traits do they share and what trait is unique to each daughter?

4. Although there are characters with overt, diagnosed addictions in *Sailing Lessons*, there are also less obvious addictions that

491

members of the Bailey family struggle with throughout the novel. What types of addictions do you see in the lives of these characters? Is there resolution and healing?

5. Compare and contrast the four Bailey women's romantic relationships. In what ways are their relationships influenced by Caleb's absence from their lives?

6. After Shannon's arrest, she remembers a nightmare she had as a child and her father's comforting words. How do you interpret this memory? What does it symbolize for Shannon?

7. Before the family scatters Caleb's ashes, Wren says a few words: "I like to think that when he finally came home to us, he gave each of us a piece of ourselves back." Discuss what piece of each of the Bailey women was restored by Caleb's return.

8. Which character's journey did you identify with the most? Did any of the characters frustrate you? Confuse you?

9. Cape Cod plays an important role in the novel; it's not just the setting, it's also a major influence on the lives of the characters. How does Hannah emphasize the importance of Cape Cod in the book? Pick a favorite passage describing the Cape and analyze the different ways the various characters think

of their home. What does the passage reveal about the character?

10. Lindy, Wren, Shannon, and Piper all react to Caleb's return in very different ways. Identify how each copes with their reunion, and the advantages and disadvantages of approaching it this way.

11. Caleb thinks that Shannon "inherited both the best and the worst from her father." Do you agree? Do you think that could be said of all his daughters, or is this statement unique to Shannon?

12. What do you imagine or hope would happen for the Baileys after the book ends? What do you think their futures hold?

13. As much as this is a story about fathers and daughters, Hannah also delves into the relationship between mothers and daughters. What insights into the mother-daughter bond did you gain from reading *Sailing Lessons*?

Enhance Your Book Club

1. Take a relaxing group trip to your local beachy spot, whether it be ocean, lake, or poolside, and enjoy being outside together, like the Baileys do.
2. In addition to its natural beauty, Cape Cod has a rich maritime history. Research one of the Cape's many charming towns and present its highlights to your book group.
3. All of Hannah's novels feature families in beautiful waterfront locations. Read *The Lake Season, Mystic Summer*, and *The Summer House* and compare and contrast the families in each book.

Books are produced in the United States using U.S.-based materials

Books are printed using a revolutionary new process called THINKtech™ that lowers energy usage by 70% and increases overall quality

Books are durable and flexible because of Smyth-sewing

Paper is sourced using environmentally responsible foresting methods and the paper is acid-free

Center Point Large Print
600 Brooks Road / PO Box 1
Thorndike, ME 04986-0001 USA

(207) 568-3717

US & Canada:
1 800 929-9108
www.centerpointlargeprint.com